Praise f

"Dark, sultry, and p... is blazing hot and will leave readers breathless."

—*Fresh Fiction*

"Has moments of humor, of tenderness and pure hot loving... Leaves a reader hungering for more of this awesome and exciting new world."

—*Long and Short Reviews*, 5 Stars

"Well-written paranormal romance featuring a couple that sizzles right off the page."

—*RT Book Reviews*, 4 Stars

"The strength of Spear's writing lies in her ability to keep the reader emotionally in tune with the characters... Spear's lush descriptions of the Amazon... will leave readers hungry for more time in paradise."

—*Booklist*

"A sizzling page turner. Terry Spear is wickedly talented."

—*Night Owl Reviews*
Reviewer Top Pick, 5 Stars

"Terry Spear makes fantasy come to life through the magical pages of her book. She packs action, romance, and paranormal shifters into one great read."

—*BookLoons*

"A sexy, action-packed paranormal romance that is sure to captivate you from the very beginning."

—*Romance Junkies*

Also by Terry Spear

Heart of the Wolf

Destiny of the Wolf

To Tempt the Wolf

Legend of the White Wolf

Seduced by the Wolf

Wolf Fever

Heart of the Highland Wolf

Dreaming of the Wolf

A SEAL in Wolf's Clothing

A Howl for a Highlander

The Jaguar Shapeshifter series

Savage Hunger

A HIGHLAND WEREWOLF WEDDING

TERRY SPEAR

sourcebooks
casablanca

Copyright © 2013 by Terry Spear
Cover and internal design © 2013 by Sourcebooks, Inc.
Photography by Jon Zychowski
Styling by Brynne Rinderknecht

Sourcebooks and the colophon are registered trademarks of Sourcebooks, Inc.

All rights reserved. No part of this book may be reproduced in any form
or by any electronic or mechanical means including information storage
and retrieval systems—except in the case of brief quotations embodied
in critical articles or reviews—without permission in writing from its
publisher, Sourcebooks, Inc.

The characters and events portrayed in this book are fictitious or are used
fictitiously. Any similarity to real persons, living or dead, is purely coin-
cidental and not intended by the author.

Published by Sourcebooks Casablanca, an imprint of Sourcebooks, Inc.
P.O. Box 4410, Naperville, Illinois 60567-4410
(630) 961-3900
FAX: (630) 961-2168
www.sourcebooks.com

Printed and bound in Canada
WC 10 9 8 7 6 5 4 3 2

To my Rebel Romance Writer critique partners who are all about rebellion: Vonda, Judy, Tammy, Carol, Randy, Betty, and Pamela. We were in another group when a really sweet woman joined us. Her abusive husband began to stalk us. He wouldn't let her contact our group and said horrible things. When we wanted him blocked, the only way to do it was ban the writer. The person moderating the group, who wasn't part of it, said we couldn't. We had no control over who could join or who could be dismissed. Only she did. So the group went completely silent.

We were afraid to correspond, knowing he was lurking, reading our emails, responding in a sick way, and reading our uploaded chapters. We took our chapters down. We could no longer critique. The group was dead unless we could change the moderator's stance.

We couldn't.

We rebelled and created our own safe haven. We're still together after forming our Rebel Romance Writer group in 2004! Thanks to my rebel writer friends who have helped me to edit my books, come up with titles, deal with deaths in the family, and do so much more. I love you!

Prologue

1782, St. Augustine, Florida

THE HEAT OF THE OCTOBER DAY MADE ELAINE Hawthorn wilt as tears blurred her eyes. She choked back a sob as men shoveled the dirt onto her mother's and father's coffins. Never again would she see her mother's bright smile or her father's raised brow when she did something he thought was not quite ladylike. Never again would she feel her mother's and father's warm embraces, or hear them telling her how much they loved her. A fateful carriage accident had brought them to this.

Barely an hour later, her uncles Tobias and Samson pulled her away from the reception to speak with her privately. From their weary expressions—and the way Kelly Rafferty, a pirating wolf himself, had leered at her at the funeral—she was in for more dire news.

"Lass, you must have a mate," Uncle Tobias said, towering over her like an Irishman ready to do battle. He was a seasoned fighter, sailor, and pirate—or as he often reminded her, a privateer, like his twin brother. Tobias never took any guff from his men. He and his brother had been born while their parents were crossing the Irish Sea from Ireland to Scotland so she believed seawater ran in their veins. They were also shape-shifting gray wolves.

In her presence, her uncles always seemed uncomfortable, fidgeting and avoiding speaking with her as if she didn't exist. Now, they were forced to do something with her. Neither had children of his own, or at least not any that either of them acknowledged.

"He has the right of it, Elaine." Uncle Samson lifted his grizzled, tanned hands in an appeasing way. "At sixteen, you need a mate. Kelly Rafferty has the only viable wolf pack in the area and has asked for you to be his mate. We have concurred."

The air rushed out of her lungs, and she felt light-headed. She grasped the side table to steady herself. Gathering her wits, she responded with outrage. "You did not even *ask* me! I will not marry that arrogant, conceited wolf! He has never been interested in me. Never! Not until he thought he might gain my parents' properties!"

That made her wonder if *he'd* had anything to do with her parents' carriage accident. Wasn't it a little too convenient? Her family had been in competition in the pirating business with Kelly Rafferty all these years—and suddenly her parents die when Elaine is old enough that Kelly can mate with her and take over her parents' estates?

"Your father should have ensured you were already mated by this time, Elaine," Tobias said, half annoyed, half gruffly as if this business was now his to deal with, and he was going to do it however he saw fit.

Expediently. From what she'd heard, Rafferty was nearly two decades older than she was and ruthless besides.

"My father would never have forced me to mate someone I did not care for! What if Rafferty was responsible for my parents' death?"

Uncle Tobias folded his arms, looking at her like she'd make up anything to get out of taking a mate. Now that Rafferty had offered for her, no other wolf in his right mind would ask for her hand. Not if he wanted to live long.

"Take me with you. Let me see the world first. Then when we return to St. Augustine, if I have not found my own wolf mate by then, we will see if Mr. Rafferty is still interested."

Over her dead body.

After much arguing with her uncles, Elaine convinced them to allow her this one boon. With great reluctance, they arranged to have her estates managed until she returned.

———

Two days into the ocean voyage, Elaine heaved the contents of her belly into a bucket while attempting to rest in the captain's quarters, sicker than she had ever been.

Everything went from bad to worse as soon as they arrived at the port city of St. Andrews, Scotland. The ship carried a new name and her uncles dressed as respectable merchants, but someone must have recognized them for who they truly were.

Word soon reached the authorities that the notorious, pirating Hawthorn brothers had returned. As armed men hurried toward them, her Uncle Tobias signaled to one of his sailors, who shoved her to the cobblestones as if she was in their way.

Men grabbed her uncles and several of their crew, led them away in chains, and tried them with barely any representation. To her horror, her uncles were hanged in the town square at the behest of Lord Harold Whittington who owned a fleet of merchant ships and claimed her uncles had plundered three of them.

Scared to death that someone would see her, believe she was part of her uncles' crew, and hang her, too, she hastily wiped away the tears rolling freely down her cheeks and tried to slip away unnoticed in the chilly breeze. Her best hope was to return to Florida and her family's estates.

As she started to steal away, she spied a broad-shouldered man observing her. He was wearing a predominantly blue and green kilt, the plaid gathered over his shoulder and pinned, a sporran at his belt, and a sword at his back—and he looked fierce. Her heart did a tumble.

She had dressed as plainly as she could in a dark-green muslin gown with a fitted jacket and a petticoat of the same color. With a cloak covering these and the hood up over her head, she had hoped to be shielded from the view of the men and women milling about. She thought she had been obscure in the crowd.

Elaine slipped away with the crowd as several men headed for the pubs to celebrate the hanging. She glanced over her shoulder. Curiosity etched on his warrior face, the man was still watching her. He appeared to be a Highland warrior of old, someone who had fought in ruthless clan battles and come out a survivor. Maybe a loyal friend of Lord Whittington who would want a noose around her neck, too.

He lifted his nose and appeared to take a deep breath, as if he was trying to scent the wind. As if he was trying to smell her. Which immediately made her think of a wolf. Her skin prickled with unease.

His eyes widened and he headed in her direction, a few other men following him. The force of powerful males made her heart trip over itself as she strove to get away but at the same time make it look as though she wasn't trying to evade him.

Her heart pumped wildly as she tried to reach an alleyway, thinking she had gotten away. She was slipping down the narrow brick alleyway when a large hand grabbed her arm and effectively stopped her.

Barely able to catch her breath, she bit back a scream.

"Lass," the man said with a distinctive Highland burr, his voice low, "where are you going in such a hurry?"

His dark brown eyes were narrowed, focused on her, yet a small smile curved his lips, as if he was amused that she thought she could evade a wolf. Because that was just what he was.

A gray wolf, tall, muscularly built, but more wiry than bulky. His hand was holding her still, not bruising her but with enough pressure that she knew he was not about to let her go. He was handsome as the devil, the crinkle lines beneath his eyes telling her he was a man who liked to smile, his masculine lips likewise not thin and mean like Kelly Rafferty's, but pleasingly full with a curve that made her think he enjoyed life in a jovial rather than a cruel way.

His wind-tussled hair was an earthy shade of dark brown with streaks of red, and he had no hint of facial hair as if he had just shaved. He was lean and hard, not an ounce of fat, and determined, his jaw set, his brows raised a little now as he examined her more closely. He was taking a good long look, not in a leering way but taking in her distinctive appearance.

The three men who had been trailing behind him were now immersed in a brawl outside the alley, fists swinging.

"Are you here alone, lass?" the man asked, his voice seductively low. He was an alpha, in charge, wanting answers.

"Let… me… go," she growled. She was trying not to make a scene.

"Come with me and my brothers, and I will protect you," he offered.

A shiver stole up her spine. He must know she was related to the hanged men. The fight was growing closer—she could hear men's shouts and cries of pain, scuffling, and thuds as some went down.

She tried to wriggle loose of his strong grip, tried to peel his powerful fingers off her arm, but to no avail. He seemed mildly amused that she'd try.

"Let… me… go," she repeated, scowling up at him.

"If Lord Whittington learns you were one of the Hawthorns' kin, it willna go well for you," the man said. "My name is Cearnach MacNeill, and those behind me…" He glanced over his shoulder, then turned back to her, and amended, "Who *were* following me are my brothers. We will see you to safety."

If he was not kin, why should he and his family wish to aid her? She didn't trust his motives.

She shook her head. "You are mistaken about me, sir. Release me at once."

He did not seem inclined to do so, but a beefy half-drunken man came up behind him, skirted around the Highlander, and slugged Cearnach in the jaw. He immediately released Elaine so that he was free to pelt the drunk.

She darted down the alleyway, glancing back to see Cearnach struggling to rid himself of the brigand. He took a swing at the drunk, and when he had knocked him back several steps, Cearnach looked for her and spied her getting away. Her heart did a flip. He appeared both troubled and exasperated.

She ran out of the alley, dashed down the street until she found another alley, and ducked down it. She would find a ship and return home on her own.

Somehow she had to figure out a way to deal with Kelly Rafferty next.

—◦◦◦—

Cearnach MacNeill swore as another lout smashed him in the jaw with a mighty punch. By the time he'd laid the man out with a couple of smashes in the face, Cearnach had lost sight of the she-wolf in the crowd. He suspected she was related to the Hawthorn brothers, which was the only way they would have taken her aboard their ship. He was almost certain that the only reason they had docked in St. Andrews was to gather their stolen goods and squirrel them away in some other location.

Did the lass know where the brothers had hidden the goods?

All he should have cared about was retrieving his family's stolen property from the now-dead brigands. When he'd looked into the girl's stricken face, he'd felt a deep regret that she'd just lost her family and now he intended to use her to reclaim his clan's goods. He was sincere about keeping her safe. At least until he could secure passage for her and send her home.

He'd seen the uncertainty in her dark brown eyes, the guarded hope he might rescue her from this nightmare. He'd felt a twinge of need—to protect her.

He picked up her wolf scent and headed for the wharves. Then he saw Robert Kilpatrick and the McKinley brothers and overheard Robert saying, "We have to get her before Whittington does."

Were they kin to the Hawthorn brothers? Most likely they wanted the same information from her as Cearnach did: where was the stolen property the Hawthorn brothers had hidden in Scotland?

She didn't stand a chance unless Cearnach could reach her first.

Chapter 1

PACING ACROSS HIS BROTHER'S OFFICE IN THE SOLAR OF Argent Castle, Cearnach MacNeill was determined not to back down on this issue with Ian, his older brother, clan chief, and pack leader of their Highland gray werewolf pack. Cearnach had promised Calla Stewart that he would show up at her wedding to lend moral support. Friends did that for friends. He would attend because she had asked him to, even though he knew his being there could stir up real trouble.

Why did she have to marry into the McKinley clan? Pirates, every last one of them, even though the pirating stopped a century ago. As far as he was concerned, they were still a bunch of ruthless brigands.

Determination was etched on Ian's scowling face as he studied Cearnach while remaining seated at his dark oak desk. He was struggling to allow Cearnach to attend his friend's wedding, worried about his safety, not happy about it, but reluctant to take a stand and say no. That was one of the reasons Cearnach loved his older quadruplet brother. He was a born leader of men with a heart of gold. Though no one would say the latter to his face. Ian was certain that he hid that part of himself well enough so he could take on the world and *them* when he needed to.

His people knew better.

The weather was dismal this fall day at Argent Castle, and the room itself was dark and gloomy. The bookshelves were filled with leather-bound volumes of the history of their clan. The rich, burgundy Turkish tapestries covering the floor, the brown leather chairs, and Ian's oak desk all took on an ominous cast, like a scene from a gothic novel.

Ian's jaw clenched like it did when he gave one of his brothers an order or at least a strong suggestion, or when any of them disagreed with him on an issue. Since Cearnach was the second eldest brother and next in command, Ian usually gave him more leeway, knowing Cearnach's heart and head were normally in the right place.

"I don't understand," Ian said finally, his dark brown eyes gauging Cearnach's resolve like a wolf attempting to see the inner workings of someone's thoughts. "You're not looking for a fight, are you? Attending Calla's wedding could stir up bad feelings we don't need with another Highland wolf clan. Especially that one."

"You're right. You don't understand. You would do whatever it took to be there for family or in choosing a mate. But you've never had a female friend who wasn't family. With me, Calla's just a friend. Being there for her is important to me."

"Aye, a friend. She tossed you a rope to keep you from drowning in the swollen river when you were a wee lad, and now you feel you owe her the same. She's made her choice," Ian reminded him, though Cearnach didn't need the reminder. "She doesn't believe she needs rescuing.

"Alpha males don't take kindly to other wolves

crossing the line. You've tried to talk her out of the mating, but she's making the commitment to Baird McKinley anyway. Neither her family nor the McKinleys will be happy to see you, Cearnach. You'll be the enemy in their midst. Some will know you tried to dissuade her from marrying the brigand. We all know what he's like. She's too stubborn to see it."

Aye, she was, but Cearnach didn't want to hear Ian telling him so. "She asked me to be there. I have to go, Ian. I'm already running late."

Ian furrowed his brow at his brother. "You're never late to anything. You're always early or on time. Doesn't that say something to you about this whole ludicrous venture? That you shouldn't be going? That you don't really want to go?"

Cearnach looked out the window at the Caledonian Forest beyond the castle walls, where the hearty breeze stirred the branches of the Scots pines while smoky gray clouds stretched across the sky. He didn't answer.

"You're not going to object to the marriage, are you?" Ian said as more of an observation than a question.

Cearnach straightened. He didn't know what he was going to do when he got there.

Sounding deeply exasperated, Ian let out his breath. "Couldn't you have worn something less… antagonistic?"

At that, Cearnach couldn't help but smile… an evil smile. He turned to face his brother. "What? My kilt? I'm proud of being a MacNeill."

"Aye, and the sword?" Ian said, motioning to it.

"Part of the formal dress. All wolves wear them to Highland weddings. I wouldn't be caught dead without it."

"Aye, but in this case they might consider you a

threat, thinking possibly you have plans to steal the bride
away, a time-honored tradition in the Highlands and still
among wolves. Here's hoping you won't have to use
your sword. Call me when you get there and after it's
done. I want to know if I have to send the troops out to
rescue you."

Cearnach bowed his head slightly in acceptance. "I'm
off, Ian. Wish me luck."

Ian shook his head. "You may need it, Brother."

Feeling disconcerted about Calla and what she was
about to do, but not worried about his own safety as he
could hold his own against any of the McKinley clan,
Cearnach stalked out of his brother's solar. He walked
down the corridor where paintings of past clan chiefs
and their mates hung on the walls, keeping watch as if
to guide the clan on its way.

Cearnach hurried through the great hall, shoved the
massive oak door to the keep open, and closed it behind
him. His boots tromping on the ancient stone pavers, he
crossed the inner bailey to the garage near the stables
where he and his brothers' cars were parked.

The gray clouds were darkening, the smell of a
rainstorm gathering power and a cold breeze whipping
around him. He hoped the rain would hold off until *after*
he reached the church. Two of his cousins were practicing fighting with swords, their weapons singing as steel
met steel.

Another couple of men were wearing their wolf coats,
lying on their stomachs, heads raised, ears perked, while
they enjoyed observing the sword play, always looking
for tips and techniques they could use themselves. They
turned to see him and bowed their heads in greeting as

the men who were sparring stopped briefly to acknowledge their second-in-command.

He nodded and continued without stopping. If he was to make it to the wedding on time, he would have to drive a wee bit faster than he'd intended. He didn't want to think too deeply about why he was going to arrive a little late. Ian was right. He never was late to anything.

But he wanted to ensure that he wasn't thrown out of the church before Calla knew he had arrived, and he wanted Baird McKinley to know that Cearnach wouldn't be stopped from making an appearance.

Out of the corner of his eye, he saw Anlan, one of their Irish wolfhounds, racing to greet him. "Not now, Anlan," Cearnach said as one of the men and the two wolves headed the dog off. Thwarted, Anlan woofed, telling Cearnach that he wanted to go for a ride.

"Fatherhood already getting you down?" Cearnach asked. Anlan's pups were two months old and ready for new homes as soon as Ian or his mate, who was the holdup really, offered them for sale.

Anlan whimpered, standing still and looking so longingly in Cearnach's direction that Cearnach knew the hound wanted desperately to go for a ride with him. Cearnach could just envision the sight, him in Highland dress with his long-legged, lanky, bristle-furred hound at his side as he entered the church.

Cearnach climbed into the silver minivan, turned over the engine, and headed out of the garage wishing he had something grander and faster to drive—like a Mercedes-Benz roadster or a Ferrari. If it wasn't about to rain, a Lamborghini convertible would have been nice.

He drove through the open castle gates and then

through the outer bailey. Out on the main road, he tore off in the direction of the church and cursed the wind for impeding his progress.

Trying to get his mind off the drive ahead and the dwindling time, he thought about Calla and the regret he felt that he couldn't have been the one for her. They just didn't have what it took to be a couple.

No matter how many times he told himself Calla understood what she was doing, he knew Baird McKinley didn't deserve her. She was making a big mistake.

An hour later, only halfway to the church and with the strong headwind thwarting his progress, Cearnach came around a bend in the hilly road to see a black Mercedes hogging the pavement in his lane. Since the other driver wasn't budging, Cearnach jerked his car off the road before they collided head-on.

Hell and damnation!

With the rate of speed he was going, the car sailed over the rocks littering the terrain, ripping up the rear tires with a boom! And another boom! The tires exploded before he could brake the car enough to stop it.

Cursing a blue streak, he cut the engine and climbed out of the car to see who the idiot driver was. Probably someone who had been celebrating a wee bit too much. He grabbed his sheathed sword and strapped it around his waist.

The black car had pulled to the side of the road, the driver hidden behind tinted windows, the engine purring.

The chilly wind tugging at his hair and kilt, Cearnach stormed toward the vehicle. He was ready to commandeer it to drive to the wedding, while letting the driver sleep the liquor off in the backseat.

When the driver's door opened, a long-legged brunette stepped out of the car. He had a hell of a time shifting his gaze from those shapely legs and a pair of sexy high-heeled pumps—her clingy red dress having risen to mid-thigh before it settled lower—to see how good the rest of her looked. Especially since he'd expected some sloppy-drunk male type.

Seeing a woman instead, one hell of a shapely woman, he hesitated, and the anger quelled in an instant.

His gaze traveled upward to take in the rest of the package. The wind blowing in her direction forced the dress's red slinky fabric to cling to her shapely legs, hips, and everything in between. The dress screamed hot and available. At least to him.

The neckline wasn't all that low, just enough to show off the swell of her breasts, but her reaction to his perusing her was what made him direct his attention upward while he bit back a smile. She folded her arms beneath her breasts, lifting them a little and making him wish he could do the honors, and then she let out an annoyed huff of breath.

More than anything, he loved her reaction and wasn't beyond pushing her a bit after she'd forced him off the road and ruined two of his tires.

"Done looking?" she asked. The hint of sarcasm amused him when he should still have been furious about what she'd done to his vehicle.

She was American, not a Scottish lass, which meant she was trouble if she was anything like his brothers Ian and Duncan's mates, except both of the women were wolves—Julia of the red wolf variety, and Shelley, a gray.

"All right," she said, now sounding *really* annoyed.

"I get it. You're a big, bad Highland warrior type of wolf, and you have to present this image…"

She knew he was a *wolf*?

Only *one way* she'd know that. She smelled his wolf scent. Only one way she could do that. She was also a wolf. He didn't hear the rest of her words as his gaze shot up to her face.

Her eyes widened, giving her a startled look as she met his gaze.

She was beautiful and elegant, not just the sweet and innocent bonny girl who lives in the cottage next door, but vibrant and ultra-sexy with dark brown eyes—*granted*, narrowed at him—and lush black lashes, high cheekbones, and full lips that were any man's wet dream.

After getting over his initial shock, he crowded her as a wolf would, checking her out, sensing her response to him, learning if she truly was a wolf. She nearly folded into the car, trying to back away from him. He seized her arm to keep her close and moved his face in to get a good whiff of her. The wind was blowing in her direction, carrying his scent to her but hers away from him.

But being this close, he smelled her. She-wolf. Gray. A hint of a seductive floral fragrance.

He took in another breath, attempting to learn how she felt about him, trying to see if she was angered, intrigued, scared. Any strong emotions would be revealed in her scent. He frowned. She smelled familiar somehow. From the scent he gathered from her, she *was* angered, intrigued, and a wee bit scared. Just as she should be around an imposing Highlander of the Old World like he was.

"Bloody hell," he said, quickly releasing her, not wanting to feel any interest in the lass. But he continued to remain in her space, continued to suck in the air around her, continued to enjoy the essence of the wolf. He couldn't help it. When a female was *this* enticing, he was all male wolf.

Then again, something more about the woman intrigued him. She was not friendly, more irritated than anything, and he figured if she had a *sgian dubh,* the traditional knife worn with a kilt, hidden in that clingy creation, she would force him to back off. She slipped her hands between them and touched his chest in a way that said, "Back off," as if she thought she could keep him at bay.

He swore the heat from her hands seared him right through his Prince Charlie jacket, vest, and white shirt, all the way to his bare chest.

She was a wolf with attitude and a total turn-on.

Large brown eyes gazed at him like a wolf who could read his every thought, every bit as welcoming and seductive as the rest of her. Dark brown hair tinted with natural highlights of red and gold softly curled to her shoulders, the wind catching it and tossing it to and fro in a playful way. Her mouth was still pursed, looking quite kissable.

One of her brows arched heavenward.

Normally he thought himself easygoing, except when someone destroyed his property. In her case, he would make a rare exception. He smiled at the realization that she wasn't thoroughly intimidated by him. If she'd been human, she would have been. Even a female wolf outside her own territory should be. But the little American she-wolf wouldn't give an inch.

"What's your name?" he asked.

"Elaine Hawthorn." She stared him down like a wolf that wouldn't be cowed, but she didn't ask his name or act as though she wanted it.

He eyed her more closely, sure he had seen her somewhere before. A long… *very* long time ago. That was the problem with living for so many years. He wasn't good at remembering new names and faces in the short term. Long term? Even worse.

Something about her appearance and something about her reaction to him had him wondering.

"Have we met before, lass?" He felt less hostile, but he still had a mission and her driving him off the road wasn't going to thwart him.

She shook her head too quickly, as if she realized he couldn't recall who she was, and she wanted to keep it that way.

"Do you know my name?" he asked, even though he assumed she'd say no. He could judge by her reaction, even if it was subtle, if she was telling the truth.

"How could I? I only just arrived in Scotland." She was too aggressive in her response, instead of just politely saying, *No, I don't know you.*

He might not be real good at names and faces, but as intriguing as she was, he remembered her from somewhere before. "I'm Cearnach MacNeill."

She frowned a little. "How do you spell your name?"

He spelled it out for her, then added, "It's pronounced like 'Care-knock' with the 'ck' at the end kind of sliding off to a 'och' sound." He waited for some form of recognition.

She gave it, even though she fought to keep her control… a subtle change in her scent, worry, maybe. Not a strong sense of anxiety. Just something vague. She licked her lips nervously, not in a seductive way. Glistening with fresh moisture, they looked too appealing.

She dropped her hands from his chest, as if she didn't want to touch him any longer and maybe trigger some deeper memory. Or maybe he was looking too interested in her in a feral way.

He hated losing that intimate touch, even though she had used her hands as a barrier to his being so close to her. The exchange felt like so much more to him.

Suddenly remembering why he was here in the first place—to attend Calla's wedding—he said, "You'll give me a ride to the wedding I'm attending. I'm already late." At least he assumed he was late. He hadn't calculated any extra time into his travel plans, and he'd already figured he'd arrive about the time everyone else took their seats in the church.

"Wedding? Don't tell me…" She put a finger to her chin, the skin beneath her eyes crinkling with wry amusement. Then she pointed at him, the point of her fingertip hovering so close to his chest that he was just waiting for her to make the intimate connection again. This time she didn't, to his disappointment. "It's *your* wedding."

"If it was, would that make a difference?" He watched her expression, seeing the sparkle of humor in her eyes. He didn't know why he'd asked, except that he could smell the way he intrigued her, just as much as she intrigued him. He really wanted to know—did it matter to her?

"It depends. I might be saving the bride from a fate worse than death if I delayed your marrying her."

At that, Cearnach grinned. He loved a woman with a sense of humor. "It's my friend's wedding."

"Ah, then that's a different matter. Can't disappoint a friend." She truly sounded sympathetic. "Why don't you have a spare tire? I guess it would be inconvenient to change a tire in all this wind while wearing a kilt." This time she raked him up and down with a sassy viewing of his whole body, her expression one of pure feminine delight.

His body tightened with need.

She was just as diligent in looking him over as he had been with her. It was as if they were sparring. Her thorough job of looking was enough to turn up the heat already making his blood sizzle.

"I would have no difficulty changing a tire in or out of my kilt." He motioned to the car where the rear tires were perfectly deflated. "As you can see, lassie, you ruined *two* tires. I only have *one* spare. Now I'm later than before, and you're driving me to the wedding."

"I'll be late for my appointment. You'll have to call someone else to help you out."

Ignoring her plans since she'd ruined his own and she owed him, he said, "If I had to wait for assistance, I'd miss the whole ceremony. So you'll take me to the wedding since my car isn't going anywhere and you helped to put it there."

Cearnach decided the only way to make the woman see his position was to escort her to the passenger side of the car and help her in, if she needed the assistance. He was always a gentleman when with women. "Only *I'll* be driving so we get there in one piece."

She balked, glanced down at his legs, frowned, and motioned to his right leg where the top of the handle of his *sgian dubh* poked out of his kilt hose. "You're already wearing a dagger."

"Part of the Highland formal dress." He bowed his head slightly, his face growing so close to hers that they almost touched.

"I know, but why the big sword also? Expecting to go to war?"

He smiled a little. "Wolves tend to carry on their traditions from long ago. We all carry swords to wolf weddings. It's… strictly for show." At least that's what he hoped it would be. Just like he hoped all the other guests at the wedding would be so attired.

She finally let out her breath but yielded, albeit reluctantly, climbed into the car in a huff, showing off a lot of leg, and quickly yanked her skirt down. She folded her arms and stared up at him as he towered over her, her expression mutinous. "You were driving way too fast. That's why you ran off the road."

"You were driving in *my* lane."

"There's only one lane out here," she retorted, brows lifted, waiting for him to disagree.

He shook his head, knowing he wouldn't win this argument, then slammed her door. He stalked around to the driver's side and got in. Despite knowing she was in the wrong—although she was not a local and obviously hadn't known the rules of the road—he did feel a twinge of regret that she would miss her appointment. Or… date, maybe. She looked as though she intended to meet someone special. Another wolf? Or just a human? Then again, if so, she probably would have called it a date, not an appointment.

He glanced at her as he started the engine. "Where were you going?"

"Senton Castle."

He pulled onto the road and continued to the church, driving even faster than before. "It's in ruins."

"I know that," she said icily.

"It's located about a quarter of a mile from here in the opposite direction from the way you were traveling. You must have missed the road that would take you there." Or she wasn't really going there and hadn't wanted him to know where she was truly meeting up with the bloke.

She frowned and looked back over her shoulder as if she could see the road leading to the castle that way. "Great," she muttered under her breath. Then she folded her arms and glanced down at his kilt. "Is it a Highland wedding?"

"Good guess. We're in the Highlands and I'm going to a wedding. Aye, it's a Highland wedding."

She took a deep, exasperated breath. "I meant is everyone wearing traditional Highland dress at the wedding, or are you the only one who will be dressed like that?" She motioned to his kilt, sounding as though she thought he was being foolish even though she had appeared to like the way he looked when she had given him the once-over.

"Is there something wrong with what I'm wearing?"

This time she smiled. "It's kind of cute, really."

"Cute?" He grunted. Sexy as hell, turned on the lassies, definitely eye candy, warrior material. But… cute?

She gave him an elusive smile, and he wondered if she was trying to get a reaction from him. He still wasn't quite sure about American humor, and he thought she might be teasing him. He hadn't meant to react so he had to concede she'd gotten him there.

"So, Cearnach," she said as she dug around in her black leather bag and pulled out a phone, "your name sounds like it must be Old World. Does it mean anything special?"

"Gaelic for victorious or warrior of the woods." He shot her a look that meant he *was* victorious, at least mostly.

Elaine motioned to his sword. "As in fighting battles?"

"As in anything I set my mind to tackle, lass." He gave her another interested look, although he meant it only in response to her calling his kilt-wearing cute. She couldn't have been serious about that.

"Hmm." She tapped a slender finger on her phone.

He thought he heard her curse lightly under her breath. "What's wrong?"

"Battery's dead." She paused, then looked over at him. "Do you have a phone on you that I can borrow?"

"Local call?"

"Of course. I need to call the guy I was to meet and let him know I'll be there later, in case he arrives early."

"So you still had time?" Cearnach asked.

"I'm always early for appointments. Besides, I didn't know how long it would take me to get here from Edinburgh. And I wanted to explore the castle a little."

"It's in ruins." He couldn't help telling her again. She looked like she belonged in a fancy hotel pub, sipping something sweet, not tromping in killer heels around a broken-down castle where she would have to traverse hundreds of stairs and slippery uneven pavers to reach the keep.

She let out a breath. "I *know* that. So can I borrow your phone?"

He patted his sporran, realized he'd left his phone

in the console in his car, and shook his head. "It's in my car."

"Terrific." She folded her arms and looked out the window, sounding more resigned than angry.

"Maybe you can borrow someone else's phone when we get to the church. What time were you supposed to meet him?"

"At two," she said.

Cearnach frowned. The lady was way off on her time. "Two? You thought you were early? It's around four." The time Cearnach was supposed to be at the church.

Her jaw dropped. "No," she said with disbelief.

"Aye. The time-zone difference has probably knocked your natural internal wolf clock off balance."

She groaned and combed her fingers through her wind-tossed hair, which made her look all the more appealing as the bodice of her dress stretched over her breasts and her skirt drew up a bit.

She dropped her hands back to her lap and shook her head.

"Did he try to contact you when you didn't arrive in time?"

She stared at her dead phone resting in her lap. "Maybe. I don't know when the phone died. The last call I managed was at the airport in Miami, and I never looked to see how charged up it was at that point."

"I'm sure he figures you're late because of your flight schedule and driving time here." But Cearnach wasn't letting her leave him until he knew for sure she'd met her party and everything was on the up and up. Besides, there was the little matter of where he'd met her before—and the fact she didn't want to admit it.

Wolves were curious by nature, and he wouldn't let her go before he knew the truth.

Chapter 2

NEITHER CEARNACH NOR ELAINE SAID ANOTHER WORD on the remainder of the trip to the wedding, but when they arrived at the church, he parked and hurried around to get her door, afraid she might think she was dropping him off and leaving. "We're here."

"Super, now you can give me my keys back." She reached out her hand and gave him a small smile.

"Nay. You're coming to the wedding, and then you'll take me back to my car so I can get a couple of tires replaced."

When she didn't move, he clasped her arm and pulled her out, then slammed the door and hauled her toward the medieval church through the car park that was filled to capacity. "We're late. Don't make us any later."

"*You're* late! I'm just forcibly detained. Why do I have to stay for the wedding? You could get a ride with someone else after the ceremony."

He knew that wasn't a possibility. "If I couldn't?" No one here would stick his or her neck out to take Cearnach anywhere, not even to loan him or the person aiding him a phone, knowing that would stoke the McKinley clan's ire. "I'd be stuck here. Besides, you've already missed your appointment. So enjoy a wee bit of Highland romance."

Which he wasn't feeling in the least, not with Calla marrying the wrong wolf. He liked her family and they seemed to like him, but he was sure they wouldn't care for him being here and upsetting things between Calla and her groom.

Elaine quickly studied the building and appeared to be fascinated by the design. She looked like she was a tourist. Maybe she had never been to Scotland before. He could just imagine her pulling out a camera and taking pictures. Yet, he'd bet that she had been. That he'd met her somewhere, and she didn't want him to recall the incident.

Before she reached into her bag for a camera, he escorted her up the stone steps and into the church.

The front pews were packed with family and friends, most of the males wearing traditional Highland dress. The tartans of different clans were on display, but predominant were the red of the Stewarts and the blue, green, and red of the McKinleys. The MacNeill plaid Cearnach wore was also a blue and green, but with yellow instead of red in the sett.

The bride wore a gown of white and the bridesmaids were in lavender—to match the purple flowers decorating the church, Cearnach thought. Calla looked devastatingly beautiful, her long red-blond hair swept up in a bun, ringlets of curls framing her face, and small flowers decorating her hair as she stood in the wings with her father. She was mostly hidden from the view of the gathered friends and family as she waited while the closest family members were escorted to their seats up front.

Lavender, lilacs, heather, and thistle filled clear glass vases around the outer walls, scenting the confines of the small church. Stained-glass windows let in a small amount of dismal light from the gloomy day.

Modern-day lights resembling candles in brass and glass flutes helped to brighten the church somewhat. Dark oak pews that had been used by Highlanders and guests for centuries during worship beckoned him to take a seat, the ends draped in lavender satin bows, ribbons, and flowers.

He glanced at Elaine to see her opinion of the wedding. She was smiling, her gaze sweeping the rest of the gathered clansmen, taking in their clothes and the chapel, breathing in deeply to capture the perfumed air and wolf scents.

As she stood there in that provocative dress, looking seductive and enticing, he wondered what Elaine was really doing here in Scotland. When had she been here before? Even though it was none of his concern, he found he wanted to know more about her: why she knew him, why he knew her, and why she didn't want him to remember their former association.

In her red dress and with her dark hair, she stood out among the gathered wedding guests, striking and utterly appealing. In one sense, she looked like she was Little Red Riding Hood among the big bad wolves, an outsider, American, not invited to the wedding—and no one would want her here because she was with him.

He noted that the bride's family was seated on the left side of the church. He was about to escort Elaine to the last pew, which was empty, when she whispered, "I would think you'd have some friends here at the wedding who could help you out."

She hadn't asked him a question so he didn't respond, not wanting to explain that he was here because of Calla, and no one else would be happy to see him.

"Which side are you here for? Groom or bride?" Elaine asked, her voice ultra-low.

"Bride." When her eyes widened, he clarified, "She's a friend."

Elaine's mouth gaped briefly, then she smiled darkly. "*Figures* she'd marry someone else."

Hadn't he just said Calla was a friend? Not his intended mate? Before he could respond, Elaine pulled her arm free from his hand. He hadn't realized he'd still been gripping her, keeping her close to him as if protecting her from any other wolf's interest.

Several of the friends and family members of the bride and groom glanced back over the pews at Cearnach and Elaine, their expressions annoyed that anyone would be this late in arriving at the church as the bride walked up the aisle with her father, the music announcing that part of the ceremony. Then the guests' eyes widened as they saw just *who* had arrived. Cearnach definitely wasn't someone they expected or wanted to attend. Like the gray day outside, the expressions on the groom's side were especially stormy.

Calla looked back and beamed at Cearnach. Her brilliant smile radiated through the church, chasing away the gloom and making him realize how important it had been to her for him to be here.

Baird McKinley, the groom, looked beyond his bride in Cearnach's direction, his face reddening when he saw Cearnach. The two men locked gazes. Cearnach's expression was a warning—*Treat Calla right*. Baird's was just as much of a warning—*Get lost and stay out of Calla's life*.

Unruffled, Cearnach stood in the pew until he realized Elaine had backtracked and was now standing in a pew on the groom's side. At first, Cearnach figured: *What difference would it make where she sat as long as she stayed put?* He tried to watch the wedding procession in progress, but two bachelor wolves standing in the pew in front of Elaine must have caught the scent of the new, intriguing lone she-wolf.

The Kilpatrick brothers moved from their pew and slipped around to the one she was standing in like a couple of wolves on the hunt. Everyone sat down and the brothers took their seats on either side of the American she-wolf, boxing her in and declaring their interest.

Cearnach growled low. The arrangement wasn't acceptable at all.

Even though she was a wolf sitting in a church filled with people, he thought she looked small and vulnerable. Hell, he thought she looked sexy and vulnerable. That was the problem.

For a moment, all thoughts of Calla and her wedding fled from his mind as Cearnach swore under his breath. He watched the Kilpatrick brothers, cousins of the McKinleys, crowd her. He didn't like the way they were declaring ownership of the she-wolf. Or the way she pulled her arms closer to her body, showing she didn't like their close proximity. He was certain she didn't want to make a scene by moving, though.

Intent on rescuing her, he rose from the bench, crossed the aisle, and stood by her pew where Robert Kilpatrick kept her blocked in.

Cearnach growled at Elaine in a low voice meant only for her ears, "Sit by me, *now*, lassie." He hadn't meant to sound so growly, but if she'd sat beside him in the beginning, he wouldn't have to rescue her now.

Appearing innocent and sweet, as if any alpha she-wolf could who looked like she did, Elaine smiled up at him and mouthed the words, "No, thank you."

The Kilpatrick brothers both patted their swords and grinned up at him as if to say, "Leave the lady alone." *They'd* see to her needs.

Over his dead body. Cearnach took a deep breath. Ian would kill Cearnach himself if he learned Cearnach had started a sword fight in a church during a wedding ceremony over an American she-wolf he didn't even know. Not that sword fights didn't break out during wolf weddings from time to time. Usually they occurred over the bride, not a guest, though.

Annoyed to the max, Cearnach restrained himself from reaching over and hauling Elaine out of the pew. He waited as patiently as wolfishly possible for her to move on her own accord. Two more of the McKinley brothers, the younger ones, entered the church, arriving late to Calla's wedding and surprising Cearnach.

They both smiled at him in such a sinister way that Cearnach figured they'd be up to something before long. They glanced at Elaine and raised their brows in wolfish speculation. They walked past him to join Baird McKinley's two older brothers at the front of the church. Which also surprised him.

Elaine didn't spare them a glance as she watched the wedding, ignoring Cearnach as he waited for her to comply with his request.

Not used to anyone saying no to him, he hesitated. Like his older brother, Ian, he was used to giving commands and having people respond quickly to do his bidding.

When she didn't move, he grasped her arm and

pulled her out of the seat, which meant her skirt brushed
over Robert's kilted lap and her bare leg touched his
long legs as she couldn't avoid them. Not surprisingly,
he wouldn't be a gentleman and stand up to allow her
through. Robert Kilpatrick smiled broadly at her. Her
face was either red with embarrassment or flushed with
anger. Cearnach couldn't tell.

Cearnach marched her across the aisle and sat her
beside him in the empty last pew, this time blocking her in.

"Highland barbarian," Elaine whispered, still frowning.

Cearnach crossed his arms over his chest and smiled.

"I didn't mean it as a compliment," she said. "Why
did you make me sit over here, anyway? I was perfectly
fine where I was. I won't have you dictating where I'll sit.
Not when you forced me to come here in the first place."

So that was what this was about—showing off her
alpha spirit. He could understand that. Alphas truly didn't
like to be dictated to. Certainly not by a stranger. He
also wondered if she had a deeper reason for not wanting to sit next to him. A reason that had to do with their
meeting in the past.

When he didn't respond, she changed tactics, saying
in a hushed voice, "Oh, I see. You sorely missed me."

"Hardly." He gave her a dark look, hiding the smile
that was trying to surface. "I didn't want you forgetting your duty in the event any of *those*," he said, his
voice couched low as he motioned toward the now
disgruntled Kilpatrick brothers, who were watching
them and not the wedding, "distracted you too much.
Besides you didn't look happy with the company you
were keeping."

She didn't respond for several moments, which meant

he'd thought right. Then she folded her arms and asked, "How long is this going to take?"

"Hours. We'll attend the reception afterward." He'd only meant to wish Calla well at the reception and leave, but something about Elaine made him want to prolong his being with her. He couldn't fathom exactly why. Maybe deep down it bothered him she was in a strange country and hadn't connected with whomever she was supposed to be meeting.

Yet…

Looking down at her, he seemed to recall he had tried to rescue her before. It wasn't just a meeting that they had had. He just couldn't remember when. Or why.

"No way. I'm not staying that long," she whispered, tilting her head to the side with a pointed look. "Don't you have any friends here who could give you a ride?"

"Not here."

Narrowing her eyes, she stared at him. "Wait. You're not a wedding crasher, are you? I'm not exactly what you'd call an invited guest either, you know."

He shrugged. "I'm a friend of the bride's. She *did* invite me. I doubt anyone else is happy to see me, though."

She snorted. "Most likely not even her, right about now."

He couldn't help but give her a wry smile.

The minister again spoke, this time garnering Cearnach's full attention. "Does anyone have an objection to the marriage?" The minister looked straight at Cearnach and Elaine, his voice elevated, sounding half annoyed with them.

Everyone in the congregation turned around to stare in the direction the minister was looking. A few of the men seated on the groom's side had their hands on the hilts of their swords belted at their waists. The bride's guests and family waited with bated breath.

Elaine finally prodded Cearnach in the ribs. *Prodded him! A Highland warrior!* He glared at her.

Frowning, she looked up at him. "Well?" she whispered, when he said nothing.

Everyone was so quiet that he heard a fly fluttering on the other side of the kirk.

When Cearnach didn't say a word to either the minister's question or Elaine's prodding, two of McKinley's older brothers stood, ready to do battle, and headed toward the back of the kirk, just to the place where Cearnach and Elaine were sitting.

The eldest one motioned with his thumb for Cearnach to leave.

Vardon.

The McKinley had never forgiven Cearnach for having kissed Vardon's mate first. Vardon hadn't even known the lass at the time. Apparently Cearnach's kiss had made an impression on the lass, and she had shared what had gone on between them. Still, one kiss shouldn't have mattered. Add that to the years of battles between their kin, and now with Cearnach being at Vardon's brother's wedding...

The problem had been that the lass's kiss hadn't done the same for Cearnach. He looked at Calla one last time as she stood so regally next to the groom. He decided she had made her choice, and that she knew he had come to see her wed as she'd asked. He could do no more, and not wanting Elaine involved in any kind of melee with the groom's family, he motioned for her to leave the pew. "We'll leave now, lass."

"I thought you were staying for the reception." She sounded surprised. Then she saw the two hulking Highlanders headed in their direction, and she moved so quickly that she started dragging Cearnach toward the door.

He hadn't wanted to walk that fast, not when he was trying to show the McKinleys they weren't chasing him off, but he didn't want to frighten Elaine further by forcing her to slow her pace.

"Truce," Cearnach mouthed to the brothers, intending to stop the fight that was bound to happen, but before he could leave the church, the bigger of the men stormed into Cearnach's path.

Vardon McKinley. Of all the brothers, he was the most volatile.

He swung his massive fist at Cearnach's face. Before Cearnach could push Elaine behind him and block the blow meant for him, she jumped in front of him, as if to protect him! Or at the very least, to stop the fight.

Vardon wasn't able to pull back in time and hit Elaine in the face. Gasps in the church resounded.

Elaine's head jerked back from the impact, and Cearnach saw red. She fell against him and cried out in shock and pain.

Roaring a string of oaths, Cearnach tucked Elaine under his left arm and unsheathed his sword with his right hand in one swift move.

"No!" Elaine shouted, struggling to free herself from his iron grip. "We're leaving." Her voice was clear and hard, as if she was in charge of the situation.

A she-wolf did *not* dictate combat rules to a Highland wolf who was ready to avenge her injury, no matter how alpha she was. Unable to quell the rage-induced adrenaline running through his blood and the need to pummel the Highlander who had struck an innocent woman, Cearnach couldn't let it go.

Even though Vardon normally bowed down to no one, man or woman, he did appear a wee bit contrite. At least he hadn't unsheathed his sword, and he had taken a couple of steps back, his face looking a bit pale.

"Get out of our way," Elaine said to the McKinley brothers, her voice a fearsome growl.

Cearnach had to give her credit for thinking with her head and not with her heart. He was still ready to kill Vardon. But he couldn't run him through if Vardon didn't at least unsheathe his sword. And he did have to think of Elaine's safety. He couldn't keep her tucked under his arm and risk her getting injured if he encouraged Vardon to draw his weapon.

She sensed Cearnach's indecision and tried to take a step forward, attempting to take charge of the situation. Cearnach wouldn't let her drag him off. Not when he still wanted to destroy Vardon.

Vardon's other brother, Hagan, waited to see what the eldest brother would do, standing beside him, looking unsure. In the past, what had happened wouldn't have been a big deal for men like Vardon. If a woman got in the way of a man's fist during a fight, the fault was her own. But Vardon had done so in a church at his own brother's wedding, in front of onlookers who might not respect him for what he'd done.

Cearnach growled in Gaelic, "An honorable man doesn't strike a woman. Be ready. This isn't finished."

Vardon sneered at him, speaking in Gaelic in return. "As you'll soon learn. Take your whore with you and get out."

Chapter 3

WITH THE MOST VALIANT OF EFFORTS, CEARNACH cooled his temper enough to get Elaine outside the church without coming to blows with Vardon. Four of the McKinley brothers gathered at his back, the tension and anger rolling off everyone in dangerous waves. To Cearnach's further annoyance, rain was now coming down in gray sheets.

"I apologize for what happened in there." Cearnach was still angered beyond reason, not finding the words to adequately describe how he really felt about what had occurred. He sheathed his sword. Then he unbuckled his sash and covered Elaine's head with it as he hurried her to the vehicle sitting on the lower end of the car park. "I shouldn't have brought you here."

He let out a heavy sigh, hating himself for having put her in danger, though he hadn't thought it would come to that.

"I shouldn't have sat on the groom's side of the church." She sounded repentant herself. "I should have stayed with you instead. I shouldn't have been talking so much during the ceremony. I suspect no one would have noticed us as much if we'd remained silent."

"They would have noticed. They weren't angry with you but with me. Where did Vardon hit you?" he growled, trying to protect her from the pelting water with the sash of his kilt.

The raindrops bounced off the waterproof wool, but water was running down his neck and soaking his shirt beneath the jacket. He couldn't cover her completely with the fabric, not unless he removed his whole kilt and wrapped her up in it.

That image quickly brought unbidden desires to the forefront. A woman wrapped in a man's plaid meant she was his. With any other woman, he would have considered such a move as protection, chivalry. With Elaine? *Mine.*

"He hit me in the cheek," she finally said, drawing him back to the current crisis. "At least he missed my eye. The place where he punched me is sore and will probably be bruised and swollen, but you know how we are. It'll fade in a couple of days."

Aye, much sooner than a human's bruises. Yet her injury wouldn't fade soon enough for him. "For your information, I didn't need protecting. Why did you get in the way? He could have killed you."

She snorted and he got the impression she thought he'd needed *her* protection.

He almost gave her a dark laugh, but shook his head instead and unlocked the car doors. She jumped into the passenger's side and slammed the door. As soon as he removed his sword and was sitting in the driver's seat, she said, "I'm freezing. Are you sure you don't have a cell phone on you?" She glanced at his sporran, the medieval-era pouch still worn with kilts today, necessary since kilts had no pockets. Because of the formal occasion, he'd worn the one with the silver cantle decorated in Celtic symbols and horsehair tassels.

After pulling his door shut, he wiped the water from

his face with his hand and turned the heater on high, though the air was cold initially and she shivered at the new assault.

He frowned at her. "No. I left my cell in the car. It would have been easier to get to it if I had an emergency." Then he raised his brows. "When a vehicle nearly hit mine, and I had to make a quick detour, and I was running so late to the wedding, I forgot it."

Feeling the anger concerning Vardon return in full force, with the burning need to settle the score still plaguing him, Cearnach gripped the steering wheel in his fists. "Turn your head so I can get a good look at your face."

Dismissing his concern, she shook her head slightly. "It's okay. We heal fast. Think nothing of it."

"You can't tell me you would have turned the other cheek so he could strike you there also." His words were as cross as he was feeling. Striking Elaine went beyond what any civilized wolf should have done. It wasn't the Middle Ages any longer. *Bastard.*

"No," she said, giving him an annoyed look. "Of course I wouldn't have turned the other cheek. But I know he didn't mean to hit me, and I'm certain he regretted it."

She couldn't know Gaelic or what Vardon had called her. Maybe *that* would have changed her mind. As stubborn as she was, she wouldn't turn her head so he could see where Vardon had struck her. Yes, they healed quickly, but her face would be swollen and bruised for a couple of days before it got better.

Her gaze still connected with his, she sighed. "Okay, though I probably shouldn't tell you this. I…" She took another deep breath and stiffened a bit, yet her gaze didn't waver from his and she said all in a rush, "I would have seized his dagger and threatened him with it if you hadn't grabbed me."

He paused, not expecting her to say such a thing. Then he smiled. "You, lass, are a woman after my own heart."

She relaxed again and he wondered if she thought he wouldn't like a woman who was willing to fight to protect herself. She would be wrong. Yet given the situation, *he* wanted to be the one defending her when he was there, not her shielding him.

He reached over and touched her uninjured cold, wet cheek. "Let me see." He gently cupped her chin and moved her head so he could observe the damage. The skin was red from the punch, swollen, and already beginning to discolor into sickly greens and purples and yellows. He growled low. "I should never have let this happen."

"You couldn't have stopped me." Her mouth was curved in the most devilish of smiles and her eyes sparkled.

She seemed to be of sturdy stock, like a bonny lass born and bred in the Highlands, but with the additional heart of a warrior she-wolf, alpha to the max. But he still wanted to do something, anything, to make the insult and the hurt go away.

Meaning to kiss her somewhere that would not be too intimate, just a light kiss on the top of the head maybe, he found he couldn't make himself do it. Not with his wolfish needs gaining momentum, the desire filling him to press his mouth against her sexy rain-moistened lips. To prove to himself that his feelings weren't one-sided.

He leaned over and kissed her mouth, gently as if she would break, not wanting to force her into complying in the event she wasn't ready for this. Her mouth softened under his touch, accepting him, allowing him this intimacy.

To his surprise and delight, she reached up and set her hands on his shoulders and pulled him closer. Already their hearts were beating at a frantic pace, their pheromones kicking up another notch.

She closed her eyes and gave in to the kiss, slowly at first, then more boldly. He groaned as she parted her lips, permitting him more familiarity. He took advantage of the moment, sliding his tongue into her mouth, tasting her, exploring her, wanting so much more.

Wolves didn't share such intimacies lightly, not with each other, not without some kind of spark that initiated further interest. They didn't make commitments with humans, so as long as the human was willing, they found mutual release with one another until the wolf discovered a mate. Then his wolf mate would be the only one for him.

So even taking it this far meant she was just as intrigued with him as he was with her. He should have backed off, kissed her on her uninjured cheek, just to say he was sorry. Yet, he couldn't help the way he was feeling about her. Not when her mouth was so appealing, tasting sweet and wet and willing. Not when he had wanted to press his lips against hers from the moment she'd gotten out of the car after the accident, and he'd finally allowed his gaze to roam to her face and see the way her lips had been pursed. *At him.* Turning him on.

As the pouring rain pelted the car in a steady rhythm, he deepened the kiss and heat consumed him. Steam covered the windows, and he felt as though they were in a time capsule far away from Calla's wedding, the church, the car park, the Highlands—off in another world. Elaine was all soft curves and feminine fragrance: her she-wolf scent and the sweet-smelling soaps she'd washed in, a hint of perfume, but most of all, the undeniable smell of her sexual desire leading him on.

They couldn't help that part of their wolf nature, the keen ability to smell subtle scents that a human couldn't, the way in which they could sense the shift in emotions—fear, lust, excitement, aggression—just from breathing deeply of the air surrounding them.

He had to force himself not to move his hands from her face, not to explore her soft womanly curves, not to taste so much more of her as her tongue danced with his, not to want *more*. With the greatest regret, he pulled his mouth away from hers, away from the heated exchange that shouldn't have occurred, away from the raging desire to take this further.

For a moment, he still cupped her face and looked into her dark eyes, reading the confusion there, not wishing to fully break contact with her. Their breathing rapid, their hearts were thumping wildly as if they'd just run a race, yet they were still running for the finish line.

Then he released her, and her cheeks blossomed in color as if she was suddenly aware of just how intimate the exchange had been between two unmated wolves.

Thank God he was wearing a kilt and no adjustments had to be made as he was ramrod stiff and ready to bury himself in her soft feminine folds. If he'd been wearing trousers and boxers, they would have strangled him.

She looked dazed as she gave him a tentative smile, then sighed. "Don't be sorry," she said, looking away and drawing closer to the heater to dry her dress. She was no longer shivering. Not after what had happened between them.

For that he was glad. He wanted to ask if she meant not to be sorry about the kiss, when he was not apologetic about that in the least.

When he didn't move the car—he was still too caught up in the profound moment he'd shared with her—she turned to look at him again and raised her brows. "I meant about the cheek."

He grunted. "That's not going to happen, lassie," he said, pausing and giving her a hint of a smile, "but about the kiss, I have no regrets."

She gave a little wolfish grin, her cheeks blushing beautifully once more, and he was ready to kiss her again. Then she turned away to pull at her dress, trying to dry it further. Not entirely resigned to leave things between them like that, he finally drove the Mercedes out of the car park and eased onto the road.

She took a deep breath and exhaled. "The wedding was beautifully done. I loved the color scheme—purple is my favorite—the lavender flowers and bridesmaids' gowns. I enjoyed seeing the men, and even the younger boys, wearing kilts. Despite what happened at the end, I did love everything about the wedding. I've never seen a more spectacular sight."

Cearnach thought he heard regret in Elaine's voice. Had she wished she had stayed in Scotland so many years ago? That she could have had such a wedding?

"Calla Stewart arranges parties, celebrations, weddings, and the like. She's very good at it. She has a real eye for artistic design, and she's great at details."

"Wow. To do so for her own wedding must have been difficult. The bride's a beautiful woman. She seemed delighted you were there."

He nodded. "I was glad I'd made the effort after I saw how pleased she appeared."

"The groom seemed just as handsome," Elaine said, not hesitating to voice her opinion. "They looked like an attractive couple. Though some of the family have a violent nature, if that man who accosted us is any indication."

"Aye, Vardon is the most aggressive of the pack."

She didn't say anything for a moment, as if pondering something, then finally asked, "Did he have a personal grudge against you?"

He didn't want to get into this. Not when he was afraid Elaine might misunderstand the situation, but he owed her an explanation after Vardon took his anger out on her. "He didn't like that I had kissed his mate—the year before he even met her."

When Elaine didn't respond, he glanced at her. She was frowning. Probably thinking he kissed all the unmated she-wolves he met. "There was no spark between us," he said, returning his attention to the rain-slicked road. "Apparently she felt differently."

Elaine said, "She told the brute who hit me? That she preferred your kissing her to his? Or something like that? Why did they end up mating if she felt that way?"

"She must have said something to him about it. They probably were having an argument about something, and she let it slip. *I* didn't tell him. As to why she mated with him, I haven't a clue."

He wanted to explain to Elaine that he'd never

experienced such a kiss with another woman, although he had the mechanics down pat. With Elaine, all his senses were heightened, clamoring for more of her—to taste and feel every inch of her, to smell her unique scent, to hear her whispered words against his ear.

"Cearnach?" Even the way she said his name with the sweetest American accent sounded seductive and sexy and like she was thinking along the same lines as he was. "So what do you think is wrong with the relationship between Calla and Baird?"

He cleared his throat, trying to get his mind off what Elaine was doing to his libido. "He's the kind of man who would dictate everything in her life. How and when she slept, what and when she ate. He's very controlling."

"Not like you," Elaine said with a definite sarcastic edge to her voice.

He glanced at her. "Where did you ever get *that* idea?"

She gave a harsh laugh.

He smiled.

He'd been unable to keep the front of her dress dry with his woolen sash, and now he noted that her dress was plastered to her skin, even more revealing now than when the wind had blown so hard against her dress earlier. Trying to act more noble than he was feeling, he looked away, hoping that the heater would dry her dress so that he wouldn't have to see so much of her.

"So if you *didn't* want him to marry her, why didn't you object?" she asked.

"I *did* object. A number of times. Just not at the wedding. If I had wished to mate with her, I would have. Actually, if I had wanted to mate with her, the wedding would never have happened. Not between her and Baird."

"Why even get married in a church? Is that something all wolves in Scotland do?"

"If we have a title, aye. We need to pass the title down to successive generations. Society expects a public wedding. Though the good citizens don't know we're wolves. Invitations are presented only to wolf kind, generally speaking."

Elaine seemed to mull that over for a few minutes, then she said, "So why did you go to the wedding? Did you think she would change her mind if she saw you there?"

"Maybe. I don't know." He kept telling himself it was because Calla had asked him to come to the wedding. Maybe secretly he'd thought she might change her mind if she saw him there and remembered all that he'd said to her. She hadn't heeded his words.

Now it was too late.

Chapter 4

Elaine Hawthorn genuinely liked Cearnach MacNeill and the way the braw Highland warrior wore his kilt, sporran, sword, and a dirk tucked in his stocking. *Hot and sexy and dangerous* came to mind. Not cute, like she'd said.

But rather than focus on that, she should be thinking about how she needed to contact the cousin she was supposed to meet. She'd use Cearnach's phone back at his car. Yet, she wished she could delay the inevitable and spend more time in Cearnach's company. Like that was a good idea. Not after the way they'd kissed and not when she still didn't know why he'd wanted to protect her in St. Andrews so long ago.

He had to know how appealing he looked to her, so she'd tested him to see how he would respond to being called "cute." She had been amused by his look of surprise, thinking that he'd be so conceited that he wouldn't care what she said about his appearance. Then he'd regained his cocky arrogance, probably figuring she had been teasing him. Most likely no one had ever called him cute.

She noticed the sidelong glances Cearnach continued to give her, wolf that he was. Her dress was way too revealing, plastered to her body as if it were a redder version of her skin. The heater was going full blast, but the air still felt cold as it hit her wet dress.

He reached down and took her cold hand in his and squeezed. "Why did you really come between Vardon and me? Did you think you could stop that Neanderthal?"

"I suppose I did. Just like you might have believed you could change Calla's mind about marrying Baird McKinley if you showed up for the wedding. I didn't give it much thought. I just instinctively stepped into his path."

"Do you often risk your neck for someone you barely know?"

She shrugged, not willing to tell him she'd always been that way—protective. She was used to being an alpha, not someone who melted into the background. Not like when her uncles had been hanged for pirating, making her fear for her life, and she had had to find her way back to America alone. That had been the hardest for her—tucking tail and running away.

"Have you ever risked getting hurt for someone who was well equipped to handle the likes of Vardon McKinley?" Cearnach asked, still trying to get her to reveal the truth.

"No," she finally said. Then she gave him an impish smile. "Not usually."

"Which means it wasn't just instinct that propelled you into action," he said, sounding smugly satisfied, as though he knew she had feelings for him and hadn't wanted to see him hurt.

She reached up to touch her throbbing face where the infuriated Highlander had struck her, her fingers shying away at the last minute. She hadn't expected to get a fist in the face, having hoped to stop the man from throwing the punch in the first place.

"If I hadn't confined you, and you had managed to grab Vardon's dirk, would you have known how to use it?"

She envisioned Vardon's dagger poking out of the top of his hose. If she'd been able to pull free, she would have grabbed that dagger and threatened Vardon with it—just to get him to back off.

She had been serious about that. "*Or* I might have gone for yours."

Silence.

She smiled.

Cearnach cleared his throat. "*My* dagger…"

"Aye," she said, borrowing his brogue. The way she said the word still sounded American to her ear.

He chuckled. "You would not have been successful."

"We'll never know, will we?" she asked in a tone meant to challenge. "But, yes, I know how to use a dirk. A lightweight sword also." Being from a family of pirates ensured that.

Thankfully, Vardon had seemed to come to his senses somewhat once he'd struck her. She had ignored him calling her a whore in Gaelic, figuring he was trying to make himself feel that what he had done wasn't wrong. Besides, he'd said it to infuriate Cearnach, not to slander her. At least that's the way she was going to view it.

She sighed, touching her lips. They were deliciously swollen from Cearnach's kisses. No wolf had ever taken charge of her to such an extent. She'd always remained detached, unaffected by men's kisses, knowing getting stuck on a human could only mean disaster. And a wolf?

She barely refrained from snorting. A wolf was even worse. At least based on her experience.

Her whole body heated again as she recalled the force

of his kiss, the passion behind it, the raw need they'd both exhibited while sharing it. She sensed something unspoken between them. That he had felt something more for her than he had felt for women in the past.

She smothered another snort at the notion before she caught Cearnach's curiosity. The kiss had thoroughly shaken her, making her want much more than was safe. For Cearnach, such a kiss was probably nothing more than what he was used to. Practiced, eliciting the same kind of response in *any* woman.

Attempting to get her mind off the way he'd made her feel, Elaine continued to pull the fabric of her dress away from her skin, trying to dry it in front of the heater.

If she had been alone, she would have slipped into the backseat, rummaged around in her suitcase, and put something else on. Now she wished she hadn't worn this particular dress. Robert Kilpatrick had told her to wear a red dress if she had one so he'd be able to pick her out of a crowd. Considering how rainy and cold it was, she would have had to wear her raincoat while she was at the castle ruins, and Robert wouldn't have seen her red dress anyway.

"Have you been to Scotland before, lass? I was worried you might pull out a camera and begin photographing the church before I escorted you inside."

She didn't want to answer him about being in Scotland before. She skipped instead to the issue of the camera and pretended to be a nice little tourist. She patted her purse. "Camera charged, new disk ready to fill up with pictures," she said proudly.

"Except now it's raining so hard that it won't make for very nice pictures," he said, sounding regretful.

She took a deep breath, recalling the scent of the wolf she'd met so long ago, loving the scent of him now and glad Cearnach didn't seem to remember her from the past. After receiving the note from her distant cousin, she'd felt that her family's pirating life had come back to haunt her. She had a comfortable savings from her parents' inheritance, yet, with cutbacks at the college and the lure of laying claim to the bounty her uncles had hidden somewhere in Scotland, she had been enticed to return.

Of course her cousin wanted a share of the booty. He didn't know all the details of where the stash was hidden. Just as she didn't have all the details, either—like two halves of a treasure map. She just had to ensure that her cousin didn't get the alpha wolf's share since *her* uncles had forfeited their lives for taking it from merchant vessels, and she'd been the one to suffer for it once they died.

"Elaine," Cearnach said as he continued to watch the road, the rain pounding the windshield.

She glanced at him. He was frowning at her—a concerned frown, not an angry one.

"Did you hear me?" he asked.

"Sorry, no. I was concentrating on drying out my dress." And thinking about lots of stuff she didn't want *him* to know about.

"We've met before, lass," Cearnach said softly, as if speaking in a strictly sweet way might make her come clean.

If she had realized who he was when she first met him after the car accident, she might have given him a different name. Still, she could tell he couldn't recall

who she was. Easy to see why. The clothes she'd worn
had covered her from head to toe. Sure, he'd smelled her
scent, touched her, looked deeply into her face, but that
had been so long ago, in a different place and time, and
she had only been sixteen.

"Where have we met?" Cearnach persisted.

She shrugged. "You must have met someone who
looks similar to me at some time or another." She
thought of telling him she hadn't been to Scotland
before, but he would sense she wasn't telling the truth.

"I... attempted... to... rescue you," he said, slowly,
deliberately, as if he was trying to recall the circumstances, or he already knew and was waiting for her to
fess up.

His mouth curved up. He gave her another sly glance,
a wolfish look that meant he wasn't going to give up. "I
will remember," he promised, his voice dark and seductive and intrigued.

He was determined, if nothing else. The game would
soon be up.

She thought back to the way he had reacted to her
when he first saw her get out of the rental car, as he
strode up to meet her in his kilt and sword, armed and
dangerous and hot and sexy. The way he'd perused her,
moved into her space, indicating he was determining
that she was a wolf like him and also attempting to learn
what her response to his close proximity would be. Was
she an alpha? Or beta? Was she skittish or had she been
as fascinated with him as he had been with her? Oh, yes,
she had been. Enthralled. *Absolutely.*

He'd seemed to like that she was an alpha. Not all
wolves would.

She appreciated that he was a first-class alpha and unwilling to bend to pressure. They'd been in a church full of hostiles, and he had held his head high, not in the least bit intimidated. She had hoped to see someone wearing a kilt while she was here, but she'd never expected to see a Highland wedding or a church full of Highlanders in kilts.

Or all wearing dirks and swords. Or ready to do battle. Or stepping into the midst of it herself and getting a bruised face because of it.

"You're so quiet, lass," Cearnach said. "What are you thinking about?"

Cearnach had stood out among the rest of the Highlanders. She wasn't sure if that was because of the way he took charge of her like a Highland warrior on the battlefield. Or maybe she appreciated him more because she sensed he really was concerned for her welfare, like he appeared to be about Calla. Why had he been that way the first time he'd met her?

This time he probably felt responsible because he'd taken her to the church. The first time they'd met, his protectiveness had been because of something else.

"Just tired," she said. "From... the jet lag, you know."

She hadn't meant to look at him, because she knew if she did, he'd probably read the truth in her expression. She glanced at him anyway.

He gave her a small smile, one that said he believed she was thinking about quite a lot that she didn't wish to share with him.

He would be right.

She raised her brows at him, smiled, and turned away. He was tall and his hair was a little shaggy, dark brown with a reddish tint. His square jaw was clean-shaven. The ferocious, dark look that he had given her when he first approached her car had made her think of a thunderstorm approaching—like the one that had finally caught up to them. His eyes were dark brown, just a shade lighter than black.

"The way you are smiling, lass, has me believing that you're thinking about something pleasant. Will you not share with me? I'd love to hear your thoughts."

She blushed. She couldn't help the way her skin flushed so easily.

"I was thinking about how you seem... so... casual at times, as if you are trying to set people at ease. That you would be kind of carefree, if it weren't for the circumstances we met under."

"Aye, that I am. So you were thinking of me and that's why you were smiling?"

Another volley of heat shot through her, and she tried not to squirm.

"Just for a moment. Are you certain I was smiling? The weather is so bad that I'm sure I was frowning quite profoundly."

"Nay, lass, you were smiling."

About him, she was certain he wanted to tack on. She didn't dare ask him what *he* had been thinking about, afraid he'd say he thought about her. She certainly didn't want to know what he was thinking of her—like, where he'd met her before.

His casual demeanor was appealing, but she thought deep down he was passionate, powerful, and forceful when he needed to be. The kiss had showed just how powerful, passionate, and sexy he could be.

Even though he wore a jacket, vest, shirt, and a plaid pinned over his shoulder and wasn't bare-chested, she could imagine him sword-fighting without the rest of his clothes. Just a kilt and boots. She liked the way she could tease the gruffness from him, and he'd parry with her in a lighthearted way. The way he was so protective of her in front of the other wolves was endearing, too.

She did feel awful that he'd ruined two tires. Not because it was her fault. He'd obviously been driving too fast, trying to make it to the church on time. Still, she did feel bad about it.

"I'll wait with you until you get someone to help replace the tires on your car," she offered, wiping rainwater from her face with some tissues from her purse.

"I can't seem to place the time or circumstance, but I recall trying to help you and… somehow you got away," he said, as if he couldn't believe anyone could escape him if he didn't wish it.

She shrugged, then drew closer to the heater again. She was trying to dry her dress, but her wet hair kept dripping water all over it. She was irritated with herself for being so off on her timing for her own appointment. Robert Kilpatrick would probably be upset that she hadn't arrived at the agreed-upon time. She was certain he had tried to contact her and hoped he realized she had phone trouble.

"Where are you staying?" Cearnach asked.

The car slid on the wet pavement, and she grasped the leather seat to keep her balance. She glanced at him. "Flora's Bed and Breakfast."

Frowning, Cearnach gripped the steering wheel as he maneuvered through another puddle of water.

"What's wrong?"

"How did you learn of *that* place? It's not listed anywhere as a rental. The bed and breakfast is for family and friends who need to stay in the area for the night."

"The man I'm meeting said it was close to the castle ruins."

Cearnach wore that dark warrior expression again. "What is his name?"

"Kilpatrick."

Cearnach stared at her, then shook his head.

"What?"

"*Which* Kilpatrick?"

She didn't like the sound of this. "Robert."

Cearnach snorted.

"I take it you don't like *him, either.*"

"He's a lecher." Cearnach glanced at her. "He's the man who was practically sitting in your lap at the church. You must have noticed."

She gaped at Cearnach, then frowned as he continued to watch the road. "Which one was he?"

"Both are Kilpatricks. The one sitting on your right was Robert. What does he want with you?"

She hesitated to say. It really was none of his business. But what difference did it make at this point? The whole situation was odd. If Robert had the wedding to get to, he hadn't allotted much time for their meeting. She wondered why not. What was Robert planning? Clearly he had chosen their meeting place to keep her far away from the rest of his family. The truth was bound to come out—to an extent. "He's…" Then she saw the humor in the whole situation and started to laugh.

Cearnach's fierce expression didn't change.

"He's a distant cousin." She gave a little shrug, loving the irony. Robert would be horrified to realize he had tried to come on to her when she was distantly related to him. "Wouldn't he be surprised to learn that if he's thinking I'm available or something."

"Distant cousin? How distant?" Cearnach asked, not sounding as though he saw the humor.

"By a couple of marriages. Maybe four times removed? I don't know for sure."

"Then he could still want you."

She wrinkled her nose at Cearnach. "This is strictly a business deal." If the man wanted her, it would only be to gain the rest of the loot through a mating.

Cearnach frowned back at her. "Doing business with the Kilpatricks can get you into a lot of hot water. In the old days, they were smugglers, pirates. They haven't changed much since then."

Her blood chilled. He was bound to make the connection between her and her uncles. She noted the irritated tone in his voice and suspected that Cearnach's family members were probably the epitome of law-abiding citizens.

Since werewolves lived such long lives, her maternal grandfather had been a pirate and had hidden treasure in the Everglades. She suspected her parents had laundered the money from the ill-gotten gains in the tavern and lodgings they rented out and maybe had been involved in their own illegal schemes. Then Kelly Rafferty had taken over.

"What exactly is the business arrangement with Kilpatrick?" Cearnach asked, the car's tires slipping on the wet pavement. He took his foot off the gas. "He's going to sell you part of the castle ruins and you can peddle tickets to tourists to see that half of the castle?"

"That's *our* castle?"

"Aye. Been in the family for generations. Once you see how much they let the place go…" He shook his head.

Automatically she went on the defensive. "Yeah, like you would do any better if you had the chance to own a castle. Years of wars and the elements beating down on a building ten centuries old, the upkeep, the taxes. I can just imagine how much the place would cost to repair and maintain."

"They sold off a lot of the ancient stone walls to keep themselves in whisky," Cearnach said drily.

She stared at him, attempting to see if he was telling the truth. He appeared to be speaking honestly.

"My own castle is in *great* shape, if you want to talk about taking care of the ancestral home," he continued.

"*Your* castle?" Now this was getting interesting. "Don't tell me you're the clan chief and a duke or something."

"No, but I'm the pack's sub-leader, and the clan chief is my older brother." He sounded proud of the fact, as well he should, as he glanced at the area where his car should have been on the side of the road. "Son of a…"

Dumbfounded, she stared at the spot in the driving rain as if looking hard enough might make the car reappear.

"It's gone. Your car. It's… not… there," she said, barely breathing.

Chapter 5

TRYING TO KEEP HIS TEMPER UNDER CONTROL AND figure out what had happened, Cearnach thought back to the younger McKinley brothers. They'd been late to their own brother's wedding, and they'd been smirking about something when they spied him in the church.

They could have been coming along the same road, seen his abandoned car, and known it was his. He'd bet Argent Castle that they'd have hauled his car over the cliffs if they could have managed. Now he didn't even have a phone so that he could call Ian.

"We're driving to the castle ruins," he said to Elaine, trying not to sound as angry as he felt as he pulled back onto the road.

"You… want to explore Senton Castle in this rain?" She sounded so incredulous that he thought she was beginning to believe he might be a little crazy.

"Aye. I have to take a look at the cliffs. Make sure there's nothing below them that belongs to me. I can't get close enough to the edge to see from here. The safest way to get to the beach to see the cliffs from down below is to park at the castle and take the stairs."

"Your car?" she asked, horrified.

"Aye."

"Who… who would do such a thing?"

"Take your pick. The McKinleys?"

"But they were at the wedding, weren't they?"

"Two of them were late."

Her eyes widened. Elaine didn't say anything for several moments, then finally looked back the way they'd come. "Why are we going *this* way?"

"This is the way to the ruins. You must have missed the turnoff, remember?" He glanced at her, noting that her damp hair was still in straggles against her wet dress. Only a small fraction of her dress had dried out.

"The road is kind of hidden," he said as gently as he could.

The lass would never have made it to the meeting with Robert Kilpatrick on time. Not when she had been lost and arrived way past the time they'd planned to meet. Cearnach wondered why Kilpatrick had left so little time for his meeting with Elaine—the wedding was only two hours later. Robert would have had only about an hour to spend with Elaine, and she clearly had expected to spend much more time. Cearnach was starting to believe that Kilpatrick was up to no good where the lass was concerned.

Without her cell phone, she couldn't call Kilpatrick, for which Cearnach was grateful. She shouldn't have any business dealings with the man unless she had someone else with her who could see the situation more objectively and ensure she didn't get ripped off.

Right then and there, he decided that he'd protect Elaine's interests until she left Scotland, if she agreed. He had failed with Calla and could do no more for her. Now Elaine seemed to need someone to look out for her. And this was the second time, he was certain.

He thought back to her name, Elaine Hawthorn, and

how it could be related to the Kilpatricks and McKinleys. They were pirates. But what about the Hawthorns?

The memories came back to him in a sudden rush. "Hawthorn," he said under his breath, both surprised and glad he'd finally figured it out.

The public hanging of the Hawthorn brothers so many years ago. Robert Kilpatrick and four of his kin had been desperate to locate the men's niece, Elaine Hawthorn, because they had believed she was the key to finding the stolen goods. Cearnach had been the one to catch up to her… and lose her in one fell swoop.

Now she was back. Suddenly, he felt possessive all over again. Wanting to protect her. Wanting to keep her.

She glanced at Cearnach. "What?"

He recalled her haunted expression when she was but a young girl, the way she'd appeared guardedly hopeful until the man slugged him and she escaped Cearnach's grasp.

"Why did you run away in St. Andrews, lass?" He spoke quietly, not wanting to put her on the defensive, and then he added, "I only meant to protect you."

He pulled into the car park below the castle ruins, which they could see off in the distance. Four towers and three of the walls were still standing. Despite how rundown some of the buildings were, Cearnach still loved seeing the ancient ruins, though his own people had fought the McKinleys a time or two in the distant past and had caused some of the damage themselves.

Elaine let her breath out in a whoosh, as if she might have finally given up on the charade, but she didn't speak.

Did she think he still didn't know who she was? Most likely, and she wouldn't come clean unless he shared with her all he knew. "You are the niece of Tobias and Samson Hawthorn. My brothers and I were passing through St. Andrews when we heard about the public hanging."

"Why would you have wanted to protect me? Yes, my uncles were hanged. I probably would have been also. Had Lord Whittington known I was their niece, he probably would have figured I had been pirating along with them. But I could barely keep my head out of a bucket the whole time I was on the ship."

"You had never traveled with them before?" Cearnach asked, not surprised. Despite the way she'd been dressed, wearing more clothes and with her hair hidden from view, she'd looked as lovely then as now, although perhaps a bit more pale.

She shook her head. "My parents had just died. My uncles were in St. Augustine visiting them when it happened. They received an offer of a mating for me back home and said yes to the man. I refused to mate with the wolf who wanted me. I coaxed my uncles into agreeing to take me with them on this one voyage. I never expected…"

She paused, her voice choking with emotion. "I never thought my uncles would be taken from me and put to death." She took a settling breath, but he noticed her eyes were swimming in tears, and he regretted upsetting her. "What would you have gained by protecting me?" she asked.

He stopped short of giving her the whole truth, telling her all he could for now. "You caught my eye when you disembarked from the ship. A flower among thistles. Once your uncles were taken prisoner, along with most of their crew, I knew the wolves would be after you, too. I could see how shaken you were when the Hawthorn brothers were hanged. I knew you must have had some close connection to them. When they were gone, I saw how young you were, how alone, and smelled on the breeze that you were a wolf."

Those—and where the loot was that had belonged to the MacNeill clan—were the most pressing concerns he'd had at the time. "I didn't know if you were a royal and able to shift to wolf form at will, or if the full moon dictated your shifts. I feared you might be in for more trouble because of that."

"I'm a royal," she said. "Because I have very few human roots many generations ago, I don't need to shift unless it's my own choice. Did you attempt to pay people to locate me?"

"Nay. I used my sense of smell." He studied her, waiting for her to explain further, and after a bit of a hesitation, she did.

"A maid came to my room saying that someone was trying to buy information about me. I didn't know who else might have figured out I was with the ship when it came into port."

"The McKinleys or Kilpatricks. They were there."

She stared at Cearnach. "They did nothing to try and stop the hangings. They didn't try to rescue my uncles or their crew, either."

"I'm certain they felt their hands were tied, lass."

"Why would you defend them?" she said, her voice angry. "You don't even like them."

"Aye, but I know venturing a rescue with all the armed guards in the square would have been impossible for them. The best they could have done was to locate you and keep you safe."

"Would they? Or would they have been afraid of risking their necks for me?"

Cearnach let out his breath, not about to hide the truth from her any longer, though he wasn't certain she would have believed him if he'd told her the reality of the situation back then. "Honestly? I imagine they wanted to see if you knew where your uncles had hidden their bounty. Maybe they would have ensured that you mated with one of their kinsman, again to keep the money in the clan."

She gave a little grunt of disgust. "*That* I can believe." She chewed on her bottom lip. "I still don't know why *you* wanted to protect me."

"Haven't you realized that I'm a defender of women and small children?"

She gave a little laugh that told him she didn't believe him—well, maybe to some extent.

She was right not to have trusted his motives back then. He would have done anything to hide her from the law and her disreputable kin after seeing how sweet and innocent and vulnerable she had looked. But he'd had pack reasons, too, for wanting to take her under his wing and hide her away.

"After searching for you for months, I assumed you'd slipped away on a ship bound for America or somewhere else." He hadn't stopped thinking about her—and the way she'd appeared so lost and tearful and fragile—for years.

Now? She was very much an alpha, sexy and gorgeous, and he wouldn't be surprised if she'd broken a lot of hearts over the years.

"What about the man you were supposed to mate back home?" he asked.

"Long story. Some other time."

That meant she wasn't going to talk about it anytime soon. He would ask again later when he had the chance and she seemed more willing to talk.

"You stay here. I'll check out the area to see if I can locate my car." He would have a long way to walk to reach the site, and Elaine wasn't dressed for the weather or a hike so he thought she should remain behind.

"Wait. I'll go with you."

Surprised at her declaration, he watched as she turned around and kneeled on the seat. Then she leaned way over the seat back to reach her suitcase and tugged at it, twisting it around until she could reach the zipper.

If he hadn't been confined by the steering wheel, he could have reached for whatever she needed, but the sight in front of him was too mesmerizing to ignore. Her red dress clung to her buttocks, showing off her sexy derriere. Like all wolves, she had to be a runner, and her toned legs and ass showed she was in great shape. His whole body jerked to attention again.

Calla was a beautiful wolf, but she'd never had a sexually charged effect on him like Elaine did.

Again he forced himself to look away, remembering the way the gown she'd worn in St. Andrews had hidden all her curves. The times sure had changed. He was damned glad he was the only one witnessing the way she looked right now, though. He didn't want another male wolf salivating over her like he was doing.

She unzipped the suitcase and pulled out a pair of boots, snagged a long raincoat, then turned back around. She sat back down on the seat. He eyed the raincoat.

Chin tilted down, she gave him an annoyed look.

"Yeah. I had a heavy-duty raincoat with me. You pulled me out of the car so fast at the church, complaining we were late to the wedding that only *you* had planned to attend, that I didn't have a chance to grab my coat."

An uncomfortable guilt washed over him. He should have asked. He should have considered the weather and how she could be affected by it.

Not about to admit it, he said instead, "Good. I'm glad you're more prepared. I wouldn't take you up there wearing that slinky dress or those high-heeled shoes and…" He considered her dress and couldn't help looking at the way the fabric was plastered against her rigid nipples or the way he could even see the indent in her belly button, which was just as sexy. "You'd freeze to death."

"I accept your apology," she quickly said, brows raised, challenging him to contradict her.

One corner of his mouth quirked up.

"I'll be fine. What about yourself?" she continued, as if he had *admitted* he had apologized to her and the issue was no longer important.

He smiled. The she-wolf was a treasure.

"Wool kilt. Water repellent. I'll remove my jacket and vest."

She sighed, eyeing his torso. "You could take off your shirt." She focused her brown eyes on his shirt, as if she was ready to help him remove it and wanted to see how he looked in just a kilt.

She could take off her dress, too, he was thinking.

What he found most engaging was that she wouldn't meet his eyes.

When he didn't say anything, waiting for her to look into his gaze and fighting the urge to grin at her, she looked up, her eyes wide and innocent. There was no earthly way that the lass had been thinking purely innocent thoughts.

Her cheeks blossomed with color. "It's not waterproof. Your shirt, I mean," she explained.

"A good point." He was still smiling, loving the way he could read her feelings so easily.

"All right." She slipped off her soaking-wet pumps and pulled on her boots while he struggled to get out of his jacket and vest in the confined space between the driver's seat and steering wheel. She tugged the raincoat over her arms and buttoned it up, glancing at him to see if he'd removed his shirt yet.

He was in the process of unbuttoning it, but when she looked at him with such keen interest and anticipation, he felt his pheromones taking over again. Just her watching him strip half naked had the darnedest effect on him. He would have felt smug, hearing the way her heartbeat had accelerated, indicating her intrigue, except that his heart was thumping just as rapidly, revealing how much he was *just* as intrigued.

As if she was reminding him of where this was going—and that this was not something more, like him removing his kilt next and then her coat and dress—she pulled the hood of her coat over her head.

That made him remember how the hood of her cloak had hid most of her features when she was but a young lass. In that instant, he felt the fates had smiled on him. He couldn't have protected her before, but he would help her this time.

He pulled off his shirt, and her gaze shifted to his torso. For an instant, he felt like he was on a wolf's version of the marriage mart. A mate mart instead. Did he meet her expectations?

Keeping a straight face, he flexed his muscles a bit, and her gaze shot up to his. Her cheeks instantly filled with color again. She might be an alpha wolf, but he realized how much he flustered her.

He tried to minimize his smile, but he was having a hard time doing so. He was having even more trouble keeping his kilt from tenting under his sporran.

She quickly said, "We could run as wolves. It's raining hard enough and no one's parked here, so no one would see us."

Her suggestion completely took him by surprise. In part because his other head was thinking for him and he needed a minute to focus on what she was saying.

"Our wolf coats would keep us drier. We'd be more sure-footed and could travel faster and farther," she added.

"Are you game?" He couldn't remove the rest of his clothes while he sat behind the steering wheel. She could climb into the backseat and take off her clothes and shift, then he could follow her.

"Not sure. What do you think?" she asked.

He'd much prefer to run as a wolf. They could smell the scents up close, nose to the ground, which they couldn't do walking upright as humans. But he was surprised she'd ask his advice. Any young girl who could escape him and his brothers while they were attempting to track her down—not to mention Lord Whittington, once he'd received the news that she was in the port city, as well as her kin, who were trying to get hold of her—seemed able to get along without seeking anyone's opinion about anything. She evaded all of them, which meant she had been a lot more capable than he'd given her credit for.

"We can shift up at the castle. There are enough enclosed rooms to shield us from prying eyes. A cellar where bread was once baked and walls to the baron's and baroness's rooms still stand. No roof, though. A chapel and a tower. A couple of other rooms, stone stables for the horses…" He paused. "Yeah, even a couple of locking restrooms. That should work."

"Okay. We can do it."

As angry as he felt about his car, he couldn't help but be pleased that Elaine wanted to help him with this. And run as wolves? Even better.

He considered the left side of her face again.

She took a deep breath and pulled her hood forward more. "The bruising will be gone before long, and you don't need to be angry about this anymore."

But he was.

"Let's do this," he said, right before they left the car. He noticed her gaze had shifted again, and she was giving his torso another appreciative look.

He smiled. Briskly in the cold wind, they walked the half-mile winding path to the castle. The walkway was mossy green and shiny wet. The rain had thankfully let up to a light drizzle. The whole area was shrouded in a blanket of thick mist, making it look surreal, otherworldly, ghostly.

The wind was still blowing fiercely across the cliffs and tugging at Elaine's hood to such an extent that she had to hold it in place around her face. The air was cold and wet as it pounded his bare chest, but he barely noticed, as hot as she made him feel from the way she seemed to enjoy his appearance. More than that, he knew that his shirt would have been soaking wet, plastered to his skin, and just about as cold.

He shifted his gaze from Elaine to the cliffs overlooking the loch that surrounded the ancient ruins on three sides and had made the place nearly impenetrable from encroaching enemies.

When they reached the mossy stairs to climb down one of the cliffs, he took hold of her hand because the steps were slippery. At least initially that was the reason, but he felt as though he was on a date with the she-wolf. Wolves didn't date. They had casual sex with humans, or they found a wolf that would be the perfect mate. Dating was a human condition.

Yet, for the first time ever, he felt like a man on a date. A very agreeable date. One that he didn't want to end.

Chapter 6

CEARNACH OBSERVED ELAINE AS SHE WATCHED THE water dashing against the rocks below, white froth splashing over stones bathed in green moss. She was taking deep breaths, her eyes sparkling with enthusiasm.

"It's breathtaking," she said, her voice filled with awe.

Just as breathtaking as she was. "Aye. Just imagine when the castle was wholly intact."

"It would have been intimidating then." She looked up at the castle that rose high above the cliff opposite the one they'd climbed down. The stairs carved into that cliff were just as steep and deadly.

He smiled darkly, thinking of how dangerous laying siege to the castle had been. "Aye, and with men at the ramparts, armed and watching every move, if we had approached it back then."

They reached the bottom of the steps, traversed a long slippery walkway, and then headed back up another hundred and fifty or so stairs until they arrived at a stone tunnel, its mouth gaping open, that led into the inner bailey of the castle.

"This is so cool," she said, staring at the moss-covered rock walls, the rainwater running off the gray stones. "To think that the people who lived here in ancient times passed this way regularly."

"Yes, but if you were a foe, you'd be dead." He pointed at the mossy stone walls that rose high above and the arrow slits from which archers could riddle an intruder with arrows before he could defend himself or escape.

She shivered, and he rubbed her arm and smiled. "You're a distant cousin of the Kilpatricks so no worries."

"Yes, but I'm with one of their staunchest enemies, a MacNeill wearing his clan plaid, although you left your sword behind. Besides, they'd probably figure I was besotted with the enemy and a traitor to the Kilpatricks' cause."

Cearnach laughed. "So you do like the kilt." He said it as a statement of fact. If she said she didn't, he wouldn't believe her.

She gave him a smile that said she liked a little more than that. The way she still held his hand—not immediately releasing it when the way was no longer slippery—made him think she enjoyed his company too.

They headed through the tunnel, their footfalls echoing off the rock walls and floor before they reached the opening into the inner bailey. Despite it being October, the courtyard was covered in soft, bright green grass that was short, as if someone came in and mowed it on a regular basis.

"Where can we hide our clothes? If we shift in the restrooms or anywhere else, our clothes could be found," she said, finally releasing his hand. "If anyone came along who was crazy enough to be out in this cold, rainy weather."

He pointed to an eighteenth-century cannon protecting the keep. "See the cannon that was used to defend the castle in later years? I'll tuck our things in there. No one would ever think to look for them there."

"You'd have to undress the rest of the way and shift

by the cannon." Her eyes honed in on his chest, the chilly rain dribbling down it.

He was used to the conditions. The strong, cold wind still whipped about but it wasn't as frigid in the bailey, most likely because of the high, four-foot-thick walls that surrounded it. But even so, a naked body would find the air cold and the light rain chilly. Still, the cold didn't bother him much.

"I've swum in the icy loch, lass. Keeps a body strong. And *virile*."

Her eyes sparkled with humor, her mouth curving up just a hint.

He continued, "A little autumn rain won't hurt."

She laughed. "I'm from Florida, and when the winter hits, even if it's not all that cold, I wear a coat and avoid the ocean."

He shook his head. Yet he was thinking how he'd like to keep her here in Scotland so she'd grow accustomed to their weather. Better than that, he knew just how to warm the lass, even if she didn't become acclimated to their weather quickly. "You'd never last in our climate when winter arrives, but I could help a lot there."

"I'll be long gone before then," she promised, giving him a small smile. Before he could respond—to tell her he hoped to change her mind, even that he *planned* to change it—she slipped into the bathroom and closed the door.

He waited outside the ladies' room while she undressed and shifted. He couldn't help thinking about her taking off the clingy, wet red dress and him seeing her naked.

When she scratched and whimpered at the door, he

broke loose of his vision of her as a naked woman, forgetting she'd be a wolf now, and pulled the door open. A beautiful, mink-brown wolf with dark brown eyes emerged. She wagged her tail and stood by the ladies' room, waiting for him to get her personal effects.

He scooped up her boots and the bundle of clothes that she'd wrapped inside her raincoat, then tucked them under his arm and strode across the inner courtyard to the outer one. Leaning down, he stuffed her things deep inside the cannon. Then he started to strip, putting each article of clothing inside the weapon as soon as he'd pulled it off.

While he did so, he watched her as she raced all over the castle ruins. She seemed to be chasing smells and unsure which way to go first because everything seemed just as intriguing as everything else. She sniffed around the stone stables, busily exploring them. Then she dashed across the bailey, glanced in his direction, looked at his kilt still riding low on his hips, then bolted up narrow, winding stairs into one of the castle towers. He'd just finished removing his kilt when she peered down at him through a broken part of the wall.

He smiled to see her head poking out of the broken structure as if the hole in the wall was a new window, her gaze perusing his naked form, her eyes catching his as he observed her reaction. If she was in her human form, would she be blushing again?

He willed his wolf half to take over. His muscles stretched, the tendons and ligaments warming as he called upon the change. Shifting felt like getting a gentle workout, but before the shifter had a chance to really experience the warming sensation, he or she was standing as a wolf, a genetic necessity to prevent humans from seeing them during the shift. If anyone observed the change, hopefully they would see a blurring of forms as if their eyes were playing tricks on them.

Now he was fully clothed in wolf fur, kneading the ground with his paws and stretching his legs before he raced to join her. Watching her explore the castle ruins and seeing her enthusiasm about running as a wolf made him feel a surge of lightheartedness, something he hadn't felt since Calla decided to mate with Baird McKinley a month earlier.

Sure, he had to see if his car was anywhere about. But with helping to run Argent Castle and the pack, he hadn't taken much time for himself of late. If his clan could only see him now. Though he was always kidded for being the most easygoing of the brothers, this was something entirely new for him—putting aside a crisis to enjoy the company of a she-wolf, forgetting duty or the pack for the moment.

He quickly joined her on the tower stairs. When she unexpectedly licked his face in greeting, he cast her a wolfish grin.

She had to know her actions were considered part of the courtship phase between wolves. Werewolves might not date, but they definitely courted in their own way. He was all too ready to go along with it.

She ran up the rest of the stairs, wagging her tail and stopping to sniff at a corner of the tower and then on the step before her while he nearly rammed his nose up her butt because of her sudden stops and starts.

He could have laughed at the way she was so delighted to cast off her human form and play in her wolf one.

Probably some of her enthusiasm was due to the long

flight, confinement on the airplane, the drive here from Edinburgh, and now her first chance to really stretch her legs, like a wild wolf released from a cage.

After circling around the tower room, she wrinkled her nose at a hole in the floor where men would have urinated when they were on guard duty. Then she stood on her hind legs to look out a perfectly round window at the water, where whitecaps frothed over the tops of moss-covered boulders. She smelled the wind for the longest time, breathing in the scents, filling her lungs, letting out the air, and doing it again. While he was smelling *her*. The way she was so ecstatic, excited, loving it.

She dropped to her paws, whipped around, and licked his cheek again. Before he could lick her back, she raced down the circular stairs until she reached the bottom as he flew down the steps after her.

She circumnavigated the inner courtyard, her thick fur coat protecting her from the chilly light rain. She poked her nose at the water-filled well, which had large, leafy plants floating on the surface as the rain splattered into the well. Then she dashed into the cellar, smelled the ovens where bread used to bake, the storage area where meat and grain had been stored, and then ran up the stairs to the baron and baroness's chambers, where the roof was long gone. She sniffed around, then headed back out again. Exploring the chapel in the same excited way, she smelled the scents that had collected over the years, none of which humans who were *purely* humans could detect.

Staying close, he took delight in seeing her joy. He realized then how easily Elaine had made him forget his mission, his anger at the McKinleys and the Kilpatricks, showing him how important life's little pleasures were.

She headed for the tunnel that led out of the inner bailey and raced down the one hundred and fifty stairs cut into the cliff like she was possessed. She was sure-footed despite her rushing because of the fur on her pads, just like when he could run on ice without slipping. He had to laugh deep inside as he easily kept up with her. He trailed just behind her, watching the upper stairs that led down, then looking up to the castle tunnel, to ensure that no one was coming or might see them.

No one was out in this weather.

Then she leaped the short distance to the beach and ran to the water's edge, snapping at the churned-up surf smashing against boulders. Whitecaps danced across small waves, as the wind blew his and Elaine's fur. The water was too stirred up for boats to be out in this weather.

She glanced out across the loch, then loped along the edge of the water, looking all along the beach and up at the cliffs.

The rain hadn't started pouring again, though as dark as the sky was, it looked like it might any minute. The outer guard hairs on Elaine's and Cearnach's thick coats repelled the water, keeping the downy, soft fur close to their skin dry and warm from the bitter cold wind.

She stopped to observe the castle, looking at it in awe and with reverence. The massive stone structure truly was a sight to behold. Anyone who had wanted to storm the castle must have had a death wish.

His own kin had put a few holes in the walls back in the early days just to make a statement concerning the Kilpatricks' thieving ways.

He stood beside her, listening to her heart pounding and the way she was panting and resting for a bit. He was damned angry about his car, but all he could think of was escorting one beautiful she-wolf out to dinner later tonight. Thinking in that direction was strange because he was always business first, pleasure second.

He nudged at her to join him and they continued searching away from the castle, around a bend in the cliffs so they couldn't see the ruins any longer. That's when he spied the debris straight ahead. The ragged remains of his minivan. His ire rose instantly.

The van looked like a flattened aluminum can, resting on its top, tires sticking straight up in the air. Cearnach raced over to the vehicle, smelling every part of the scraped and gouged metal, and analyzing the scents. He smelled the two younger McKinley brothers—the same two brothers who had arrived late at the church.

Elaine was taking in the scents also, sniffing around the vehicle as if she was one of his wolf pack, not a stranger who shouldn't want to be involved, not someone who was related to the men who had done this. She would memorize their scents and know them again if either of them got close to her.

Her tail was down, while his was straight out, fully alpha, aggressive, in charge. She wasn't cowed, but she wasn't happy, either. He quickly moved to nudge her face in a show of solidarity. She licked his cheek in understanding, maybe trying to tell him how sorry she was. She wagged her tail a bit, but it was a sad kind of wag.

He hoped he could get to his cell phone so he could tell Ian where he was and what was going on. He moved back to the minivan and tried to reach in through the window with his right front paw. The glass shattered, but the gap between the roof and the door now was too narrow to even reach in with his foreleg. He scraped his leg on the broken glass, cutting it and swearing inwardly, growling outwardly.

When he stood, he saw Robert Kilpatrick's red curls crest the bluff right before he saw the rest of Robert's head. "Hey, Cearnach, whatcha doin' out here, mon, wearing your wolf coat and running with your new girlfriend? Better take care or you might get stranded. Then where would you be?" He gave a harsh laugh, his green eyes glittering with menace, then he hurried away from the cliff.

Cearnach would climb the cliff and pay Robert back if he could, but the cliffs were so steep here that he'd have a better chance of climbing them if he were a mountain goat.

Then he began to think of what Robert meant. *Stranded.* How could they be stranded unless… *hell.* Cearnach ran full out toward the castle ruins.

He glanced over his shoulder to make sure Elaine was keeping up. She was following, her face grim and her tongue hanging out.

When he reached the path, he looked back again, but he had to stop the men if they were attempting to steal Elaine's rental car. She was close, nearly to the path. He jumped up and climbed the few feet to the stone path, then ran as fast as his legs would carry him up all the stairs and around the walkway that wound through the cliffs until he could see the car park.

Her car was gone. The car park was empty.

Damn it to hell.

Despite the rain, he could smell that two of the McKinley brothers had been here on this path. Why would they have been *here*?

He glanced back to see if Elaine was following him. She was nowhere in sight. His heart plummeted. He dove back the way he'd come. He was fairly certain that none of the McKinleys would harm them. The brothers were just annoyed enough about Cearnach crashing the wedding—to their way of thinking—and stirring up trouble that they wanted to pay him back. He hadn't thought they'd go to these lengths.

He ran as if his life depended on it, frantic that Elaine might have come to harm, or that they might have somehow gotten hold of her. But he was certain she would be growling, baring her teeth, charging, and snapping her jaws if anyone had tried to approach her, and he would hear her feral outrage.

When he reached the bottom of the long, narrow steps, where they had headed for the beach, he didn't see Elaine. His heart slamming into his ribs, he looked up at the steps leading into the tunnel that took them into the inner bailey. She wasn't anywhere that he could see. Not on the stairs, the path, or the beach.

He smelled the air. She'd been here recently. He ran for the steps leading to the castle tunnel, and by the time he'd come to the entrance, she was entering it.

He'd never seen a more beautiful sight. He wanted to hug the life out of her now that he knew she was all right. She paused, looking upset, but with her tail held out straight behind her.

Even before he joined her to nuzzle her, to greet her and tell her how relieved he was to see her safe, he knew that she'd learned their clothes were gone, stolen from the cannon.

Chapter 7

ELAINE HAD FEARED THE WORST ONCE SHE REALIZED Robert Kilpatrick and his kin—her kin also, as much as she hated to admit it—had planned to steal her car. Had they found the clothes in the cannon?

She smelled the men's scent on the stairs and where they had moved all over the place looking for where she and Cearnach had been. They would have smelled their scents and discovered their clothes in the centuries-old weapon.

Before she even poked her nose inside, she knew her clothes were gone, and she felt her whole body tense in anger. At first, she had stared dumbly at the ancient weapon as if by looking at it hard enough and peeking in again, she could make their belongings reappear.

She smelled the scent of the two men who had brushed up against the cannon and recognized them as the same two who had approached them, one being Vardon, who had hit her.

Seeing Robert Kilpatrick gloating over what they'd done to Cearnach's car infuriated her. *The bastards.* She should be on her cousin's side, but not when she didn't know him and he'd done this mischief. And not when she had seen the way Cearnach had acted in the church. He hadn't protested Calla's wedding or disturbed the ceremony in the least. Well, maybe a little. Angered that the men would steal her belongings and Cearnach's and destroy his car, she growled softly.

She felt utterly defeated. Everything she'd brought with her on the trip was in the car. Passport, driver's license, money, clothes, credit card—everything was in there. The vehicle was insured under her name. Which meant she was liable for the car, too.

Because they were werewolves, they couldn't go to the police about matters like this. Not with the concern that someone might end up in police custody. A confined wolf who couldn't control his shifting could spell danger for all their kind.

Cearnach licked her face and urged her to come with him.

She hesitated, though she really didn't have any alternative. Most likely he intended to take her to his castle, and his pack would help her out. What made her hesitate was the knowledge that running through the countryside as wolves could be a dangerous business. Even in Florida, where wolves no longer roamed free, she had to be careful. She'd been mistaken for a German shepherd once, or at least a mixed breed of some sort.

A *dog*. She humphed to herself. Worse? A dogcatcher had actually caught her and taken her to the pound. Nothing worse than being caged up with a bunch of noisy dogs when she was a wolf! Since they'd caught her early in the morning, she'd had to stay there until everyone left for the night. Thankfully, the workers had left a couple of windbreakers hanging on a coatrack, so when she left, she hadn't been completely naked.

She didn't want to leave Senton Castle, the place where she'd had all that belonged to her in Scotland. Then she reminded herself that those belongings were just stuff. The Kilpatricks and McKinleys could

destroy them and she would have a hard time recoup-
ing her losses, but she was alive and well and so was
Cearnach, and that was all that truly mattered. Though
she couldn't help biting back a bit of annoyance concerning him. If his car hadn't nearly hit hers on the
road, she wouldn't be here now. She would have
met with...

Robert Kilpatrick. Well, if she'd been on time.

She snorted. If she'd met him first, she probably
would have thought *he* was one of the good guys. What
a horrible thought.

Trying to make the best of a bad situation, she ran
through the tunnel alongside Cearnach and back down
the steps. The wind was blowing hard, and fog cloaked
everything in a misty gray curtain as she and Cearnach
made their way to the beach. They loped through glens
and woodlands, behind a hill hiding them from the
view of a farmhouse, alongside a creek where the trees
kept them well hidden, stopping only to drink at the
water's edge. Cearnach stayed glued to her side as if
he was afraid for her safety and was protecting her at
all costs.

She and Cearnach had been running and alternately
loping, a less tiring gait, for maybe an hour when she
wondered just how far his castle was from the ruins. By
car, maybe not so far. But he was probably taking her
in a roundabout way, avoiding farms and houses and
towns, and keeping to rivers and creeks and unsettled
areas. The unrelenting rain had started up again.

After the second hour on the run, she was getting
tired. When he saw her falling back, he began to walk
beside her. Both of their tongues were lolling out of their

mouths as they tried to cool their bodies, which were overheated despite the cold weather.

Elaine explored a little, figuring she'd never have the chance to run as a wolf in the wilderness of Scotland again and, in any other circumstance, would never do something so dangerous. She touched her nose to moss-covered stones, the feel soft and velvety, and listened to the wind rustling the leaves of nearby trees and the sound of water trickling in the creek just beyond them. Everything—the grass, the leaves, the moss covering ancient stone walls—was emerald green.

She ran in the Ocala National Forest and elsewhere in Florida in the heat, so she enjoyed this—the cooler weather, the wetness, no worry about rattlesnakes or alligators or other animals. When she'd run in the Everglades, she'd come across a protective bear and her cubs, and smelled the scat from a black panther, although she hadn't seen him.

She felt relatively safe here—at least from other wild animal predators. Man was another story.

Furry russet-colored cows grazing in a field caught her eye. Their short faces were bent and nibbling on rain-soaked grass until they sensed the wolves' approach. They were funny-looking creatures compared to American cows. But she was certain the Scots would think the same of the long-faced cows in America.

They mooed and moved together away from the perceived threat, as if Cearnach and she wanted to eat a cow on the hoof. She never hunted in wolf form, not unless she was in dire straits. If she was starving and lost in the wilderness, she'd make an exception, but she usually went after fish.

No farmhouse was in sight, which was a good thing. That meant no one would be worried about what was upsetting the livestock and come out to shoot at them.

A half mile farther, a gray stone farmhouse sat back off a road. The farmhouse wasn't a problem. The dogs living at the stone building were.

Two border collies suddenly appeared, running at a full gallop, headed straight for Cearnach and Elaine, and intent on chasing them away. They were ultra-fast, extremely clever, hardworking sheepherding dogs. Elaine knew their herding instinct was actually a wolf characteristic, but instead of taking an animal down as wolves would on a hunt, the border collies had been bred to eliminate the killing instinct and would circle and gather, rather than using brute force to guide the herd.

One of the collies had a red face and white chest; the other was black and white. Both were equally aggressive. They were in full pursuit as they ran across the glen, barking at Cearnach and Elaine, alerting anyone in the house that someone or something had invaded their land and they needed backup pronto.

Cearnach and Elaine turned to face them down, growling in their fiercest manners, staring them down like pissed-off, ready-to-pounce wolves. The dogs were tenacious. Their stares matched the wolves'—the instinct so bred into their breed that they wouldn't back down.

Cearnach nudged Elaine to run ahead while he continued to turn back and snap and snarl at the dogs. They knew better than to get too close to the much bigger *Canis lupus* with his much larger teeth and bite. But they were just as aggressive. With the two of them sticking together, they encouraged each other to keep pushing.

Elaine stopped until he joined her, and she growled again along with Cearnach to show their own unified force. The dogs stopped and sniffed the air, testing to determine the wolves' resolve, judging if they were angered or afraid. The collies stood their ground, not moving an inch forward as the wolves held their glare.

As soon as she and Cearnach raced off again, the collies ran after them, but they weren't getting as close this time. They were leaving their own territory, and they didn't need to protect it as firmly. They still wanted to make an impression. *This is ours! You stay out!* But they were beginning to drop back.

She and Cearnach were concentrating so much on the threat of the collies that they didn't see the man riding shotgun in an old rusty pickup truck until it was almost too late. He waved at his companion to get closer and the window opened. A rifle poked out and pointed straight at them. Cearnach quickly steered Elaine toward the river. That meant they could hit her in the butt instead of the side. *Pleasant thought.*

The powerful report of the weapon sounded like an explosion and echoed across the glen, making her heart hitch. She immediately jumped into the water, where she stumbled over the moss-covered rocks. Chest-deep in the water, she slipped on the stones and the current lifted her and swept her away.

In the great hall of Argent Castle, Ian paced, agitated over Cearnach's stubborn refusal to leave well enough alone instead of listening to his advice. He'd thought of sending someone to watch his brother's back, but he hadn't wanted to make Cearnach think that Ian had no faith in him. And he knew that if Cearnach had been able to stay at Calla's wedding and reception without being asked to leave, he might not be home for hours. But Ian didn't believe that his brother would hang around that long. And he had a nagging feeling that something had gone wrong.

His ghostly cousin, Flynn, was hovering nearby as Ian tried to get his concern under control. Flynn was wearing the ancient MacNeill plaid pinned over his shoulder, his hair wild and unkempt. Cearnach had always stuck up for Flynn, despite his cousin's rakish ways, which had gotten him banned from the clan and ultimately murdered by the angry husband of a lass Flynn had dallied with.

Ian ran his hands through his hair and scowled at Flynn's accusatory glare. "He knows what he's doing. He'll be all right."

Ian wasn't as sure as he tried to sound. Hearing footfalls stalking in the direction of his solar, Ian knew his youngest brother, Duncan, was coming to talk to him about Cearnach.

As soon as Duncan knocked on the door frame and Ian said, "Enter," his brother stalked in, wearing all black and looking ready to do battle. Ian could smell the wind and pine and rain surrounding him. He knew his brother had been up on the ramparts waiting for Cearnach's return. "He's been gone too long," Duncan said.

Ian didn't have to guess who Duncan was referring to. Duncan bowed his head slightly to Flynn in acknowledgment, then shifted his stormy gaze to Ian. "Do you want me to gather some men?"

"Even if he just stayed for the wedding, he still

wouldn't have had time to drive all that way home yet," Ian cautioned.

"Did he call you when he arrived?"

That's what had been bothering Ian. His brother hadn't let him know he'd arrived, although he should have reached the church hours ago. He was good about keeping in touch. All his kin were. So why hadn't Cearnach called? Trouble was all that came to mind. His brother was in trouble.

"Send six men to the church and scout around."

Duncan arched an eyebrow. The order was clear. Ian didn't want Duncan to lead them.

Ian folded his arms. He'd already tried to convince Cearnach not to go to the wedding. He wasn't about to explain himself to each of his other brothers concerning this matter. Then he shook his head. *Hell.* When had he become such a softy? When a little red she-wolf had turned his world upside down, that's when.

"I need you here. If the men report that nothing is the matter, then we have no cause for concern. If there's trouble, I'll need you to take care of the matter."

Armed with his sword sheathed at his back and a dirk in his boot, Duncan didn't respond, his expression one of battle readiness. Ian didn't want Duncan killing someone before he knew all the facts. That was one of the reasons Ian led the pack, not Duncan. That plus the fact that Ian was the eldest and Duncan the youngest by several minutes.

"Duncan?"

"Aye, Ian, but if anything's happened to Cearnach…" He let his words trail away.

Flynn withdrew his ghostly sword and sliced through

the air as if he would take on the men who dared harm
Cearnach himself.

"Aye, Duncan. *We* will deal with it," Ian said.

"In the harshest manner possible," Duncan said, as if
seeking clarification.

Duncan had to know that if any harm came to their
brother, Ian would stop at nothing to pursue those
responsible. "Aye."

Bowing his head in deference to his brother's leader-
ship and position, Duncan turned around to give the word.

"Duncan, let your mate's Uncle Ethan go with them."

Duncan stopped in the doorway and offered a small
smile over his shoulder.

The American had been giving Ian trouble ever since
he'd arrived with Shelley's family, but only because
the Scots-born, transplanted Texan was a born leader of
men. "He won't be in charge."

"Aye, one of our cousins will be."

"Better make it Oran, then. He's about the only one
who can butt heads with Ethan and still remain on top."
Besides Ian and his brothers, that was, and Oran could
barely keep the lead over Ethan.

Oran had a ready sword hand and a temper to match
his red hair. Muscular and ready for a fight, he would
face any foe. He had a steady head also, and he was
perfect for the job.

"Shelley's uncle will be grateful for the opportunity."
Then Duncan left the solar, and Flynn scowled at Ian
and took off after Duncan.

Julia, Ian's lovely red-wolf mate, entered the solar,
her expression shadowed with worry. "Are you going
after Cearnach?"

Ian gathered her up in his arms, kissed her lightly on the lips, then hugged her tight. "He'll be all right. He's a warrior at heart. He'll be all right." He repeated the words as if by doing so, he could make them true. But he wasn't sure.

Cearnach should have called him.

Chapter 8

CEARNACH DOVE AFTER ELAINE INTO THE ICY WATER, his heart skipping beats as he saw her lose her footing and the force of the river carry her away. He followed after her, paddling as fast as his legs could go to catch up. She looked worn out, trying to keep her head above water, dipping her nose in, then lifting it and sneezing. She was unable to keep her footing on the slippery rocks and pull herself out of the river.

In their favor, the sunlight was quickly fading. The farmers who had been shooting at them could no longer get close enough to the river while driving the truck, and Cearnach doubted they could see the wolves swimming in the dark water.

The roar in the distance warned Cearnach that the waterfall was coming up. The currents quickened, pulling them faster toward the sound of the falls.

All in a rush, the memories of the panic he'd felt when he'd been showing off to Calla as a young lad came back to him. He'd been teasing her, saying that he could hop from boulder to boulder without getting wet, while she'd played with an old rope, pretending to be fishing when no one in her clan would allow her to do such a thing.

With a shout of terror, he'd lost his footing on the slippery rocks and fallen into the swiftly moving water. Numb with cold, he had tried to reach the shore but couldn't. He wasn't all that old then, not as muscled, not as strong. She'd raced along the bank, shouting his name and desperately throwing the rope out to him, hitting him twice—once on the shoulder, once on the head—before he finally was able to grab hold.

She had quickly wrapped it around a pine tree and held on with all her might as he'd climbed onto the shore, choking on water that had gone down the wrong way.

Then he had collapsed on the frost-covered ground like a fish out of water, gasping for air.

Now it was his turn to rescue a she-wolf instead of a she-wolf rescuing him.

He was so close to Elaine that he could almost touch her. He didn't want to startle her, so he bumped her side to let her know he was there and would help her. She yipped in surprise.

He woofed, letting her know it was just him. She cast him a quick look of relief over her shoulder.

With his powerful legs, he swam beside her, steering her away from the falls and toward the boulders littering the sides of the river. She slid over them, still unable to gain her footing. He pushed her again, moving her toward the beach, his whole body pressing against hers, offering a wall of muscle that she could lean against, protecting her while he worked at keeping her from being carried over the falls.

Almost there.

She stumbled on the slippery stones, but he kept nudging her toward the shore, wishing he could put an arm around her as a human or lift her out of the water and carry her to safety. As soon as she reached the shore, she scrambled over the rocks and ran straight for the trees, a spurt of energy apparently charging through her.

He shook the water from his fur, then hurried after her.

She shook herself as soon as she was in the woods. Sheltered from prying eyes, she collapsed on her side in the creeping ladies' tresses and twinflowers, panting with relief and exhaustion, her wet mink fur clinging to her, her eyes closed. Fatigued, soaked, and beautiful.

He joined her, thanking God that she hadn't gone over the falls. He was also glad that the farmer hadn't managed to shoot either of them. He hoped the men would believe he and Elaine had been big dogs, not wolves. Strict rules governed the keeping of wolves in Scotland. If anyone truly thought that he and Elaine were wolves running loose, a bounty might be placed on their heads. Shoot to kill. All of his kind would be threatened then.

He lay down next to her and rested his head over her neck as if they'd been friends forever. That she was his to protect from all dangers. She opened her eyes, gave him a tired wolf smile, licked his cheek, and closed her eyes again.

He sighed and settled more comfortably against her, responding to the wolfish showing of trust on her part in allowing him to rest his head there. Trust on his part also that she wouldn't snap at him to give her space. For the moment, he felt he had finally accomplished what he'd hoped to do the first time he met her. Help her. Take care of her.

But this time he realized he wanted to get to know her better. Take her home to his family. Wine and dine her. Learn all he could about her. Keep her here. *Permanently.*

He closed his eyes and breathed in the wet wolf smell of her, basked in the warmth of their bodies touching, and listened to her breathing growing steadier, sleepier, until he was sure she had fallen asleep.

They weren't too far from the castle now. Though he suspected that Ian would send out the troops, worried that Cearnach hadn't called to say everything was all right, concerned that the McKinleys had harmed him. He was sure that Ian would have some heartburn over him bringing a cousin of the Kilpatricks home with him. *Or not.* Being mated to Julia Wildthorn, werewolf romance writer, had softened his brother up a bit. In a good way.

Cearnach hadn't meant to, but resting next to the enticing she-wolf, her blood pulsing through her veins, and listening to the steady thump of her heart led to him dozing off for a couple of hours. He woke to the smell of an elusive pine marten rummaging around nearby. The slim creature was mink brown in color with a yellow bib at its throat, around the size of a cat, and a member of the family that included mink, otters, and weasels. It was scrounging for something to eat.

The animals were territorial, so Cearnach had smelled the scat left in the area by the marten. It was a predator, reducing the populations of gray squirrels, but when it came to wolves and martens, territorial lines went out the window. Since he was downwind of the mammal, Cearnach raised his head to let the marten know he had company.

Because of the movement, the marten saw the two wolves, its eyes widening in horror, and quickly scampered away. Elaine stared in the direction the animal had gone, and then she sat up. Cearnach stood and nodded in the direction they needed to go. She got up, leaned her head down, and licked the cut on his foreleg that had occurred when he'd tried to reach his phone through the broken window in his demolished minivan. She whimpered.

Touched by her concern, he nudged her face, telling her he was fine.

The castle was not too far now. No sliver of a moon could be seen in the darkness, though the rains hadn't started again. A heavy mist cloaked everything in shades of wet gray, which was perfect for wolves who shouldn't have existed in Scotland and didn't want to get caught out in the open.

They finally reached the long drive that led to Argent Castle, the portcullis and wooden gates still open. Most likely because Cearnach hadn't returned yet. Some of his clan had to be out searching for him.

Before he could escort Elaine to the gate where lights illuminated the entryway, he heard a car engine rumbling as it approached the castle, the headlights peering into the gloom.

To be on the safe side, he kept Elaine hidden in the woods with him. The car didn't sound or look familiar.

In the kennel where they were rounded up for the night, the wolfhounds began to bark, warning of intruders.

The black BMW's tires crunched on the gravel drive, then stopped as the car parked outside the gates. The occupants—the driver and a passenger—remained inside as if waiting for an invitation. Cearnach glanced up at the castle towers flanking the gate entryway. One of his cousins was watching from each of the cylindrical towers. One was calling on his cell phone, warning Ian they had company, and the word would soon spread throughout the pack.

Cearnach watched and waited, intending on lending wolf teeth to a fight if that's what was needed here. But his priority was keeping Elaine in the woods, quiet and safe for now. She stayed close to him, her body touching his, her tail straight out. She was tense, alert, and appeared ready for a skirmish.

Duncan, his youngest quadruplet brother, was headed for the gate, already armed with a sword, shirtless, and wearing only black trousers and boots. Two other clansmen flanked him, looking ready to shift and fight a battle to the death. Another two in wolf form hurried to catch up to lend backup.

Cearnach wanted to let them know he was all right, but he didn't want to let anyone know Elaine was here with him, in case these men were the McKinleys or Kilpatricks and they had finally figured out that the rental car they had stolen was their distant cousin's. He was afraid they'd attempt to take her with them. Not forcibly with all the muscle the MacNeill had in place, but in more of a placating way: *We're your kin, these people are not, and we have your belongings. Come back and we'll make it up to you.*

The driver's door finally opened and redheaded Robert Kilpatrick got out. Cearnach stifled a low growl. Elaine barely breathed next to him, but then she growled even lower than he did. She was just as pissed off at Kilpatrick as he was.

When she took a couple of steps closer to the edge of the woods, Cearnach nipped at her, warning her not to go any further. He didn't want them catching sight of her. She turned to look at him, trying to read his intent.

He breathed in deeply, trying to settle his own

concern for her. She gave him an almost imperceptible smile. She wasn't angry with him. *Good.* He didn't want her to think he was that controlling. Even if he was pushing it at the moment.

The passenger door opened and Baird McKinley exited, surprising the hell out of Cearnach. Had he left his own wedding reception and bride to come here? Calla must have loved that. Unless she had known what had happened and forced him to come here to check on Elaine and him.

Cearnach was ready to tear into Robert, but he had a more important mission right now. Keep Elaine by his side and out of sight.

"What are you doing here?" Duncan asked, not giving the men a chance to speak.

"Your brother came to my wedding." Baird acted like that was a reason to wage war in and of itself.

"He stole your bride?" Duncan asked, as though he assumed such and approved. "Time-honored tradition."

Cearnach had never considered that the pack might have believed that. Now with Baird here, his actions made it appear that way. Cearnach couldn't believe Duncan was defending him for stealing Baird's bride. The pack must have thought Cearnach was off somewhere with Calla consummating the mating! He had to set his family straight as soon as he was able.

Elaine bumped his cheek in a playful manner as if amused that his kin thought he was off mating Calla when she was only supposed to be a friend. He licked her back, wanting to tell her that he wanted *her,* and *not* Calla. For a second, he closed his mouth and quit panting. He hadn't meant to be so obvious so soon in their relationship.

For a moment, his and Elaine's gazes locked, alpha to alpha in a purely wolfish way. She knew what he was thinking just as he knew her own thoughts and desires. Humans would look away from such a gaze if they didn't know each other well, the eye-to-eye contact too intimate between a man and woman who had just met, unless they were having a bit of conversation and wanted to show their interest in the topic.

Wolves didn't break eye contact that easily if they were attracted, regarding each other, or reading each other. It wasn't just their mutual gazes, but the special scents they gave off that told *how* fascinated they were. Both breathed in deeply to learn what the other was feeling, as if the men having a confrontation in front of the castle gates suddenly didn't exist.

Baird kicked at the gravel in a frustrated manner, catching Cearnach and Elaine's attention again. He scowled, but before he could respond, Robert raised his hand in a motion that said they'd come in peace. "We're here because..." Robert paused, looking as though he was weighing his options: tell the truth or draw this out a little longer. "Hell, he's stolen my cousin," he growled.

Elaine again began to move toward the driveway, growling softly. For a moment, she appeared ready to show Robert what she thought of him in a purely wolf demonstration.

Cearnach quickly moved in front of her, blocking her. She didn't growl at him or act annoyed. Instead, she nudged his cheek with her nose as if to say she wasn't going to confront her cousin over his lies, even though she wanted to. Cearnach could envision her racing up to Robert, her beautiful wolf teeth bared, and him falling back, shocked out of his human skin. As a wolf, he wouldn't be as easily intimidated. In his human form, Robert wouldn't stand up to her half as well. Not as alpha as she was.

Duncan stared at Robert for a moment as if he was processing that new turn of events, then suddenly burst out laughing. "Your cousin? You have five male cousins. Which one did Cearnach take a fancy to?"

The other men standing beside Duncan looked like they were trying to hold straight faces but were barely managing.

"Elaine Hawthorn. We want her turned over now," Robert said, not in the least amused.

"There's no one here by that name. My brother hasn't returned. If you've harmed him in any way…" Duncan said, offering the threat but not finishing what he was going to say.

Robert glanced at Baird, who nodded in agreement.

"All right, so she's not at Argent Castle right now. But if she comes here, call me. I'll pick her up." Robert's voice was forceful but worried now.

"Why… *if she's your cousin*… would she come here?" Duncan asked, his expression darkening. "Is she with Cearnach? Did you threaten them?"

Baird said, "You tell Cearnach for me that if he comes near Calla ever again, he's a dead wolf." He got back in the car and slammed the door.

Robert let out his breath. "Elaine Hawthorn is our cousin. I want her returned at once, should she come here." Then he climbed into the driver's seat, slammed his door, and drove into the turnaround built especially for tourists who thought they could visit the pretty castle without invitation—not that any tourist was ever invited to visit. Once Robert was headed toward the main road, he sped off, spitting gravel in his wake.

"Hell, what was that all about?" Cearnach's cousin shouted from the tower.

"Cearnach's got to be in trouble," Duncan said, pulling out his phone.

Once the car was out of sight, Cearnach nudged Elaine to come with him, though she seemed a little reluctant. He was certain she was unsure about meeting his family when she was kin to the McKinleys and Kilpatricks, and she could see none of them liked that pack.

He licked her face, and then she took a deep breath and ran alongside him as they headed for the gate where Duncan and the other men had turned around and had begun to stalk in the direction of the keep.

"Cearnach!" his cousin shouted from the left tower. "Hell, he does have the Kilpatrick's cousin. If the little lady is her. Way to go, mon!"

Cearnach suspected his brother Ian would not be pleased.

Turning, Duncan grinned at him and then looked Elaine over. "Here I thought you'd stolen Baird's bride. Instead, you've taken a Kilpatrick cousin hostage?" Then he grew serious and shook his head. "I knew that if you went to Calla's wedding, you'd start a war between wolf packs. But I am glad to see you safe."

Start a war? He had saved a wolf—a she-wolf—to his way of thinking.

Cearnach and Elaine trotted into the inner bailey, while two of the men shut and locked the gates as Duncan jogged to keep up with the wolves.

Barking in the kennel started up all over again. This time the wolfhounds let out happy barks welcoming Cearnach home.

"I just didn't think it would be over a different she-wolf." Duncan punched in a number and said into his phone, "Ian, we've got trouble. Cearnach just arrived home in his wolf form, no sign of his vehicle, and he's brought Robert Kilpatrick's she-wolf cousin home with him." Duncan raised his brows at Cearnach.

"I know. I thought he had only male cousins. She's definitely all female. Robert said Cearnach took her hostage. She was with Cearnach in the woods and didn't make a move to go with her cousin, so I'll let Cearnach explain what's going on. He's headed into the keep now. See you in a minute."

Duncan opened the front door to the keep and followed Cearnach inside. "Glad it's you and not me this time." Then he smiled, the look pure evil.

Chapter 9

WALKING INTO THE GREAT HALL WITH ELAINE AT HIS side, her body pressing lightly against his, Cearnach wanted to protect her from his overenthusiastic kin. The heat from the fire burning brightly at the hearth warmed the air, but with the word quickly spreading through the pack of Cearnach's return, his laird brother, Ian, met Cearnach, Elaine, and Duncan in the great hall. The large room seemed to grow hotter with every new body that appeared. Not to mention that Cearnach and Elaine were still wearing their wolf coats, damp as they were.

Voices and footfalls added to the chaos as the aroma of lamb stew cooked in red wine wafted in the air. He and Elaine turned their attention toward the kitchen, and he heard her stomach rumbling. He assumed she was as hungry as he was.

She stuck close to him and seemed bothered by all the attention they were getting. The word most likely had spread that Cearnach had trouble with the McKinley clan. And that she was one of them.

Their financial guru of a brother, Guthrie, was running to join them, speaking on his phone. "Yeah, Oran, bring the men in. Cearnach's back safe. No car, though, and he's a wolf. He brought a she-wolf home with him." Guthrie raised his brows at Cearnach and grinned. "No. She's not Calla. He's brought a *new* she-wolf home. Talk to you later when we know more."

A mob scene ensued, made up of his brothers' mates, their families, his mother, his aunt, and cousins, as well as at least half of the pack crowding around. They made him appreciate having a family even more, and he realized just how much of a sorry excuse Elaine's kin were to her.

She deserved a loving, caring, decent family. Everyone did.

The men looked like they were ready to grab their swords like Duncan had done, while the women appeared more worried about the she-wolf in their midst. They crowded in, inspecting her, making sure she had no injuries.

Cearnach wanted to take Elaine to his room so she could shift. But Julia Wildthorn, Ian's mate and mistress of the manor, motioned to Elaine to go with her.

"Come, I'm sure we can find some clothes to fit you," Julia said, waving at the stairs.

He hadn't even considered that Elaine would need something to wear once she shifted out of her wolf fur. He smiled at himself.

Duncan's mate, Shelley Campbell, also American, and Cearnach's mother and aunt went with Elaine. *Poor lass.* When his mother and his aunt got through with her, Elaine would want to claw her way out of the place, unable to leave fast enough, even if it meant joining up with that bastard Robert Kilpatrick. Cearnach wished he could have warned her before they reached the castle what she might be in for. He should have considered it before. All he had thought of was getting her home safely.

More than anything, he wanted to protect her from

them or anyone else who might treat her poorly because of her familial connections.

Cearnach followed them up the curving stairs and slipped off to his own bedchamber where he quickly shifted in his bathroom, and cleaned and bandaged his bleeding arm. The cut he'd received from his shattered car window wasn't too bad and would heal in the next couple of days. He yanked on a lamb's wool sweater and a pair of well-worn jeans.

Someone knocked at his door. Cearnach left the bathroom.

"My solar," Ian said, looking fierce.

Cearnach bowed his head. His brother's expression said he was ready to gather the troops to right any wrong as soon as Cearnach gave the word. Cearnach put on his socks and boots, then left his bedchamber. When he reached Ian's solar, he found his brothers were already gathered, looking anxious to hear the news. He shut the door and took a seat on one of the leather sofas.

Observing him, Duncan stood rooted to the floor, his arms crossed. Guthrie sat down on one of the high-backed plaid-covered chairs, his back as stiff as the chair. Knowing him, he was pondering the financial ramifications of the matter. He was always thinking along those lines as their financial advisor.

His arms still folded across his chest, Ian leaned against his desk, but he wasn't fooling anyone. He was wired and looked like he was only trying to put Cearnach at ease and not jump to rash conclusions.

"Julia's father and grandfather asked to sit in on the discussion, but I wanted to know how bad this was first. They don't know the parties who are involved so I didn't want to have to go into a lot of history. Shelley's uncles were also ready to sit in on the war council," Ian said.

That meant they had a lot more muscle, in the form of Americans of Highland descent, to aid them this time around if they needed it.

"We don't need to go to war, Ian," Cearnach said, though he was still ready to battle Vardon for what he had done to Elaine. He wanted their properties returned, including a minivan like the one they'd destroyed, before he would agree to anything. Giving Elaine up wasn't part of the bargain.

Duncan scowled at him. "You arrive without your car, running as a wolf with a lass you must have saved from them, and you're saying everything's fine?"

Cearnach laughed.

His brothers frowned at him. He couldn't help himself. The situation did sound as if that was enough to start a fight, but they had the Kilpatricks and the McKinleys by the balls as long as Elaine stayed with them safely inside Argent Castle.

"All right, all right. The McKinleys destroyed my car and stole the lass's rental vehicle."

Duncan growled, "Sounds to me that that's enough of a reason to want to exact revenge."

"Oh, aye, they'll pay," Cearnach assured him.

Ian remained quiet and thoughtful, judging without speaking. That's the way he ruled the clan, learning not only what was said, but what wasn't.

"Who is she?" Guthrie asked, brows raised, his tone of voice sounding as if he might be interested in the new she-wolf for himself. "She doesn't appear to be anyone we know. Duncan told us Robert Kilpatrick said you had stolen his cousin."

"Elaine Hawthorn. American." Not wanting to feed his brothers' speculation about his own interest in Elaine, Cearnach fought telling Guthrie to stay away from her. He gave him a fierce look instead, which would garner the same result. All his brothers saw his reaction and could guess just where it was coming from.

Ian and Duncan exchanged knowing glances. American wolves could be a handful.

"You met this Elaine Hawthorn while she was attending Calla's wedding?" Ian asked, trying to sort out the situation.

"No. Elaine ran me off the road."

Duncan laughed out loud, then smirking, offered an apology, not meaning it in the least. He was still grinning from ear to ear. To see him that lighthearted when he thought they were ready to battle the McKinleys and Kilpatricks was uncharacteristic for him. Duncan poured a glass of whisky and handed it to Cearnach, as if welcoming him to his world of dealing with an American she-wolf.

Cearnach tossed down the smooth, warm liquor. "She was in my lane. To avoid hitting her, I ended up driving off the road and blew two tires. The lass gave me a ride to the wedding."

"But all did not go well at the wedding," Ian guessed, head tilted down, his expression severe. He looked like he would be considering battle moves as soon as he knew who the key players were that he needed to target.

"Two of the older McKinley brothers ordered us

out." Cearnach left out the part about Vardon striking Elaine in the face. Everyone would see the damage soon enough, and that would stir up the pack's ire just as much. "When we returned to where we'd left my car, it was gone. I had the idea they might have dumped it over the cliffs near the Senton Castle ruins. So Elaine and I found the destroyed minivan."

Duncan swore in Gaelic.

"Robert Kilpatrick taunted us from the cliffside, threatening to leave us stranded. We tore off to stop them, but the McKinley brothers had already stolen our clothes and Elaine's rental car."

"They must have suspected she was your girlfriend and that's why she was with you at the wedding," Ian said, thinking out loud.

Cearnach wasn't about to tell them that she'd sat on the groom's side until he moved her to his side of the church.

"What was she doing here? Is she vacationing in Scotland? If she was visiting her kin, why wasn't she at the wedding already?" Ian asked.

Cearnach hated to tell his brother about her connection to the Hawthorns who had stolen the MacNeill merchandise.

"She was supposed to meet with Robert Kilpatrick— her distant cousin—about some business deal."

Back to battle mode, Duncan shook his head. "I can't believe you brought a Kilpatrick lass under our roof."

Ian raised his hand to silence Duncan. "What kind of business deal?"

"She didn't say. He was making the move on her at the church, but he didn't know who she was, and she didn't realize he was the one she was supposed to be meeting. I'm sure now that they've got her passport and driver's license, they realize their mistake."

Guthrie laughed. "I should say so. They left one of their kin in your hands to protect when they were too stupid to know any better."

Cearnach wished he could've seen their reactions when they discovered their cousin was in his care. Stunned silence? Cursing and bellowing? Any reaction would have been worth seeing.

"I'm sure they believed she was my new girlfriend and thought my bringing her to the wedding was an insult to Calla. But Calla wasn't upset about my being with Elaine. I'm sure the McKinleys and Kilpatricks intended for us both to pay for the insult, though."

Duncan cast one of his darker smiles and poured himself a whisky. "The joke's on them. She's with us now."

Ian frowned at Duncan. "He can't keep her as a hostage. She's American and *is* related to them."

"What if she's really a spy for them? She knew Cearnach was headed to the wedding, and she forced him off the road. Then she offered him a lift. What if she's behind all of this?" Duncan asked, his wary nature suddenly kicking in.

Cearnach's cautious temperament as a wolf had considered and dismissed the notion. She was American and had too recently arrived. Her cool behavior toward the Kilpatrick brothers at the church told him she hadn't known them, nor had she appreciated that they moved into her space. Though she also hadn't liked Cearnach dictating where she would sit.

The excitement she had exhibited while exploring the ruined castle was real. The terror he had seen in her eyes when she realized her clothes and rented car had been stolen was just as genuine.

"She's an innocent in all this," Cearnach said.

"Yet she's one of them and she's entering into some kind of business arrangement with Robert Kilpatrick," Duncan warned.

Two hundred years ago, the Kilpatricks had entered into a "business arrangement" with the MacNeills that took them into a bloody battle that had lasted for months between their clans.

So what was it all about this time? It might have nothing to do with the two clans, but what if it did? Or what if it had something to do with the stolen merchandise her uncles had hidden in Scotland before their untimely demise?

If it was about the MacNeills' stolen goods, they couldn't let her hand over the loot to the Kilpatricks and McKinleys. It was a matter of pride. If she thought they would allow her to keep at least half of the proceeds, she didn't know anything about her cutthroat cousins.

In any event, Cearnach believed that Elaine didn't know what she was getting herself into. Just like Calla marrying Baird McKinley.

He wanted to help Elaine in whatever way he could while leaving her kin out of the matter.

In the elegantly fashioned guest bathroom where everything was brass or gold trimmed, the walls marbled tile, the shower and separate whirlpool tub stylish, Elaine felt like she was in a luxury hotel instead of an ancient castle as she finished dressing in a pair of black jeans and a long-sleeved, pale blue jersey, the clothes compliments of Julia.

Ian's mate was a red wolf—Elaine could smell the difference—while everyone else she'd encountered thus far were gray wolves. Julia was a natural redhead with deep red-orange curls resting on her shoulders, translucent ivory skin, and olive-green catlike eyes that made her appear like she had Scottish roots.

Duncan's mate, auburn-haired Shelley, had offered Elaine a pair of black leather boots because their shoe size was the same. Her eyes were a lovely shade of blue-green, and from the way she gazed at Elaine, Shelley seemed sympathetic to her predicament. She was of average height like Julia and wore a sweatshirt emblazoned with a silver Rampant Lion, silver belt buckle, black jeans, and a pair of black cowboy boots.

Was she from Texas?

As if reading her mind, Julia said, "I was living in California, Shelley in Texas, but we all had roots in Scotland. And you?"

"Florida," Elaine said, thinking she was family to a bunch of pirates from Florida. Related to the pirates of the McKinley and Kilpatrick clans. She was the enemy in their midst.

"We've gathered some clothes for you to wear for tonight and the next several days, and left them on the dresser in the guest room," Julia said, having concluded that Elaine was their houseguest for the long term.

Elaine had to admit she liked the way the mistress of the house, the alpha pack leader she-wolf, had welcomed her as if she was a long-lost friend. Or already part of the family.

The two American she-wolves remained standing. Cearnach's Aunt Agnes was seated on a blue brocade chair and introduced to Elaine as Cearnach's mother's sister-in-law, although the two referred to each other as sister. Aunt Agnes's silver hair was tucked up in a bun, her gray eyes studying Elaine like a wary wolf.

Julia's mother-in-law, Lady MacNeill, was seated on a matching blue chair, and a small curio table was situated between the two women. She barely allowed Elaine to join them before she took charge, though Elaine thought it was Julia's place to do so as the clan chief's mate. His mother's red-gold curls streaked with gray were piled on top of her head in an elegant coif. Her green eyes were sharp and observant, and she wore a lacy green dress as if she was attending a formal tea. All she needed to finish the look were a hat and pair of gloves.

"What happened to you and Cearnach?" his mother asked, her voice sharp and accusatory, as if everything that had happened was Elaine's fault before she'd heard any of the story.

His Aunt Agnes studied Elaine, her expression more guarded, as she waited to hear the full story before she condemned her. At least that's what Elaine thought.

"I'm Elaine Hawthorn and I met Cearnach when he nearly ran me off the road earlier today. He ended up with two flat tires near the edge of a cliff instead."

Cearnach's mother's mouth gaped, then she snapped it shut and narrowed her eyes. "Are you sure the fault was not your own?"

"In a hurry to reach the church on time, he was speeding. He was an accident waiting to happen." Elaine frowned back at the woman. She wasn't about to allow his mother to turn this around and make her out to be the bad guy.

Julia and Shelley smiled at Elaine, and she got the impression they were on her side.

Cearnach's mother gave a ladylike snort. "How did you hurt yourself? Was it from the near-accident with my son?"

Ah, the bruise on her face. She didn't think the woman would appreciate that she'd stepped in front of her son to protect him from Vardon McKinley. She-wolves didn't have to defend an armed alpha male wolf, after all.

"Well, speak up, young lady," the woman snapped.

Elaine wondered how the other women could put up with her. She straightened her back. "Vardon McKinley did it."

Everyone stared at her with wide eyes. The mother's brows drew together. "Because you were with Cearnach at the church?"

"In a manner of speaking, yes. But not on purpose. I tried to stop the fight headed his way."

Julia and Shelley grinned. Aunt Agnes's eyes widened. His mother just stared at her.

Okay, which way was this going to go? His mother would hate her for trying to protect her son, or love her or... well, something in between.

The mother tapped her finger on the arm of the chair. "What will Cearnach say about this?"

She didn't believe Elaine? What did she think? That another version of the story existed?

"He will probably say he was pissed off that I moved in front of him to..."

"Protect him?" Aunt Agnes asked, speculation in her gray eyes. "Do you always rescue alpha males from others who are ready to rip their throats out, or was today somehow special?"

Oh... my... God. Elaine was being attacked by two female wolves at once? She thought the mother had exclusive rights to the exercise.

"Okay, listen," Elaine said, her hackles raised. She could fight the most capable of she-wolves any day, and she wasn't about to be intimidated by these two old women. "Cearnach nearly hit me head-on. He was speeding, and if he hadn't been going so fast, we could have easily maneuvered around each other. As it was, we didn't. Then, he forced me to take him to the church. But wait, he wouldn't let me drive my own car because he didn't think I could get us there in one piece."

His mother smiled a little at that.

Elaine paused, waiting for his mother to object or contradict or something, but all eyes were upon Elaine and everyone kept quiet, waiting to hear the whole story.

"Okay, so we get to the church and go inside. I'm not about to be told where I'm to sit. I wasn't a guest and I was annoyed with Cearnach so I sat on the groom's side since he was sitting on the bride's side."

A gasp from the aunt made Elaine stop. When nobody said anything, Elaine continued. "The Kilpatrick brothers boxed me in, but I didn't know they were my distant cousins."

"Distant cousins?" His mother managed to sound shocked and angry at the same time.

Uh-oh. She'd thought his mother had already received the bad news.

"Yes. But I didn't know it at the time. Cearnach made me move to the bride's side."

Aunt Agnes said, "Did Cearnach know you were related to that family?"

"No." Elaine waited for her to ask something else, but the woman just nodded.

"Then two of Baird's brothers decided to show us out of the church. Only one, Vardon, was really angry. I figured it would come to blows. I wanted to stop it because I didn't want Cearnach and Vardon fighting in the church, upsetting Calla's wedding. She seemed like a lovely girl. I tried to get between Cearnach and Vardon to diffuse the situation, but Vardon threw a punch and hit me."

When no one said a word, Elaine shrugged like it was no big deal.

Julia sat down as if she couldn't take any more. Shelley looked worried, her brow deeply furrowed.

"Well, what else?" his mother asked.

"We left. We discovered Cearnach's minivan was destroyed."

His mother growled.

"They stole…"

"They?" Aunt Agnes asked.

"The Kilpatricks and McKinleys," Elaine clarified. "They stole my car and our clothes. We had to run as wolves to get here."

No one said anything. Then, her face tight with anger, Cearnach's mother rose from her chair. "You caused all kinds of trouble here today. That *won't* be the end of it."

Chapter 10

ELAINE GAVE AN ABRUPT LAUGH OF DISBELIEF WHEN she heard Cearnach's mother's condemnation. Somehow she knew Cearnach's accident, the church incident, the destroying of Cearnach's minivan, and the stealing of her rental car would become her fault.

"Of course. I flew all the way to Scotland just to meet up with Cearnach on that road and cause all of these problems for your clan."

His mother actually offered a small sour smile—of amusement or conjecture, Elaine wasn't sure.

"I'll get some ice for your cheek." Shelley gave her a meaningful smile, saying she was supportive of Elaine's cause, and squeezed her hand with reassurance on the way out.

Julia's brow furrowed. "I'm surprised Cearnach didn't kill Vardon for striking you. Cearnach's the nicest man you'd ever want to meet, usually as cheerful as can be, but he'd risk his life for others to keep them safe from harm."

"He *did* unsheathe his sword." Elaine didn't want anyone to think he hadn't made the effort. "But I told him not to fight."

His mother's brows arched. "A she-wolf told my son not to fight?"

"Vardon didn't unsheathe his sword so Cearnach couldn't fight an unarmed man. I'm sure Cearnach was also afraid I might get injured if he fought Vardon." Elaine didn't mention that she thought Cearnach had been ready to kill Vardon over what he'd done and had needed all of his willpower to let it go and escort her outside.

"You were already hurt." Julia's voice was hard and unyielding. "Cearnach will not let this insult go if he sees Vardon again." She took a deep breath and changed the subject. "So what is your business here? Are you staying somewhere already?"

"I had plans to stay at Flora's Bed and Breakfast."

Everyone exchanged glances. Round two in the battle with Cearnach's mother. Elaine could understand his mother wanting to know everything about a prospective daughter-in-law. But she and Cearnach weren't considering such a thing, not that she didn't fantasize about it. Who wouldn't when the wolf wore a kilt slung low on his hips, his chest bare, and the smile in his eyes and on his lips made her whole body heat with desire? Not to mention the kiss that had steamed up the car's windows and made her temporarily lose her mind.

She wanted to tell the woman the truth—not about the fantasy part, though—but Elaine held her tongue, not wanting to even go there.

"Kilpatrick's mother, Flora Kilpatrick, runs it. They're first cousins to the McKinleys, one of the ones whose wedding you attended today," Cearnach's mother said hotly. "I thought you said you didn't know them."

"I hadn't met them before today," Elaine said, defending herself. "Only after we left the church and I said I was to meet with my distant cousin Robert Kilpatrick did Cearnach tell me who I'd been sitting next to."

Julia let out her breath. "I bet the McKinleys insisting that Cearnach leave went over really peachy with him."

"He appeared resigned to let Calla live her life the way she saw fit. She seemed perfectly happy. When we returned to where Cearnach's disabled vehicle was, it was gone. He thought maybe the McKinley brothers had pushed it over the cliffs. When we went to investigate, we found it had been destroyed."

"You went with him to look for it?" Julia asked curiously.

"Sure. I wasn't going to stay in the rental car waiting."

"You went as wolves." Julia hadn't asked a question but was more circumspect, as if she was seeing the picture more clearly now.

"Yeah. We could observe more, smell closer to the ground, see if we could sense any sign of the McKinleys. We didn't find any. Not until we explored the beach, discovered his car, and returned."

"You found your clothes and rental car gone."

Elaine nodded, trying to push back the tears that suddenly appeared. She'd thought she was dealing with the situation well. She'd trusted Cearnach to take her someplace safe until she could get her money and ID back, at the very least. She hadn't expected his kin to be so hostile. She was feeling the ramifications of losing her rental car on top of cutbacks at the college, the long trip here, not getting enough sleep, and then being run off the road, shot at, and nearly drowned... and now Cearnach's mother was interrogating her.

She looked at the floor, trying to get her emotions under control.

Julia moved closer to her, patted her shoulder, and assured her, "We'll get everything of yours back."

"Why exactly *were* you here in the first place?" Cearnach's mother asked, as if Elaine had slipped into the country to sabotage her son and she wasn't buying Elaine's declaration of innocence.

"I was supposed to meet with Robert Kilpatrick concerning a business arrangement."

Cearnach's stern-faced aunt laughed. No one else seemed amused.

Aunt Agnes asked Elaine, "Do you plan to mate with Robert Kilpatrick?"

"Heavens no. We're related."

"Distant cousins, so you claim," Lady MacNeill said.

"Well, no, I have no intention of mating with him or anyone else in Scotland."

"Good," Cearnach's mother said. "We saved you from some horrible business scheme, my dear. Believe me, we've been through a financial swindle of epic proportions with an American businessman recently and know just how awful that can be. At least this is a good thing."

Elaine couldn't tell them she intended to find a pirate's stolen treasure. Her uncles had been commissioned to steal from merchant ships loyal to their country's enemies. So one could rationalize that her uncles had been doing their nation's work for a grand cause and not that they were… pirating exactly. But whoever they'd stolen from wouldn't think of them as anything other than pirates.

"How are your kin related to Robert Kilpatrick?" Cearnach's mother asked, her voice darkening.

"My great-grandfather was his great-grandfather's brother."

"Your great-grandfather was Padruig?"

Elaine barely breathed. Cearnach's mother knew him? This was so not good. "Yes."

"*He* was the one who started the war between our clans years ago," Cearnach's aunt said, her lips pursed and eyes narrowed. She looked at Elaine as if she personally had advised her great-grandfather to go to war with the MacNeill clan eons earlier.

So much for Cearnach taking her someplace safe until she could get her ID and everything back. But she had nowhere else to go.

"What did you say your name was again?" his mother asked.

"Elaine."

"Your *last* name."

She hoped that her uncles had not accosted any of the MacNeills' ships.

"Hawthorn."

His mother seemed to mull that over, then her face turned red. "The Hawthorn brothers. Pirates, both of them. The men who Lord Whittington had hanged in St. Andrews?"

"Privateers," Elaine countered. "Fighting for the American cause."

"Och!" his mother said in outrage, her face reddening. "Tell that to the men who lost everything."

Elaine's heart tumbled over itself, and she gritted her teeth as a sudden shimmer of tears swam in her eyes. Had her uncles killed the sailors? She didn't think they were that cruel, but what did she know, living as sheltered a life as her family had given her?

Except for after they died and she had to deal with Kelly Rafferty on her own.

"I've got to straighten this out with Robert." Elaine looked away from his mother's harsh glower before the woman could see how upset she was. She knew that kind of woman. She would not be moved by tears, taking that reaction as a sign of weakness. "I need to get my things back and talk to him about the... uh... inheritance."

"That's what this business arrangement is about? An inheritance?" Cearnach's mother asked.

"Um, yes."

His mother looked like she wanted to ask more, but Julia took charge. "Come. Let's join the men. I'm sure they'll have a plan of attack."

Elaine frowned at her. She didn't want the clans fighting over this.

"Just a figure of speech. After what happened to you and Cearnach, I doubt they'll want you doing this on your own."

Elaine wasn't sure what to think about the MacNeills' offer of help. In a way, she wished she could have it since at least Cearnach seemed genuinely interested in her welfare. Yet she wondered if they would just create more trouble if she allowed them to get involved. She didn't want to tell them the whole truth—that she was after her uncles' treasure. What if some of it belonged to the MacNeills?

She sighed. If she hadn't met Cearnach's family, it wouldn't have mattered. But now that she'd met them, she felt obligated to do the right thing and turn the treasure over to his family if it had belonged to them.

"You… don't have any dogs, do you?" Cearnach's mother suddenly asked Elaine.

Elaine was so startled by the question that she didn't respond right away.

"You know, dogs?" his mother said, impatiently waving her hand as if conjuring up visions of dogs.

"No. No dogs."

"Good."

Julia frowned at her mother-in-law, appearing to be surprised by the question, too. Then she escorted Elaine to another room down the long hall and knocked on the closed oak door. The men's conversation inside the room went silent.

Ian said, "Yes?"

"It's Julia. Elaine wishes to speak with Robert and get this matter taken care of."

Duncan opened the door. Cearnach was already moving toward Elaine and Julia, looking grim-faced, a man with a definite mission, like he was ready to do battle on her behalf.

Julia quickly introduced the brothers: Ian, the pack leader and her mate; Guthrie, their financial advisor; and Duncan, in charge of warfare. All eyes were focused on Elaine's swollen and bruised cheek.

The air was already sizzling with tension when she walked in. When everyone saw her injury, she felt the whole room would explode.

Shelley quickly joined them and handed Elaine an ice pack. She pressed the cool ice to her cheek while Ian looked to Cearnach to explain.

"Vardon McKinley did it when he tried to hit me. Elaine attempted to stop the fight." Cearnach stood so close to her that she could feel the heat radiating from his body, reaching out to her, warming her.

Ian's phone rang. He read the name on the caller ID. Shaking his head, he said to his brothers, "The Kilpatricks." He set his phone on the desk and didn't answer it.

They had to know she was here. She felt mixed emotions over that. She was worried about bringing the MacNeill clan into this, although it was her kin's fault for putting her in this predicament in the first place. And she felt self-righteous satisfaction that after having been so ruthless toward her and Cearnach, the Kilpatricks had lost her to their enemy.

"After what they pulled, we're not going to just turn her over to them," Cearnach said, as if he was in charge of the pack and dictating terms.

Ian took a seat at his desk and leaned back in the chair. "She's their kin. I doubt they plan to harm her."

"Ha! They've already treated her shabbily. What if she had been shot while running as a wolf?"

Ian's expression turned stormy. "You mentioned *nothing* of this to me."

"A sheepherder's dogs barked until the farmer investigated to see what was disturbing the peace. Oglivie, you know how he is, and another man chased after us in a pickup and tried to shoot us. What if they'd injured Elaine?"

Duncan snorted. "Her kin don't deserve to have her back."

She wholeheartedly agreed, but she wasn't sure Ian wanted to keep her here, which could stir up more trouble between the clans.

Cearnach remained beside Elaine, his fists clenched in anger. "What if they're furious with her for having been with me? You can't turn her over to them."

"I'm not going to. They have to make full restitution of your vehicle and hers. Your clothes, sword, phone, and anything else they took. If they can't do that right away, she'll be our honored guest until they do," Ian said. He looked at Elaine as she stiffened, and she thought his dark expression was a warning. She had brought this trouble to the clan; he was the clan chief and would decide what happened to her.

After Rafferty, no one had dictated what she could do, so she was used to being in charge of her own destiny. She didn't like anyone thinking he could tell her what to do.

Ian's phone rang again, and this time after he looked at the caller ID, he shook his head. "The McKinleys." He set his phone back down on the desk. "They can stew overnight about what they did to the lass and Cearnach. Guthrie, make sure the place is locked up tight. Next time they see her, they can show their kin a wee bit more Scottish hospitality."

"Aye, Ian." Guthrie hurried out of the room to take care of the task.

"Elaine and I need to have dinner." Cearnach slipped his hand around her arm. "I'll get us something to eat."

"You don't cook," Ian reminded him. Though his brother's tone was dark, Cearnach thought he heard a hint of amusement in his voice.

Cearnach gave him a small smile. "Maybe I can manage a pizza. Or..." He sniffed the air. "Maybe Cook's got some of that lamb stew left."

"The way this clan eats, I doubt it," Duncan said.

"Then I can take her to Scot's pub."

"Not without an armed escort. Call ahead and clear out the place before we arrive," Duncan suggested.

Cearnach was thinking of a quiet dinner for two. Just Elaine and him where they could discuss what they would do next. Not a mob scene with his clansmen watching over them.

"Did the rest of you not eat already?" Cearnach asked. At this late hour, he knew they had.

Ian and Duncan glanced at each other and looked as though they finally got the message.

Julia and Duncan's mate, Shelley, smiled. His aunt and mother didn't look pleased.

"Cearnach," his mother said, her brow furrowed, "a word with you."

When he hesitated, fairly sure she would lecture him about getting involved with his enemy's kin, he couldn't believe it when she said, "Please."

It was the first time he'd ever heard his mother say the word, and he knew everyone present was just as shocked.

"I'll take Elaine down to the kitchen, and you can join her in a few minutes," Shelley quickly offered.

Cearnach didn't care how nicely his mother asked, *if* she even asked him nicely, or if she tried to order him about. She wasn't the one to determine what would happen to Elaine.

Chapter 11

IAN'S PHONE RANG ONCE AGAIN IN HIS SOLAR, AND everyone looked at him as if he was about to hear some earth-shattering news—a call to battle, a final ultimatum—from one of the McKinleys or their cousins. He glanced at the caller ID and frowned. Looking at Cearnach with a raised brow, he greeted the caller with a brief, "Calla."

Cearnach couldn't have been more astonished.

"Yeah, Cearnach is safe here. I'll let you speak with him." Ian held the phone out to Cearnach.

Cearnach crossed the floor to Ian and took the phone. He breathed in deeply and said, "Calla."

"You're all right?" she asked, and he heard a hint of tears in her voice.

He hated that Baird or his brothers had upset her. "Aye, I'm fine, Calla. You… heard about my car."

"Aye, the bastards. I'm so sorry."

"You had nothing to do with it, lass."

"Is… is the woman with you?"

"Aye, Elaine Hawthorn. Robert Kilpatrick's distant cousin. They stole her rental car and left us stranded."

Silence.

"Calla?"

"Aye, I know. That's why I called. After I left the church, I learned Baird and his brothers and the Kilpatricks went after Elaine's car. Except they didn't know at the time that she was the one who was to meet with

Robert. I was worried when they were concerned you and Elaine hadn't made it to Argent Castle yet. They were furious you came to the wedding, but even more so when I called it off."

Cearnach didn't say anything for a moment, too astonished. "But you got married."

"We didn't exchange our vows yet. I'd explained to Baird that I'd invited you, so when Vardon hit Elaine and made you leave the church, I was furious. I'd told him before the wedding that if he did anything to discourage your being there, I'd call off the marriage. Despite my warning, he still had his brothers throw you out. He said he had nothing to do with it, but he lied. I saw him give them a slight nod, issuing the order to have them remove you. So as soon as you left, I walked out."

Cearnach smiled. "I'm glad to hear it."

"If I'd learned they'd destroyed your car beforehand, I would have made a public spectacle of Baird. Is Elaine all right?" she asked, sounding genuinely concerned for the American.

"Aye. She's here with me now." Safe and secure, and he meant to keep her that way.

"Good. Keep her there, Cearnach. Let them continue to be concerned. Robert's stored her rental car in his garage so it's protected for the time being. They're still worried that Elaine might not have made it safely to Argent Castle. Ian wouldn't answer his cell phone. So they've turned wolf to find your trails. I'm sure they'll soon discover you made it home and will be demanding Elaine's release."

"They can demand all they want. Are you going to be all right? About calling off the mating?"

Calla gave a ladylike snort. "My family has been really quiet about the whole situation. I think they're secretly pleased I didn't marry Baird but afraid to say so. What's Robert's cousin like?"

Sexy as hell was what came to mind. Cearnach smiled at Elaine. "Travel weary, and she's hungry. I'm about to fix her something to eat."

"I'd like to meet her before she returns home to America," Calla said. "She's really pretty. I saw her poke at you and heard her say that if you were going to object to the wedding, you should do so. I had to smile, although Baird was scowling up a storm. I like her already. Keep her away from Robert. Make him pay for what they did. I think Vardon feels bad about hitting her when he meant to hit you, but you know how they are. No apologies to anyone. And, Cearnach?"

"Aye, lass?"

"Thanks. For telling me what I didn't want to hear. I've got to go. Dad wants to talk with me. He says to tell you hi. Take care."

"You as well. 'Night, Calla."

When the phone call ended, he took a deep settling breath, glad that Calla had not married McKinley, but he knew it wouldn't be over that easily. He was certain Baird would attempt to convince her to marry him, if nothing more than to save face. Although knowing him, he'd probably blame Cearnach. He handed the phone to Ian. "Calla called off the wedding."

Duncan gave a dark laugh. "No wonder they were angry with you, Cearnach. So she finally listened to you."

"Yeah, well, I don't think she would have done so if I hadn't been there and they hadn't reacted the way they had. They proved to Calla what I'd been talking about all along." Cearnach turned to Elaine. "Ready to eat?"

"I'm not all that hungry," she demurely said.

She looked tired and ready to go to bed, which immediately made him think of sharing his mattress with her and wishing she was thinking along the same lines. "Keep me company then after I speak with my mother? I'm starving." He took her arm and led her into the hall, away from his family. He hoped he could whip up something that would appeal to her.

His mother came out into the hall looking determined. He said to Elaine, "I'll be down in a moment." In truth, he didn't want to leave her for a second longer. Even while he'd stood next to her in Ian's solar, he'd wanted to do so much more.

Elaine seemed to know what he was thinking. She took his hand in hers and squeezed, then reached up and kissed his lips briefly as if she was afraid to do much more in front of his mother or Shelley.

Hell. But when he saw the devilish smile in her eyes and on her lips, he knew her sweet, innocent kiss was intended to entice him. *Vixen.*

He pulled her hard against him, looked down into her dazzling dark brown eyes, and kissed her for all it was worth. All the pent-up worry about her and the men that had been shooting at them, and the anxiety about her being injured in the falls… all of that came rushing back to him.

He didn't stop at a sweet, chaste kiss but gave her what he was feeling—relief, desire, and a craving for her so strong that he didn't want to curb the emotions. When she melted in his arms and kissed him back, pressing her soft body against his arousal, he deepened the kiss.

Both their hearts were pounding as he leaned his forehead against hers, breathed in deeply, smelling her own arousal, and gave her a small wicked smile. She cast just as devilish of a smile back at him.

He kissed her again, then let her go, his body still hot and hard and wanting from holding her. "I'll be down in a moment," he said, his voice rough with need.

She nodded.

Shelley was grinning as she took Elaine's hand and led her toward the stairs. Cearnach stood staring after them until they disappeared, not caring how his mother might react to his impulsivity. But then he noticed that his brothers, his aunt, and Julia had observed the whole thing, too. Fine. They could assume what they would.

Julia was wearing a small smile of approval. His aunt's brows were raised, a hint of disbelief in her expression. Guthrie shook his head as if he finally got the point that he didn't have a chance with the little gray wolf. Duncan's brows were furrowed. He probably figured Cearnach was going to start a war between clans if he took the she-wolf as his mate. Ian closed his gaping mouth and glanced at their mother to see her take on it.

"Coming?" his mother asked, her voice brittle.

He followed her to the library, where three walls were covered in books all the way to the ceiling. A large floor-to-ceiling window was situated between two of the bookshelves, providing a view of the garden during daylight. One whole section of a bookcase had been dedicated to Julia's werewolf romances as well as some of her favorite authors' romance stories.

A book with a hot-bodied military man and a wolf on the cover lay on one of the tables, apparently someone's recent read. He could just imagine Julia insisting that Ian wear a dog tag for her next book. He wouldn't go for it, Cearnach was sure. No self-respecting wolf would wear something called a *dog* tag.

After his mother was settled in an overstuffed reading chair, he closed the door. He didn't move any farther into the library, his whole posture stating that the audience with his mother would be as brief as possible. He crossed his arms in a defensive manner and studied her.

"In the old days you would have killed a wolf who hurt a woman like that. Are you going to kill Vardon, Cearnach?" his mother asked, her tone serious.

In fact, if he hadn't known her better, he would have thought she was giving him permission to do just that. He certainly hadn't expected her to ask such a question. He cast his mother a wry smile. "Is that what this is all about?"

"Mate with her," his mother said.

His jaw nearly dropped to the floor. He had half expected his mother to tell him not to get interested in the woman and to get her out of their castle at the earliest convenience. That she was a source of danger to their people.

But mating? He was stunned as hell that she would even suggest such a thing. He wanted to ask if she'd been nipping the brandy with his aunt before he and Elaine arrived.

His mother shrugged. "She's protective of you, a good quality in an alpha female. She's able to stand up to me. I like her."

He ground his teeth, studying his mother's set expression—the one she used when she was determined to have her way. He knew she had to be interested in something beyond just liking Elaine.

His mother was a crafty wolf, always thinking of what would benefit the clan, the pack. She wasn't impulsive in the least.

"What else, my lady mother? What are you thinking?"

"She knows where our stolen property is hidden. She's a Hawthorn, niece to those rogue wolves who were pirates. You will help her to locate the stolen goods and keep her safe at the same time."

Keeping her safe was what he had in mind. And more. But he didn't like where this was headed as far as the stolen property was concerned.

"The Kilpatricks, who obviously want it, won't get a farthing, and we'll keep all of it," his mother continued.

He frowned.

She quickly said, "Through a mating. We won't take it away from her. We'll keep it in the family. It's ours anyway. You know if they get hold of her, they'll plan the same thing—to get the stolen goods. Worse"—she cast him a concerned look—"one of *their* wolves will mate her."

"Like hell they will. What about *her* feelings in the matter?"

His mother smiled slyly. "From what you've demonstrated, dear boy, you already know what you're doing in showing everyone in the clan you've claimed her. And she… you. No need for you to ask me how it's done. Of all my sons, I always thought you would be mated first. It's past time."

It was true that he'd loved the lassies since he was a wee lad. Ian had been too busy running Argent Castle and the pack once their father had died. Duncan had been much more interested in quelling battles until Shelley walked into his life. Guthrie couldn't quit thinking about numbers and the pack's finances. No female wolf in the near future for him.

"She protected you, Cearnach. She stood up for you and risked her own safety. You won't often find that to be the case. Not when she didn't know you all that well. In the old days, a woman who could fight her husband's battles when he had to leave the castle was a real boon to a marriage. Many a castle was kept out of enemy hands because of a wife's canny wit and, more than that, a backbone and drive enough to make it happen."

"I'm not running the castle. Ian is."

She waved her hand in dismissal. "Don't be so obtuse, Cearnach. You want the girl. Make it happen." She gave him a wicked smile. "She said you were at fault for ruining your tires."

He raised his brows.

She nodded. "I have to agree with her. It was your fault. Now go cook something for the lass and make it good. I know she said she wasn't hungry, but have her eating out of your hands."

He shook his head. "A mating is for a lifetime."

"Aye, you think I don't know that? Everyone can see the way you feel about the woman. I raised you, you know. I probably understand you better than you do yourself. You want her. Don't you dare deny it. She feels the same for you."

He let out his breath. "I wanted to give time for us to get to know each other and for her to feel like she was part of the family first."

His mother scowled. "Don't give her a chance to get to know the family. She's mating you, not us. We don't want family issues to change her mind."

He laughed. He suspected Elaine might enjoy their family and all its quirks and not be put off by it. Unless his mother had ruined that chance.

His mother smiled. It was a calculating, evil kind of smile. He wasn't sure what she was up to, but he knew she was planning something. "Lust is only the beginning. You don't think your father lusted after me until he wore my father down into letting him have me? Of course the feeling was mutual."

If Cearnach had been human, he might not have wanted to hear the details. As a wolf, he knew his father and mother had been very much in lust and in love. He was glad she'd had so many good years with his father before he died. Though her relationship with Ethan, Shelley's uncle, wasn't the same, he thought they were growing closer every day. He'd even witnessed Ethan kissing his mother briefly in the gardens, and she hadn't even clouted him one. Just turned a rosy pink. Ethan had smiled in his indomitable way.

"Did you treat Elaine as though you wanted her to become one of our pack?" Cearnach asked, frowning.

"Och, Cearnach, you cannot be serious. She doesn't need my coddling. She's a fighter—a good one at that. Agnes and I went at her with a two-pronged attack, and she still came out on top."

He groaned. "You want me to undo the damage? Do you think I'm a miracle worker?" He let out his breath in annoyance.

"I can be the bad guy and you're her savior."

Cearnach shook his head. "I think she sees herself in that role."

His mother chuckled with wry amusement. "Aye, then she can be yours instead."

He shouldn't have allowed his mother to speak with Elaine first. "Is that all you wish of me, my mother?"

"Aye, go sweet-talk the lady. I'll speak with you later."

Shaking his head, he stalked out of the library and down the hall, wondering just what his mother had said to Elaine during their exchange. He hoped Elaine wasn't too upset over the whole affair.

Left to their own devices, he figured he and she could work out their relationship just fine. But he had to keep his mother *out* of it at all costs.

Now it was time to repair the damage.

Chapter 12

CEARNACH'S TALK WITH HIS MOTHER FILLED ELAINE'S thoughts—though she was trying not to think about it—as she walked with Shelley through the great hall where cushioned chairs, sofas, and pillow-covered benches were situated in front of a large fireplace. Flames flickered, casting light against the shadows, the wood crackling and snapping. Elaine felt oddly at home here. She could see the clan gathering here for special activities, particularly when the weather was wet or cold.

Yet her thoughts instantly returned to what was being said between Cearnach and his mother. Did she always rule the roost? More importantly, what she was saying to Cearnach about Elaine now?

As Shelley led her into the kitchen, Elaine was impressed with the newness and size, having expected it to be less than modern and much smaller. But it had to feed a fairly large wolf pack—around thirty or more, she estimated. She wasn't used to thinking in terms of pack life.

To her surprise, the need to belong to a wolf pack like this one crept into the marrow of her bones. To be understood by others of her kind. To be protected and to protect.

A long honey-oak table was situated next to a wide window overlooking the gardens below, a hedge surrounding them. It made her think of a labyrinth where she could get lost with Cearnach, just strolling and talking like two people on a special date, as small brass lanterns illuminated the paths, a touch of warm yellow light on a dark gray night. The tall hedges hid most of the gardens from view, giving only glimpses into the sectioned-off, outdoor living rooms, making them seem mysterious and intriguing.

The table in the kitchen seated about twelve. Pack members could drop in for a quick meal between working various jobs at the castle and beyond, she assumed. She'd passed through a formal dining room on the way into the kitchen where a dark mahogany table and chairs took center stage. The table would seat around twenty people, and the high-back chairs wore forest-green brocade with braid trim edging the seats. Paintings of local scenery were displayed on the walls, showing snowcapped mountains, dark blue lochs, fields of purple heather and yellow gorse, and the dark green forest.

In the kitchen, racks held glistening stainless-steel serving ladles and pots and pans that hung over a large, freestanding island. All the counters were golden granite flecked with black. Three stainless-steel fridges, two dishwashers, and three ovens filled the kitchen, plus a microwave built into the cabinets on one wall. Elaine couldn't begin to imagine the chaos that must ensue when everyone came in to eat. Unless the pack ate their meals in shifts.

She'd never considered what it would be like for a working pack to live together on an estate like this. The teasing, the camaraderie, the sharing of stories and jokes and good humor. Used to eating her meals alone in front of a TV screen after work, she thought how nice it would be to actually enjoy wolf company instead.

Shelley poked around in one of the fridges. "I have to admit I never make meals here. When I was back home, I cooked some, but lots of times I just microwaved meals. Here they have a woman who cooks for the pack. When I met Duncan on Grand Cayman Island, he was our chef extraordinaire.

"It's an ongoing joke. Ian's brothers say they can't cook, except maybe to make a pizza if Cook isn't around. But I caught them all making ham-and-cheese omelets and mimosas one morning when I slept in late and they had missed the morning meal, too. Which meant Cook wasn't going to fix them breakfast. It also meant that not only can Duncan cook, but so can his older brothers."

Amused that the brothers played such a game on their pack leader, Elaine smiled. "Do you think Ian really knows the truth?"

"Probably. He seems to know *everything* that goes on in the castle."

A pretty brunette hurried into the kitchen, her cheeks flushed, her dark eyes wide. She appeared to be about Shelley and Elaine's age and smelled of the outdoors, rain, and wind. "Oh, I can't believe it. I take one night off to visit a girlfriend, and our whole pack is ready to go to war with another pack."

She smiled brightly at Elaine as if that was a good thing, that she knew who had started it, and she wholeheartedly approved. Then she turned her attention to Shelley. "What are you doing? You don't cook."

"Attempting to figure out what Cearnach and Elaine

can eat for dinner. I was thinking of making them sandwiches and a salad."

"I'll do it. I'm Heather MacNeill, Cearnach's cousin," she said, offering her hand to Elaine. She smiled broadly again.

Elaine shook her hand and smiled back. She really hadn't expected everyone to be so friendly, all but Cearnach's mother and aunt. They were Old-World Highland nobility and probably thought Elaine was some uncultured, uncouth American nobody.

Well, kin to pirates. That was worse. Particularly because Elaine's kin had stolen from Cearnach's kin. Not to mention being old-time enemies.

"You will have to fill me in on all the details of what's going on." Heather peered into the fridge as Shelley stepped aside and let her take over. Heather glanced over her shoulder at Elaine. "Where's Cearnach? My brother, Oran, said that Cearnach was glued to you."

"His mother is talking to him," Elaine said, not at all happy about it.

Heather lifted her chin a bit, then frowned. "Oh."

Elaine thought that one little word said it all. The talk wouldn't go well. "I'm not all that hungry." Too many butterflies were flitting about in her stomach. After the long flight and running with Cearnach to get here as wolves, she was ready to collapse and *try* to sleep. Though everything was so unsettled that she wasn't sure she could.

"*I* am hungry," Cearnach said, stalking into the kitchen like a ray of sunshine on a gloomy day. He instantly gave Elaine an appreciative smile and wrapped his arm around her shoulders as if saying, "Mine."

For the first time since they had arrived at Argent, she really noticed what he was wearing—a pair of well-worn jeans, the fabric soft and faded, and a lamb's wool sweater just as soft, with grays and browns woven into ancient patterns. Hiking boots finished the ensemble. He looked like he was ready for the great outdoors. The sweater made her take a second look. She wanted to run her hands over it, under it, feel his muscles bunching like when he'd worn no shirt at all.

Heather straightened and looked at him. "What would you like to eat?"

"Anything that's easy to make," Cearnach said.

Elaine couldn't believe how considerate he was. Most men she knew would ask for the world if someone else was doing the cooking.

"What about some of the stew Cook made? I didn't get a bite of it either, but it smells delicious." Then Heather frowned as she shoved things around in the fridge. "There don't appear to be any leftovers." She started pulling packages of food out of the fridge. "I can make up a fresh batch."

"Are you sure it won't be too much trouble?" Elaine asked.

Heather waved a hand of dismissal. "No. I love to cook. I heard you're an American and you ran Cearnach off the road, which is how you met so fortuitously."

Cearnach shook his head as if he couldn't believe meeting like that would become the topic of conversation, but at least he was smiling.

"He was driving too fast for a one-lane road," Elaine said, one brow raised as she crossed her arms beneath her breasts.

Heather grinned at her and pulled out a peeler, then began removing the skin from a potato. "I like her. Don't chase her off."

Cearnach grabbed a bag of carrots and celery.

"Here, let me do that." Shelley extracted a knife from the drawer and took the vegetables from him. "You wouldn't want Ian to know you can cook. Not after you and your brothers have guarded the secret for so long."

"I can manage," Cearnach said.

Elaine wondered why he was so intent on offering when the ladies treated him as though he was just in the way.

Heather grinned at him, and Elaine assumed she knew him so well that she had figured out what his game was. "Go, Cearnach. You can show off to the lady some other time. Take Elaine to the garden room. Someone's started a fire in the fire pit so it should be nice and toasty warm. Talk with her. Take her for a stroll in the gardens. The rain has stopped. I'll have something palatable ready in half an hour or so."

A strange look crossed Cearnach's face, one of questioning, Elaine thought. She'd gotten the impression he had planned to take care of this in his own way, and now his cousin had thrown him totally off stride. Had he really intended to show her he could cook? How utterly sweet of him.

She'd never known a man who could switch plans so quickly and not be a little rattled, though. His cousin just smiled, feigning innocence, but the look appeared more calculating than angelic to Elaine.

A setup. That's what Elaine felt was going on here. A means to move a romantic relationship forward at a jackrabbit's pace instead of a snail's. She got the impression that Cearnach didn't often show interest in a she-wolf around his clan members, and Heather was pushing for something to happen.

"Do you want to take a walk in the gardens, lass?" Cearnach asked, finally taking his cousin's cue as he motioned gallantly to the door with a gracious sweeping gesture.

"I'd love to. Thank you, Heather and Shelley, for preparing a meal for us." Even if Elaine didn't think she could eat any of it, she appreciated their kindness.

"You're so very welcome. It's not every day we have such an uproar in the pack." Heather waved a hand at the coats hanging on a rack. "The yellow one is mine. Feel free to use it."

"Thanks," Elaine said, and Cearnach quickly helped her into it.

Cearnach threw on a black rain jacket and escorted Elaine out the kitchen door. He wrapped his arm around her shoulders and kept her close, as if they were lovers already, as he guided her along a brick walkway, down steps, through a four-foot-wide living boxwood arch, and into the gardens.

"The steps are mossy and wet and slippery," he explained, as if that was the real reason he was holding her close.

She slipped once and he tightened his hold on her in response, so she had to agree he was right.

She loved the intimacy between them, the closeness, the warmth of his body pressed against hers. She loved getting away from the castle, his kin, and the overwhelming feeling that everyone wanted to know more about her when she had always been a very private person... and wolf. Still, she wanted to learn what his mother had said to him. Not that she meant to defend herself. In truth, she wanted to know how difficult it would be for her to stay here until she got her car and personal items back.

Leaving him was another story. For the first time ever, she really cared about someone. The spark between them was so intense that she wanted to explore further possibilities. How could she when their families were so at odds?

She took a deep breath. "Your mother..."

"Later," he said.

The news couldn't be good.

She tried to concentrate on the gardens, the way the small brass lanterns lighted all the paths, the water glistening on the smooth stones. Yew hedges rose high around the gardens, as massive as stone walls, only bright green and living.

He held her tightly against his side, heating her all the way to her core. Her nose was cold and so were her toes, but the rest of her was heating up just fine.

Hedges sectioned off the various gardens, and she could hear the pleasing sound of water as it spilled over stone fountains into lower basins or into small pools of water. The fountains were visible through vine-covered, wrought-iron trellises or hedges trimmed into living archways. A misty fog draped the area as Cearnach moved her from one garden section of herbs to another with flowers, past a garden with a waterfall, a glass greenhouse, and separate garden rooms for every interest.

She smiled when she saw the building made of glass walls with corner stone towers that mimicked the castle and its towers situated on four corners of the curtain wall. A roof made of skylights showed off the stormy gray night, and the warm, orange flames of the fire beckoned them inside.

She peered through one of the windows as he opened the door. Soft moss-green couches wrapped around the fire pit, connected in a gently curving fashion like a stream winding through woods. Brocade pillows generously embroidered in gold thread with Celtic designs covered the couches, while pots of plants hung from the rafters or sat high above on small shelves beneath the massive windows.

Cearnach escorted her inside where the warmth encircled her, then closed the door and locked it. She raised her brows. He smiled and pressed a few buttons on a panel. Shades began to slide down over the windows.

Her mouth dropped open as she watched the room, which had been bared to the gardens, suddenly become private.

"We can have real privacy here or in my bedchamber." Cearnach offered to take her coat.

Somehow, she didn't think either place would be safe.

He helped pull off her coat, then draped it on a coatrack that looked like a wrought-iron, leafless tree.

"We need to talk," he said with all seriousness, yet his eyes held dark interest, not at all what she would expect if he was going to tell her she needed to leave Argent Castle at the earliest possible moment.

She tried not to stiffen too much as he removed his coat, hung it up, and led her to one of the couches. He sat down with her but not too close, as if he needed to keep his distance.

She sank into the soft cushions, saw a bottle of wine and two glasses set next to it, and thought of the way Heather had been so flushed when she had hurried into the kitchen.

"I take it your mother wants me out of here as quickly as she can manage."

"Wine?" he asked, already pouring her a glass.

She accepted the glass and sighed before she took a sip. She knew she shouldn't drink anything after not having eaten for so long. With the meal, fine. Or after the meal. Not before.

For the first time in a long time, though, she felt she needed the fortification, wishing everything could be different between them.

Cearnach studied Elaine as she pressed her lips against the wineglass, recalling when she was so young in St. Andrews. He wondered how innocent she'd truly been. Had she known what her family had worked at? Where they had gotten their wealth?

Not caring what she'd known back then, he shook his head and lifted his glass of wine. "My mother said she wanted me to mate with you."

Elaine had just taken a sip of wine and choked on it. Sputtering and coughing, she tried to catch her breath, her eyes tearing.

He patted her back, wishing he had waited until after she swallowed the mouthful of wine before he made the comment.

She held up a hand, tears in her eyes, as she indicated she would be all right.

He still rubbed her back, craving the intimacy between them. She didn't move away and, in fact, leaned a little closer to him as if wanting more of his touch. He wanted to give it. But they had to talk.

When she finally caught her breath, she hoarsely said, "You can't be serious. She hates me. From everything she said, her posture, all of it."

"No, Elaine," he said tenderly. "My mother can be hard to read. I believe she sees in you something of herself. A fighter. Someone who would protect one of her own when she had no stake in risking her own neck. She likes you. That's saying something, believe me."

She gave a harsh laugh. "If the way she reacted to me indicates she likes me, I'd hate to see her when she hated me."

"She tests a wolf's mettle. You have what it takes to impress her."

She let out her breath softly. "I didn't think she appreciated what I'd done—standing up for you against Vardon."

"Hmm, lass, enough to suggest I mate with you. She wouldn't make a proposition like that flippantly."

Elaine laughed again, softer now, more amused than bitter. "Did she choose your brothers' mates for them?"

"No." He recalled how angry his mother had been when she learned Ian had taken Julia as his mate but hadn't bothered to consult her. When Shelley became Duncan's, his mother had actually been glad that the she-wolf had helped to recover their money, so she was more than willing to open her home to her. Shelley's Uncle Ethan was an added benefit because Cearnach could see that his mother was becoming quite smitten with the American.

"So why does she think she can decide who *you* mate?" Elaine asked.

"She thinks I'm in lust with you and that can turn into something deeper," he boldly said, watching her reaction. Elaine had to know how much he wanted her already, and not just because of the way she heated his blood with sexual craving.

Her eyes sparkled in the soft lights, her mouth curving up. God, how he wanted to cup her face in his hands and kiss her like they hadn't a second to lose.

She finished her glass of wine and poured herself another. "So what has that to do with anything? Lust is lust. It doesn't necessarily lead to a long-term relationship. Not between wolves who mate for life."

He cocked a brow. "She believes that the feeling is mutual." He knew the feeling was mutual because Elaine's pheromones told him so. Because of the way her heart raced when he drew close to her. Because of how he felt the air sizzle with sexual tension between them. Aye, the lass lusted for him as much as he did for her. There was no denying it.

The glass of wine that Elaine was about to sip from stopped at her lips, and she studied him before lowering it again and saying, "Okay, so if we're being brutally honest here, what is this really about?"

He admired her for her insight. He wasn't about to hide the truth from Elaine. Best to get it all out in the open. He leaned back on the pillows covering the couch, observing her reaction to what he was about to say although he wanted to pull her close, kiss her, forget talking, and get to more pleasurable business.

She sipped her wine, then set the glass down, pressed

her back against the soft cushions, and folded her arms, ready to hear the naked truth.

"The Hawthorn brothers…"

As soon as he mentioned them, she stiffened slightly. She was uncomfortable right away. Her past had come back to haunt her.

"…stole the goods from three of our merchant ships. The word was that they hid the goods somewhere in Scotland."

Her lovely, dark brown eyes narrowed fractionally. Not enough that most would have noticed, but a wary wolf would see the shift in her response.

"My mother wants us to become mates. I help you to locate the goods and you get to keep them, but they stay in the family," he said.

Elaine narrowed her eyes even further. "I see. You agreed to this scheme?" Her tone was icy now.

He hated how he'd turned a blossoming friendship into something else. A business relationship no longer in the least bit friendly.

"No. My mother dictates, but we do as we see fit," Cearnach said easily.

She relaxed a little, but the hostility was still smoldering beneath the surface. "Thank you, Cearnach, for being honest with me."

"I wouldn't want it any other way."

"I didn't know my uncles had stolen from your family before your mother told me. I'm sorry for what… for what they did."

"Aye. I doubted you knew much about any of their operations."

"I didn't." She took a deep breath. "The truth is that

once I learned the goods probably belonged to your family, I would have given them back anyway."

"Aye, lass," he said, believing her even though her expression said she was ready to argue her point.

"You believe me," she said. Her reaction was half question and half statement, indicating just how surprised she was.

"Aye, lass. You are not a pirate like your kin."

Tears filled her eyes. "Your mother said something awful happened to your men. That they lost everything. Did… did my uncles kill some of your people?"

"Nay, Elaine. They were privateers and believed they were fighting for a good cause. We fought them, of course, but when we knew we were undermanned and outgunned, we gave up. Lives were worth more than a few measly trinkets. I have to admit that I lost a favored sword to your Uncle Tobias. I was but a lad and wouldn't stop fighting, though my *da* ordered me to. Tobias Hawthorn fought me until he knocked my sword from my grip. He said he wanted me to join his crew but instead took my sword for safekeeping.

"I was the only one of my brothers who had traveled with my *da* on that trip. Duncan chided me that he wouldn't have lost his sword. Truth be known, Ian is the best swordsman of all of us, and *he* might have kept his sword. Maybe not. We were all just lads then. After the theft, we were short on funds and had a harsh winter to get through, but we managed to survive."

"You fought my uncle?" she said, disbelief threading her words.

"Aye. He had no intention of killing me. He could easily have done so, as large as he was compared to how scrawny I was in my youth. He showed he had honor."

Elaine swallowed hard, tears misting her eyes. "If we find the treasure…" she said, taking his hand—and all at once he was back to his original need to move closer and make this personal. To see the heated look in her eyes right before he kissed her sweet mouth. To feel her soft curves plastered against his hard muscles. That's what he wanted—but then she continued talking, and he realized her touch had made him lose all thoughts but one.

"…I want those families who suffered the most to share whatever is found," she said. Then frowned. "Are you listening?"

He tried to contain his wolfish smile because she was being brutally honest with him and that had nothing to do with where his thoughts had roamed of their own volition. "Aye, lass. You are nothing like your uncles. I imagine they'd be rolling in their graves if they knew what you'd offered to do with their loot."

"*My* loot," she corrected him, giving him a little smile.

He pulled her into his arms, loving her, unable to keep the distance between them, and she was kissing him and running her hands up under his sweater, her fingertips warm and soft as she teased his skin.

But he had to know more. He had to before they could go any further.

"What happened when I lost you in St. Andrews? What happened to Kelly Rafferty? The man your uncles said you had to mate?"

Chapter 13

SITTING ON THE SOFA IN THE GARDEN ROOM, CEARNACH wanted nothing more than to take Elaine right then and there. The way her hands had slid up his chest underneath his sweater and the way she was kissing his mouth with such pent-up need, her tongue teasing his lips, stroking his tongue, made his fingers tangle in her hair as he tackled her mouth with just as much enthusiasm.

He told himself he had to know what had become of the man who had mated her, but he couldn't get his feelings for her under control. Until a knock sounded at the garden room door. Cearnach frowned, looking down at a tussled Elaine, her lips swollen from their kisses, her cheeks high with color, her hair tangled. She was beautiful.

"Stay," he said, not wanting her to move an inch until he took care of the matter.

She smiled up at him, her brows and the corners of her mouth lifting as she took a deep breath and relaxed even more against the cushions, her expression saying she was more amused than annoyed with him that he would command her in such a way.

When he reached the door, he found covered dishes sitting on the table outside, Heather and Shelley's scent lingering in the air. He loved his family.

He carried the trays inside, closing the door with his boot.

Elaine had moved to the table but finished off her wine as if it would brace her to speak to Cearnach about that bastard Rafferty. He wanted to return to the sofa, to pull her into his arms, and comfort her while she spoke. But he needed to get some food down her.

Cearnach studied her as they ate the hearty lamb stew Heather and Shelley had prepared. Or... at least he ate the food. Elaine merely moved chunks of celery and lamb meat around in her bowl.

The warm fire, the orange-red flames licking the air, the aroma of the stew, and the wine all added ambience, he thought. The golden lights silhouetted her, and she looked like a wolf goddess. *His* wolf goddess.

She leaned her chin on her hand, resting her elbow on the table, and he wondered if her tired posture had to do with the wine. Then she perked up a little, and he thought she was going to eat. Instead, she refilled her empty wineglass. He raised his brows, wanting to ask if she normally drank that much or felt the need because of what she'd been through today.

"Okay, here's the story. Kelly Rafferty was furious I had left St. Augustine with my uncles." She tipped her wineglass one way and then the other, watching the wine tilt like waves on a shifting sea. "I meant to sail home after my uncles were hanged." She swallowed hard.

"I planned to secure as much of my inheritance from my parents' estate as I could and then flee the city." She looked down at the table. "Pirates attacked our ship." She glanced up at Cearnach, eyes narrowed, and gave a little snort of derision. "Imagine that. Sailing on the high seas wasn't safe at all. Worse, the ship was one of Rafferty's.

"He wasn't the captain of the vessel, but one of his men recognized me, which was probably good since some of his men were ready to treat me as fair game. He locked me in the captain's cabin to keep me safe so I wouldn't be spoiled goods. They returned home with all haste. You see, I was the biggest treasure of all. They didn't want to anger Rafferty if they should somehow lose me before they could turn me over to him."

Cearnach clenched his hand around his fork, afraid of where this was headed and not liking it one bit.

"My parents maintained a manor home, a couple of lodging houses, and three ships. When Kelly forcibly took me as his mate, he owned all of it."

Cearnach growled low, wanting to kill the bastard.

"He'd actually been in competition with my family for years before that. So mating with me was strictly a business arrangement. He possessed me and everything I could bring to the relationship. I was the perfectly reticent mate, waiting for his return each time he went out on a voyage."

"I have a difficult time imagining you being reticent," Cearnach said, stabbing a chunk of potato and wishing he could have protected her so long ago.

She humphed. "I prayed he'd perish every time he went out to sea. Rafferty had bodyguards, werewolves who were completely dedicated to him and who would have died before they let anything happen to me, including allowing me to escape. Not that I didn't try. When he returned home, his men told him that I had tried to run away, and Rafferty beat me for it. No one raised a hand to stop him. It was his right to do with me as was his will. He would have done the same to any of his men, had they gotten out of line. Or he would have done worse."

"He better be dead," Cearnach growled.

She nodded and suddenly looked even wearier as she sank down in her chair.

He noticed the dark shadows beneath her eyes, but he had to know more before they retired for the night. He still hoped she'd eat some of the stew.

"Did you have children?" He could hardly bear the thought of the pig lifting her skirts and rutting into her like some wild animal. Cearnach was certain, given her description of the man, that he couldn't have cared about pleasuring her.

"No. I protected myself. I didn't want children who would be treated as harshly as I was. Nor did I want to bear any males who might have been forced to become pirates. Not having any children emasculated him in front of his men. He couldn't produce one child. He blamed it on me, and rightly so. I won't deny I took evil pleasure in knowing he worried about his own manhood."

Rafferty's distress over his inability to procreate wasn't enough to compensate for what Elaine had experienced at his hands, Cearnach thought.

"What happened to him?"

"As privateers, my uncles had some honor. Maybe not a whole lot, but they believed in part they were justified. Not Kelly. He never served as a privateer. All that he stole, he kept for himself, except for the proceeds he had to share with his men. On an earlier voyage, he cheated his men out of their share of the loot. When he went out on the next one, he didn't come home.

"His men said the quartermaster, Terrance, killed

him in a squabble over his share of the loot. He was supposed to have received twice the usual share, like the captain, for seeing that his orders were carried out and managing the day-to-day operations of the ship, administering punishments, and dividing up the loot. The crew threw Terrance overboard to make him pay for murdering the captain. They gave Kelly a burial at sea. I envisioned the captain and his quartermaster floating there together as their ship sailed away. A perfect end to their despicable lives."

She took a long breath. "I don't believe it happened that way. One of his men had overheard Kelly and Terrance speaking in the library of my parents' home about cheating the crew when the two men had had too much whisky to drink, celebrating their return and the loot they'd stolen. Before their next voyage, which was to be their last, the word must have spread among his crew and the men mutinied. That's loyalty among thieves for you."

Cearnach didn't care how the bastard had died as long as he was dead. "What happened to you?"

She shrugged as if it didn't matter. Deep down he knew it did. Everything that had gone on in her life had made an impact of one kind or another.

"The men figured I was part of the spoils. Probably payment for what Rafferty hadn't given them, even though they had his ships. They didn't know what a fighter I had become. Only two of them were guarding me the afternoon they received word that Rafferty was dead and one of the men had taken over as captain of his ship. They didn't expect me to shift and use my teeth.

"After I'd dealt with them, I sold the properties and

moved. Robert Kilpatrick finally found me, saying he'd been contacted by a solicitor in Scotland concerning some correspondence that had to do with our family. The lawyer was reviewing old records and needed to locate me.

"My uncles had mentioned the goods and where they were hidden in a roundabout way, in case anything ever happened to them. They didn't give me sufficient information to know what the treasure was or where it was kept. For two years, Robert had tried to locate me to see if I knew anything about where the treasure was hidden, or if I at least had the other half of the puzzle."

She offered Cearnach a wicked smile. "He tried to learn what information I might have without giving up the fact that he knew something of the matter. If he'd gotten the rest of the clues from me, I wouldn't be here today. I had the impression that his kin knew nothing about what he had discovered. That he was keeping the treasure secret from them so he could have the spoils and not have to share them with the others. Especially when he planned to meet me at the castle ruins two hours before Calla's wedding. I assumed he didn't want the McKinleys to know what he was up to. Or maybe even his own brother."

Cearnach could see Kilpatrick doing that. "If you hadn't come to Scotland, that would have been my great loss." He couldn't imagine not having met her again today. He would never return to Senton Castle's ruins without remembering how she had looked there earlier this afternoon, first as a human, observing the castle with such awe and reverence, then exploring it like a wolf—eager, excited, loving it.

Elaine turned to him. "So, all I have to do is mate you, and we can go on a treasure hunt. For your peace of mind, I'm not mating you. You can let your mother know that, too."

He loved her pragmatism and fighting spirit. He also saw the challenge in her eyes. He was certain she was waiting for him to contradict her, to say he wanted her. She had to know he did. That he recognized she wanted him also.

He cast her a predatory grin, tilted his chin down, and reached under the table to take her hand from where it was resting in her lap. Her gaze latched on to his, and he knew she could see the desire he had for her as plain as he could see the interest in hers. "We'll see about that."

He was named "victorious" for a reason. He was often victorious in anything he set his mind to accomplish. And he was determined to have her.

He released her hand and finished his stew.

"All these years, you've never been mated?" Cearnach asked, not believing Kelly Rafferty could have been the only one she'd mated with.

"Oh, sure, several times… *nearly*."

The inference that she'd been mated several times got to him, until she clarified with *nearly*. As beautiful and fun to be with as she was, he wasn't surprised she could have been mated many times over, although hearing it bothered him deep down. He couldn't fathom why any wolf wouldn't have followed through.

She took a deep breath, then said brightly, her tone incongruent with her body posture, "A lot of wolves took interest in me over the years. They just always vanished before anything could come of the relationship."

"That's hard to believe." He meant it. Why would any of them show interest and then quit the relationship? Not when she was as intriguing as she was.

She smiled a sad kind of smile. "Maybe so, but it's true. I began to believe I could easily attract attention, but no one was interested in mating me for a lifetime."

That's why she thought he couldn't want her? Because the others had skipped out on her?

Why would they change their minds overnight like that? He pondered that for a moment more, then a realization dawned. "They were betas."

"How… did you know?"

"No alpha who wanted you would vanish without making you his. So they had to be betas, unsure whether being mated to an alpha would work out. Why your interest in betas? You need an alpha."

Like me, he wanted to say.

She gave him a ghost of a smile. "An alpha would have been like Kelly Rafferty—in charge, beating me when I didn't do as he wished, in control of my money." She gave a half shrug. "I didn't need a mate for that."

Cearnach clenched his fists and wanted to kill the wolf himself for hurting Elaine. "You're certain he's dead?"

Though the point was moot. No alpha who had taken her to mate would have left her alone all these years. Not one as controlling as Rafferty had been.

He would change her mind. Not all alpha males were like that bastard.

"Yes, he's dead. His men wouldn't have come for me if he hadn't been dead. They'd know he would have killed them."

She looked so tired, her eyelids drooping, the swelling

and bruising on her face from where Vardon had hit her making her look all the more done in. Cearnach took her hand again and rubbed his thumb over her soft skin. "We can talk more tomorrow. Did you want to eat any of the stew?"

She shook her head. "Too tired."

"All right." Then he made his claim, unwilling to put it off any longer. "You need a mate." He kissed her cheek, deciding this once and for all. "And a family. You'll have both with me."

Her eyes widened and her lips parted.

He knew she would disagree with him for now, but he would sway her one way or another. She needed a family, a pack, him.

She said softly, tears glittering in her eyes, "You'll vanish before we do it. That's the way it always happens. A wolf promises me the moon, and then he disappears as if he didn't have the courage to tell me to my face that it wouldn't work out between us."

His jaw dropped. He couldn't conceal his surprise. She was agreeing to be his mate? He was expecting to work a lot harder at it than that. He was ready.

He had to be sure that she was.

He stood, then pulled her from her chair and into his arms, and hugged her with all his might, relieved as hell that she wanted him as much as he wanted her. At least he believed so. "Not this time, lass. You're exhausted. I'll take you up to your guest chamber. I'm not losing you again."

The way her sweet body called to his, if she hadn't been so fatigued, he knew they would do a hell of a lot more than talk. Just a touch and his pheromones were stirring, and so were hers, communicating with one another, saying it was way past time to get on with the more primal—and pleasurable—side of wolf business.

"Are you going to prove to me why I should mate you?" She looked at him with such a sweetly devilish look that he wondered if the wine was doing the talking. Yet the challenge was there again: *Prove to me you truly want me. Make it happen.*

He decided she was being wholly truthful with him, and he was going to ensure she agreed to a mating... when she was well rested in the morning.

He would prove to her that he meant what he said. He was no damned beta wolf. Nor was he an alpha like Rafferty. He would give her all that she deserved and more.

Unable to help herself, Elaine yawned, then smiled at Cearnach. She could tell he wasn't sure if she was ready to be his. She wasn't. Not until she was feeling more clearheaded. "Sorry."

After that, no holds barred.

"You're tired, lass. We'll decide a course of action tomorrow, once you tell me more about this business transaction between you and your cousin Robert Kilpatrick."

Hoping to come up with a solution for the situation with her cousins after she had a good night's sleep and she could think more clearly, Elaine agreed.

Gallant man that he was, and without waiting for her to agree, Cearnach slipped his arms underneath Elaine and lifted her. She let out a little gasp of surprise. As wobbly as she felt from drinking too much wine, she didn't think she could have stumbled all the way to the castle on her own two feet.

Having told Cearnach so much of her past, she felt drained. She didn't feel cleansed, as she'd thought she might by finally telling him what had happened to her so long ago. She felt weary.

Some of the tiredness was due to the jet lag and the stress of the day; some of it was the wine. She couldn't believe she wasn't staying at the bed and breakfast owned by the Kilpatricks and instead was sleeping in a stone castle owned by an enemy clan.

Yet, Cearnach wasn't the enemy. He was someone who cheered her even when the situation was dire, gave her hope so she felt she had a new lease on life. Odd thing, that. She hadn't thought about Kelly for a long time now, but returning to Scotland had brought the memories all back.

She gave in to her fatigue and rested her head against Cearnach's hard chest as he carried her back to the castle—her braw Highland warrior in a soft lamb's wool sweater and jeans. She felt more than saw a few people stare in their direction as they entered the castle and made their way to the stairs.

Cearnach nodded at a knot of people seated next to the fire that she noticed out of her peripheral vision.

Was Ian there? His mother?

She had never been the focus of so much attention, and it was somewhat overwhelming. Yet on another level, she felt special.

"Sorry," she said softly again, snuggling closer to Cearnach as he carried her through the castle.

"For what?" He kissed the top of her head and made his way up the stairs.

"For all the grief you're going to get over having brought me here."

"I've had worse, lass."

She laughed at him. She had expected him to disagree.

He smiled down at her, but he didn't say anything, and she let the issue go.

Cearnach carried Elaine into a guest bedchamber where clothes were stacked on top of a light oak dresser for her use. He set her on her feet, but she still felt a little shaky, gripping his arm to keep her balance. The immense bed sitting center stage immediately captured her attention. Surrounding the bed were heavy burgundy curtains made of velvet and embellished with swirls of gold thread. She walked over to the bed and ran her hand over the soft curtains.

Glancing back at him, she witnessed the curve to his mouth, one raised brow, and his arms folded across his broad chest as he watched her. The sweater was nice, but she kept thinking of his beautiful naked chest when he was wearing only a kilt, and she smiled warmly at the memory.

With such a predatory look on his face, was he envisioning her in the bed? Maybe with him in it while he lay beside her… or on top of her? She thought his smile was more wicked than sweet.

Her cheeks instantly blossomed with heat. "Thank you for everything, Cearnach." She was drained of all energy after having run and swum as a wolf, not to mention fighting jet lag. She felt she could just as easily curl up on the lovely gold-and-burgundy Turkish hand-knotted rugs covering the floor and fall asleep.

At first Cearnach didn't move. Then, as if he'd made

up his mind about something, he closed the distance between them, and she knew he'd give her another kiss. She wasn't sure she could handle another of his kisses while she was alone with him in a bedroom.

His large hands took hold of her shoulders, the heat seeping through her shirt, the power of his touch drugging her. He leaned down and said in a wickedly husky voice, "A kiss before you sleep to give you pleasant dreams. I promise you more tomorrow."

He didn't ask permission, although at this point, she wouldn't let him get away before he fulfilled his promise.

He kissed her, leaning against her, sharing his heat and power and interest. His tongue plundered her like a pirate taking possession—and as she devoured him in the same way, she knew this exchange was taking another step closer to making their relationship something more. Permanent. Forever. Giving in to the lust, the sexiness, the wolfish fascination for another of her kind was something new for her.

She was already wet for him, her breasts heavy and achy for his touch, her nipples taut peaks of desire. Needy, craving his mouth, his fingers, his caress.

"I want you." His voice was dark and fathomless, husky with craving.

Before she was ready to end the kiss or think of where this might lead, he hugged her tight—wrapping his muscled arms around her body, keeping her close as if she was the most precious thing to him—and rested his cheek on the top of her head. She loved the way his body surrounded her, wishing they could take this further.

Then he groaned.

A lusty groan of unfulfilled passion, of regrets and desires that she could so relate to. He was holding back.

Appreciating him and his family, loving that she'd have a chance to sleep in a medieval castle, she hugged him back. She felt the hardness of his erection pressed against her belly, knew he needed release as much as she did, knew he desired more. Yet despite knowing what a mistake that could be if they gave into their primal urges... she wasn't ready to let him go. She wasn't thinking clearly, either. She'd had too much wine.

Curbing her own wolfish needs, she finally said, "Good night, Highlander. Until tomorrow, then."

He sighed deeply and looked into her eyes, his own simmering with lust.

"'Night, lass." His voice was rough with restrained need. He kissed the top of her head, then moved away from her and winked before he shut the door. When he closed it on his departure, she suddenly felt bereft. She hadn't realized how seeing a family, a working pack, would affect her. She'd always thought being part of a family was someone else's dream. Not her own. Not since her parents and uncles had died.

She never felt that way about human families, considering them something different, alien to her. After the disaster with Kelly Rafferty, she'd struck out on her own, avoiding wolf packs wherever she went. What if she'd ended up in another abusive relationship?

Yet unexpectedly, she felt she was missing out after seeing the teasing between members of Cearnach's clan, the anxiety on the brothers' faces, the worry for Cearnach, and the concern for her. The gathering of the family to take her in, to counsel her about the apprehension they had about her dealings with her kin. Even his mother's telling him he should mate Elaine. How Cearnach's family had treated her like she was one of their pack, their clan.

She couldn't help being surprised to be accepted into a wolf pack of perfect strangers, when in a human's world she had kept herself apart. Friendly, but not too much so.

No matter how much she had behaved as a human among their kind, she was always well aware that she wasn't one. That her senses were so much more attuned, that she could detect emotions and feelings just from their scents. That the wolfish side of her had to be controlled when she got angry, and she'd want to shift and show them her teeth.

That she had to run as a wolf from time to time, to enjoy nature as her other half. The halves were what made her whole—one didn't exist without the other. She was wolf and human all in one. For the first time in a very long time, she enjoyed being with others of her kind who could understand just how she felt, who could look deep into her soul like she could into theirs. They were equals, not all that different from her.

Even his mother—what a surprise it was that she wanted Elaine to become part of their pack. She knew the woman hadn't said so lightly. That felt comforting in an odd way.

Yet, Elaine had to keep herself from falling into a false sense of security, remembering that they were family and she was still an outsider, kin to an enemy clan.

Sighing deeply, she removed her clothes and slipped into the borrowed, silky, pale blue nightgown sitting atop the dresser that made her feel like a fairy princess. A lace-trimmed bodice dipped low, showing the swell of her breasts. Long flowing sleeves trimmed with lace tickled her knuckles. An ankle-length edging trimmed with lace swished as she walked.

The fabric was opaque enough for modesty, although when she glimpsed herself in a gold-gilded mirror, she noted that her nipples stood out against the material. She swirled around, loving the luxurious, silky feel of the gown, feeling sexier than if she'd just climbed into bed naked, which was how she usually slept—like most wolves did.

The fatigue catching up to her again, she climbed onto the bed and pulled the bed curtains closed, then slipped underneath the burgundy covers. The comforter was velvety soft, covered in rich, gold floral embroidery, warm and comforting as she burrowed beneath it. The sheets smelled like they had been washed in sweet fragrant roses, and she breathed in deeply to enjoy the scent.

She felt small and pretty and at home in this huge bed. What would have made it even better was Cearnach sleeping with her here. Not sleeping. Making love.

Then her thoughts turned to meeting Cearnach again after all these years, how she'd felt about his offer of assistance so long ago, wishing he could have helped her, and wondering what would have happened had she accepted it. How different might her life have been if she had stayed with Cearnach back then?

Now he was offering to assist her again, protecting her against her kin while attempting to help her locate the goods her uncles had hidden away.

She couldn't avoid thinking about the heat that had

erupted between them and the desire to do something about it.

She sighed and closed her eyes in the dark room, needing to sleep, not believing she could shut off thoughts of Cearnach kissing her in the car... how his tongue had danced with hers, the way he let her set the boundaries yet was so enraptured in the kiss that he'd quickly become the aggressor—passionate, craving more, just like she had.

Now tonight, kissing him again had felt just as right. She knew he was having as difficult a time reeling in his desire as she had with him. She suspected they would become mates sooner rather than later. As long as he didn't change his mind, or someone or something didn't change it for him.

With a heavy sigh and forcing herself to push away the images of Cearnach and what she had to do concerning her cousins, she finally succumbed to sleep.

Only to be awakened a couple of hours later by a soft, whispered breath touching her cheek. She tried to ignore the sensation. Tried to tell herself she was dreaming.

"Elaine," a male voice whispered, the voice so disembodied, so wispy, so soft that she didn't pay any attention to it.

She was so tired that she assumed it was her imagination in her partly dream-filled, slightly inebriated consciousness.

Until a chilly hand brushed over her silk-covered breast.

Chapter 14

LYING ON HER SIDE, ELAINE WOKE ENOUGH TO REALIZE the man's hand that had felt her up *wasn't* a dream. Heart pounding, she jerked her head around to see who it was, expecting Cearnach and not sure how she would react. Angry that he would sneak into her bed. But wanting him, too.

Yet, no one was beside her on the mattress in the dark. As a *lupus garou*, she could see some in the pitch blackness. A shiver stole up her spine.

With the blood rushing in her ears, she did what any red-blooded woman—whether half wolf or strictly human—would do under the circumstances. She let out an ear-piercing scream to wake everyone in the whole castle.

She scrambled to get out of the bed and away from the intruder. Her feet and legs became tangled in the silky sheets and velvet comforter. Panicked, she twisted and jerked. Freeing herself, she shoved aside the heavy curtains, desperate to get out of the bed where the man had to be hiding under the comforter.

In her haste, forgetting just how high the mattress was, she leaped from the bed, catching a foot in the curtain and the long nightgown, and went down on her knees with a thump.

Ouch! Dull pain radiated through her kneecaps, and she cursed under her breath.

Not wanting her back to the man, she spun around and sat in the dark, staring up at the bed, studying the outline of the draped canopy, listening for any rustling in the sheets or creaking of the box springs.

She saw no movement. Heard no sound.

With her heart racing and her breathing so rapid that it made her light-headed, she watched and waited to see the man clamber out of the bed before the whole household came running.

No one left the bed.

Arrogant bastard!

What was she thinking? She would shift and take care of the intruder herself. Before she could pull off the nightgown, a door across the hall banged against a wall. Footfalls rushed toward her room. *Cearnach?*

The door to her chamber opened with a whoosh. Cearnach shouted from the threshold, "Elaine!"

His gaze swept the room, searching for her.

"Here," she said quickly. Warm relief at seeing him washed over her chilled body as he stood in the doorway.

Looming large, silhouetted by the hall light, Cearnach was scowling. He was wearing only black boxers and holding a sword as if he was ready to kill the intruder.

On some wolfish level, she had known he hadn't been the one touching her. She would have noticed the delicious, tantalizing scent of him. Yet when she thought about that, she realized she hadn't smelled any sign of a wolf in bed with her. Just the rose-scented sheets.

He hit the light switch with his free hand, momentarily blinding her.

"Are you all right, Elaine?" he asked, his voice dark with concern.

Still sitting on the floor, her aching knees tucked up close to her chest, she squinted in the bright light and pointed at the bed. "Yes, I'm… I'm all right. A man was in there."

Cearnach rushed forth and yanked the curtains open.

Wearing a plaid haphazardly thrown on, Duncan hurried into the chamber, sword in hand, looking just as dangerous. Ian was right behind him, and Guthrie next, both wearing boxers, both also carrying swords.

She would have laughed to see so many braw Highlanders ready to defend her, but she was still so shaken that she managed only a small smile.

Cearnach shook his head at his brothers, letting them know there was no one in the bed, which was impossible for her to believe.

He reached down and helped Elaine from the floor, then pulled her into his warm, comforting embrace. She realized then just how icy cold the floor had been.

"Are you okay?" he asked again. This time his words were spoken soothingly, not brusque with concern that she might have been injured.

"Yes, I'm okay."

He brushed the top of her head with a kiss. "What exactly did you see?"

"Nothing. I didn't see anything. I thought maybe… maybe he was hiding beneath the covers. I felt… I felt a hand touch me."

"Are you sure you weren't having a nightmare?" Cearnach sounded more hopeful than certain.

She trembled in his arms, not sure why she was so shaken, when normally not much shook her. The fact she hadn't seen the man, only felt his icy touch, the way his breath had caressed her ear, the way he'd said her name, unnerved her something awful. She could deal with someone she could see. Not something like this.

The brothers all shared looks, and she suspected they thought she'd been having a nightmare. She knew the man had been real. He had to have been. She couldn't have dreamed it.

"Flynn," Ian said, his voice a growl, "damn you. Stay out of this guest room. Leave the lass alone."

Flynn? She hadn't remembered meeting anyone by that name.

"No one else is here. I would have noticed if he opened the door and left," Elaine said. Then she frowned. "Unless you have secret passages in the castle. A secret paneled entrance into the room."

That's when she looked around at the walls again and wondered if a secret entrance was hidden behind one of the tapestries.

"You didn't tell her about him, did you, Cearnach?" Duncan's tone was a warning, and she didn't like the sound of it.

"Flynn MacNeill's a ghost, one of our cousins, Elaine. He has a passion for dallying with the ladies," Cearnach explained. Then he looked at the ceiling and said in a voice rough with barely controlled anger, "Flynn, if you weren't already dead…"

"Remind him that we can always hire someone to do an exorcism," Ian said.

"He's harmless, although he annoys the lassies sometimes." Duncan waved his sword around as if he was slicing the ghost in two anyway. "Did you want anything from the kitchen, lass? A glass of milk to help you sleep?"

A ghost? She didn't believe in such things, though she tried to always keep an open mind. She shook her head and rubbed her arms, feeling the goose bumps trailing up and down them.

"Good night, lass, then," Duncan said. "If he bothers you again, just call out. We'll chase him away."

"Thank you, Duncan."

He bowed his head, then left the room.

Guthrie cleared his throat. "Same with me." Then he stalked out of the room after his brother.

"I'll take care of her," Cearnach told Ian, and she realized that since Ian was the pack leader, he felt responsible for her.

Cearnach was clearly showing he was the one who would take care of her as he kept her pressed against his hard—and getting harder—body.

Ian bowed his head slightly, gave Cearnach a look like he'd better be careful with their guest, and exited the bedchamber.

"My room or the guest room?" Cearnach asked.

"What?" She wasn't sure if he was joking or not, yet he looked damned earnest.

He didn't let go of her, as if he was her bodyguard now and taking this seriously. "He's harmless, but he can be persistent if he likes a woman. I'm not leaving you alone. Either you join me in my bed or I join you in yours."

"What if I sleep with Heather?" Not that she wanted Cearnach's poor cousin to have to share her bed with a perfect stranger just because of a pesky ghost, if that's truly what had been harassing her.

Cearnach snorted. "Flynn loves to torment her. If

you join her, he might decide to visit the two of you at one time."

She raised her brows, not sure she believed him. Then she shook her head.

"You don't want me to stay with you the rest of the night?"

"No, thanks." Yes, she did. She was afraid to return to bed. Afraid of not being able to fight some unseen ghostly entity, and she feared experiencing the same thing again. But then again, she didn't feel that sleeping with Cearnach was a safe bet, either. Not until she'd had a good night's sleep.

"I'll be all right," she assured him, not sounding half that sure of herself.

"If you need me, my chamber is just across the hall."

"All right." She hesitated to pull away from him and return to the bed. Despite the lamps lighting the room, the bed now looked dark and ominous, and she couldn't shake loose of the fear that a body that didn't exist was hiding under her covers.

Cearnach helped her onto the mattress and even tucked her in, which she found endearing. He didn't act like she was being foolish, even though she couldn't help feeling that way. If the intruder had been real, it would have been a different story.

"Do you want me to wait with you until you fall asleep?"

She shook her head no. She wasn't a child, even though she was feeling like one now. Yet, she appreciated the way he and his brothers had treated her—as though she had nothing to fear, and they didn't think she was crazy—and that they were at her beck and call, no matter what.

"I'll see you in the morning, then." He kissed her on the cheek, squeezed her hand, pulled the curtain shut, and then retreated from the room.

The door gave a soft *thunk* as it closed.

She snuggled under the covers, feeling suddenly isolated, trying to envision just what had happened. No matter how much she tried to explain away the cold hand on her breast or her name whispered in her ear or the wisp of icy breath on her cheek, she could think of only one thing—the man had been real. Not a ghost. Not a figment of her imagination.

He *was* real.

Despite closing her eyes and willing herself to sleep, she couldn't. Like having her house broken into once when she had been sleeping and then fearing the same thing would happen again, she couldn't relax her tense muscles, couldn't shut down her fears. Only this time instead of fearing the thieves would return, she waited for a ghostly touch and whispered words to come again.

———

Cearnach paced across his chamber, furious with Flynn. *Damn him.*

His ghostly cousin would never give up the lassies. Liking them way too much had been his downfall in the first place. But Flynn didn't always bother them, not unless he really liked them or he really disliked them.

Cearnach wondered if the fact that Elaine was kin to an enemy clan had bothered Flynn. Or did she really intrigue him?

"Leave the lass alone," Cearnach growled under his breath. "I mean it, Flynn."

Flynn did not make an appearance in Cearnach's bed-chamber, nor could he feel Flynn's presence in the form of chilled air in this room. He had noticed it right away in Elaine's room. Particularly in her bed. He was furious that Flynn would molest her.

Of all the cousins, Cearnach had been the closest to Flynn. He supposed it had something to do with them both being jovial sorts who saw most circumstances in a good light. Flynn just couldn't quit dallying with the lasses, not even when they had been married, not even now that he was just a ghostly version of himself.

Cearnach was ready to return to bed when another shriek erupted from Elaine's chamber.

"Flynn, damn you," Cearnach roared, throwing his door open again and storming across the hallway to Elaine's chamber. She was *not* sleeping the rest of the night alone! He wouldn't allow his cousin to bother her all night.

Cearnach yanked open her door and felt a soft body crash into his before it registered that the body belonged to Elaine.

"It's all right," he said, wrapping his arms around her in a comforting embrace, loving the silky soft feel of her, wishing she was in his arms for reasons other than Flynn scaring her.

She was trembling worse than before.

"He was there again," she finally managed to get out, sounding angry, exasperated, and uneasy.

His brothers stalked down the hall ready to do battle again. "Cearnach?" Ian asked.

"Aye," Cearnach said. The temperature in the guest chamber was much colder than in his. "Flynn is up to his old tricks."

"We'll find an exorcist on the morrow, mark my word!" Ian shouted. "Do you hear me, Flynn?"

Cearnach knew Ian wouldn't do it. Flynn was their kin, even if not in the flesh any longer. Though Ian tried to hide his feelings from his people, Cearnach knew he'd always regretted having sent Flynn away from the pack before he was murdered. Not that the reason he'd been sent away hadn't been Flynn's own doing. He was still family. After he was killed for another of his transgressions, Ian had felt some responsibility. That if he'd kept Flynn at home, he would still be alive today.

Not that most of their kin truly believed that.

"You're coming with me," Cearnach said to Elaine, not about to let her argue with him over the matter.

She wasn't arguing this time, he realized as he nodded to his brothers and led her into his room, then shut the door.

Elaine took a deep breath and tilted her head up to look at him, brows raised, her look hopeful. "This isn't a trick to get me into your bed with you, is it?"

Cearnach laughed out loud. "No, it's not a trick. You saw the look Ian gave me. He wants me to behave myself with you, but Flynn is not someone we conjure up out of the blue. I'll tell you more about him later." He helped her into his bed. "I wonder just what Flynn is up to."

"I don't… I don't believe in ghosts."

He thought she didn't sound as sure of the statement as she wished to be. He wasn't going to tell her what she wanted to hear—that she was right. That Flynn didn't exist. Because he did, and he might end up living longer at Argent Castle than any of them.

"Will he come back tonight? I mean, if I feel a hand on my breast again, would it be his?"

So much for her not believing in ghosts. Cearnach frowned at her. "He'd better not bother you again. Not with me here. I won't be fondling you unless you wish it."

She smiled a little at that but then shook her head. "Do you think he knows I'm kin to one of your enemy clans?"

"Aye, he knows. He hears and sees everything." Cearnach shut the bed curtains on her side, then went around the bed and climbed in and pulled his curtains closed. As soon as he was under the covers, he reached over, not waiting for an invitation, and pulled her into his arms. She was his to protect from her flesh-and-blood kin *and* his ghostly cousin. He wouldn't let her worry about any more visitations in the night.

She was cold, chill bumps traveling over her soft skin, and she was still trembling. He couldn't warm her up quickly the way his body was urging him to do, but he enjoyed feeling her pressed against him, seeking his heat and protection.

She didn't say anything for several minutes, and he thought she might have fallen asleep, but then she said, "He won't try to make me think you're attempting to take advantage of me in the middle of the night and cause friction between us, will he?"

He thought about that, wondering if Flynn would feel he was protecting Cearnach from the she-wolf. He could see him doing something to cause trouble between them if he thought he was being noble in defending Cearnach.

"I don't know, Elaine. I've never brought a woman to the castle before. I'm not sure what's going through his mind."

She snuggled closer to Cearnach, her head resting on his bare chest, her arm linked around his waist, stirring a fresh need in him to have her. "He won't come between us," she said with firm resolve.

Flynn was causing more trouble than Cearnach could deal with—keeping his hands wrapped around the lass in a gentlemanly way, fighting back the urge to stroke her skin, to lift that filmy piece of gauze cloaking her body, and join her in the ultimate bliss. Mate with her for life.

"Good night, lass. Pleasant dreams." *Damn you, Flynn, for bothering the lass.*

On the other hand, Cearnach was glad to have Elaine in his arms tonight, the first of many, he hoped.

It wasn't until early the next morning when Cearnach woke to find Elaine's borrowed gown bunched at the waist, his hand resting on her bare ass, her leg thrown over his legs and the most painful arousal he'd ever experienced to realize Flynn had not troubled them for the remainder of the night.

Cearnach quickly moved his hand off her derriere before she caught him. He smiled when she moaned in protest. At least it sounded that way to him.

He needed to disentangle himself from her bare limbs, and they should join his kin for breakfast before too much speculation about him and Elaine began to surface. Even if his kin didn't share much of what they thought might be going on between Elaine and him, he didn't want to fan the flames of conjecture any further.

Yet, she was sleeping so soundly that he hated to disturb her. Especially after what she'd been through the night before.

Continuing to sleep with the she-wolf could cause more difficulties than either of them could handle— until he could convince her that it was time to mate, and that had to happen before she began to make plans to leave Scotland.

Chapter 15

ELAINE WOKE SLOWLY IN CEARNACH'S PROTECTIVE and warm embrace, and realized several things at once. She'd actually slept the rest of the night undisturbed. She was relieved that she'd had no more issues with the *ghost*. But now she was in an untenable position, her gown gathered around her navel, Cearnach's hand resting on her buttock, and her naked leg locking him in place as if she was a pirate and had captured him, and he was her prisoner. *More-than-willing prisoner.*

She wanted to keep the fantasy alive. Except she'd exchange the pirate's cabin bed for this one in the castle, which was much more her style. Rocking on rough seas was not, considering how sick she got when traveling by ship.

He still wore the pair of black boxers, but that didn't hide the fact he was fully aroused and that she was pressing against that rock-hard erection. She was imagining him entering her, making love to her, mating with her like two wolves would for life. Did he still want to do that with her?

She'd felt his hand slip from her ass, and she'd let out a slight moan in protest, not intending to, trying to pretend she was asleep. It hadn't worked.

Maybe he was still asleep. She missed having his hand on her skin, feeling sexy and dangerous and ready for more.

She tried to move her leg off him without disturbing him, but as soon as she lifted her leg, he groaned in a half dissatisfied, half husky way. She glanced up at him. He was smiling down at her smugly, his face covered with a shadow of stubble.

"Ahh, lass," he drawled with his sexy Scottish burr, "seems I chased Flynn away for you last night."

He ran his hand over her arm, the silky fabric sliding up and down, his touch gentle and loving.

She quickly moved away from him, yanking down the gown so that the hem was around her ankles again. "You… weren't in on this with your ghostly cousin, were you?"

Cearnach laughed, the sound rich and husky. He reached over, tugging playfully on a length of her hair. She breathed in deeply and smelled his delightful masculine scent. Now her own light scent mixed with his. She never imagined she'd spend the night in a male wolf's bed when he wasn't her mate.

She sighed. "Bathroom?"

"In there," he said, motioning toward her side of the curtained bed.

She sat up and pulled aside the black velvet curtains and for the first time really saw his chamber. One wall was covered with swords and dirks and shields—some old and battle-scarred, some shiny and new. His chamber made her think of an Old World armory that would have been the prized possession of a museum on Scottish weaponry. She thought he should have a suit of mail to make the room complete.

Large, bulky dark oak dressers and armoires filled the room. On top of one, a brass framed picture of Cearnach caught her full attention. He was crouched among a dozen Irish wolfhounds—some lying at his feet, two looking up at him with adoration, some standing beside him, four sitting in a semicircle around him with eyes focused on the camera, and three pups climbing on his lap. He gave the impression that he was the alpha leader of a pack of wolfhounds, his elusive smile and the twinkle in his eyes as he looked into the camera making it appear as though he was observing her. Who wouldn't love a man who loved animals?

Her gaze shifted to the remaining walls, which were covered with sketches of intricately carved Celtic knot designs for the wooden handles of daggers.

"My hobby," he said, watching her as she turned to look at him. He motioned to the sketches. "I design them and sell them to shops looking for hand-carved individual creations."

"They're beautiful," she said, marveling at the detail on the handles of the weapons. "You did all of these?"

"Aye. Our smithy makes the blades. I work the handles."

"They're truly artwork."

"Thanks, Elaine." He cast her a small smile. "Not all lasses would appreciate my collection."

She gave his bared upper body an appreciative look. "I do."

His smile widened and he leaned across the bed to grasp her arm in response to her comment. She quickly hopped down from the high bed and hurried into his bathroom.

"Coward," he teased in a husky, sexy voice.

"I'm not a coward," she said from the bathroom, finding it as luxurious as the other that she'd used when she shifted and dressed in the borrowed clothes. This one was all in black and white streaked marble, the counters and the floor in solid black stone, and the shower in white. She ran her hand over the cool, sleek marble.

She peered out of the bathroom at him as he now sat on her edge of the bed, smiling at her in the most wicked way, his chest and legs bared, his erection outlined as it stood at attention underneath the satiny fabric of the boxers.

She said, "I'm trying to protect your reputation."

"My reputation," he said, his voice taking on an even huskier tone.

"Oh, aye," she said, attempting to copy his delightful brogue.

"It's already in tatters." He smiled at her.

She chuckled. "Which has nothing to do with me, and I want to keep it that way."

He cocked one brow. "It has *all* to do with you."

"It has all to do with your cousin *Flynn*." She glanced around at the bathroom and realized she didn't have any clothes with her here. She would need to either get them out of the guest bedroom and return here, or shower over there.

Flynn wouldn't bother her now that it was daylight, she assumed. If he had meant to get her and Cearnach together, he'd already done so.

She left the bathroom.

Cearnach stood in front of the bed, stretching his muscles, his brows raised as he watched her, probably wondering what she was up to. She tore her gaze away from his muscled chest and arms, perused the bulge in his boxers with interest, and curbed a smile. He was just too sexy for a morning wake-up vision in the flesh.

She waved to the guest room across the hall. "I'll use the one in the guest chamber since my clothes are there."

"Ah," he said, giving her rumpled appearance a long, fascinated look. "I'll escort you down to breakfast as soon as you're ready to go."

At least no one was about when she left his room and rushed across the hall to her chamber.

She closed the bedroom door, then hurried into the bathroom to take a shower. The guest room was well equipped with travel-sized soaps and shampoos, packaged guest toothbrushes, and mini tubes of toothpaste, perfect for a guest whose kin had stolen her suitcases. After brushing her teeth, she pulled off the gown and tucked it over the gold bath towels on the towel rack, then entered the glassed-in shower stall.

She was in the middle of soaping her hair with the sweetest-smelling lavender shampoo, the hot water sluicing down her body making her nearly moan with pleasure, when she felt a hand brush across a nipple.

She screamed, opening her eyes at the same time, and realized too late that the soap was running into them. She saw no one in the second of reprieve she had before her eyes filled with tears mixing with shampoo.

Rubbing frantically to get the burning shampoo out of her eyes, she heard the door to her chamber open.

"I'm all right," she called out to whoever it was, suspecting it was Cearnach since his room was so close and he was so protective.

Footfalls moved across her chamber, headed for the bathroom anyway. She still couldn't see, her eyes tearing up as she continued to try and wash the soap out of them.

"Elaine," Cearnach said, standing outside the glass door of the shower stall.

She shook her head, barely able to see him through her stinging eyes. He was wearing a towel, soap in his hair and a scowl on his face. She shoved the door to the stall open. "Come in."

"What happened this time?" Cearnach asked, sounding annoyed with what he suspected was his cousin's unsettling her, but then he caught sight of her naked body covered only in a light coating of soapy water. He dropped his towel on the countertop, then stepped into the shower and closed the door.

"I don't think he wants me here. Not the way he keeps hassling me."

Cearnach moved in behind her and began to wash the shampoo out of her hair, gently, lovingly as if they were already mated. He didn't say anything as she continued to try and wipe the soap out of her eyes. They felt better, but they still stung and tears reappeared as they tried to wash away the sting.

Yet something about his protectiveness, his wanting her—his pheromones were so hot she could smell them over the scent of the shampoo, the water, him—the way he was declaring his interest, yet not pushing until she agreed, and his tenderness touched a need so deep that she couldn't deny she also wanted him in a desperate way.

"What did he do?" Cearnach sounded angry, although he was attempting to couch that anger.

His voice broke the magical spell he'd cast over her.

She hesitated to tell him, afraid he'd be so furious that he'd want to exorcise the ghost, and she didn't want that. She supposed, as far as spirits went, Cearnach and his kin were family and Flynn deserved some happiness. Not that she wanted him touching her.

"Elaine?" Cearnach wasn't saying her name as a question but more as a command. "Tell me. What did Flynn do to you?"

"He touched my breast." She was thinking that Flynn had to be a breast man. Or… had been. Well, still was.

She heard Cearnach gnash his teeth. He didn't touch her, beyond rinsing out her hair, and she finished washing, then cast a look over her shoulder to see him watching her, rinsing out his own hair, looking primal, but not with regard to her, she didn't think. More that he was ready to kick a Highland ghost's butt.

"Thanks, Cearnach. Sorry," she said. Then she frowned. "No one heard me, did they? I mean, they were probably miles away in the kitchen." She hoped.

"I met Ian in the hall and told him I had this under control."

While Cearnach had been naked, wearing only a sheen of soapy water, shampoo in his hair, and a towel around his waist? Not that she'd want Ian to come to her rescue in the state she'd been in.

She groaned and left Cearnach to finish washing by himself, grabbed a towel from a rack, and wrapped herself in it. There was no going back. One little near car collision had changed her life. No—the first time she'd met Cearnach, she'd felt the intrigue, the desire, the need. He had been like a dark wolf angel when she first met him, although she was not sure of his intentions. Yet deep down she had known he was the kind of man she needed in her life.

Looking like a man with a mission, his brown eyes nearly as black as coal, Cearnach exited the shower stall, water dripping all over his skin. He retrieved his towel off the counter and wrapped it around his waist, his gaze fixed on hers. "I believe we have rather a situation here."

"Situation," Elaine said, leaning back against the counter, holding her towel closed, and observing the intense look on Cearnach's face.

"Aye." He was studying her, watching her expression closely, which meant he was coming to some sort of conclusion that he was worried she wouldn't like, she thought. "I believe Flynn wants me to stick close to you. For whatever reason."

"Ha!" she said. "I've never heard of anything so crazy in my life. Your dead cousin is trying to match-make from the grave?"

Cearnach smiled a little at her words and shrugged. "Maybe. I can't think of anything else. When he's bothered the other lasses and they bring it to Ian's attention, Ian threatens to exorcise him. It always works. Flynn lies low for days, weeks, months even. Sometimes he goes somewhere else to dally with the lasses. He's never continued to pester the same woman right after we've taken him to task for it. Certainly not twice in a night, and then bright and early the next morning. Not like this."

"What if he's doing so because he wants you to leave me alone since I'm kin to your enemy? Maybe he's really concerned for you and wants to chase me off."

"Then what he's pulling is having the opposite effect." Cearnach drew close to Elaine, his hands cupping her face, his eyes taking on a heated look. "He's smart enough to know it. Sleeping with you in bed, sharing a shower but not being able to touch you like I'd like, none of these things are conducive to my leaving you alone. You do realize when I'm with you, he doesn't bother you?"

"I wonder…" She looked up at Cearnach, her eyes still bleary with tears from the darned soap.

"Aye?"

"Would he have bothered me if I had used your bathroom while I showered?"

"It's hard to say. If he hadn't unsettled you in there, it could have been that he was off haunting someone else for a time, and so we wouldn't know the truth of the matter."

She observed Cearnach, willing him to tell her the truth. "Do you honestly believe if I had stayed in your bathroom, he wouldn't have touched me?"

Cearnach shook his head. "I don't know, lass. I suspect he might have pulled the same thing, attempting to push me into going to you."

She touched Cearnach's chest with her fingertips, looking at the way his nipples were already hard little pebbles. "If I didn't know better, I'd say you… really did put him up to it."

He chuckled. "Conspiring with a ghost to catch a lady's attention? Like I'd need encouragement when it comes to you."

Yet, the ghost *had* pushed them together, if she was going to allow that's what had plagued her in bed and in the shower. Not that either she or Cearnach had much control over the way their pheromones jump-started every time they drew close to each other. That was the problem with being a wolf-shifter. They could smell the interest from another wolf, and if they felt the same way, that special intriguing scent kicked their own into high gear.

Right now, they were in a race to reach the finish line, only they were both slamming on the brakes because reaching that line meant a mating for life.

She kissed his mouth lightly, just a very sweet, innocent peck on the lips, but she knew he wasn't satisfied with that. Not that she was, either. He smiled just a hint, watching her expression, waiting for her to do more than just give him such a barely there kiss, waiting for her to take this up another notch. He was not pressuring her too much—not kissing her back, not encouraging her—as if he knew that once he got started kissing, they'd end up in bed together.

For one rare moment, she wanted to toss away her cautious behavior. She'd already made up her mind that she needed and wanted him. She wrapped her arms around his neck and kissed him, not sweetly or innocently, but like she was a she-wolf starved for affection, and he was the male she had chosen for her mate.

Because he was. For the first time ever, despite having thought she'd found her mate several times over, only to have them vanish before a mating could occur, she knew that Cearnach would always be there for her. That she felt something deeper, more primal for him than she'd ever felt for any other wolf. Cearnach was hers.

Cearnach growled in response, sampling her mouth, tasting, smiling as she nipped his lips, loving that she'd finally made the decision to take this further. Cearnach had realized when Elaine screamed in the shower that his ghostly cousin was attempting to get Elaine and him together. *Again.*

At first, he hadn't been certain. This time, he was. Her towel was slipping, her eyes closed as he pressed his tongue between her lips, enjoying the way she slid her tongue over his in a mating dance. He was ready to explode, listening to her heart beating so fast, smelling her lavender and she-wolf fragrance, recognized that as delicious as she smelled, she was already wet for him.

Instead of removing their towels, he slid his hand between the opening of hers, found her soft, moist feminine folds and began to caress. Her low moan against his mouth turned him on all the more. He dipped his fingers deep inside of her and felt how wet and receptive she was for him. She dug her fingers into his arms, holding on for dear life so she wouldn't collapse.

She panted and softly groaned, pressing herself against his questing fingers. She was like a flower blossoming to his touch. Except for the growls. Those were wolfishly endearing.

He wanted to carry her to the bed, yet he was afraid that if he did, he'd want to take this so much further than she might be ready for.

Instead, he listened to the way her breathing hitched, felt the way she moved against his fingers, arching her pelvis, and sensed she was near the peak of climax when it hit her. He loved the way she buried her mouth against his throat, trying to stifle the rough cry of his name as she came.

"Oh, yes," she groaned, then reached down to touch him.

He kissed the top of her head and withdrew his fingers. "Let's get something to eat. Downstairs," he clarified, not wanting to push this to a conclusion before she was willing.

Her eyes were glazed as she yanked off his towel, her voice dark and commanding. "Your bed or mine? We finish this, Cearnach." She smiled a little, her expression determined, yet playful.

"Finish," he said, his hands caressing her shoulders, so soft and silky, as he studied her gaze.

She wrapped her arms around his waist in a loving embrace and placed her head against his chest. She said in whispered words, "You should never have let me get away the first time."

"Oh, aye, lass. Of that I am well aware. I can't tell you how much I regretted losing you the first time." He tilted her chin up and looked into her eyes. "You don't feel pressured, do you? Either by my mother or Flynn? Or... by me?"

She gave a little laugh. "Hardly." Then her expression changed to something more serious, her brow slightly furrowed. "I don't want you to get away from me, either. Every time I declare I want to mate with a wolf, he agrees, but before we consummate the relationship, he disappears."

"You're mine, Elaine, and I'm not going anywhere." He lifted her towel-clad body into his arms and kissed her forehead as she sighed, then carried her to the guest bed, though he wanted to claim her on his own mattress.

Chapter 16

SOMETHING FELT OFF FOR CEARNACH ABOUT MATING with her here in the guest chamber. Like she was still just a guest, when he wanted her in his room, his bed, his.

But he didn't want to carry her across the hall to his chamber and risk running into anyone, either. He reminded himself he'd mate with her there later, many times over, to make it right.

"A penny for your thoughts?" Elaine asked as she observed him. "You're not having second thoughts, are you?"

He heard the pain in her words, that maybe she believed he was already thinking of abandoning the idea and didn't want to prolong the inevitable.

He smiled and was sure that he looked as wolfishly predatory as he felt. "We're not delaying this." He peeled off her towel and tossed it to the floor. Then he slowly climbed over her, deliberately rubbing his chest and arousal and legs over her soft, bare skin, leaving his scent on her, claiming her in a not-so-subtle wolf way.

She knew exactly what he was doing, and her smile showed just what it meant to her as he lay next to her on his side. His gaze locked on hers as his fingers teased one of her rigid nipples, circling it and touching it. She lifted her fingers to caress his chest.

His skin sizzled everywhere she trailed her fingers, making his erection jump with need.

Unable to enjoy just the feel and look of her sweet body, he leaned in to kiss her, showing her every ounce of passion he possessed—the primal need and craving to make her his mate before one more male looked at her as though she was available.

He pressed his tongue into her mouth, leaning his body against hers, parting her legs with one knee, and straddling her, his arousal thick and rigid. He wanted more than anything to lay claim to her. Now. Forever.

He slid his fingers into her soft, wet heat, feeling the warm slickness from her climax. She moaned, bucking against him, her body arching as if she was pushing him to finish this.

His blood ran hot as every muscle flexed with need. His mouth caressed her collarbone. She shivered as he touched her, explored her, and enjoyed her soft skin, her exquisite fragrance tantalizing him.

His mouth captured hers. Their tongues twisted and danced together as if mating of their own accord. He ran his fingers through her hair, gripping the silky, damp locks. Liquid fire rushed through his veins, his cock straining against her thigh, his body rubbing against the muscle, her hips rising, forcing him to press harder against her.

He inserted two fingers into her tight sheath. Tight like a virgin, he thought to himself. She would have had encounters with human males, and of course she was mated to that slug of a bastard centuries ago, but when was the last time she'd been with a man? She felt too tight for it to have been recently. He was glad to know it. She was his. No one else's.

He licked her taut nipple, taking it in his mouth,

tugging gently with his lips. She moaned and cupped his head against her breast, writhing beneath him, her pelvis lifting against his throbbing erection. He kissed her across her breast, the valley between, and her right breast until he reached the other nipple, pushing her thighs open for him before pressing his erection against her hot, wet core. Not entering yet. Teasing. Wanting her to come when he did.

"Oh, Cearnach," she moaned, as he slid two fingers into her again, then pushed as deep as he could go.

She spread her legs farther apart for him, and he declared against her mouth in Gaelic, "You are mine."

"As you are mine," she whispered back.

He lifted his head and stared at her. Had she known Gaelic all along? Had she known what Vardon had called her?

Swearing in Gaelic, Cearnach gazed into her molten eyes. She lifted her hands and pulled his face back to hers, kissing him thoroughly, their tongues dueling as if in a medieval fight, making him forget all else but her.

It was time. Time to make her his. He pushed the broad head of his penis into her, slowly at first until he was fully inside her. Thrusting carefully, he pushed deeper, mating with her, their hearts beating so loudly that he barely could hear anything else.

"Yes," she whispered. "Oh, yes."

This was what he'd wanted from the moment he'd seen her: him wrapped around her soft curves, Elaine's wet heat wrapped around him in the ultimate joining.

He swept his tongue across her parted lips, thrusting his cock deep inside her and feeling as though he was the first man in centuries to explore her core.

Her sheath softened for him, allowing him to thrust deeper as the raw craving within him grew.

She was beautiful, her face flushed, her breathing fast, her body moving against him like a siren encouraging his every move.

Her chocolate eyes were smoky with lust, her fingertips touching his muscles, his skin, leaving a trail of heat.

She slid her legs around his hips and dug her heels into his ass, her breathing suspended as he sensed she was ready to explode. He groaned out loud, unable to hold back any longer. He felt the end coming, tried to hold on, felt her muscles contracting around him. Then he let loose, rocketed with the orgasm, and felt her body shuddering with ripples of climax. He loved the wolf beneath him, the sexy, loving woman who would share his world until the end of his days.

He groaned and settled on top of her, still sheathed in her wet, slick heat, wanting to remain joined like this for hours. With her. Together. As one.

For a long time, they stayed like that, breathing deeply of each other, listening to their hearts beating in unison, feeling the warmth of their bodies pressed together, sharing the knowledge that they were joined as wolf mates for life.

He hadn't realized they'd fallen asleep until he woke to find Elaine cuddled in his arms, the bed curtains still open, and the day growing later. The world outside the keep was full of activity as he heard the clanging of swords in practice sword-fighting, horses clip-clopping on the stone pavers as they were being taken out for exercise, the barks of their Irish wolfhounds and

Duncan's mate's standard poodles as they raced around the inner bailey, the shouts of his people as they called out to each other.

"Elaine," he said softly, wanting to hold on to this moment forever but knowing they had to get up and face the day. Which meant facing his clan, his pack, his family and letting them all know they had a new she-wolf as part of the family.

"Hmm," she said, her voice dreamy. She tightened her hold around his waist, her eyes still closed, her lashes fanning her cheeks.

He ran his hand over her bare arm, caressing and loving the way she felt—warm and silky soft. "You know Gaelic," he said.

"My parents taught me the old ways."

He hated that she'd known what that bastard had called her. He kissed her cheek. "I'm sorry for what Vardon had said."

"He was trying to make himself feel better for striking me. He didn't mean it."

Cearnach looked at Elaine in wonder. "You are a treasure. I'll return to my chamber and get dressed while you slip into your clothes."

She raised her head and looked at him, her expression a little skeptical. "What if your ghostly cousin returns?"

Not having considered such a thing, he frowned at her. "He better not." His voice was dark with threat. Then he took a deep breath and rethought his cousin's interference. "I'm pretty certain now that Flynn got his way, he will leave you alone. At least he better."

Elaine sighed, hoping Cearnach was right. She rolled over onto her back and surveyed the rest of the chamber—the richly woven Turkish tapestries hanging on the walls, the thick bottle glass covering narrow arrow-slit windows. Antique oil paintings of lochs, heather-covered hills, snowcapped mountains, and bubbling streams hung from some of the walls.

One painting stood out from all the rest. A red-blond, long-haired Highland cow stared at her with warm brown eyes half hidden under bangs that nearly reached the tip of its nose.

"That is a painting of the first cow we ever stole from our neighbors," Cearnach remarked as he caressed her shoulder, his voice hinting of self-righteous satisfaction.

She turned and frowned at him, surprised to hear that his own clan was not above reproach when she had worried what he thought of her family and their pirating past. "Your kin stole from others?"

"'Tis an Old World tradition, lass. They stole one of our kin's brides before she reached the kirk. We stole a cow in retaliation. Well, six, but who's counting?"

Surprised that they'd be satisfied with cows in the lady's place, she frowned. She would have envisioned a fierce battle between the clans lasting for days instead. "Wasn't the lady worth more than the cows?" Where was the romance in that?

His mouth curved up a fraction more, his dark eyes alight with humor. "She orchestrated the whole charade. The man she wanted to mate couldn't make up his mind and hadn't believed she'd marry someone else. When she agreed to marry one of my kin, the Highlander finally took her seriously. And rescued her, or so he believed. In truth, she'd arranged the whole affair through one mishap or another so that she never make it to the kirk. At least she hadn't wanted bloodshed between the clans."

"Your kinsman must have felt awful to lose his bride before she even arrived at the altar. He must have been heartbroken."

"Once he learned of her deception and we were able to convince him that she was not worth any bloodshed, he was all too willing to go on a raid, steal the cows, and forgo the lass. Within a fortnight, he had found a new bonnie lassie to wed."

"Wow, that was fast."

"The first lassie had not been the right woman for him. When he found the right one, he realized what a mistake he could have made with the other. The one he married had been living within our castle walls, her father the blacksmith, and not until that day had he ever taken notice of her."

"I'm glad he found the right woman, then. Did the other clan retaliate for your stealing the cows?"

"Aye. They said if we'd taken one, that would have been enough."

Elaine laughed. "What did the woman think of that?"

"She was not happy with her husband. She made him sleep with the other men for several days, we'd heard. We always wondered if he regretted rescuing her from our clansman."

Elaine smiled, then realized perhaps the MacNeill clan was not above stealing like she'd thought they were—and her kin weren't so bad after all. He might believe differently. Yet her uncles had felt justified in what they had done, hired to do the pirating as privateers. So anyone could justify anything, truly. Not that *she* agreed with any of it.

"You said last night your clan gave you grief over some other woman," Elaine asked.

"Calla."

Elaine took a deep breath, not wanting to hear that he had feelings for Calla that he couldn't admit to. "She's just a friend, you said."

"Aye. Most of the wolves in my pack didn't believe it. They thought we had to be more than friends. When she told me she was mating with Baird McKinley, many of my family members believed I'd fight him for the right to have her as my own mate. Calla is more like a sister to me, like Heather, my cousin, is."

"Just a friend." She realized that he truly meant it.

She considered staying here in the guest chamber and dressing, then frowned and dismissed that notion. "I don't trust your ghostly cousin." She pulled away from Cearnach, got off the bed, grabbed her towel, and wrapped it around her. Then she bundled up some clothes. "I'll go to your room with you while you get dressed."

"You sure you don't want to dress here first?" He climbed off the bed and joined her.

She shook her head. "No. We need to get down to the kitchen and have breakfast before everyone assumes the worst."

He smiled at her words, wound his hands in her hair, and kissed her hard. She melted against him. He loved that his kisses and touches turned her into melted wax.

"They'll know the truth before long. But this works for me." He kissed her cheek, pulled away, then stalked into the bathroom. Once he snagged his towel off the floor, he secured it around his waist. He returned to her and clasped her hand in his and led her to the door.

As soon as he opened the guest chamber door,
Cearnach saw his mother and aunt coming down the hall
as quietly as they could, when they would usually be
talking their heads off. They had to have been attempting to eavesdrop, trying to learn what he and Elaine were
up to. For Elaine's sake, he hesitated to leave the room.

To his surprise and delight, Elaine didn't stop. She
hauled Cearnach across the hall to his room and gave
both his aunt and mother a bright smile. "Good morning."

His bedroom door was still open from when he'd
thrown it aside to save Elaine in the shower. He nodded
to his mother and aunt, not about to say a word, moved
Elaine into his room, and shut the door.

"Omigod, could that have been any more embarrass-
ing?" Elaine whispered as she slipped a pair of jeans on
under her towel, her cheeks crimson. "After they saw us
both wearing only towels in my guest room, there was
no way to rectify the situation."

Since she was an alpha, Elaine had reacted in a way
that he should have expected: in his mother's face with
a "get used to it" attitude.

He was much more the diplomat, trying to smooth
situations over that had gotten a wee bit out of hand. Not
Elaine. He loved her for it.

"Think nothing of it, lass," he said, not about to mention that his mother and aunt had to have heard what
sounded like his mating with Elaine.

With wry amusement, he was surprised to see Elaine
so shy with him now, or perhaps she was afraid someone would come knocking at the door and confront him
about what had just occurred.

He jerked off his towel and headed for the bathroom

to shave. He was one satisfied wolf. He reminded himself that Elaine had been alone for years. That meant he had to do everything in his power to make her feel at home with his pack, family to his kin, and satisfied that she'd chosen him for her mate above all others.

Still, a vague worry continued to plague him concerning Flynn. Why had his cousin felt that the need for Cearnach to mate with Elaine was so pressing that he would harass her like he had?

Cearnach was certain Flynn knew something was wrong, and it all had to do with Elaine and keeping her safe.

Chapter 17

CEARNACH HAD A DEVIL OF A TIME LEAVING HIS
bathroom and dressing in his bedchamber, while Elaine
watched him as if she was starving for more loving, a
saucy smile in her expression. His gaze had to have been
just as interested as she pulled the soft, pale blue sweater
she was wearing down over her bare breasts. He was
thinking of pushing it back up and tasting the treats poking at the fabric even now.

"Hurry up, Cearnach." She smiled at him in the most
devilish way. "If you dress any slower, you're going to
forget that we were headed for the kitchen to grab a bite
to eat."

A bite to eat. He wanted more of her. One little taste
would start a craving in him that couldn't be satisfied.

"Remember, I didn't have any supper because I was
too tired to eat the delightful stew Heather and Shelley
made for us last night."

He sighed and took her hand. "Let's go before I
forget I have chores to do today and decide to take the
afternoon off to spend with my mate. You do realize we
have to get married now."

She frowned a little, not as though she was concerned, but more pondering the notion as if she hadn't
considered it. He kissed her cheek. "Remember when
I told you at Calla's wedding that nobility have to get
married to carry the title to the next generation."

Then she smiled at him, more amused than anything. "Is *that* a proposal?"

He chuckled. "I guess I could have worded that a little differently."

"You think?" she teased, and he loved her for it.

Before he could get on bended knee and try again, she added, "I want something *really* simple."

He would give her anything in his power that he could. But, because of the size of their pack and his mother and aunt's involvement, a modest wedding wasn't going to happen.

He was about to say so when someone knocked on the door.

He growled as he released her hand and stalked to the door, trying to get his annoyance under control and expecting that his mother wished a word with him.

When he opened the door, he saw Duncan and Guthrie standing there, not at all who he had expected. Both were smirking at him. His brothers had to have a death wish if they thought to disturb him when he was with Elaine in his bedchamber. Something had to be amiss.

Duncan folded his arms and leaned against the door frame. "We've got company. Baird McKinley, his brothers, and Robert Kilpatrick and his brother are at the gate. They want to speak with Elaine."

Cearnach snorted. "Tell them I'm planning on pressing charges."

Guthrie laughed. "They said they'd contact the police and say you kidnapped Elaine. That she's being held here against her will."

They all knew no one would be contacting any police over the matter.

His brothers shifted their gazes to a point behind him. Cearnach turned.

Brows furrowed, Elaine strode toward them, looking like she'd take his brothers on in an instant. Both Guthrie and Duncan were fighting a smile. Not in a condescending way, but with respect for her alpha-ness.

"When *they* stole my car?" she growled, standing next to Cearnach. "They would have a hard time convincing a cop that Cearnach is in the wrong when they left me no choice but to go with him. Plus, there's the little matter of their having destroyed Cearnach's minivan." She said to Cearnach, "I'll go with you."

Cearnach frowned down at her. He'd rather she stayed far away from her kin, as he was still worried she might be talked into leaving with them if only to clear things up between them, maybe learn about the stolen goods, and reclaim her car and personal effects along with Cearnach's.

"I'll speak with them. I'd rather you stayed safely here," Cearnach said.

Instead of disagreeing with him and insisting she accompany him, she slipped her hand around his and gave his fingers a squeeze that said, "We're in this together."

Bloody hell. No words could have undone his steadfast resolve faster than her touching him in such a loving way.

His brothers' eyes widened. Not because of what she had done, but because of Cearnach's hesitation. If he'd been his indomitable self, he would have stated emphatically that she would remain behind. His hesitation said volumes to anyone who might be watching. That the she-wolf knew just how to play him. And that he would go along.

She added, "I'll insert my two cents worth if they give you a bunch of lip."

He'd never understand the strange phrases Americans were fond of saying.

He shook his head but tightened his hand on hers, confirming they were unified in this.

"We're accompanying you also," Duncan said. "The portcullis is down so they won't be coming in. We've got men posted around the wall walk, watching them."

"Are you certain you want to go with us, Elaine?" Cearnach asked one last time, knowing what she would say even before she squeezed his hand marginally.

"Yes."

"I'm sorry to have dragged you into this, lass."

She let out her breath. "I'm not used to pack politics."

"A loner?" Cearnach asked as they followed his brothers through the hallway, down the stairs, and through the great hall until they were outside the keep and striding across the inner bailey.

He knew Duncan and Guthrie were listening to their conversation, as quiet as they were. They normally ate up the stone pavers with their lanky strides. Both were walking slower to maintain Elaine's pace and sticking closer to them.

"Yes, by choice. I'm not a follower," she said.

"Oh." He realized then that if she'd had no remaining family in the States and she hadn't mated with a wolf with a pack that she'd stayed with, she had indeed been a loner.

She gave him a small smile and pulled his arm around her waist as if declaring she was fine with joining his pack. "The cobblestones are slippery."

They were, he had to admit. He knew her cuddling

against him meant much more than that, though. She
was declaring that she wanted him just as much as he
wanted her—again.

His brothers cast them a look over their shoulders
as if to see what she had done to make the comment
about the slick stones, both slightly raising their brows
in unison when they saw them wrapped up together.

"Path's slippery," Cearnach said to his brothers, grinning and giving Elaine a squeeze.

———

Cearnach saw Robert Kilpatrick first, scowling, his face
as red as his hair as he watched him, Duncan, Guthrie,
and two of their cousins walk Elaine to the outer gate,
the iron portcullis firmly in place. More of the MacNeill
clan stood atop the wall walk armed with bows and
arrows as they observed the talks. Four of Cearnach's
clansmen had shifted into wolves.

Robert's carrot-topped brother, Edmond, and Baird
McKinley stood beside him. Baird's four brothers were
milling about some distance from the gate near their
two vehicles as if to show they were the backup muscle
but giving enough space to indicate they had come in
relative peace. From their dour expressions, all of them
looked ready to do battle.

Cearnach glanced at Elaine, whose head was held
high, lips thinned, eyes narrow. Her whole tension-filled
posture said she was angry and she wasn't about to take
crap from any of them.

As soon as they reached the portcullis, Robert opened
his mouth to speak as Baird speared Cearnach with a
glacial stare.

Everyone's attention shifted abruptly to Elaine when, to Cearnach's surprise, she spoke first. "I'm Elaine Hawthorn, daughter of Hans Hawthorn, the third; son of Hans Hawthorn, the second; son of Hans Hawthorn, the first. You are?" she directed at Robert.

"Robert Kilpatrick, my brother, Edmond, and our cousin Baird McKinley. I missed meeting with you earlier at Senton Castle, *cousin*." He sounded as though he was trying to emphasize the point that she was on the wrong side of the gate, that she belonged with them and *not* standing with the MacNeills.

"We did meet already, Robert. At the church. Remember? There was a little matter of you stealing my rental car and personal items."

"Send her out here now," Baird growled at Cearnach.

"I'm not going anywhere," Elaine said to Baird.

Baird looked at her. "I'm talking about Calla."

Calla had gone into hiding? Cearnach had thought she was at her father's home.

"Calla's not here," Cearnach said. "If she were, I wouldn't send her to you unless she wished it."

Robert cleared his throat and motioned to one of the vehicles they had come in. "We'll take you to the bed and breakfast now, Elaine. I'm sorry for the… mistakes made yesterday. Had I known that you were the bonny lass sitting beside me at the church—"

Looking beautifully obstinate, Elaine folded her arms. "I want my car and all my belongings…" She looked up at Cearnach as if she needed his permission first, even though this was her home now and she didn't need it.

He nodded, giving her a small smile, which he knew would irk her kinsmen.

She took a deep breath and continued. "I want them brought here."

"You can't stay here," Robert said as if she was considering sleeping in a dungeon and as if he could dictate to her. Then he got more to the point. "We have a private matter to discuss."

"She's not going anywhere with you," Cearnach said, wanting to make that perfectly clear.

Elaine didn't take her eyes off Robert, watching for every reaction like a wolf would. Like an alpha wolf. "You owe Cearnach a replacement minivan and whatever else he lost in his vehicle, including his clothes and sword."

"They're not our friends." Robert gave Cearnach and his men a cold glare, then turned his attention back to Elaine. "You don't know the history between us."

"That may be so, but your history has nothing to do with me. And you know what? Cearnach protected me from hunters when my own kin left me in an untenable situation. More than untenable. Potentially deadly."

They had to have known what might happen when they stranded them without vehicles or clothes, and Cearnach and Elaine had no choice but to run in their wolf coats across territory not their own. Cearnach assumed they had figured she was a new girlfriend of his and it didn't matter what had become of her... or him. He was more than irked that they valued her life so little.

"We didn't know who you were," Baird growled. "You don't side with our enemy if you know what's good for you."

"Are you threatening me?" Her tone of voice had darkened, she-wolf in battle mode. "You didn't believe I was related to Cearnach, did you?"

Robert shook his head.

"So then why would you have stolen my car?"

One of Baird's older brothers spoke up. "We thought you were Cearnach's new girlfriend. His bringing you to the wedding was an insult and upset Calla."

"I see. Instead, I was part of your extended family and had every right to be at the wedding. Did my being at the church truly upset Calla?"

Baird huffed out an annoyed breath, folded his arms, tilted his head up in an arrogant way, and didn't speak.

Elaine straightened and clarified her situation. "Cearnach had a little accident. I gave him a lift to the church. I didn't know him before this. Then again, I didn't know who you all were, either."

"Okay, so we start over. You come with us, and you can have your car and belongings back," Baird said, his voice dark with annoyance.

Cearnach didn't trust Baird. The man had to recognize that Cearnach felt protective of Elaine, and he suspected Baird would use that vulnerability to get back at him for Calla standing him up at the wedding if he could.

"Where's that brother of yours, Baird? Vardon? I demand an apology from him," Elaine said.

He was standing beside the second car, looking angry, his hands fisted at his sides. Cearnach imagined that Vardon wanted to punch her again, except not by accident this time. He'd kill him before the wolf ever got close to her again.

Baird glanced at Kilpatrick and the irritated looks they shared said that no way in hell was Vardon going to apologize.

"You got in the way," Robert said. "He didn't mean to punch you. He was aiming for Cearnach."

Cearnach growled under his breath. Vardon was a bastard for not apologizing to the lass, and her cousin Robert just as much of one for defending Vardon's brutal behavior. Cearnach opened his mouth to tell him so, but Elaine was running the show.

"That doesn't excuse what happened. Accident or no accident, he missed Cearnach and struck me. I'll have an apology. He doesn't have to get down on bended knee, unless of course he wants to, but a sincere, heartfelt 'I'm sorry' will go a long way," she said, her voice cold with fury.

Robert and Baird's faces couldn't have hardened any further. Cearnach and his kin were grinning. Cearnach heard a few snickers from his own people. He could just imagine everyone envisioning Vardon on his knees in front of Elaine, pleading with her to accept his apology.

No one said anything for a moment.

"You can't stay here," Robert reiterated. "It's an insult to our name. Beyond that, they'll tell you that the stolen goods came from their ships and that you have no right to keep the goods."

So the matter was no longer private? Good.

"If they had belonged to the MacNeill clan?" Elaine asked.

Robert scowled. "Don't tell me the scoundrel has already set you against your own kin. You can't mean to give him the goods."

Rapid feminine footfalls echoed on the stone pavers behind Elaine and Cearnach and the others with them. They turned to see his mother and aunt approaching.

Cearnach frowned at them, not wishing their interference. What now?

"Robert Kilpatrick." Cearnach's mother's voice was sharp. She sounded like she was scolding a small child as she stood on the other side of Elaine, close, protective like a mother wolf. "I thought your mother raised you better."

His eyes narrowed. "This is between Elaine and me and no one else."

"Seems you made it our business when you stole the lass's car. Be off with you. She's with us now and perfectly content to enjoy our hospitality. Whatever financial dealings you had planned to discuss with her are over. Do you understand?" She turned her sharp eyes on Elaine, who quickly closed her gaping mouth and smiled a little.

Cearnach liked it when his mother was giving someone else hell.

"What part of 'I'm not going anywhere with you' did you not comprehend?" Elaine asked Robert. Then she did the unexpected—slipped her arm around Cearnach's waist and said, "I'm ready for breakfast and a walk in the gardens."

Every one of her kin looked as though they wanted to thrash her soundly. Even though they didn't know her, they would expect her to remain loyal to them through kinship, no matter the circumstances.

Cearnach was proud of her. "You heard the lass. When her wishes are met, she'll grant you an audience."

The looks on their faces said they could kill Cearnach right this very minute.

Standing beside Cearnach, Duncan gave a murmured, "Aye."

Before anyone could say a word, Cearnach wrapped his arm around Elaine's small waist and headed her back to the keep. His brother and cousins hung around the gate, waiting for the McKinleys and the Kilpatricks to vacate their lands.

"You know they'll test your resolve," Cearnach said to Elaine. "They suspect you'll want to return home before long and need to finish your business here. They'll try to force you to come to them on their terms."

"Too late for that," she said, giving him a wicked smile. "Seems I've made my bed and I'm staying in it."

He chuckled low, planning an early night for both of them.

Chapter 18

CEARNACH ESCORTED ELAINE BACK TO THE KEEP FOR breakfast, and she was hopeful that everyone was away working at their jobs so he and she would have some privacy.

"I do have a question for you." He led her through the great hall.

He sounded so serious that she looked up at him expectantly.

"I never considered how my bedchamber would look to a prospective mate."

"It's fine," she said dismissively. She really didn't care as long as *he* was part of the scheme.

"Nay, it's not. It's a warrior's haven. You decide how you want to decorate it."

"The guest room isn't mine any longer?" she asked, a teasing laugh in her voice.

"Nay, it is not." He was smiling, but he had a possessively dark tone to his voice. "You belong in my bed. Our bed, now."

"Hmm," she said, snuggling closer to him as he walked her through the dining room. "How about purple? Lavender and thistle purple."

He groaned.

She laughed. "So much for *my* input on redecorating."

He chuckled. "Hopefully we can agree on something, but if we can't, I'll be man enough to deal with it.

Purple sheets, purple floral paintings. As long as you're wrapped up in the sheets with me, that's all that matters."

She sighed. "My room back home is like a garden."

Brows raised enquiringly, he looked down at her.

She smiled up at him. "Not all floral. But I love plants. So it has green walls, a mural of a garden, and a large window with plants hanging from it."

His eyes sparkled with humor. "Aye. So we'll take over the garden room, and that will be our new bedchamber."

She laughed. "I'm sure your clan would love that."

"Anything for you, Elaine," he said, kissing the top of her head.

She knew then he was the right man for her.

When they arrived in the kitchen, the smell of sausage and baked bread still permeated the air, and the room was toasty warm from all the cooking. Heather was talking with Shelley about her poodles. Both quickly turned speculative gazes their way. So much for everyone being off somewhere else, busy with their chores.

"Good morning," Elaine said, the yummy scents making her stomach growl.

"Morning," both the ladies said in greeting, smiling broadly.

Elaine suspected they had purposefully hung around to see her and Cearnach. She loved the way they made her feel at home with the pack.

"Anything left to eat?" he asked as he surveyed the kitchen counters.

"I made sure Cook left you both something to eat. You know how she is. If you don't come down to the meal on time, you fix your own meals. I told her that Elaine was a guest." Heather looked from Cearnach to Elaine as if she knew Elaine was more than just a guest. "I mentioned to her that you had to rescue her from Flynn half the night. You know how much trouble Flynn's given Cook." Heather pulled two plates out of the fridge. "She's broken so much clay crockery that she's resorted to plastic."

"What does he do to her?" Elaine asked, frowning.

"Startles her. She used to scold him something fierce when he stole food from the cellar as a lad. So now he gets her back."

Elaine glanced at Shelley, but she just shook her head. "He hasn't bothered me at all. Duncan keeps saying it's because Flynn knows he'll do something drastic and Flynn's spirit will be put to rest. So he's left me alone."

"He pesters me," Heather said. "He used to when we were kids. He still does. Nothing naughty. Just scares me when I'm in the kitchen. He rescued Ian's mate, Julia. He reacts differently to people, depending on who they are and how he relates to them."

Elaine hoped now that she was mated with Cearnach, Flynn would leave her alone.

Heather put out silverware for them and Shelley brought them a small pitcher of milk. "Coffee? Tea?" she asked.

"Tea," Cearnach said, "the Scottish whisky one."

"Coffee for me, thanks." Elaine wrinkled her nose at Cearnach. "Scottish whisky tea?"

"It's made of China tea marinated in Scottish malt whisky," Heather said. "He can breathe in the rich aroma of the whisky from the freshly brewed tea, but the tea itself is nonalcoholic."

Cearnach winked at Elaine. "You might try some, lass. They say it grows hair on your chest."

Shelley and Heather laughed. Cearnach smiled and buttered his bread.

"Ian said you were planning to wash the dogs today, but if you don't have time…" Heather said.

"I do have time. I planned to do it after Elaine and I had breakfast." And mated. And talked with her hostile kin.

They both smiled at Elaine, then headed out the kitchen door.

Once the door snapped shut, Elaine let out her breath. "Is it just me who thinks so, or are your clansmen really that interested in what you do with your time?"

He laughed. "Let me put it this way. You're the first woman I've ever brought home. The rumor about us having met before has spread, and the gossip is that we had planned this meeting all along."

"That I would run you off the road for a clandestine meeting?"

He reached over and took her hand and squeezed. "All part of the master plan."

She sighed. "Here I thought I was only coming to Scotland on a treasure hunt. But you know what? I don't need the treasure any longer."

Cearnach studied her expression. She looked so sincere that he realized she meant what she said.

She sighed. "Everyone in my family took risks. I was the one wolf who usually only ventured into what I considered safe territory. I'd thrown caution to the wind when I'd ventured coming to Scotland the first time with my uncles, to escape from Rafferty. And now this time, wanting to find my uncles' treasure.

"Some of it was because I figured they owed me for agreeing that Rafferty could have me as a mate. Some of it was plain, old-fashioned curiosity. What had they hidden and what was its ultimate value? I hadn't wanted my cousins getting their hands on it. Now? It really doesn't matter. But as to your family, nothing's going to change the fact that I'm kin to the McKinleys and Kilpatricks, Cearnach."

"What do I care of that, lass? You are not truly one of them, except by blood. Not by actions."

She humphed. "Your family will not see it that way."

"It won't matter to them, Elaine."

She chewed on her bottom lip, her gaze locked on his. Then she seemed to trust in what he said and nodded. "Okay, if you say so."

Well, maybe she didn't believe him all the way. "I'm serious."

She took a deep breath. "What if Ian objects?"

She *didn't* have faith in Cearnach. He reached out and took her hand in his and held on tight. "He won't, lass. Believe me. He knows we're meant to be together." Everyone else probably knew it, too. "Tell me what you know concerning the location of the treasure."

"Uncle Tobias said that he had an uncanny fondness for buttered and salted porridge and sweet Scottish shortbread. He was referring to both himself and his twin brother, Samson. They did everything together."

Cearnach raised a brow, wondering how that had anything to do with the hidden treasure, but he kept quiet.

"It was his way of saying the bounty was in Scotland." She looked so sincere that he tried to keep from commenting or laughing at what he didn't think could be real clues to where the goods were hidden. More likely it was the lass's very vivid imagination.

"He said the loveliest loch he ever swam and fished in was surrounded by mountains with a picturesque waterfall nearby."

"That narrows it down a wee bit," Cearnach said, "but it still could be hundreds of places, if this refers to the treasure at all. Even if we could pinpoint one particular loch, the goods could still be buried anywhere in the surrounding area for miles around." From what she'd offered as clues, he figured there was no chance she'd ever find what she was looking for.

She forged onward, sounding as though she didn't think it would be that difficult a task once he knew the rest. "A mound of rocks covered in moss and surrounded by a stand of Scots pine was his favorite place to sit for a while and commune with nature."

"I didn't think he and his brother ever left their ship except to board another and take the merchandise."

"They must have at some point in their lives."

Cearnach nodded. "All right, but moss-covered cairns are everywhere in Scotland. Oftentimes, particularly that long ago, they could have been gathered up and used to fortify some castle's walls or some other building. Large-scale pilfering of the ruins of castles to use on clans' own castles was quite the thing in centuries past."

She pondered that for a moment as she stirred her spoon around in her nearly empty bowl of porridge.

He finally asked the question he was trying not to ask. "What made you think you could find it, lass, from the clues you have?"

"I have only *half* the clues. Robert has the others. Or so he says." She looked steadily into Cearnach's eyes. "My uncle said he left the key with a woman who was the only one who could unlock his heart and find the treasure hidden within."

Cearnach folded his arms. "What if he was being poetic? And his words had nothing to do with treasure?"

She gave a ladylike snort. "*Neither* of my uncles were the poetic sorts."

"Okay, then let's say it is about a treasure. The woman could be dead, for all we know. Even if she wasn't, do you have any clue as to who she was?"

"Me," Elaine said quietly, her eyes shimmering with tears. "He told me that right before we disembarked from the ship that day in St. Andrews. It was me."

Cearnach rose from the chair and helped her to stand, then hugged her tightly. "I love you, Elaine. You are the key to *my* heart." He didn't want her to be sad. She'd had enough of that with losing her close family members, enduring a forced mating with a wolf bastard, and losing other wolf suitors. He meant to make her happy.

She gave him a teary smile. "I can't express how much being here with you and your family means to me, Cearnach."

"Aye, you've shown me how much it means to you. You are my joy." He kissed her and gave her one last heartfelt hug as she squeezed him tightly back. "Come on. I've got to bathe the dogs, and then we'll tackle the mystery of the treasure further."

Before Cearnach could escort Elaine to the kennels, his mother sent word via a lad that she wished to speak with him. She rarely made a summons, and when she did, they always were important.

What was his mother about this time? "Sit in the

sunroom for a minute, Elaine, will you? I'll be but a moment," Cearnach said, taking her there instead.

Cearnach briskly walked to the library where his mother was sitting at a small writing desk. "Is it done yet?" his mother asked.

This was why he had been summoned? To learn if he'd truly been mated with Elaine? This was too much.

"My lady mother," Cearnach said, exasperated more than he'd ever been with her meddling ways. "Aren't you off to London with Aunt Agnes to shop for new dresses or some such thing?"

Her brow wrinkling with annoyance, his mother waved for him to be quiet. "You know how Agnes loves to do research? How she has volumes of history concerning our family's past and everyone related to us or that we've had dealings with?"

Not good news, he suspected. "Aye." He folded his arms and frowned. "So what has Aunt Agnes dug up?"

"The lass is truly wealthy, Cearnach. *Your* lass. Which could be trouble. We're worried about her association with Kilpatrick."

Feeling the same unsettling concern for the lass, Cearnach nodded.

"She has four estates she manages here in Scotland. Has she told you about them?"

His frown deepened. "Nay. What do you know of them?" He suspected the lass had not known of the estates or she would have mentioned it.

"She owns Senton Castle, two manor houses, and a keep. I've told Ian and he's contacting her solicitor. He wants to ensure that Kilpatrick isn't trying to steal her properties away from her. Why did Kilpatrick want to meet her at Senton Castle? It's so isolated that no one in the world would know she was going there, just him. The cliffs below the ramparts are deadly. It would be easy to drag a much slighter woman across the broken wall and toss her to her death." His mother's brows rose.

"The properties would still be in Elaine's name," Cearnach said, frowning.

"Aye, and he could forge the documents, sign them over to himself, and have someone loyal who worked for him as witnesses to the transfer. But he'd have to get rid of the only one who could prove the documents were forged. The lass herself."

He'd considered that Elaine might have come to harm in meeting with Kilpatrick at the isolated ruins, especially when Kilpatrick thought to have a chunk of her treasure and wouldn't want to give up a farthing of it. The properties would add an even greater incentive. "You didn't know about this before you suggested that I mate the lass, did you?" He had to ask. He had to know the truth.

His mother waved her hand dismissively. "Of course not. What do you take me for? A thief? As for you, you didn't know either, so she won't believe you married her for her money. Go," she said flippantly. "I just wanted to let you know you're a man of many estates."

"They will be the clan's. Ian will control them." As was usual for a pack that worked together as one big family.

"Oh, I know that our kind normally puts all our wealth into one pool of funds. This is different because she has not lived with a pack. He'll let her keep them for her own, if she wishes it. He'll want her to be as happy with being with us as we are to take her into the fold. Oh, and Cearnach, I want to see Elaine soon so that we can discuss the wedding."

He hoped that Elaine would be all right with his mother getting involved with the wedding planning, but he couldn't be more pleased that she was so delighted that he had mated Elaine.

Then he considered his bothersome ghostly cousin and wanted to put that business to rest as well. "My lady mother, why has Flynn been bothering Elaine so?"

"You know how he is. He either pesters a woman because he likes her or because he doesn't. He liked Elaine from the start once he heard her speaking about protecting you from Vardon."

"He was there when you were talking with her?"

"Aye. He was hovering so close that he was giving me chills, though he wouldn't show himself. Since you are his favorite cousin, he wanted to know if the lass was the right one for you."

"He didn't push the mating for some other reason, did he?" Cearnach couldn't settle his concern that Flynn had been snooping around and learned something related to Elaine. Something that could harm her.

"Perhaps. If so, he hasn't enlightened me. If he's going to speak with anyone, it's usually you. Although he did confide in me that he truly likes the lass."

"He's avoiding me. Which isn't normal. His absence makes me think he's afraid that I'll learn the truth about some matter."

"Nonsense. He wanted you to be happy. That's all. He could tell you were taken by the lass and he wanted to see the two of you mated."

Cearnach growled. "He molested her. If I could get my hands on him, I'd show him just how I feel about his touching Elaine twice last night and again this morning."

"I understand." His mother was smiling as she looked back to her correspondence. "Go, keep her company. I'm certain she's anxiously awaiting your return."

He studied his mother further. He sensed she felt what he did—that Flynn knew something but wouldn't tell them what. He didn't think she knew what it was any more than he did.

He shook his head, hurried out of the library, and went to the sunroom where Elaine was watching out the window. He glanced out to see what she was smiling at. Heather and Shelley walking the dogs.

"The poodles are beautiful," she said. Then she looked up at Cearnach and smiled. "What would your mother have done if I said I owned a pair of dachshunds?"

He laughed and walked her outside the keep and onto the path to the kennels, pulling her close, trying to keep her warm in the chilly breeze. At least it wasn't raining today, though dark clouds melded together in a fluffy gray blanket covering the sky. "My mother would have loved them." He looked down at Elaine. "You don't really have dogs, do you?"

She laughed. "No. Though Shelley said something about Julia falling in love with the wolfhound pups and having a hard time letting Ian sell them. Maybe I could have one of those for my own?"

Cearnach shook his head. "Ian will have a fit."

She frowned up at him.

He smiled. "But for you, I will ensure you have your pick."

She beamed up at him. "What if I can't choose? And I want more than one?"

He laughed. "That's why we have so many wolf-hounds already."

Cearnach thought again about Flynn. He couldn't rid himself of the notion that something more was going on here.

"Lass, I wonder, could there be any other reason Robert Kilpatrick wanted you to meet him here at the ruins? Did you know you have holdings in Scotland?"

Chapter 19

SPECULATING ABOUT HOW DEEPLY CEARNACH WAS becoming involved with Elaine, Ian took a small force of men for protection as he and Julia rode their horses through the Caledonian Forest. The cool autumn breeze flowed through the pine trees, scenting the air. He glanced at Julia, finally comfortable with riding a horse.

She had wanted to get away from the castle and think about a new scene in the latest werewolf romance novel she was writing. He'd do whatever was needed to please his mate—even wear blue jeans and a black Stetson hat, which still didn't feel quite right. He thought she was thinking about her book until she spoke.

"I overheard your mother talking to Cearnach about Elaine and how she wanted him to mate with her."

Ian frowned. Not because she'd overheard his mother and Cearnach's conversation, but because of the gist of it and that Cearnach hadn't said a word to him about it.

"What did she say?"

"Something about stolen goods that would be part of your pack's holdings instead of Kilpatrick's."

"Stolen goods?" Ian rode on, pondering that. "What did Cearnach say?"

Julia scowled at Ian. "You can't be serious, Ian. Cearnach can't take Elaine as his mate based on such a thing."

"Julia, sweeting, you must realize that none of us

listen to my mother when she's on one of her crusades. I still want to know how Cearnach responded."

"He didn't stand up to your mother!"

"That's not his way. He might appease her, smile sweetly, act as though he agrees, and try to talk some sense into her, but he'll ultimately do what is right."

Julia didn't say anything as the horses' hooves clip-clopped on the leaf-littered ground.

"So what did he do?"

"He did just what you said he would do," Julia retorted.

Ian gave a muffled laugh. "Cearnach is a diplomat. He always does what's right, even if it doesn't seem so at the time."

"You mean like attending Calla's wedding?"

"Aye. See what a mess that's become? Yet he had to do it for Calla's sake. Now she's seen the light and left Baird McKinley. Cearnach did what was right, what he had to do." He glanced at Julia and studied the way the breeze caught her red hair, the way it caressed her cheeks, and was ready to take her back to bed with him.

He drew close to Julia's horse, leaned over, and lifted her from her saddle. She gasped in surprise. He set her on his lap, and she smiled up at him. "You should have warned me you were going to do that."

"You should have been listening to me. I am the laird, you know."

"A sexy one at that." She kissed his mouth with tenderness, then longing and passion.

"We return to Argent Castle." He took her horse's reins and rode back toward the keep. Had it not been for the recent trouble with the McKinleys and Kilpatricks, he would have made love to Julia in the woods. "They will be all right, Julia. Both Elaine and Cearnach," he reassured her.

"I hope so. I like her. I don't think I've seen anyone stand up to your mother the way she did. And Cearnach is more than fond of her."

Ian sighed, knowing just where this was headed with his brother. He approved, but he wished Cearnach would tell him that it was done. The sooner, the better.

———

Before Cearnach and Elaine walked through the outer bailey heading toward the kennels, Elaine asked him, "What do you mean I have properties in Scotland? How do you know?"

"I did some checking into Senton Castle's ownership some years ago. A man by the name of Hans Hawthorn III, owned it. You mentioned to Robert McKinley that Hans was your father?"

Her lips parted as tears welled up in her eyes. She nodded. "My father," she choked out. Then her eyes widened as realization dawned. "My father owned it?"

"Aye. So that is why you're the owner of the castle. Not the Kilpatricks and McKinleys, though they lived there for many years."

"It's now in ruins." Then she added wistfully, "But so beautiful. I can't believe it's mine. I wonder why he and my mother left there."

"I don't know. It's something we can check into. As far as the other properties that are in your name, we don't have the details yet."

He quickly told her what he knew, which was very little. "We haven't any idea of their value. Ian is contacting your solicitor about them, and we'll learn the details as soon as we can." Cearnach changed direction on the subject, still concerned about Kilpatrick's bid to meet up with her. "What if Kilpatrick learned of these properties and thought somehow to take them from you?"

Frowning, she walked with Cearnach outside. "It's possible, I suppose. It would make sense as to why he wanted me to meet with him. That it was about more than a treasure that might not be all that valuable." She continued walking in silence for a few steps, then asked, "Why didn't I know about the properties all these years?"

Before Cearnach could speculate, she shook her head and answered her own question. "I changed my identity after I sold off my parents' estates. Some of Rafferty's pirate crew still thought to make me part of the bounty that they received after murdering Rafferty. I knew Rafferty was dead, yet I kept looking over my shoulder, worried that he'd come back for me.

"He did, you know. Not after he died, of course, but before that. His ship would be a month late in returning, and I'd be so hopeful he'd died, and then when I thought I might be free, he'd return. So that's the way I felt. That I'd be shopping at market, I'd turn, and then there he'd be, that menacing, cruel grin on his face, his eyes locked onto mine, telling me to get home before he even spoke a word.

"I kept moving, reinventing myself over the years. I had to anyway since I didn't have a wolf pack that could hide my longevity from others. Humans would begin to ask what my secret was to looking so young when they were aging and I was not. So moving was essential." She frowned up at Cearnach. "Do you think Kilpatrick wanted me at the castle ruins to somehow force me to turn the deeds over to him?"

"It's possible." Cearnach wasn't about to tell her otherwise. He didn't trust Kilpatrick.

She shuddered and he wrapped his arm around her shoulders and pulled her close. "Then it was good that you ran off the road, and I met you first instead," she said.

He smiled down at her. Someday, he supposed they'd tell their children how they'd met—her version and his.

Cearnach caught the eye of Logan, the blacksmith's sixteen-year-old son. Logan was practicing sword-fighting with another young man, but he lowered his sword and looked hopefully at Cearnach as if he wanted to join him and Elaine in the kennel.

Full of the devil at sixteen, Logan reminded Cearnach of himself at that age. Logan loved animals more than anything else and didn't care for working in the smithy like his father did, to his father's disappointment.

Cearnach nodded and Logan raced toward them.

"Don't run with the sword, lad," Cearnach cautioned him, continuing on his way with Elaine to the kennel.

"It's not real. Just a play sword." Logan frowned. "Laird said if you were too busy protecting your girlfriend…"

Cearnach gave the youth a quelling look meant to guard his words.

"We all know she's kin to our enemy, the McKinleys and the Kilpatricks, but lots of people say you're protecting her from them. So doesn't that make her your girlfriend?" Logan glanced at Elaine and gave her a big smile, then frowned when he saw her bruised face.

"She is a friend," Cearnach said. *Mate.*

"They say Vardon McKinley hit Elaine. Are you going to kill him?" Logan asked.

"No, he's not going to kill Vardon," Elaine said firmly.

"Someone ought to. Oran was saying that Vardon has beaten women before. He doesn't deserve to live." Logan swung his sword at a fake opponent. "Some of our kin said Flynn's bothering Elaine. Do you want me to talk to him? Not that I haven't already. I told him to leave the lass alone… or else." He cast Elaine another big grin.

"He spoke with you?" Cearnach asked.

"Aye, said she was a bonny lass, and if you hadn't been interested in her, he was."

Cearnach shook his head. "If he won't listen to Ian or me, he won't listen to anyone."

"Maybe he'll listen to me," Elaine said. "I hadn't thought to talk to him. Not that I ever saw him."

Both Cearnach and the lad looked at her, then at the same time said, "Nay."

"He doesn't pay attention to women?" Elaine asked, sounding irritated.

"Ask Lady Heather," Logan said. "He pesters her all the time."

Cearnach glanced down at Logan. "Did you have something you wished to speak with me about other than Flynn and the like?"

"Oh, aye, while you protect the lady, do you want me to bathe the dogs today?"

"Did your father give you leave to do so?" Cearnach asked.

"Aye. He said that I was to help you wash them."

Cearnach opened the kennel door, then closed it behind them. Yips and happy woofs greeted them.

"One of the wolfhounds, Sheba, had pups about eight weeks ago. All the rest are adult dogs," Cearnach said.

Elaine looked through the metal gate. "Ah, they're *adorable*."

"You want all of the dogs out at once?" Logan asked.

"Aye."

"Do they all live out here?" Elaine sounded disappointed, and he thought about her comment concerning the dachshunds.

If she chose one of the pups to keep for her own, would she want it to sleep with her in her bed? In *their* bed? He had other plans for their bed.

He glanced back at her as she peered into the huge cage where Sheba lay curled up on her bed while her pups ran to the cage door.

"They're not family pets?" she asked.

He heard the distinct dissatisfaction in her voice. "They're like family, lass. They only come out here to sleep at night. During the day, they join the family in various activities. They're only here right now because this is bath day, and we needed them gathered in one place. After their bath, they get to be walked and join other family members for the rest of the day."

Logan busily opened all the cage doors. The wolfhounds were huge and ferocious-looking with their shaggy, wiry coats, bristly hair over their eyes, and chin whiskers giving them an old-man appearance. They jumped all over each other, vying to reach Cearnach to earn his attention, while others were checking Elaine out thoroughly—the newcomer to the clan.

Cearnach opened the door for Sheba. Elaine was grinning broadly as she tried to pet all the rambunctious dogs at once. Elaine looked so sweet, right at home with the dogs as the pups licked her all over in greeting. He chuckled under his breath.

Sheba rose, stretched, then trotted over to greet them.

He crouched down to pet her pups as they scrambled over each other to lick and bite him.

"They're huge for being eight weeks old. I had a yellow Labrador retriever. Her pups at this age were so much smaller, like the difference between a young fawn and a baby moose."

Cearnach laughed. "Aye. The adult males are taller than a man when standing on their hind legs. Come on," he coaxed the pups as he took Elaine's hand and walked through the kennel and into a large shower room with stainless steel benches on one side, a sink on another, and hoses hanging from one wall.

Logan greeted the dogs competing for his attention, but he was checking Elaine out, watching the way the dogs were nosing her, smelling her, brushing up against her, and how she was petting them all.

"You have what? Fifteen adult wolfhounds, ten puppies, and two poodles?" she asked, trying to count them.

"Aye. Sheba's pups will go to good homes," Cearnach said. "Most of them. If Ian can convince Julia, that is."

"How do you know which you've washed and which you haven't with all this chaos?"

"Logan will take the washed dogs into the drying room as soon as I've finished with them."

"Do you want me to help?" Elaine asked, sounding eager.

He smiled at her. "They're awfully"—one jumped up on him and he finished with—"rambunctious. They'd probably knock you over. Especially as the floor gets wet."

He began to rinse one of the dogs, though two others tried to tackle the spray. The dogs bumped into Cearnach, who ignored the distractions. Then he turned off the hose and set it on its hook before he began soaping down the dog.

He glanced over to see what Logan and Elaine were doing. She was sitting on one of the benches, cuddling three puppies at once while all were delightfully licking her throat and chin and nipping at her fingers. She was grinning and chuckling. Logan was watching her, beaming.

As soon as Cearnach rinsed the dog, Logan came to take him to the drying room and whispered, "If you don't want her to be your girlfriend, she can be mine."

Before Cearnach could respond, Logan, serious as could be, led the wet dog off to the drying room.

Cearnach glanced back at Elaine and saw her washing one of the pups in the large sink. He smiled and shook his head. She would fit right in with the pack.

By the time Cearnach had begun to work on Anlan, father of Sheba's pups and the last of the male wolfhounds he had to wash, Dillon, the most mischievous of the males, had spied the hose with a devilish gleam in his dark brown eyes. Cearnach knew what he was up to before the dog lunged, but he couldn't thwart Dillon fast enough.

The dog grabbed the hose and gave it a tug, sending a stream of water Elaine's way. The water blasted her in the chest and she squealed in surprise.

The stream of water swung wildly as Cearnach wrestled the hose away from the dog's tight grip. The spray came back around and hit Elaine's face as she tried to get out of the way.

By the time Cearnach feinted releasing the hose and Dillon loosened his grip to re-situate his teeth for a better hold, Cearnach had pulled the hose free. Elaine was already sopping wet and wiping her eyes. Logan looked on in horror, then he ran back into the drying room and raced out again to give her a clean, dry towel.

She wrung some of the water out from her sweater. She was soaked to the skin, revealing all, which for Cearnach's consumption was fine. But for the lad, no.

"Logan, why don't you go up to the keep and ask Lady Julia if she has something dry that Elaine can wear?"

"Aye, I will." Logan raced through the shower room.

"Walk," Cearnach warned and shook his head.

"Were you like that at his age?" Elaine asked, her eyes and lips smiling as she wiped the water from her face.

Cearnach chuckled. "And then some. Though I would have helped you to remove your sweater and towel-dried you."

She laughed, then began washing the mother dog. "Not if a man older than you was watching, and he had some interest in the girl who was more the older guy's age."

"It would depend," he said, joining her, unable to help his feral gaze from roaming over her sexy, wet body.

He finished washing Sheba, then rinsed her off and took her into the drying room. When Elaine joined him, he reached over and shut and locked the door.

Elaine frowned. "Logan can't get in."

"That's the general idea."

Chapter 20

ELAINE EYED CEARNACH WITH INTRIGUE AS HE secreted her away in the dog kennels' drying room. Smiling at her with lustful intent, he shifted his gaze to the wet sweater clinging to her breasts. She smiled back at him. "What do you have in mind?"

"Helping to dry you off a wee bit, lass," he said with a devilish glint in his eyes.

All the dogs were curled up on mats, some of them mostly dry and sleeping, some licking their wet fur, others sitting and watching Cearnach and Elaine, their tails thumping enthusiastically on their beds. Cearnach drew off Elaine's wet sweater and tossed it on a bench. She felt wickedly exposed as he towel-dried her breasts while warm air from the heater vents swirled around them. The smell of citrus shampoo and wet dog and a couple of wet shifter wolves filled the room.

"You're nearly as wet as me." She reached up and touched the damp shirt outlining his hard muscles. Wanting to expose his brawny chest, she'd tugged his shirt barely past his navel before he took charge.

He yanked his shirt off and tossed it on the bench with hers. She picked up another clean towel and ran it over his beautiful pecs and abs—beach-body perfect, making her think of him lying on Pensacola Beach with her, enjoying the sun and surf.

"I'll never wash the dogs again without thinking of

you in that wet sweater, or like this, half naked in the drying room." He cupped her breasts, then ran his fingers over the extended nipples, taut and sensitive. Her breathing suspended as she gloried in the sweep of his fingers against her flesh. "There's a room off this one for the person who stays with the dogs when they have new pups. The sheets have been changed since no one's slept in here for the last month."

Thank God for that! She could envision pushing a wolfhound off its damp bed to make room for two wolves who wanted to find a soft spot to make love—yuck!—or having to run back to his bedchamber in the castle in wet clothes in the chilly breeze in front of those working on the grounds and inside the stone building. Cearnach kissed her lips gently, then moved her into the room where a twin bed covered with a light blue blanket and comforter sat against a wall, a wooden table and a chair beside it. Shades were pulled closed over the one window, and she noticed a sink and toilet in a half bath off the room.

Just as Cearnach reached for Elaine's jeans zipper, they heard movement beyond the locked drying-room door. *They froze.*

"Cearnach, I've got the lady's clothes for her," Logan said, trying the door to the drying room, the doorknob twisting back and forth. "Cearnach?" Then the lad grumbled under his breath, "She is *too* your girlfriend."

Cearnach grinned down at Elaine. "Leave them on one of the dry benches, Logan. You can come back in half an hour and exercise the dogs," Cearnach said.

Elaine and Cearnach waited, listening, until they

heard Logan slosh across the wet floor, then slam the door to the kennels.

Cearnach smiled and shook his head.

Elaine pulled off her jeans in a hurry, worried some-one else would interrupt them, as Cearnach quickly shucked the rest of his clothes. Then he lifted her in his arms and carried her to the bed.

Pulse quickening, she smiled up at him, loving the heat of his naked chest pressed against her, the feel of his hard muscles bunching as he laid her on the bed.

He stretched out on top of her, claiming her—all that sinewy strength and virile heat rubbing against her. Kissing her mouth, slowly, luxuriously, he moved his body against hers, working his stiff cock against her mound. She groaned with feral need, wanting him inside her now.

She slipped her arms around his neck, pulling him close, holding him against her. Spreading her legs, she willed him to enter her, her tongue teasing his smil-ing lips, his eyes already clouded with desire. She loved his passion, the way he couldn't seem to get enough of her, the way he loved her just as much as she loved him.

"Elaine," he groaned as she pressed her tongue into his mouth. She felt the heat between them building, his body rocking against hers, his erection pressing against her damp heat, urgent, relentless, not entering her yet, but close.

So close.

She angled her hips, trying to capture his erection so that she could sheathe the throbbing part of him that would join them together as one.

His hands shifted again to her breasts, cupping, massaging the flesh. His fingers toyed with her nipples, making them hard and sensitive and just as needy for his touch as the rest of her. She arched against him, aching for him.

He bent his head and licked a nipple, then the other, while her hands moved down his back, stroking, touching, loving the feel of his heated skin, his hardworking muscles.

Then before he seemed ready, she bent her knees, digging her heels into the mattress, willing him to penetrate her. Cradled between her legs, he reached between them and stroked her sweet spot, harder, faster, until she was soaring toward the burning hot sun, ready to explode. Then it hit her. Shudders of fine ecstasy filled her body as her heat enveloped him.

Sweet wolf, he was everything she ever wanted in a man, someone who could give her the sun and moon and love her as she did him.

She wrapped her legs around his back, locking her ankles together, urging him to fill her with his cock, to find his own release deep within her.

He slid slowly inside her, saying her name in his sexy Scottish way, which turned her on all the more. He drove deep, trying to satisfy the savage hunger, then pulled out slowly. As soon as she lifted her hips to take him back inside her, he moved inside her again, deepening the penetration, burying himself to the hilt while he kissed her neck and throat and chin.

Her pelvis met his as they continued to rock together, the bed squeaking, their hearts beating frantically as he pinned her against the mattress. Urging him on, she felt his body working, his thick cock sliding into her. Pleasure. Rapture.

All of a sudden, he held still, buried deep, and then he increased the plunges, racing to the end. Taking her with him. A starburst of delicious fulfillment shot through her as he spilled his seed inside her, jerking with release. She sagged beneath him, satiated as the waves of contractions moved through her, loving him and the pure joy of being with him.

He pumped into her several more times as if milking every last drop, depositing a wolfish treasure deep inside her, then moving around so that she could rest on top of him on the small mattress.

For a long while, he lightly stroked her arm as they lay there, their breathing ragged, their hearts beating wildly as they cuddled. She ran her finger over his chest. "What are you thinking about, Cearnach?"

He leaned down and kissed her head, then wrapped his arms around her in a bear hug. "How I should never have lost you the first time I saw you in St. Andrews. And how I'm going to love making up so much lost time between us."

She couldn't agree more.

Cearnach snuggled with Elaine, nearly falling asleep on the small bed, the warm air circulating around them. He couldn't remember a time when he'd been happier. But he had to get dressed before Logan returned to walk the dogs.

He again considered that bastard Rafferty and his crew. Elaine said she'd killed a couple of them that had been guarding her, but he couldn't stop wondering what had become of the rest of them.

She kissed his chest and looked up at him. "What are you thinking that has you frowning so?"

"Do you know what happened to the rest of Rafferty's men?"

"I'd heard that some had died at sea during storms, some due to encountering ships that had more guns, some due to hangings. Three were murdered near where I relocated. I don't know about the rest. If they didn't make the newspapers, I had no way of knowing."

"The stolen goods your uncles had hidden?" He combed his fingers through her silky hair.

"They may be long gone by now," she warned. "What was the merchandise that my uncles stole from your ships?"

"Pearls, twenty hogshead barrels of sugar, gold dust, indigo, silver plate, emeralds, silk. All very valuable back then. Some just as valuable today."

"Oh," she said.

"You had no idea?"

She shook her head. "I thought the joke might be on Robert if the treasure was something perishable, like the sugar. I can just imagine what centuries-old sugar would be worth. Are the goods so valuable now that you still want the treasure that badly?"

"Only to keep it out of Kilpatrick's hands because *he* wants it so badly."

"Why, after all these years, would they want the treasure? For me, I wanted to see what my uncles thought so precious that they risked their lives to obtain it. Like you, I agree that Robert doesn't deserve it. So if anything, I want to keep him from having the spoils as much as possible."

"I understand. The MacNeill merchandise might not have been hidden in Scotland, though," Cearnach said. "It became my duty to learn why your uncles had sailed to St. Andrews when I witnessed what happened to them and to see if that shed any light on where you'd vanished to. Had they had business there or elsewhere? We assume that was just where they docked. Beyond that, they could have had business at some other location."

She closed her gaping mouth, and he realized she really hadn't known what her uncles had planned for her. Perhaps they had wanted to see their relations, ensure that one of them would suit her as a mate, and leave her with the family to give her a chance to be with someone other than Kelly.

"The Kilpatricks and McKinleys were in the city of St. Andrews when your uncles arrived, as if the meeting had been planned. Had your uncles intended to rendezvous with them? But circumstances prevented it?" he continued.

"They said nothing about what they intended to do," she said, then studied the ceiling as if trying to recall the voyage and everything that had been said between them. "Yet they seemed… disquieted. I thought it was because I was aboard ship."

"Some believe a woman on a ship can bring disaster."

"So I've heard." She cuddled against Cearnach, idly stroking his naked chest while he brushed his fingers over her silky hair, delighting in the feel of her molded against his body.

He took a deep breath and exhaled. "You said you thought Kelly Rafferty might have murdered your parents. Did you ever learn the truth?"

"I believed he did. I questioned everyone I could, even his men. They told him I had been looking into my parents' deaths and what I suspected. He took it out on me—for questioning his honor. I even asked him when he was in a drunken state if he'd done it, figuring he was too inebriated to realize what he was revealing to me. He hadn't been drunk enough, and I paid dearly for it with a broken jaw and wrist.

"Even after word reached me that he'd died, no one would tell me the truth, as if his ghostly person would come back to haunt them. I admit that for years I feared he'd return and take up where he'd left off. I had nightmares about him forever, about his brutality, both physical and emotional. I know he had my parents murdered if he hadn't actually done the deed himself."

Angered that anyone could do violence against her, he caressed her arm, her body pressed against his, wishing he could take away all of her past pain.

"The whole scenario was a little too convenient. My parents' carriage suddenly veered off into the river when they had been on their way to a party that night. For what reason? No one ever knew. The carriage sank so fast that they were unable to get out. But the horses were saved. The horses, as if they were the only thing of value and not my parents' lives. That's partly why I believe he had something to do with the carriage *accident*. The horses were safely returned home, and neither was wet."

"My God, Elaine." He took her hand in his and found that her fingers were ice cold. He held her hand against his chest and rubbed it to warm her. Again he regretted having lost her all those years ago and felt sickened that he couldn't have protected her. "What about the other half of the details that would lead to the loot? Isn't it with your suitcase or purse?" The game would be lost, but why would Robert still want Elaine to meet with him?

"In here," she said, tapping her head. "He won't get it from me."

"I wonder if the stolen goods could be hidden on one of the properties you own."

Elaine frowned. "Wouldn't Robert have learned of them and already investigated?"

"Possibly."

"Then he wouldn't need me for finding the treasure."

She snuggled closer to Cearnach, loving the sound of his heartbeat beneath her ear and the way he was caressing her hand. She hoped Cearnach wasn't condemning her too much for not standing up more to Kelly Rafferty. She'd always felt she was a caught animal, unable to get free of his men when he was away and terrified of him when he was home, yet she had tried to show him her alpha side.

Sometimes he loved bullying her to show she wasn't as alpha as he. Other times he seemed to love that she'd stand up to him and he would leave her alone.

"I'm sorry for letting you get away from me the first time," Cearnach said, hugging her tight.

This was where she belonged. With him. Like this.

"I ought to get up and get dressed before Logan returns," Cearnach said, not sounding like he wanted to let go of her.

"Yes," she murmured.

Before they could leave the small bed, Cearnach turned his head in the direction of the door.

"Someone's coming," Elaine whispered, hearing the sounds of footsteps.

"Logan," Cearnach guessed.

"Have you seen Cearnach?" Ian asked beyond the drying room, the door still locked.

Ian.

Chapter 21

SOMEONE POUNDED ON THE KENNEL'S DRYING ROOM door. "Cearnach, Elaine's solicitor is here. She needs to speak with him. You and I will also listen to what he has to say," Ian said.

"Hell," Cearnach said, running his hand over Elaine's hair. "Guess we've got to face the world."

She groaned. Then she sat upright and whispered, "Ian said my solicitor is here?"

"Aye." He hadn't thought the solicitor would show up this quickly, either. Ian must have made the man fear the wrath of the pack.

She wrapped the towel around her and pushed at Cearnach. "Go, get the dry clothes Logan brought for me. Mine are still wet."

Cearnach put his damp clothes on.

"Why would a lawyer be here to speak to me?" Her eyes were wide.

"It probably has to do with your properties and the management of them. I'm sure that's what the solicitor is here to talk with you about."

"Did your mother know about this before she suggested you mate with me?" she asked. Then she shook her head. "She didn't. We had only just met. I bet that would have been an even greater incentive for you to mate me."

Cearnach sighed. "You are priceless to me, lass. With

or without your holdings. With or without the treasure."
He smiled in a much too predatory way. "With or without your clothes."

He sighed. "Let me get the dry clothes."

He left the room and stalked through the drying room where the dogs had left their beds to crowd around the door, desperate to greet Ian. Cearnach unlocked and opened the door. The dogs rushed out as Cearnach came face to face with Logan and Ian, both giving him accusatory looks. The dogs eagerly greeted them, bouncing around and jumping up in a wild frenzy of doggy love.

"The clothes?" Cearnach was not about to explain himself in front of Logan. Well, to Ian either.

Logan handed him the clothes.

"We'll be right out, Ian." Cearnach shut the door.

"How'd they take it?" Elaine took the borrowed pale-pink sweater and jeans from him and hurried to dress.

"I'm certain they knew it was coming."

"I'm not getting married." She pulled on the light sweater and looked up at Cearnach, who was staring at her in surprise. "Wolves don't get married. I don't have any family and…"

"You have us." He pulled her into his arms and held her tight. He didn't want this to be an issue between them, but she had to marry him. He understood her reluctance because she had no family—at least that would be welcome. "You have my family and extended family."

"No one would sit on the bride's side of the church."

"Oh, aye, the place will be packed. Mark my word."

"Wolves don't get married," she said again. "I never planned to be married if I found… found the right mate for me."

"If something should happen to Ian, I would gain his title." He sighed and kissed her forehead. "It's nothing to worry about now."

"That's easy for you to say. You wouldn't have to do anything but show up at the ceremony."

He smiled. "We fight the battles, lass. You plan the fun stuff."

She snorted.

"My mother will insist on helping."

She sighed at that.

"Tell her to stay out of it if you want. It's up to you."

"If it was up to me, I wouldn't have a wedding!"

"Except for that."

Cearnach took Elaine's hand and led her through the front door of the kennels. As soon as they walked across the inner bailey, several people greeted them, small smiles on their faces.

Elaine's cheeks flushed beautifully. "They know," she whispered to him. "Don't they?"

"Aye, I imagine so."

She frowned. "Your mother will think it's her doing."

Cearnach didn't say anything.

"Flynn will think it's his."

Cearnach finally smiled down at her and pulled her to a stop. "But I will know it was *your* doing."

"Mine?" she asked, looking up at him, her gaze questioning.

"Oh, aye, lass. You hooked me from the very beginning." He wrapped his arm around her shoulders and pulled open the door to the keep, then escorted her inside.

Though they had jobs to do, Duncan and Guthrie were milling around in the great hall. When they heard

Elaine and Cearnach crossing the stone floor, both turned to watch them.

Duncan, not one to mince words, spoke right up. "Is it done?"

Cearnach frowned at him. "We haven't spoken with Elaine's solicitor yet," Cearnach said, not about to discuss mating with Elaine with his brothers.

Duncan gave him a small smile, knowing just from his response that he'd taken Elaine for his mate.

Guthrie raised his brows.

As Cearnach and Elaine walked by his brothers, he cast a glance over his shoulder at them, giving them a look, reminding them not to spread the word until he was ready to tell everyone. Duncan would speak with Shelley about it, and he was certain Ian had told Julia already.

When they arrived in Ian's office, he introduced Elaine and Cearnach to her solicitor, a wiry, little gray-haired man with a laptop computer and a big black briefcase. The man smelled like a gray wolf.

"I've been managing the lass's estates for years," Mr. Hoover said. "Samson and Tobias Hawthorn gifted the properties to her centuries ago, and the estates have earned enough money to pay the taxes and upkeep all these years. I... couldn't locate her once I learned her uncles had died. I did try. Once I discovered where she'd gone, she had already disappeared again.

"You own Senton Castle and all the land around it. Your parents married in the chapel there when the castle was still standing. Grand affair, if I do say so myself," Mr. Hoover said to Elaine. "Here are the property descriptions and locations." He passed a pile of papers to her.

"They were married at Senton Castle? Why did my parents leave there?" she asked, tears forming in her eyes.

"Many years later, they left when they couldn't maintain the castle. Wars, famine. One of those wars resulted in the death of your older brother."

"Brother?" Elaine asked, sounding horrified. "I had a brother?"

"Two, but one was stillborn. The other was ten when you were born. Fighting broke out and he was beyond the shelter of the castle walls at the time. Your parents were distraught over the death of their male heir." Mr. Hoover looked at Ian as if the fault was his.

That had Cearnach thinking about the times they'd bombarded the castle with cannon fire.

"Your parents left the castle in your uncles' care shortly after that. Not wishing to remain in Scotland, your parents started anew in Florida. While your uncles were away sailing the seas, the Kilpatricks and McKinleys ran Senton Castle into the ground. Your uncles bought the other properties also. All of them were bequeathed to you."

"I'd had no word. My parents never mentioned any of this to me."

The solicitor nodded. "You were young."

She hadn't been for years. Cearnach frowned at the solicitor.

Mr. Hoover cleared his throat. "We did try to locate you, Miss Hawthorn. You'd changed your identity and moved so many times over the years…" He spread his hands in a gesture of helplessness.

He glanced down at his notes. "You own two manors and a keep in Scotland that have been continuously rented out at a goodly income for years. The properties have been well maintained and are in good shape. All but Senton Castle, which as you probably have learned is in…"

"Ruins, I know," Elaine said, frowning.

"Did the Hawthorns store any merchandise at any of the locations?" Cearnach asked.

"You mean, sir, the merchandise stolen from ships while they were away at sea?" Mr. Hoover inquired, his brows raised.

Elaine barely breathed.

So the old fox knew. Cearnach nodded. "Aye, that's what I mean."

"Nay. Several warehouses full of stolen merchandise were captured and sold to pay off those whose property had been taken at sea. Some of the merchandise had already been moved before the authorities learned of the locations."

"None of the merchandise was left at the manor houses?" Elaine asked, glancing at the documents, then passing them to Ian, who began to study them in earnest.

"Nay."

"Did my uncles leave me a key?"

"To the manor houses and keep, aye. Several. To the warehouses, several more. But those I didn't bother to pay the rent on. No need when they held no more goods and the storage space wasn't being used. I turned the keys over to the owners of the warehouses years ago. Most of the buildings don't even exist any longer."

"So no merchandise that my uncles might have stolen is left," Elaine said, sounding both disappointed and relieved at the same time.

"That we know about, nay. That doesn't mean they didn't hide some in another location that I don't know about. I brought you the deeds and wished to offer my services to continue to manage your properties, should you so desire."

"Why didn't you contact me about this? As soon as you could?" she asked, her cheeks growing flushed, her whole posture stiff.

"We couldn't locate you."

"Maybe early on," she retorted. "But my cousin found me. Why couldn't you have?"

Mr. Hoover sat even more rigidly in the chair, his jaw tightening with tension. "He hired someone to locate you and told me you were coming here to meet with him. I asked how he had located you. He said he had friends in low places, laughed, and wouldn't say anything further. Even so, it took him ten years after he…" Mr. Hoover paused, glanced at Ian and Cearnach, then focused again on Elaine and hesitated to finish what he was going to say.

"He… *what*?" Elaine asked, her voice terse.

The solicitor ground his teeth. "Your uncles had told me never to contact your relations in Scotland, but a renter offered a substantial amount of money to buy one of your manors ten years ago. I didn't know what to do. He decided to keep renting. If you were no longer living…" He sighed. "I had to find you, to let you know you had properties and learn what you wanted to do with them. I thought maybe one of your cousins might know your whereabouts.

"I contacted Robert Kilpatrick since I handle his estates also. I didn't tell him about your properties, although I'm certain he assumed that the only reason I would try to learn where you'd gone was because you had an estate. He said since I couldn't find you, he'd have someone else search for you. It wasn't easy. He had several false starts, and then finally you changed your name back to Hawthorn and returned to Florida a month ago. As soon as Mr. Kilpatrick could verify it was you…"

"How did he confirm it was me?" she asked warily. "I'm certain there are tons of female Hawthorns in the state."

"Aye. I don't know for sure. He wouldn't say. I assume he used a wolf living in the area to check on you and substantiate that you were one of us, for one thing. You were the only Hawthorn she-wolf in the area."

"But once you learned she was living in Florida, you didn't contact her," Cearnach said. "*We* contacted *you* once we discovered she had estates in Scotland. You didn't bother to try and speak with Miss Hawthorn before this."

A bead of sweat broke out on the solicitor's upper lip. Matching beads appeared on his forehead. "Aye. Mr. Kilpatrick said the lass was coming to Scotland, and he would tell her I wished to speak with her. She vanished after she had arrived, and he was trying to locate her again. He said he didn't know where she'd disappeared to."

Elaine folded her arms. "All right, so what if I wanted to sell the properties? Not that I'm saying I want to, but if I did?"

Mr. Hoover cleared his throat. "You can't."

Her eyes widened.

He glanced at Cearnach as if he was afraid the alpha

would take him to task. "I mean to say that not all the properties can be sold. The keep and Senton Castle must go to your heirs, Miss Hawthorn. No one is permitted to sell off the properties as long as they're supporting their upkeep. The manors are a different story."

"Have they incurred any profit? If so, where has the money gone?"

"A bank, Miss Hawthorn." He stiffened. "You're quite a wealthy woman. All the money is there. You can have your own accountant verify that the expenses and receipts all are correct."

She raised her brows, showing a slight upward tilt to her mouth.

Cearnach stared at Elaine as the beautiful she-wolf sat straighter, her lips parted. Her uncle had told her *she* was the key to his heart, to the treasure. Not in goods, but in land holdings.

She took a deep breath. "Had my uncles planned to settle down here? In Scotland?"

Mr. Hoover shook his head. "They were seafarers. The ocean was their bloodline. They wanted this for you. For the child that neither of them had."

Tears reappeared in her eyes, and Cearnach took her hand and squeezed it.

Mr. Hoover watched the intimacy between them and pulled out a handkerchief and dabbed at his brow.

"Why did they want me to mate with Kelly Rafferty, then? Did you know about that?"

He swallowed hard and gave a jerky nod, his gaze settling on hers.

"Then why?"

"You were so young. You needed protection."

Cearnach snorted.

"Something to fall back on," Mr. Hoover hastily said. "After your uncles died, you disappeared. Four months later, word reached us that pirates had attacked the ship you'd been traveling on. It was nearly a year before we learned you had become Rafferty's wife and then that he had died. If we could have located you, you would have had the income to use as you saw fit all these years. Did… did you want us to continue to maintain your estates, ma'am?"

"I will have Guthrie MacNeill verify the accounts," Elaine said. "I'm certain he will manage them from now on." Then she looked at Cearnach as if she realized that since she was a mated wolf, it would be his business also.

She took a deep breath and Cearnach bowed his head slightly to her, acknowledging that he was in agreement, knowing what she was about to say and wanting her to know he was behind her on this. "I'm mated to Cearnach now. So we'll need to make the deeds out in his name also."

Ian let out his breath. "Hell, Cearnach."

Everyone looked at Ian.

He shook his head and folded his arms, but didn't say anything more. Cearnach knew he'd hear an earful as soon as he was alone with his brother. He should have told his brother that he and Elaine were mated before anyone else—particularly someone not of their pack.

Frowning deeply, the solicitor cleared his throat. "Do your kin know about this?"

"The Kilpatricks and McKinleys?" Elaine shook her head. "No one else officially knows here, either. I don't plan to tell my kin. It's none of their business.

After the way they treated me, I don't claim them as my own clansmen."

"Can I… speak with you *privately*?" Mr. Hoover asked Elaine, looking more than concerned.

"I'm mated. So whatever you have to say can be said in front of my mate."

The solicitor looked a little gray.

"What is it that you wished to speak to me about in private?" she asked when he didn't say.

"Nay, Miss Hawthorn. I will have to confer with your cousins as to whether they wish for me to share this information with more than just yourself."

"Who's paying you for your services, Mr. Hoover?" she asked, her back and tone of voice stiff, alpha-like.

"For the management of your properties, you are, miss. Uh, I guess, I'm no longer managing your properties if the MacNeill clan will be responsible for them in future. For this other matter, your cousins are."

"My cousins," she said.

Cearnach was about to rise from his chair to force the solicitor to say what he had wished to say, but Elaine stayed him, a hand on Cearnach's arm. "If you can't share the information, it really doesn't matter," Elaine said. "I want to see each of these places. Would it be possible?"

"Aye. The occupants of the two manors are human. I've told everyone that you have arrived in Scotland and might wish to see your properties. One of the buildings is an ancient keep. One of our kind lives there."

"A kinsman of mine?" she asked, her brows furrowing.

The solicitor hesitated to say, then shook his head. Lying? Hiding some truth?

"Can I see them today?"

"They're spread out over Scotland. One of the properties is located about three hours from here." He pointed to one of the manor houses on the sheet of paper Ian was looking at. Mr. Hoover closed up his laptop. "I'll see about changing the names on the deeds." He rose from the chair.

Cearnach and Elaine stood.

Mr. Hoover bowed his head a little, looking like he wished nothing more than to leave immediately. Why? Because of the news about Elaine and Cearnach's mating?

Cearnach suspected her kin would be furious, and the little man did not wish to be the bearer of ill tidings.

"Aye. Good day, ma'am, sir, my laird."

"Will you show him out, Cearnach?" Ian asked.

Cearnach felt torn. He didn't want to leave Elaine alone with Ian, afraid of what he might say to her while he was gone.

"I'm not going anywhere," Elaine promised Cearnach, giving his hand a squeeze, her smile a promise that everything would be okay.

He kissed her cheek. "All right." Then he gave Ian a warning look, which made his brother give him a raised brow in return. Cearnach reluctantly escorted the solicitor out of Ian's office and shut the door.

Elaine retook her seat.

"My mother didn't force this on you, did she?" Ian asked, his eyes narrowed as he studied her response.

"No. Not Flynn, either. Cearnach said *I* forced it upon him."

Ian didn't say anything for a moment as if he was taking that in, then nodded as if he agreed. She'd expected him to laugh or smile or something. Not just seriously agree.

"You were the one we were trying to track down for weeks in the St. Andrews area. Cearnach was certain someone evil had taken you hostage, and he needed to rescue you."

"I'm sorry he worried about me for so long."

"We all did." Ian leaned back in his chair and folded his arms. "What do you think the Kilpatricks and McKinleys want with you?"

"If no merchandise is hidden anywhere, or if it was discovered years ago, then I don't know why they would want to have anything further to do with me."

Ian shook his head. "They wouldn't want you to be mated to one of us. Certainly not to Cearnach, of all people."

"Why him?"

"His friendship with Calla. Now she's called off the wedding between her and Baird. They wished to speak with you about some matter, and now you're here and siding with us."

She made an annoyed little huff under her breath. "That was easy to do after all they'd done to Cearnach and me."

"Aye, but they won't see it that way. They'll feel justified in everything they've done."

Cearnach stalked into the solar. "Was anything important discussed while I was gone?" He took a seat next to Elaine again and put his arm around her shoulders.

Ian laughed. "You must have run the solicitor out of the building."

"Duncan met me on the stairs and is giving him the royal escort out."

"Not only have you created ill will with Elaine's clan over Calla but now also concerning Elaine," Ian said.

Cearnach shrugged. "Couldn't be helped. That clan is bad news."

Ian nodded. "I'll ask Guthrie and Duncan to see if they can learn anything about what the solicitor alluded to. I suspect we will have more trouble."

"They won't give back my ID and the rental car and all," Elaine said.

"I suspect not. But we have our ways," Ian assured her.

"By force, you mean?" she asked.

"If we have to, aye."

"What do you think this is all about, Ian?" Cearnach asked.

"I believe that Elaine's kin know where more of the stolen goods are hidden. Or maybe not exactly where, as they would have already procured them. Somehow Elaine is the key."

"Just because of the clues I have. When Robert tells me what he knows, hopefully we can decipher the location, if anything still exists," Elaine said.

Ian looked at his desk as if he was deep in thought. "I'm not sure."

"What are you thinking?" Cearnach asked.

"Did they ask you to share what you knew about the treasure without coming to Scotland?" Ian asked Elaine.

"Yes. But I wouldn't tell them what I knew, assuming they'd find the goods and cut me out of them entirely."

"Are you certain?" Ian asked.

She frowned at him. "Of course, I'm certain. They were all a bunch of pirates."

"Nay, lass, that's not what I mean," Ian said gently.

"Are you certain that Kilpatrick was only interested in the information about the treasure? If you had given it to him over the phone and not bothered to come to Scotland, would he have been satisfied?"

"What are you saying?" Elaine asked. "That they wanted me just as much as they wanted the goods?"

"Aye, that's what I'm thinking. Though it could very well be that it's just your information they want."

But from the tone of Ian's voice, that wasn't what she thought he meant at all.

Chapter 22

As they sat in Ian's solar discussing the reasons why Robert Kilpatrick wanted Elaine in Scotland so badly, Cearnach asked her, "Could it be that your kin wanted to get hold of your properties because they are profitable?"

"It's possible that's what this is all about." She sighed. "I don't wish to delay this any further. I want to see the properties," Elaine told Ian. "I want to see if they might hold the goods my uncles stole from you and just take a look at the places also."

"I'm certain your cousins would have searched them thoroughly. It appears to me that your uncles used the stolen goods to make sound investments. These, in turn, are now back in MacNeill hands, but are more valuable than the original goods your uncles stole from us," Cearnach said, as if worried she might be disappointed.

She agreed he might be right. Yet, she wished she could have seen the goods. She envisioned a dragon hoarding its treasure. She had hoped they were more than a few barrels of useless stuff. She'd never realized her uncles had been good at making investments. Her mother and father had been, but she'd always thought of her uncles as the kind of men who lived off of one cache of stolen goods to the next. Never did she imagine that they could have been wealthy landowners.

It saddened her to learn she'd had an older brother,

lost to an earlier war, whose death had upset her parents so much that they'd moved to the Americas. Had they worried about losing her, too? Why hadn't her parents ever told her about him? Or about the other son who died before he was born.

"If you wish to survey your lands, I'll make the necessary arrangements. You will have a guard force at all times," Ian said.

She frowned, not wanting to create more work for his clansmen. "Do you believe that's really necessary?"

"Aye. I don't know what the McKinleys and Kilpatricks are up to where you're concerned. You're one of us now. I won't permit either you or Cearnach to travel alone until we learn that the treasure doesn't exist or discover some other reason why Robert is so desperate to see you—alone."

"I don't want you or your people to feel put upon."

Ian and Cearnach gave each other smiles. "The thing of it, lass," Ian said, "is that we live for adventure, train to fight, and protect. I will have a time choosing some clansmen to accompany you without offending those who are not chosen."

Elaine smiled at that. Instead of a group of men taking a step backward when asked for volunteers to accompany them, she envisioned kilted warriors, swords in hand, all stepping forward.

"If you're sure…"

"I am, lass."

Elaine stood and said to Cearnach. "I want to go on a treasure hunt. The first manor Mr. Hoover mentioned is not too far from here."

"I'll send word at once to have a force of men attend

you," Ian said. "As to the keep, it's about five hours
south of Argent Castle. I'll ask Guthrie, Duncan, and
Oran and a few other men to check out the place. The
men will be thorough. The renter might be one of your
kinsmen, despite what your solicitor said. I didn't care
for his hesitation when he responded after you pointedly
asked if the wolf was related to you."

"Make sure they take notice if the property is near a
loch or has a waterfall nearby."

"Aye, lass. They will make sure of it."

—⁓—

Despite not expecting to be overly impressed, Elaine
was when they arrived at the first estate.

Heavy stone walls and massive oak doors gave the
immediate impression of the medieval three-story building being just as hardy as the Highlanders accompanying her.

"No loch," she said to Cearnach, thinking of what her
uncle had eluded to.

"Aye. No waterfalls near here. No pile of rocks."

Two vanloads of warriors joined them as Elaine
knocked on the door of the manor, the renters already
informed of their visit. Wide-eyed, a matronly woman
stared at all the men standing around.

"My husband's kinsmen," Elaine said, "wanting to
see the property also. They'll just look at the grounds.
My husband will accompany me on a brief tour of the
manor. The others will remain outside."

"Of course, Mrs. MacNeill. Come in. I'm Tricia
Haverstein."

Calling Cearnach her husband when he wasn't—and

when her kind normally didn't wed, nor had she ever planned such a thing—felt odd.

Inside, she toured the seven bedrooms, all with fireplaces and small glazed glass windows. Antiques filled each room, and all the walls were papered in floral designs. The older woman related details about the place as they moved through it. About all the people who had made changes to the building over the years. How at one time the manor was a monastery. She pointed to the window seats. "Prayer seats for the monks."

Three spiral staircases led from one floor to another in the same manner as the stairs at Argent Castle, for protection in case of invasion. The kitchen looked old with its stone walls and fireplace, but was modernized with new appliances. A wine cellar where Elaine thought a treasure might have been hidden proved to hold nothing but racks of wine.

The woman motioned to one of the racks. "At one time a ship sank and casks of wine were brought here to be enjoyed by the vicar and the parson. It was called the 'right of wreckage' in the Middle Ages."

"Finders, keepers," Elaine mused.

"Aye."

"Thank you for your time, Mrs. Haverstein."

They left the manor, and when Elaine climbed into the car with Cearnach, she said, "The other manor is only three hours from this one."

Cearnach studied her for a moment, then nodded. He called Ian and okayed the trip to the next medieval manor.

They stopped for a meal at a quaint little eatery and then they were off again.

The next manor was similar to the first, with ancient,

beautiful oak doors and floors, stone walls, and antique-filled rooms.

Like the other, the place was not near any water. "This couldn't be where they hid the treasure," she said. "No loch. No waterfalls." She couldn't help the disappointment in her voice.

"Aye, but remember the properties are worth far more than the merchandise your uncles stole. And they are yours."

"Ours," she reminded him.

"They are that." He called Ian to let him know of their progress. "I'll tell her. See you later." He set the new phone down on the console. "They haven't brought your car to the castle yet, Ian said."

"Do you think they will?" Elaine asked.

"I don't know, lass. Because you wouldn't do as they asked, maybe not. It's time to go home."

She worried now what other measures Ian might take to get her property back and restitution paid for Cearnach's vehicle. She hoped it didn't mean a battle between wolf packs.

—∙⁄∖∖∿—

Duncan and Guthrie and the other men scouted the area surrounding the keep that Elaine owned. No one was at home, but they noted the smell of a gray wolf and suspected he might be Elaine's kin and trouble. If they'd been human, they would have had to abide by human laws, such as those against illegal search and breaking and entering. But shape-shifting wolves had their own set of rules to live by. It was the only way their kind could live among humans without detection and survive as long as they had. Using a key, Duncan, Guthrie, and Oran entered first.

Even though his attention should have been on searching for hidden places within the keep, Duncan kept wanting to look through the drawers of the desk, learn the contents of the computer sitting atop it, and rifle through every cabinet, nook, and cranny in every room of the keep.

"He's not any of the McKinleys or Kilpatricks we know," Guthrie said, watching Duncan as he stared at another confounded bureau drawer.

Then he jerked it open and began searching through it. "He's been here forever. Long enough to have known her uncles."

Guthrie turned to the other men with them. "Search everything. All the drawers, cabinets, everything for any clue as to who he is. Or any connections he might have with the Kilpatricks, McKinleys, or Elaine."

Either the guy was a neat freak or he had a maid who was one. Socks were rolled up in one drawer. Briefs in another. Sweaters were neatly folded in another.

Duncan made a mess of them, not bothering to neaten up after himself. Guthrie smiled at him, knowing that with the way a wolf could smell scents, the renter would realize another wolf had handled his property. No sense in trying to hide the fact.

They returned to the office, and while Guthrie worked on breaking through the wolf's security code on his computer, Duncan searched through all the drawers in the room, then began to pull books off a shelf and flip through each and every one of them.

Duncan found nothing, which was more than odd. He turned to watch Guthrie.

No matter how good his skills were at hacking, Guthrie was unable to get into the man's computer. He glanced at Duncan, then at the mass of books thrown on the floor in a heap. Guthrie knew Duncan wouldn't intentionally make a mess of someone else's place unless he had good reason. To make a statement. To make the wolf beware. Elaine now had family, a new family, to protect her. Duncan couldn't help feeling antagonistic about the wolf who lived here.

"What do you suspect, Duncan?" Guthrie asked, standing.

Oran and his brothers came to the doorway of the office, shaking their heads as Duncan considered them. "We didn't find any clues," Oran said.

"There's nothing personal here anywhere. How can anyone live so long in a place and have nothing that would clue others in about his habits, interests, lifestyle?" Duncan said. "I have a feeling he's connected somehow to Elaine, her family, something. And it's not in a good way." That's all Duncan had to say. A wolf's instincts were often right.

"Okay." Guthrie sat back down at Mr. Hazelton's computer. "Let's see what we can learn about old Samuel here."

—⁓—

Much later that evening, Cearnach and Elaine returned to Argent Castle, where she almost felt at home. Calling a massive castle in a different country "home" seemed strange. Actually, being at the castle wasn't what made her feel that way, but being with Cearnach. He was home for her.

Most everyone had retired for the night, although Ian told Cearnach that his brothers and cousins were still at the keep, trying to break into the renter's computer. No sign of the man as yet. And no indication that he was related to Elaine or that any treasure was hidden within.

"I'm worried about them," Elaine said to Cearnach.

"They'll be fine."

Dismissing her concern, he told her they were warriors, used to business like this. She still couldn't help herself. She hadn't thought they'd do anything more than she and Cearnach had done. Search the place. Not try to break into his computer. But Cearnach had warned her they would be thorough.

She could see that Cearnach had only one thing in mind as he hurried her up to their bedchamber. As soon as he shut the door, she yanked aside the curtain on her side of the bed. He turned to see her sitting on the mattress, yawning. She attempted to fight the tiredness that racked her body, but she couldn't shake it off. After the ghostly problems last night and the jet lag from the day before, then washing all those huge pups earlier today and running all over Scotland searching for treasure, she was exhausted.

Cearnach stalked toward her, his gaze predatory, not in the least bit tired. He crouched before her and pulled off one of her boots, then the other. "It's late and way past time for bed."

She smiled at him and cupped his face, then lifted it to look up at her. "If anyone had told me I'd be sleeping with a Highland wolf in a castle in Scotland…"

"*Mated* to a wolf," he corrected her. "There's a vast

difference. Last night, you slept with a wolf. Tonight, you're with your mate."

Mated to a wolf. She liked the way he said it. The connection that now stood between them for the rest of their days.

His warm fingers stroked up her belly underneath the sweater, higher until he ran his hands over her breasts and squeezed them. Already his erection was heavy against her thigh, his breathing rough, hers getting rougher. She'd never known being with a wolf could be this good.

He pushed the sweater up, exposing her breasts. Cool air from the room mixed with his heated breath to make her nipples stand at attention. Her breasts felt heavier, achy, needy. Just like the area between her legs was feeling needy. Then he licked her nipples, tasting, swirling his tongue around one and then the other.

He raised his mouth to hers, his soft sweater brushing her bare breasts as he rocked his erection against her leg, simulating being inside her. Her mouth caressed his, her tongue sweeping out to lick his, her teeth gently nipping his lips in a wolfish way.

He groaned with need, his fingers combing through her hair as she tugged at his sweater to pull it up. To feel his heated skin rubbing against hers. The pleasure of his mouth on hers, his tongue teasing her own, his body sliding against hers, all made her want to be naked, to have him deep inside her... now.

"I want you," she whispered against his mouth. Her hands glided down his bare back and managed to slip into his jeans. He wasn't wearing any boxers. Good. She cupped his ass. "Now." Her hushed voice came out a low growl.

He smiled, then whispered in Gaelic, making an ancient connection with her—not just a wolfish one, but a Highland one as well.

She loved hearing the words that said he loved her, and she repeated them to him even though hers had an American accent. He seemed to love the way she said the words, no matter what her accent was. Then he stripped off her sweater and then his, tossing them to the floor.

This was more like it. Her bare chest to his. Skin to skin. Nipples to nipples, his just as erect as hers were.

He nuzzled her face, kissed her throat, and licked it, sending a new wave of heat coursing through every blood vessel. The pleasure was so intense that she felt her sex wet and prepared for him.

He brushed his lips across her throat, then lower, licking a trail down between her breasts all the way to her navel, his fingers working feverishly to unfasten her pants. He unzipped her jeans, then plunged his hand inside between her legs, feeling her wetness, his fingers entering her, cupping her, demanding.

She was on fire, the sensation of his touch, determination, and urgency sending her up in flames. Waves of orgasm struck as if the sun had just warmed the room, the bed, and her, even though it was dark out, cold and gloomy.

His jeans and hers were on the floor before she realized just how fast he could move.

He climbed on top of her, pressing her thighs apart. He pushed his cock slowly into the center of her being, deepening the drive, not in a hurry, although he looked as though it was killing him to hold back. His mouth sought hers and she took him in, his tongue slipping inside, deep and penetrating.

She wanted him to make love to her as fast and furiously as he was able. She tightened around him—her sheath, her body, her legs, her arms, her lips around his tongue—holding the powerful wolf in her grasp. He was hers. Every glorious, muscled bit of him. And she loved him.

Feral need demanded action as Cearnach slid deeply into his mate, his love, her erotic scent assaulting his senses and making him plunge deeper, faster. He wanted to go slower, but the way she was digging her heels into his arse and her nails were gliding down his back, the way she clenched his cock and rocked upward to meet his thrusts, he couldn't hold on. Then she sucked on his tongue and he nearly lost it.

He'd wanted her ever since he'd made love to her in the kennel. Wanted to taste her and feel her clenching him in the most pleasurable way, to hold her close like a mate would, to love her.

She was the only one for him. The girl from so long ago. The woman now cradling him between her legs. He thrust his aching arousal into her, her pulse and his rapidly beating in unison, the tiny waves of pleasure wracking her body and feeding his own need to make her come again.

Pulling his mouth free from hers, he nuzzled her face, then licked her jaw. He clutched her hips as he pumped into her, her body grinding against his, the blood pooling in his groin, the climax so close that he barely breathed.

Then he came, explosively, deep inside her, bathing her in his seed.

He thought briefly about the puppy Elaine wanted

from Sheba's litter and how soon she'd have her own werewolf litter to love, too. He'd make sure of it in the most pleasurable of ways.

———⁓———

In the middle of the night, Elaine woke with Cearnach's body wrapped soundly around hers. She heard the muffled sound of the dogs barking in the kennel, alerting of trespassers or something. She couldn't sleep until she discovered what the matter was.

She untangled herself from Cearnach, pulled aside the curtains, and left the bed. After crossing the floor, she opened the window to look out. The air was cold and damp, and she shivered.

That's when she heard wolves howling farther away in the woods surrounding the castle. Were they some of Cearnach's people? Running as wolves in the woods tonight?

Or were they some of *her* kin? Why, if they were McKinleys or Kilpatricks, would they be prowling the woods here?

She returned to Cearnach's side of the bed and said softly to wake him, "Cearnach."

He didn't stir. She walked back over to the window and saw men on the wall walk looking in the direction of the forest. She couldn't sleep anyway, so she might as well find out what was going on. She quickly yanked on her sweater, jeans, and boots, then left the bedchamber, half expecting others from the keep to also be headed outside to learn what the matter was. Unless the wolves were just the MacNeills—then no one would be paying any attention to them.

She considered that she might look foolish, worrying about something she had no need to be concerned about, but she was checking the matter out just the same.

Chapter 23

WOLVES STILL HOWLED IN THE WOODS BEYOND THE walls of Argent Castle, calling to Elaine as she left the warmth of the keep and headed for the gates in the frigid weather. Gray clouds blocked any sign of stars clinging to the heavens tonight. She realized she should have borrowed Heather's coat again.

She also realized she couldn't see anything beyond the walls surrounding the inner bailey, which was the point of being protected by massive walls of stone. The heavy oak gates were closed for the night so the only way she would see what was going on outside the castle would be to climb to the top of the castle wall. She imagined that the stairs to the wall walk were encased in the two towers flanking the gate.

Brass lanterns lighted some areas—the doorway to the kennels, to the horses' stalls, and to the castle. Since only *lupus garous* lived here, they could see well enough in the dark.

Six men were watching the forest from the top of the wall walks, four on one side of the gate, two on the other. She didn't recognize any of them and hoped they wouldn't mind her joining them up there.

She hurried across the courtyard, and when she reached the doorway to one of the gate towers, she yanked at the door handle, half expecting it to be locked. It wasn't and the door squeaked open, alerting anyone above that she was on her way to join them.

When she reached the wall walk, the four men were looking in her direction, not at the woods.

"Lass," the one said, his eyes wide, appearing startled to see her there. "Does Cearnach know ye are here?"

She shook her head. "He's still asleep. I couldn't wake him."

"I'm his cousin, Oran," the man said. He was smiling with boyish charm, yet he was all muscle and braw warrior and tall like the rest of his kin. He was one of Heather's brothers. "Ye just didn't give him the right incentive to wake."

Her face blossomed with heat, and she quickly walked over to the wall and peered out at the woods. "Whose wolves are howling? Yours?"

"Nay, lass. Yours."

The only reason they were interested in her being family was because of the stolen goods. Maybe... her properties as well. She saw eyes glowing in the woods. Wolves' eyes. They stopped howling, watching her as she observed them. They obviously knew who she was. Was Robert Kilpatrick among them? The brute Vardon McKinley?

"Why are they here?" she asked.

Oran pointed to the private drive.

She glanced to the left and saw a car sitting some distance from the closed gate on the gravel drive. Lanterns at the castle entryway cast light that shimmered off the wet silver metal. Heart thumping erratically, she paused for a fraction of a minute, so stupefied to see the car sitting there that she didn't recognize it as hers. When realization dawned, she whipped around and headed for the stairs in the tower.

She couldn't be more excited. She was certain the battle between the clans would be averted with just that one gesture of appeasement.

"Wait, lass," Oran commanded, hurrying after her. "Where are you going?"

"To get my car. All my belongings. I have to make sure it's all there."

"We can't open the gates," Oran said, as he followed her down the stairs while the other men remained watchful on top of the wall walk. "No' until they're opened come morn."

Ignoring him, she finally reached the gates and stood there staring at them as if they'd just magically open. She turned to scowl at Oran. "I want my rental car and my belongings. They've left it here as I asked, as they should have. They probably figured I wouldn't talk with Robert until he met my demands."

"Perhaps." Oran folded his arms across his broad chest, his brow lifting. "Perhaps not. The car will be here when Ian gives the word that we can open the gates to retrieve it in the morn."

"At least call him on your cell phone and let him know it's here. That he doesn't need to go to war over this."

"Lass, unless the castle is on fire, we dinna disturb our laird in the middle of the night. Especially not since he picked a mate."

"Fine. I'll wake Cearnach. He's next in command, right?"

Oran's mouth kicked up at the corner a bit. "If Ian isn't here, aye."

"He isn't. He's *indisposed*." She stormed back toward the keep as fast as she could manage. She imagined her rental car vanishing before she was able to return for it, just like before.

Oran chuckled. "Cearnach has his hands full."

"But will she be returning when she wakes him?" one of the men hollered from the top of the wall walk, humor lacing his words.

Elaine snorted. Cearnach would want to see if his stuff had been returned as much as she did hers.

Annoyed with Oran, Elaine hurried to the stairs to Cearnach's bedchamber. When she reached his door, she opened, then closed it. She heard nothing but his quiet breathing and knew he was still sound asleep, never aware that she'd left him alone in the first place. She rushed around the bed to his side and yanked open the curtains.

His eyes popped open, and he grabbed a sword sheathed beside the bed that she had not noticed before.

Eyes wide, Elaine quickly moved back out of the path of the Highland warrior, afraid he wasn't awake enough to realize she wasn't a threat to him. "It's just me, Cearnach," she said in a rush.

"Lass, what are you doing out of bed?" Then he frowned. "Flynn hasn't been bothering you, has he?"

"No. I heard the dogs barking and then wolves howling and went to see what the matter was. The McKinleys and Kilpatricks were prowling through your woods in wolf form."

"Ah, that's the trouble." He sheathed his sword and reached out to snag her hand.

Before she could dodge away from his quick action,

knowing just where this would lead if she didn't, he had her by the wrist, stopping her, his mouth curved up, warning her that she shouldn't have awakened him. He pulled her into bed with him. "You're freezing. You shouldn't have been running around the bailey without being more properly dressed. I'll warm you up."

He tugged off one of her boots and then the other.

"They brought my car back," she said, trying to free herself, but he was all muscled arms and legs and body, claiming her as he pulled the covers over them. Yet she thought if he knew the importance of why she wanted to leave the bed and wanted him to go with her, he'd agree and help retrieve her car. Surely.

"Even your nose is cold, lass," he said, kissing it.

So much for him being interested in the return of her car.

"Cearnach," she said sharply, trying to get him to pay attention to her. "My rental car—"

"Will be there in the morning if you have come to tell me they delivered it and it is beyond our gate, which is closed for now. It won't be opened without Ian's approval, and he would not give it at this time of night…"

"Because he's with his new mate, your cousin said."

"Aye, true enough."

"Well, since you're second in charge…"

"When Ian is not on the premises or otherwise indisposed."

"Then he's otherwise indisposed…"

"If the matter is of the utmost importance." He kissed her cheeks, his hands caressing her breasts, his thumbs stroking her nipples.

"It is."

"Nay, it is not. The gate stays closed, except like last night when the pack was waiting for our return and the others who went searching for us. Keeping the gate closed now means security of the pack. The car can wait until morning. This can't." He pressed his heavy, hard erection against her thigh. "Lass," Cearnach said, with such longing that she couldn't have fought him to come with her outside even if she'd wanted to.

The men at the wall walk had been right. Once she woke Cearnach, he wasn't about to let her leave his bed again that night. As much as she wanted her car back, and everything else her cousins had stolen, she wanted these stolen moments with Cearnach more. She also realized he was right about leaving the gate closed. She had been alone for so long, dealing with issues on her own, never with a pack to worry about or to be concerned about her. The notion was so alien that she couldn't get used to it.

"You smell of the wind and fresh air, of the piney woods and the moisture from the thick mist." He breathed in the scents that had collected in her hair like those of a wolf that had gathered interesting smells in her fur while exploring the woods, returned to the pack, and shared the scents with the rest of the members.

"You smell of sandalwood soap and sexy man," she murmured against his mouth.

He took that as an open invitation to another mating.

"Why didn't you wake me?" he asked, sliding his hands beneath her sweater, his hands hot against her cold breasts.

"I tried," she said, leaning back against the bed and closing her eyes as she absorbed the feeling of his fingers splayed across her aching breasts.

"Not hard enough," he said, pushing the sweater up until her breasts were exposed. "You're ice cold. You shouldn't have been running around outside without me." He licked a nipple. "Certainly not without wearing a heavy coat when you're not used to our weather."

He leaned across her waist and licked her other nipple.

She smoothed his hair down, her eyes watching him, a small smile playing on her lips. "I love you."

"I know you do," he said.

He grinned and her smile broadened, right before she tried to push him aside. He didn't budge. Instead, he clasped her wrists with one hand and held them above her head. Then with his mouth, he trailed kisses from her low-cut jeans to her throat and her mouth again.

"You think you're one hot, bad wolf and in charge of me, don't you?" she taunted.

"One hot, sexy Highland wolf armed and not wearing his kilt," he said, tugging her jeans button open, then pulling the zipper down.

He smelled her scent: intrigued, excited, and sexually aroused.

"You'll have to let go of me if you want me naked."

"Nay, lass. I know what I'm doing." He flipped her over and pinned her down with his body, his hands sliding underneath her, over her belly, up to her breasts until he had handfuls of the beautiful soft mounds. His body moved over hers, letting her feel his growing desire for her.

"Hmm," she groaned, even though she didn't want him to know how much he was turning her on.

He slid his hand down the front of her jeans, lower until he cupped her mound. He held her like that, as if he held her treasure in the palm of his hand, waiting for her reaction.

"Cearnach," she pleaded.

He inserted his middle finger into her as deeply as he could.

"More," she whispered.

He pulled off her sweater, then kissed her naked back. He pushed her hair aside and licked her neck.

She shivered, loving the sensation, and tried to turn over.

"Nay, lass. I'm in charge. The big, sexy Highland wolf, remember?"

"Bad wolf," she said, and took a deep breath of his musky scent, validating his level of arousal.

He chuckled. Grabbing her waistband, he slid her jeans over her hips and buttocks, down her thighs and shins, until he could tug them off completely and toss them to the floor.

He pushed her legs apart, his arousal already painful with readiness. Kissing her shoulders and back and neck, he slipped his hands under her breasts and gave them another gentle squeeze.

"You shouldn't have left the bed, lass," he said again.

She murmured a gratifying sound, not agreeing with his words, but with what he was doing to her body. Her nipples were sexy peaks, and he could smell her arousal, wet and ready for his penetration.

He kissed each buttock as she barely breathed.

He was throbbing already with pent-up need. Kissing her ear, he stroked her clit and rubbed his body against her soft globes, making her moan. She smelled and tasted and felt and sounded delicious. His fingers slid into her creamy sex, then stroked her swollen nub. Opening for him, she spread her legs, knees drawing up so he had better access.

He groaned with the need to penetrate her, to release the burning craving to have her.

He entered her folds with his hot, rigid penis and pushed hard.

"Oh, yes," she panted, as he pulled his hips back, then plunged into her even more deeply. She moved against him, encouraging him, driving him.

His hand slid back into the thick curls covering her sex, and he stroked her bud again. He could feel her fever pitch, the rising tide nearly swallowing her whole, and then the crash as she buried her mouth against the mattress and screamed his muffled name.

He stiffened, driving into her until he felt the release coming. He jerked with the sensation, felt the shudders of her climax squeezing his cock in a pleasurable, wet, hot way, and collapsed.

He wanted to stay like this, buried inside her, pinning her to the mattress, keeping her in his bed where she belonged, not running around the inner bailey seeking a way to get to her rental car.

Tomorrow would be soon enough to learn what they could about the car.

Chapter 24

THE NEXT MORNING, TANGLED TOGETHER AND HALF asleep, the bed curtains drawn around them and hiding them from the world, Elaine cuddled against Cearnach. He was the most consummate, tender lover she'd ever had, and she was thinking that she never wanted to let go of him when a knock sounded on the bedchamber door.

Cearnach growled at the interruption of their half sleepy bliss. Elaine stroked his arm with a soothing caress. He uttered a low, "Hmm," that was part loving her touch, part rough with need.

Guthrie said beyond the door, "Cearnach, a word with you." He sounded gruff and concerned.

Cearnach groaned, moving out from under Elaine as she stirred. She realized then that she had captured him again in the middle of the night, her leg resting over his, locking him in place. He was hers. She loved possessing him when *he* thought he possessed *her*.

Only this time they were completely naked.

She wasn't awake enough to fully register the worry in Guthrie's voice. Or maybe it was that Cearnach didn't seem to think the world was coming to an end in the way he moved, stretching his sleeping muscles and giving her a view of a hot body that was muscled, toned, and with an erection that had her taking a second look. She was ready to pull him back into bed with her.

As if he knew just what she was thinking, Cearnach winked at her, then threw on a pair of boxers and went to the door and pulled it open.

"Aye, Guthrie? What's so wrong that you couldn't have waited until *later* this morning?" He sounded like a growly Highland bear.

"Oran said that Ian wished to let you know he is having the gate opened and wanted you to be there."

The car! How could she have forgotten all about it? Cearnach did that to her. Just the way he had worked his magic on her, bringing her to a thousand pleasures with his touch half the night.

She quickly sat up, wanting to leave the bed, get dressed, and race down to the gate. But she had no clothes near enough to the bed that she could grab. Guthrie stood on the threshold of Cearnach's room, though he couldn't see her for the curtains drawn around her side of the bed.

"I'll be down at once," Cearnach said. He sounded like he was ready for battle.

"Me, too," Elaine called out from the curtained bed. She wasn't going to be left out of this. "Close the door so I can get dressed."

"Ian doesn't want any women in the inner bailey until we ensure it's safe for everyone." Guthrie sounded as tactful as a man could be who was giving her orders.

"I'm going," she reiterated, not about to be stopped in her mission.

Cearnach cleared his throat and said to Guthrie, "We'll be right down."

If he thought to change her mind, Cearnach was welcome to attempt it, but she wasn't buying it. She half expected Cearnach to close the door, ending the discussion with his brother. But he didn't.

"Ian won't like it," Guthrie said to Cearnach.

"He doesn't have to like it." Elaine spoke as if the conversation included her. She wasn't being left out of this. "The car is registered in my name. I want to make sure everything's there."

"You can do so once the car is within our gates and everything is secure. He's your pack leader now, lass." Guthrie acted as though she needed reminding.

"See you in a moment," Cearnach said to his brother. The door shut, then Cearnach opened the curtains to her side of the bed and smiled down at her. He was all warmth and energy, and if not for the car business, she would have tugged him into bed again.

Frowning up at him, she let out her breath. "I won't be coddled."

"Or dictated to," he said.

"Right."

He touched her cheek with a gentle caress, eyeing the bruise that remained. "If you have your heart set on doing this, hurry and get dressed as Ian won't wait for us once he's decided to do something."

She quickly climbed out of bed, then headed for the bathroom. "He really doesn't expect a force of Kilpatricks and McKinleys to attack, does he?"

"As a battle-trained warrior and leader of men, he always prepares for the worst."

She didn't believe anyone would attack whoever retrieved the car. Not when the castle was so well defended. And not if Robert wanted to meet with her.

She quickly washed off in the shower, barely drying

herself, then struggled to get into a pair of jeans and sweater, her skin still wet in places.

As if he knew her thoughts on the matter, Cearnach said, "We wouldn't put it past them to offer a show of force. They will not like that they had to return your car here instead of you coming to them."

She joined him in the bedroom and sat down, but before she could slip on a pair of boots, Cearnach leaned over and pulled one on for her. He wasn't just doing so to help hurry her along. Smelling her scent, he was checking how she felt about this whole issue. He would recognize that she was both afraid and pissed.

She ruffled his hair with her hand. "I'm not worried." She slipped her other boot on. Well, maybe a little worried. She was concerned for everyone's safety, should her kin attack them. She was much more pissed, and she hoped that scent reigned over all else.

"You smell delicious," he murmured, looking up at her as he crouched at her booted feet, his hands shifting to her knees, then sliding higher.

He pushed her knees apart, suggesting he wanted her again. Moving in between her legs, he cupped her face in his large hands and kissed her mouth tenderly and lovingly, his tongue darting into her mouth gently, and then hungrily as a groan escaped his lips. Liquid heat poured through every inch of her, making her instantly wet for him. He smiled, so wickedly sexy, and took another deep breath of her, his smile growing.

"You are so bad," she said, shoving at his shoulders, but she didn't budge him.

"What?" He feigned innocence as he rose and towered over her, pulling her to her feet.

"For making me want you so badly."

He chuckled, grabbed her hand, and headed out the door.

His mother was on her way down the hall and quickly said, "I want to speak with Elaine."

"Later, my lady mother."

His mother furrowed her brows. "She can't go out there. It's too dangerous."

"I will protect her." He headed down the hall.

His mother snorted. He glanced over his shoulder at her.

"They'll pull something. They're pirates," his mother warned.

"Aye, of that I'm well aware."

When she and Cearnach left the keep and made their way across the inner bailey, she saw a small crowd of men and wolves gathered near the gates to the entrance of the bailey. She realized after they opened the wooden gates that the defenses protecting the front entrance included three portcullises with an area in between each other where invading armies could be scalded with boiling water or struck with arrows, reducing their chances of successfully entering the inner bailey. All of the portcullises were down.

She still thought that the pack's extreme caution was unwarranted, though what did she know about Highland wolf fighting?

As soon as Ian and his brothers turned to see them approach, Ian gave her a bow of his head in greeting. Guthrie had his arms folded across his chest, his brow furrowed, and appeared very annoyed with her.

Duncan gave her a small smile.

Ian said to Cearnach, "You'll stay with her?"

"Aye."

So Cearnach would be forced to babysit her. "Cearnach can go." She didn't want him to feel obligated to stand beside her the whole time.

A few of the men chuckled. The wolves quit panting and swung their heads from looking at her to observing Ian.

"You're my responsibility, Elaine, first and foremost." Cearnach sounded proud of the fact.

Ian said to Duncan, "Ready?"

"Aye," Duncan said and pulled out his sword.

"What if the men—saying that there are any out there, hiding, waiting—have guns?" Elaine whispered to Cearnach.

"Not sporting enough." Cearnach folded his arms as he stood so close to her that his body was touching hers. She felt pleasure, warmth, and security in the intimate contact on this cold, windy, damp day.

Men lifted the first of the portcullises, which made a grinding sound all the way up.

Duncan and Ian headed toward the next one, six wolves walking beside them.

"Are the wolves still out there?" Elaine asked, her voice hushed. She hadn't heard them in the middle of the night again.

"They might be. We don't want to take any chances."

The second portcullis whined as it was raised, and the men and wolves continued on their way.

Another dozen or so wolves, men, and Guthrie still stood protectively near Elaine.

The last of the portcullises was opened, and when

Cearnach's brothers and the wolves reached the final gate, Ian waited to give the order to open it.

He glanced up at the tower. Oran nodded that it was all clear. Ian said, "Open the gates."

The gates creaked open as two men put their backs into moving them aside, the oak so heavy she imagined only muscled men could manage.

Then she saw her vehicle—undamaged. Thank God. Water droplets collected on its shiny silver surface, but the Mercedes looked the same as it had when she saw it last night; only in the daytime the scene appeared a lot less scary. A thick fog still clung to the trees surrounding the castle, and she couldn't make out the long curving drive because of the heavy mist.

Tension was riding high as everyone in the inner bailey waited, barely breathing. She heard the swishing sound of a few swords being unsheathed to the left and right of her position as Ian and the other men and wolves headed beyond the gate and moved toward the car.

Every muscle in her body was straining with tension, and she could tell Cearnach's were the same by the way he stiffened next to her. All eyes were on the men exposed beyond the castle walls. Several were standing on top of the wall walk, and she noticed then, they were equipped with bows and arrows. She felt she had suddenly become immersed in a Highland battle.

Ian approached the driver's door of the vehicle, and she worried that her cousins might have planted a bomb inside. What if she had been the one to drive it into the inner bailey? They would know she wouldn't. That one of the men would.

The wolves sniffed around the car, and she wondered

if they could detect the smell of bomb-making material. Sure they could, as sensitive as their sense of smell was.

Duncan made a move to open the door. She held her breath.

He pulled the door ajar and the buzzer sounded, indicating that the keys were in the ignition. The car had been sitting in the drive all night with the keys in the ignition? *Great*. Someone could have stolen it. Then she rethought that scenario. The MacNeill men probably had been watching the vehicle from the wall walk all night long. If anyone had made a move to get near it, their archers could have prevented it.

Duncan jerked the passenger's door open. Ian leaned inside. The trunk lid popped open.

Ian's cousin Oran peered into the trunk, sword ready. "All clear," he shouted.

So they thought her rental vehicle might be like the Trojan horse, bearing armed soldiers instead of gifts? Or in this case, her clothes and Cearnach's?

She started to move forward now that the car was safe, but Cearnach seized her arm and glanced down at her, wearing a fearsome expression. "Wait."

The single word was both a command and a plea. He wished to protect her above all else.

She nodded, acknowledging that he knew the Highlanders and their tactics better than she did. Ian got into the car with Duncan and they drove in through the gates.

Guthrie said to Cearnach, "We finally broke into the man's computer at the keep that Elaine owns."

Expectantly, Cearnach and Elaine looked at him, waiting to hear what he'd learned.

Guthrie frowned. "Nothing. He's lived centuries like us undoubtedly. Yet there was nothing in the keep or on his computer to say a thing about him. As if the place was a model home. Clothes in the drawers, and necessities in other drawers, food in the kitchen. Nothing personal. Not one thing. No financial statements, bills, nothing."

"Which means?" Cearnach asked.

"He knew we'd investigate the place. Maybe that Elaine would, and he didn't want her to know anything about him."

Without warning, wolves snarled and growled in the woods, and then attacked.

Cearnach shoved Elaine behind him as a pack of at least a couple of dozen wolves raced out of the woods flanking the drive to the castle. In the inner bailey, Ian and Duncan threw open the doors to the car and hopped out. Some of the wolves went after Ian and Duncan, none getting too close to the men's swords, while the six MacNeill wolves were fighting with those of the McKinleys'. Another dozen or more McKinley wolves ran through the gate, targeting the rest of the men in the inner bailey.

Damnation! Cearnach couldn't protect Elaine like this. "Run to the kennels," Cearnach shouted. "Lock yourself in."

The kennels were much closer than the keep, if she could just reach them in time.

Guthrie and Cearnach swung their swords at two of the wolves while the others were fighting her cousins in wolf form.

Something more than wanting the treasure had stirred them to fight. Did they think Calla was staying at the castle? Was Baird going to war for her? Was the treasure worth a lot more than they had imagined, and Kilpatrick would do anything to get hold of it?

Elaine barely made it into the kennel, slamming the door behind her, as a wolf crashed into it, unable to turn away fast enough.

Cearnach pivoted to fight a wolf, glad Elaine was inside the kennel. Yet he still wished she was safely inside the keep and that he'd insisted that she stay there in the first place, even if it hurt her fiercely independent pride.

Chapter 25

THE DOGS IN THE KENNEL WERE BARKING SO LOUDLY that Elaine could hardly hear anything else as she slammed the kennel door, her heart pounding furiously as she quickly locked herself in.

For the briefest instant, she thought maybe Cearnach had been right. She should have stayed in the keep until they knew for sure everything was safe.

She shook her head. She couldn't have done it. If she had to do it all over again, though, she'd have armed herself with one of Cearnach's swords. She knew how to use one.

Secure the back door, she thought, but before she could turn to race that way and lock it, a man said in a harsh voice, "Hello, dear sweet Elaine, my mate, my darling." Though his voice was roughened with age, it couldn't be anyone other than Kelly Rafferty. "'Tis a treasure you were seeking, lass, when you returned to Scotland. 'Tis a treasure you have found."

The blood drained from her face, her head becoming so light that she could barely stand. *Kelly Rafferty. Him.*

She turned around, afraid to see him, and saw the brute, older. He had the same leering expression as he devoured her with his green eyes. His long red hair hung around his shoulders and he was naked.

"You," she said, gasping out the word and wondering

if he was like Flynn, a ghostly visage, not real. She had to admit he looked damn real.

"Who hit you?" he said darkly, his gaze focusing on her bruised cheek as if he wanted to kill the bastard himself. *He* was the only one allowed to beat on her.

She reached up to touch her bruised face but stilled her hand.

He couldn't be real. She couldn't be mated to two wolves. She wanted to die. She probably would be dead as soon as Kelly knew she'd taken Cearnach as her mate. No, he'd want to keep her, abuse her, ensure she knew she was his property forever.

"*I* am the treasure you are seeking," he said again as he moved toward her, and she realized that he must have slipped around the back of the kennels as a wolf while everyone else was a distraction. "You are mine."

No, no, no. She hadn't been his for centuries.

"You're dead," she said, her voice a whisper.

She couldn't seem to catch her breath, to react. She'd feared and hated this man for the year they'd been together. She'd wanted to escape him, free herself from her bond to him. Every time he'd struck her, she'd wanted to fight back and kill him.

She'd known beyond a doubt, with all the passing years, that he was dead.

He had to be dead.

He smiled, the look so sinister that she knew he'd take a belt to her again, break her jaw, beat her until she barely lived. She wouldn't let him this time. She wouldn't let him beat her ever again.

"Why come for me now?" She backed toward the locked door, her legs wobbly from the shock of seeing

him, her thoughts in turmoil as she tried to recall anything that would have clued her in that he had always
been alive.

"I killed the last of my crew that had left me for dead,"
he said, standing still, not drawing any closer now.

"No, no," she said, recalling the words of one of his
men who had come for her. "Your crew said that your
quartermaster murdered you because you cheated him.
After he killed you, they left *him* for dead because of
what he'd done to you. *He'd* betrayed you. Not them."

A sinister light glowed in his eyes. "My quartermaster? So they thought to make you feel they were justified
in killing Terrance? He'd punished them for infractions
on the ship, and the men wanted him dead also. They
quickly turned on both of us, knowing that if one lived,
the survivor would make them pay for their traitorous
deeds. Which I did anyway. I never cheated my quartermaster out of his fair share of the treasure. He was worth
his weight in gold to me."

Despite his apparent fondness for Terrance, Rafferty
was a cold-blooded murderer, a pirate, a thief, a demon.
So were his men. Cutthroats, every last one of them.

The only good she'd seen in Rafferty was that he'd
loved his father, as much as he could love anyone. The
drunken, whoring man had drowned himself acciden-
tally after going on a drinking binge while Rafferty was
away at sea. It was the only time she'd ever seen Kelly's
eyes moisten with tears. Yet he'd quickly hidden his
feelings behind a mask of indifference, swearing that
his father's love of whisky had been his undoing.

"I hired men to watch you for years. Ever wonder
why all those beta wolves who'd expressed an interest

in you suddenly just… vanished?" he said, breaking into her thoughts, his tone cold and imperious.

Her stomach fell. He was crazed with vengeance and willing to murder.

"You… killed my suitors," she whispered, barely able to get the words out. "You were dead," she said again. "Your men told me so. You never returned to dispute their claim."

Innocent. The men who had courted her had been innocent of any crime. She'd never suspected they'd been murdered. Just disappeared from her life. She'd always believed they had chickened out, been afraid to take up with an alpha.

She clenched her teeth and narrowed her eyes. He'd murdered them.

She knew—even if he hadn't come clean with her when she'd asked him before—that he had killed her parents. "You… murdered… my… parents."

"Lass," he said, coaxing her to see him for what he truly was. "You cannot still believe that. I never harmed your parents. I was there to pick up the pieces of your shattered life after they had that unfortunate carriage accident."

Unfortunate. Her thoughts were whirling around and around as if in a tidal pool, threatening to drown her. He'd had so much control over her life once her parents died. What if her uncles had survived?

Her mouth dropped open. How had Lord Whittington known to arrest her uncles? Who had told him they would be arriving at port?

She'd always suspected that someone they'd stolen from had recognized them when they disembarked from the ship. What if Lord Whittington had prior warning instead? What if Rafferty had known all along where her uncles were going? And had planned to murder them to ensure they didn't get in the way of him mating with her?

Rafferty had been furious when her uncles said they were taking her with them instead of allowing him to marry her right away. But why not have a ship accost them at sea?

Because she would have known it was Rafferty's ship, his men, his plan. He had already set the wheels in motion to destroy her uncles in another way.

He would have known where they were going. She could see him planning this from the start. He could have sent word ahead to let Lord Whittington know her uncles were arriving in St. Andrews on an approximate date.

"You knew about my uncles. That they were hanged," she said.

"Aye, of course. When I caught up with you, you were beside yourself with grief. Though you would not share with me what had happened, I learned soon enough what had become of them." He shrugged. "They met their fate as so many of our kind do."

"You had nothing to do with it?"

He didn't even attempt to hide the wicked way his lip curled up. He stretched his hands out in appeasement and sighed. "They knew not to take you with them. I warned them."

"You murdering bastard. You would have had them killed anyway, whether I had joined them or not."

He sighed and changed the subject. "I've been here all along. You are my mate and now we are finally together again. You cannot have another. I encouraged

Robert Kilpatrick to entice you to come to Scotland to find the Hawthorn treasure—'tis me, lass." He looked demonically pleased with himself.

"You… you *paid* him?" Her cousin was even in on this? He had known she was still mated?

"Aye. Only he disappointed me. He stranded you with one of the MacNeill brothers. You cannot know how infuriated that made me. By the time he learned that you were his cousin, the same one he was to bring to me, it was already too late."

Rafferty folded his arms, still too far away from her, but as soon as he drew close enough, she could only think to do one thing. Jam her knee into his naked groin. Bring the murdering bastard to his knees.

"Can I tell you how encouraging it was for me to spy you on the ramparts late last night and how discouraging that I could not reach you?" he asked.

"Why have you come for me now? Why not earlier?"

His gaze narrowed on her. "I thought you might have paid my men to mutiny on the ship. That you paid them to have me killed. I know you wanted to. They murdered my quartermaster first as he came out of my cabin, thinking it was me. He didn't stand a chance. Poor Terrance."

"Ha! You cheated your crew. You and your quartermaster." She remembered clearly that day, hearing the men talking about the spoils and how the captain and the quartermaster had cheated their crew. One of the men guarding her had overheard, too. He'd glanced her way as he escorted her to the parlor, as if wondering if she'd tell her mate that one of their men had learned the truth. Then the man gave her a small smile, as if to say that if the men mutinied, she would be free of her husband

and not to stand in their way. If she warned her husband, there would be dire consequences for her also.

"Your men wanted vengeance. Their actions had nothing to do with me," she said.

"I nearly died," he said, as if he hadn't heard her, caught up in the past, a faraway look on his grizzled face.

She realized then that he'd thought he was invincible. That by ruling with an iron fist, he could force his men to do as he bid, no matter what. He'd been wrong. The money his crew thought they were owed had been enough of an incentive to mutiny.

"You were dead," she said again.

"Nay, Elaine, my love. I *nearly* died. Vengeance was mine. After years of tracking down my would-be murderers and learning that you were not behind the mutiny, I finished the last of them off and contacted your Kilpatrick cousin, recalling he had some interest in you."

She wanted to close her eyes and reopen them to see him gone.

"Tell… me… the… truth. My parents. You murdered them. It wasn't an accident."

He shrugged. "I don't know why you insist on learning the truth. There were too many of us in competition. I wanted their ships, their manors, and you in the bargain."

"You didn't really want me. You wanted the properties that my parents bequeathed to me."

"That's where you're wrong, love. I wanted you. Desperately, I wanted you. Your father would not agree."

Her lips parted in surprise. Her father had tried to protect her?

"If you wanted me so badly, you wouldn't have waited that long to come for me," she growled.

He let out a heavy sigh of exasperation. "You're right. You always were a canny lass. I was shipwrecked on that blasted island. And then I didn't remember who I was for over a century. I didn't recall that I had a mate, or that I was the captain of a fleet of pirate ships, or that my blood-thirsty crew had thrown me overboard to fend for myself.

"I didn't even remember I was born in Ireland, but everyone said I had an Irish accent, and I had to be from there. So when I was able, I returned to Ireland. I recalled having been a sailor, so I began to work aboard ships again. Then the memories came flooding back. All of them at once. You. My men. The treasure. The mutiny. I had to make things right. First, the men had to go." He stalked toward her again.

Her heart beat frantically. She had to keep her head. If he struck her, he could knock her out. He'd done it before. One blow to the head.

She would be defenseless against him. What did he plan to do? He couldn't spirit her away from here. Not like he was now, naked, not with the castle defended by the MacNeill clan, who would fight him to the death.

The dogs in the kennel were still barking wildly about the commotion outside, though a few were quiet, watching her through the gates of their kennel rooms. No one but the dogs would even hear her scream.

Would she have enough time to turn and unlock the door, or could she catch him off guard and knee him where it would hurt most?

"Your solicitor told Robert you mated a MacNeill. You can't have another mate. If you come quietly with me, I won't have him killed like I did the others who dared approach you with the notion of mating. Wolf law,

Elaine. I was first. The others who wanted you are all dead. In this case, I have every right to take my pound of flesh. Remember that."

Unless you are dead.

"He's not the only reason you should leave here, Elaine, sweeting. You remember Calla? The pretty wolf whose wedding you attended?"

Elaine's stomach fell and Rafferty smirked. "Aye. Lady MacNeill called her to arrange your wedding to her son, and she was on her way here when I… stopped her. The she-wolf is conveniently tied up. I don't care anything about her, so if you'll leave with me, I'll release her unharmed. The time to make a decision is running out."

The bastard could be lying. Then again, what if he wasn't?

"They won't let me leave," she said.

"Make a run for it, dearest. Unlock the door. The car's in the inner bailey. Jump into it and drive off. It's the only chance you'll have at getting away from them. You know you can't have the MacNeill bastard who wants you. Cearnach? Is that his name?"

She couldn't stay here. Not with Cearnach when she was still mated to Rafferty. She had to leave Argent Castle. She had to get away. Away from Rafferty. Away from this new home that she couldn't have.

But Robert had her ID, her money, everything.

No, it was in the car. If she could disable Rafferty and get to her rental car and all her personal items, she could escape. But Calla. What if he really had Calla?

If he wanted Elaine to run, that wasn't a good thing. He needed her beyond the castle walls.

She couldn't just kill Rafferty, either, or she'd be just like him. Not that she had anything she could use to kill him with. Unless she shifted. And only if he remained in his human form. She knew he wouldn't let her strip off her clothes, shift into the wolf, and tear into him.

An odd mist formed behind Rafferty. She stared past him, just as a hefty, younger man appeared, wearing what looked like an ancient plaid and a pirate's kind of shirt.

"Flynn, my lady," he said to her in greeting, bowing slightly.

"You're…" Her mouth gaped. She glanced back at Rafferty, but he didn't seem to see the apparition.

Flynn looked as real to her as Rafferty did.

"Why are you here?" she asked Flynn, feeling foolish for even speaking to a specter.

"I told you," Rafferty said.

"To save you, lass. Cearnach is busy." Flynn unsheathed a sword, but she didn't hear the telltale swishing sound of metal pulling from the leather scabbard. That was because there could be no sound. His sword and scabbard were as much apparitions as he was. He sliced the sword through Rafferty, but it had no effect on the man.

"Do you know if Calla is safe?"

The ghost frowned. "Nay, lass."

Rafferty took another step forward, stretching his hand out to grab her wrist. "I'm here because you mated with me and you belong to me. We could go together to the car with my arm securely around your neck, threatening to choke you to death if you don't go peaceably. You know I don't make idle threats."

No, he didn't.

She whipped around and unlocked the door. Her

heart was beating as if it was trying to get out of her chest, but she couldn't breathe.

She yanked the door open. Saw the mayhem in the bailey. The fighting and snarling wolves. Saw Cearnach sword-fighting with a man she didn't know. Heard the dogs barking even louder behind her now. Knew she'd never see any of them again.

If only Rafferty had died long ago.

She bolted for the car, the driver's door still open, and jumped in, jerking the door shut before Rafferty in the form of a wolf tried to join her. His body slammed into the door with a loud thump.

Keys in the ignition, she flipped the engine on and jerked the steering wheel to the left, turning hard until she'd maneuvered through the battling men and wolves. She saw Cearnach glance up from where he was fighting, saw the look of horror on his face, his sword lowered in his hand, watched his brothers look in her direction with disbelief, and that blasted Kelly Rafferty racing after her in wolf form.

He'd never catch up to her. Ever again.

Not if she could help it.

Then she saw Cearnach running for the garage. "No, Cearnach!" she shouted from the car. Tears trailed down her cheeks.

She wanted to die.

Chapter 26

CEARNACH WAS SO ANGRY THAT HE COULD BARELY think straight except for the need to go after Elaine. What in the world was she doing? He'd thought she'd be safe in the kennels. He knew he'd been wrong when he saw the wolf racing out of the building after her and Elaine heading for her car. At first, he'd been stunned. He thought she meant to get into the car for protection, lock the doors, and stay there until he could kill the wolf.

When she drove off, he couldn't figure out what was going through her head.

"Elaine," he said, half groaning her name.

Duncan was right behind him, his boots tromping against the pavers. Out of his peripheral vision, Cearnach saw Guthrie headed for another car.

"Where the hell is she going?" Duncan yelled.

"Damned if I know," Cearnach said, climbing into the car and slamming the door.

As soon as Duncan shut his door, Cearnach tore out of the garage, men and wolves scattering to get out of his path.

The wolves and men from the enemy clan took off toward the gate, escaping, as if they'd finally gotten what they'd wanted: Elaine beyond the protective walls surrounding the keep.

"She can't believe that her leaving will stop the fighting."

Actually it had, damn it, but how could she believe they couldn't deal with her kin in a satisfactory manner?

"Did you recognize the wolf who was in the kennels with her?" Cearnach asked, unable to suppress his anger and concern.

In the rearview mirror, he saw Guthrie barreling down the drive after him and Ian giving orders in the inner bailey, waving his hands, red-faced and angry. Not at his brothers. He knew they'd do whatever was right to bring Elaine back to the pack. Ian was furious with her kin for attacking them at Argent Castle.

"He wasn't any of the McKinleys or Kilpatricks," Duncan warned. "He'd been in her rental car. I smelled his scent when I opened the door and took a good whiff. I smelled him again when he ran past me to get to her. Worse?"

Cearnach glanced at his brother.

"He's the wolf who's been living in her keep."

"Why? Who the hell is he?"

"A henchman of her clansmen?" Duncan guessed.

Cearnach shook his head. "It's personal between Elaine and him. Whoever he was, he forced her to run. Now she's beyond the keep and beyond our protection." He mulled the situation over further, but he couldn't come up with any logical explanation.

"You don't think whoever it was told her where the stolen goods were located, and she had to get there before someone else did, do you?" Duncan asked, then shook his head as if dismissing the idea. "She probably doesn't know these roads that well. I doubt she'd be able to find any place quickly. She looked terrified when she raced past us."

Cearnach recalled how she'd missed the turnoff to Senton Castle before. He didn't think she'd easily find her way anywhere quickly without someone to guide her.

"Where is she going?" Cearnach asked, thinking out loud and not expecting Duncan to know any more than he did.

"I'm not sure." Duncan put his cell on speakerphone and called their brother. "Ian, we're pursuing Elaine. We have no idea where she's headed."

"What happened?" Ian asked.

"We don't know. The wolf who was with her in the kennels forced her to run. That's all we can figure."

"Bring the lass back," Ian said. "Whatever she's afraid of, we'll straighten it out. We'll be cleaning things up here. Let me know what's happening and where she's headed. I'll send backup as soon as you have some idea."

"Aye, Ian. Thanks." Duncan rested his phone on his lap. "Are you sure she went this way and not toward Edinburgh and the airport?"

"Why in bloody hell would she be going there?" Cearnach growled.

"Just a thought, Cearnach. I haven't any idea why she would. Or why she would leave our protection."

"Her solicitor wanted to speak to her alone," Cearnach said. The notion continued to bother him. Something had been wrong from the start.

Duncan didn't say anything.

Cearnach let out his breath. "It was something important. Something he said he'd ask Kilpatrick if it was all right to discuss with her."

Duncan pulled out his cell. "What's his name?"

"Hoover."

"Is he a wolf?"

"Aye."

Duncan searched for the number, then finding it, tapped on his cell and put it on speakerphone. "Mr. Hoover? This is Duncan MacNeill."

"Yes, sir? What may I do for you?"

Cearnach thought the solicitor sounded defensive, like a wolf backed up against a wall, even though he couldn't know why someone from the MacNeill wolf pack was calling him.

"I'm calling on behalf of Elaine Hawthorn, mate of my brother, Cearnach. You had some news for her but didn't wish to give it to her. Some important news. I need to know what it was." Duncan was all business, his voice taking on a tell-me-or-else tone. Most wolves would bend to the pressure.

"I'm sorry, sir. I can't give that information out to anyone but—"

Typical solicitor response. Wouldn't work with alpha male wolves who expected an answer… pronto.

"Fine. We'll come call on you, and then you can decide if your answer is still the same," Duncan said, his voice so dark that even Cearnach glanced his way. Duncan gave Cearnach an evil smile, his brows elevated just a fraction.

"Sir, if you're threatening me—"

Cearnach couldn't help snorting.

"I'm making a promise. I don't threaten anyone," Duncan said.

Cearnach smiled at that. With just a look, Duncan could change any beta wolf's mind. Hoover was definitely a beta wolf.

Hoover cleared his throat over the phone. "Sir—"

"*Just*… tell… me."

Despite Duncan's ability to get what he wanted out of someone, the man still hesitated. Then probably envisioning Duncan coming to meet him at his office and dealing with the wolf face to face, the solicitor said, "Kelly Rafferty's come for her. He paid Kilpatrick to seek her out and encourage her to come to Scotland."

"Kelly Rafferty? Who the hell is that?" Duncan asked, glancing at Cearnach.

Cearnach nearly grabbed the phone out of his brother's hand. "He's dead! Damn the man."

He knew Elaine wouldn't have lied about it. Why in the hell had the man kept the truth from her about his being alive for so long? Then the realization hit him. That's why she'd run!

Duncan stared at Cearnach, then said, "Who's Kelly Rafferty?"

"Elaine Hawthorn's mate," the solicitor said.

Elaine's cell phone rang, nearly giving her a stroke as she headed away from Argent Castle in the direction of Edinburgh. Robert Kilpatrick had charged up her phone? She lifted it off the seat as she drove as fast as she was able on the narrow, winding road.

"You can't mate with Cearnach," Robert said vehemently.

Elaine glanced in the rearview mirror. No sign of any car yet. She drove faster on the twisting road, hoping she wouldn't end up in the trees, her car disabled like Cearnach's had been.

"You knew all along, didn't you? That Rafferty was still alive."

"Oh, aye, lass. You've come home to him. The near-death experience changed him," Robert said as if he was assuring her that the man was someone she'd want to be with again. "When he could, he made his way here. He's been living here as a respectable businessman. He owns three pubs and a hotel. He gave up on ships after he was able to make his fortune and settle here."

Elaine didn't believe Rafferty was a changed man. She understood his need for revenge, that he'd killed the men who'd tried to kill him. But he'd murdered the men who'd wanted to mate her, her parents, and her uncles by having them turned in. None of them had deserved to die.

Tears filled her eyes and she choked back a sob. He hadn't changed. He was the same as before. She didn't want to be mated to him any longer. But wolf law only allowed a mating for life. They didn't believe in divorce, and most never re-mated if they lost their mate early on. The bond between them usually was too great and no other wolf would do.

"I was supposed to meet with you to coordinate a meeting between the two of you later. He was certain you wouldn't go to him if he tried to arrange the meeting himself. Then you didn't arrive and I had to go to the wedding and try to figure out a way to find you... again," Robert said.

For all these years, she'd felt happily secure in the knowledge that Kelly Rafferty was dead.

"Did you know he killed my uncles? Your kin, too?" she asked.

"*Lord Whittington* had them hanged."

"Because Rafferty told him they were arriving in St. Andrews!"

Robert didn't say anything.

"You knew. You wanted their stolen goods. You bastard." She hung up on him. He was just like all the rest—thieving pirates who cared nothing for their distant relatives except for the money they could help them get from the dead.

She drove and drove and drove. The maps she'd used to find her way here were gone. At least her suitcase and purse and clothes all seemed to be in the car.

Then she remembered Calla. She had to get hold of her. To see if Rafferty had lied about holding her hostage. She called information for Cearnach's mother and heard the older woman say, "Elaine, where are you?"

"Did you call Calla to have her go to Argent Castle?"

"Aye, about your wedding. Where… are… you? My sons are frantically searching for you."

"Have you talked with Calla recently?" Elaine asked in a rush. *Please, please, Calla, be okay.*

"Aye, I told her to wait to arrive here until after the fighting ended between the wolf packs. She couldn't come here in the midst of it."

Elaine bit her lip, trying to judge the time that had passed. An hour? Two? "Call her and make sure she's okay."

"She's here, dear. Right here with me. What is this about, lass? Cearnach is ready to have a heart attack over you vanishing like you did."

"There… there won't be any wedding. I had to know Calla was safe."

Elaine stared at the landscape she was passing—a small house in a glen, fenced-in Highland cows, a creek half hidden in woods.

Everything seemed familiar as she drove farther away from Argent Castle. She was sure she was heading back to Edinburgh where she could return the rental car and get a flight out to anywhere that she could. Not to the States, though. She couldn't return there yet. Not without him finding her too quickly.

"Elaine? Calla arrived at Argent Castle a few minutes ago. What's wrong?" Cearnach's mother asked, her voice troubled.

Thanking the heavens Calla was safe, Elaine realized she was in real trouble. "I'm sorry for everything," she said with tears in her voice. "Don't make any wedding plans. There won't be a wedding."

Before her almost mother-in-law could say anything, Elaine cut off the connection and stared at the road she was on, finally recognizing a few of the landmarks. She'd been so shook up that she hadn't realized she had gone the wrong way. She was on the road to Senton Castle.

Like a wolf returning to its own territory, she was back home again—at her family's castle.

She was so turned around. So angry with herself that she could scream. She hated getting lost more than anything else in the world. How could she do this to herself now?

If she continued past the castle, she had no idea where she'd end up.

She pulled into the parking lot at the castle ruins to turn the car around, figuring that she'd have to drive to the nearest city she could find and get directions, when three vehicles rushed in behind her.

Heart nearly failing, she glanced over her shoulder to see them tactically blocking her in. They must have been following her. The road twisted and turned so much that as long as they kept back far enough, she wouldn't spy them. Or maybe they had suspected where she was headed from the direction she had taken and had come straight here. As if she'd come here of her own accord.

Or had they planted a device in the car that would make her easy to follow? Sure, that's why Rafferty had suggested she take the car and run. Oh, how could she have fallen so easily into his trap?

Her heart was pounding so wildly that she didn't know what to do. They'd blocked her in and she had no way to move the car. As a woman, she had no defenses. As a wolf, sure, but if anyone had a tranquilizer dart, she wouldn't stand a chance against her kin, either.

She could run. But they could shift and run after her. Males could catch up to her with their longer legs.

She didn't have a choice.

She closed her eyes. She could only do one thing. Attempt to return to Argent Castle. God, how could this nightmare get any worse?

As much as she hated to, she had to solicit the MacNeills' help to get away. Like Cearnach had intended to aid her so many years ago.

She shoved open the car door, yanked off her clothes, and heard the men shouting, "She's shifting!"

Car doors were thrown open. She willed herself to be a wolf, and before anyone could strip or chase after her, she dashed off. She would never be Rafferty's punching bag again.

She would have to find a way to defend herself in the future. Arm herself. Be prepared. Kill him if he ever found her again.

She raced toward the castle ruins, wishing she had an army of men who could rain arrows down on her own kin. Then she tore down the stairs until she reached the walkway and leaped to the beach. She would have to find her way home. No not home. To Argent Castle. Cearnach's home. Not hers.

He'd be so angry with her. She didn't want to face him. She'd ask Ian instead. He'd probably be just as angry with her. She'd mated with his brother when she should never have done so.

What a mess she'd made of things.

All because she'd returned to Scotland, wanting the treasure, just like her own family whose greed had made them pirates.

She ran as fast as her legs would carry her, knowing some of her kin would turn wolf and follow her. Had they picked up Rafferty, too? Probably. He was much older than her. He probably couldn't keep up with her or the rest of them like some of the younger, stronger wolves.

If they got hold of her and could stop her from running, Rafferty would catch up to her, too.

———◈———

Cearnach had been flooring the gas nearly the whole time and hadn't seen any sign of her on the road ahead. *Which way did you go? Which way, Elaine?*

Duncan's phone rang, and he lifted it off his lap. "Yeah, Guthrie?"

"She's running as a wolf. Up near Senton Castle. Five wolves are trying to track her down. Three are McKinleys—Vardon, Baird, and another brother. And both the Kilpatrick brothers are in hot pursuit," Guthrie said.

Cearnach was already turning his car around.

"How the hell did you know she went that way?" Duncan asked.

"You went one way, I went the opposite," Guthrie said.

"Where's the wolf who met her in the kennel?" Duncan asked.

"Up on the walk to the castle. He's in wolf form still, but he's older, and I figured he's letting the younger wolves chase her down and bring her back to him. Or he's planning on catching up to them if they can grab her and hold her for him." A pause followed. "Hell, he's run after them."

"They're dead wolves," Cearnach growled. Then he frowned. "Why would Rafferty hold back?" Cearnach asked. "He's alpha. I didn't see that she'd been physically abused when she dashed out of the kennel. He's a hitter. He had to know she'd been with another male. And now, up on the walkway. Why would he let the others go after her first? He should have been the first one after her. Why would the bastard have held back?"

"He's older, in charge? Paying the money for her kin to bring her to him? Above chasing her down? In the kennels, he couldn't afford to beat her. Injured, she wouldn't have been able to escape him, or us," Guthrie said. "She appears to be headed south toward our castle."

"Bloody hell," Cearnach said, thinking of how she

knew the way on foot, smelling their scents, tracking better than she could find her way while driving a car. She would face the farmer's wrath again, the dogs, and the falls.

He pulled off onto another road.

"This isn't going to take you to the ruins. Where are you headed?" Duncan asked.

"To intercept her, fight the other wolves, and take her home."

"She's mated to another wolf," Duncan warned.

"Aye." He cast Duncan a dark look that told his brother just what he had in mind.

Duncan nodded. "Aye. Guthrie, you get all that?"

"I don't understand," Guthrie said.

"The wolf who was watching from the pathway is Kelly Rafferty, Elaine's mate. He was thought dead since a year after her uncle's hangings," Cearnach said.

Duncan snorted. "If he's waited that long to reclaim his mate, he doesn't deserve her."

"He beat her, killed her parents, and I suspect, murdered the men who became interested in mating her. He forced the mating. He's a dead wolf," Cearnach said. "She should have known she didn't have to run."

"I remember when she got away from us in St. Andrews, Cearnach," Duncan said. "She was frightened then, had no family to call her own. This is the only thing she knows how to do. To her way of thinking, she's dishonored our clan, the pack, you. She has no family to fall back on. She won't return to Rafferty, so she intends to disappear again."

"Aye, she's a woman. She doesn't think like a warrior," Guthrie said.

"If you don't kill him, I will, Cearnach. She should never have run. She's one of us now," Duncan said.

"I'll kill him," Cearnach promised.

"Where do I need to go to meet up with you?" Guthrie asked.

"A quarter mile south of Oglivie's farm. She'll be headed for the river, and we'll need to stop her kin from pursuing her and keep her from crossing the river," Cearnach said.

"Oglivie's got two border collies," Duncan warned.

"Aye." How well Cearnach knew.

"Meet you there," Guthrie said.

"Be careful," Duncan told him.

"And you."

"She won't make it to the river." Duncan set his phone back on his lap.

"Not without me to help her." Cearnach headed down another road.

Duncan frowned. "You're going to intercept her earlier? You're not going to include Guthrie in the fight?"

"I have to do it this way."

Duncan sighed and folded his arms. "That means facing five wolves."

"I wanted Guthrie with us. But I can't describe the location adequately so that he would find it. The best I can do is to have him meet us beyond the Oglivie's farm and his dogs. We'll rescue her, then take her to the car, then get in touch with Guthrie."

"All right." Duncan made another call. "Ian, she's running as a wolf, headed back to Argent Castle from Senton Castle and pursued by some of the Kilpatricks and McKinleys. We're going to intercept them."

"Why did she run? She has to know we'd protect her," Ian said over the sound of men shouting in the background at Argent Castle and the dogs barking wildly.

"She learned she has a former mate who's still alive."

Ian snorted. "The pirate Rafferty? The wolf is a dead mon. Guthrie with you?"

Cearnach swore under his breath. When had Ian learned the truth?

"Not exactly," Duncan said to Ian.

"How many wolves are after her?"

"Five. We can manage."

"Duncan, I know how capable the two of you are. But you have to include Guthrie. I don't want to lose either of my brothers or the lass."

"Cearnach doesn't think he can guide him to the right location."

"*Try.* I'll send men to Senton Castle to grab their vehicles and hers. This time *they'll* be stranded. Give them a taste of their own treachery."

Duncan smiled. "Aye. Revenge is sweet, Ian. I'll call Guthrie."

Cearnach could envision his pack members driving the cars back to Argent Castle while Kilpatrick and the others had to return home as wolves. Let them face Oglivie's gun and dogs. He hoped if the farmer saw the pack of wolves, he'd be drinking a wee bit much and believe he was seeing things.

"Guthrie," Duncan said, "change of plans. Head north of Oglivie's farm."

"Aye, meet you north of that location."

Duncan shoved his phone into the console between the front seats and began yanking off his clothes.

"Another five miles to go yet, brother," Cearnach said.

Duncan smiled. "Aye. If you get stopped, just say I'm your pet dog. I'll give the nice policeman a big grin."

Cearnach knew his brother would, too.

The five miles seemed to take forever. When they reached the place Cearnach had in mind, he pulled the car off the road into a turnout and began to strip. Duncan was panting, waiting for him to open the door for him.

Cearnach reached around his brother and pushed his door open. Duncan jumped out of the car and shoved the door closed with his nose.

Cearnach pushed his own door open and locked the doors with the electronic keypad. Thankfully, they had a keypad on the outside door panel on their cars, so there was no worry about getting back into their vehicles after they were done with business.

After shifting, he pushed the door closed with his paws and joined his brother. Duncan greeted him, nose to nose, then the two ran to where Cearnach was certain Elaine would be headed. When he didn't find her scent, he figured she hadn't made it this far, and his heart began skipping beats. Hell, what if the wolves had already encircled her much closer to Senton Castle? What if they had forced her to return to the car park already?

He went north, hoping to reach her quickly. They were now northeast of the Oglivie farm.

Guthrie would be able to detect their scent once he'd reached where they'd left their car and begun to run on foot. Their paws would leave their scent, easy for him to locate.

Cearnach heard growling about a half mile away. He recognized the vocal sound at once. It was Elaine's warning growl—long and low and threatening. Not quite like when she had stood beside him in the woods outside Argent Castle and growled at Baird McKinley and Robert Kilpatrick. Loud this time as if warning them that if any got near, she'd rip them to shreds.

Fear for her engulfed him. He tore after her, his brother racing beside him. His stomach was knotted, every muscle tensed, adrenaline coursing through his veins.

Male snarls and snaps greeted her as she responded in kind. Her cousins were trying to force her to return with them, and she was telling them in wolf terms—*no way*.

Someone yipped twice.

Not her. He remembered the sound of her yip when he'd startled her by coming up behind her in the river.

Then a yip sounded from her.

Cearnach saw red.

Chapter 27

IF HIS TONGUE WASN'T LOLLING OUT OF HIS MOUTH AS he ran, Cearnach would be grinding his teeth. He'd kill the bastard who had frightened her so.

He knew her cousins would be pissed off at her. They'd take out their frustrations on her because of her perceived disobedience.

What did her cousins plan to do with her? They couldn't knock her out with drugs, not while pursuing her as wolves. They had to be trying to corral and take her back to the cars parked at Senton Castle and to that bastard Rafferty. That's all Cearnach could imagine they'd try to do.

He wanted to call out to her, howl, bark, to let her know her Highland warrior was on his way. But he didn't want to alert her kin that he was coming to rescue her, afraid they might deal with her more harshly if they thought their time was quickly running out.

Instead, he moved swiftly over the glen and through the woods, scattering birds, and then he dashed across a shallow stream, sending the water flying, trying to judge where she was.

Dogs began to bark south of them. Oglivie's collies. He frowned and glanced over his shoulder, couldn't see anything but trees. He and Duncan were too far from the farmhouse for the collies to come this way. Unless... Guthrie had to be passing the farm. Cearnach briefly worried about the old man getting into his rusty pickup truck and trying to hunt Guthrie down.

Then Cearnach saw Elaine standing proud and tall, tail straight out behind her, her fur standing on end to make her appear more threatening. Five male wolves circled her, ganging up on her, bigger, meaner, more powerful. She was just as aggressive as they were. Every time one moved in close, she charged him, and the wolf would veer out of her path.

Trees surrounded the area on all sides but one, and that backed up on a swiftly moving river.

It was a game for them. A well-executed game. She knew it, but she had no other options but to keep them at bay.

They were trying to wear her down. Five against one. They were resting in between. She was tense, and with one perpetually attacking her, she didn't have time to rest. Even so, everyone's tongues were hanging out.

He noted then that Vardon's ear dripped with blood.

She had bitten him? Her mouth was bloodied. That's who had yelped? The biggest, strongest of the wolves?

Damn, the woman had balls.

He saw the blood streaking down her right hip. *Someone* had bitten *her*.

Cearnach turned his head to look at Vardon again. The wolf's mouth was bloody also. He was a dead wolf.

Vardon and Robert saw Cearnach and his brother first. Their mouths snapped shut, their ears perked, and their gazes focused on the bigger, more dangerous male wolves.

They realized at once who Cearnach and Duncan were. Knew that they had a real fight on their hands now, not just with a she-wolf who was battling five males at once. The odds were still in her kin's favor, but the odds were a wee bit better now.

She swung her head around to see what had taken the wolves' attention. At first, Cearnach saw the relief in her expression and then the sorrow. She was mated to him but couldn't be. The other wolves quickly moved around to face the oncoming males, but only Vardon need have worried about fighting a male.

Cearnach hit Vardon so hard with his body in a frontal assault that the wolf fell backward and landed hard on his side with an oompf. He quickly scrambled to his feet as Duncan growled low, warning the other wolves not to interfere.

Cearnach attacked Vardon again, ripping at his other ear, the flap dangling and bloodied. Vardon howled in pain and anger, then swung around to bite Cearnach, but then paused, looking past him.

Cearnach didn't dare look to see what was happening behind him. A wolf never turned his head away from another that he was fighting if he wanted to live.

Guthrie gave a low growl, letting Cearnach know he had arrived. So now they were more evenly matched in the event that the other wolves wanted to fight this out.

Vardon growled at Cearnach and lunged again, but Cearnach tore viciously into him, ripping at the skin of his throat. The wolf fell back and ran even farther away, turning quickly in case Cearnach was following him. He wasn't. He was standing his ground, not about to put more distance between him and Elaine.

Vardon's gaze shifted to another wolf. Out of the corner of his eye, Cearnach saw which wolf it was.

Baird.

He'd inched closer to Cearnach, wanting to attack next. Cearnach was certain Baird was still angry that his presence at the wedding had changed Calla's desire to mate with Baird.

As soon as he took Baird on, Vardon attempted to move in closer to Elaine. Guthrie ripped into Vardon. The other wolves watched and waited, Duncan keeping an eye on them as Cearnach fought with Baird.

Baird was too angry, too wild in his actions, too unfocused, making mistakes that he probably wouldn't have otherwise. Cearnach was about to make some headway with the wolf when a snarling wolf came out of the woods and hit him broadside.

Elaine barked and tore into the male wolf. *The newcomer.* The one that had to be Rafferty. His eyes nearly black with rage, his fur a little grayer than any of the wolves here, he was still strong.

He swung his head around to bite Elaine as Duncan charged Vardon, and Guthrie went after Baird.

Cearnach attacked Rafferty with a snarling, growling bite to the face.

The Kilpatrick brothers and the remaining McKinley brother could have made a difference, but none of them advanced. Suddenly, those wolves turned their heads and listened to sounds from the direction of Senton Castle. Tires crunched on gravel. Car doors slammed. One, two, three, four, five, six. The three wolves looked back at the ones still fighting, then ran off toward Senton Castle.

Cearnach knew they'd never reach their vehicles in time to stop his kin from using their lockpicks to break into the vehicles and move them to a new location.

With his concentration back on Rafferty, Cearnach knew he had to kill him. The pirate wolf would never lay another hand on Elaine's sweet body, never mar her creamy skin, never break another one of her bones, never say another cruel word to her or kill anyone that she loved.

For being an older wolf, Rafferty was well matched in size and strength. Cearnach was glad for that. Taking down an old wolf who was too weak to defend himself wouldn't be his way. Though he had to remind himself he couldn't let the wolf have a chance at Elaine again, ever.

Their teeth clicked as enamel struck enamel. Both Cearnach and Rafferty fought to get the upper bite, then leaped back away from each other to attack again. Cearnach noted that the other wolf was pushing him toward the river. Did he think he could drown Cearnach the way he'd so easily dispensed with Elaine's parents? Did he think that since he had survived his crew's mutiny and been left to fend for himself for who knew how long in the ocean, he had the advantage in the water?

The idea that Cearnach had nearly drowned as a young lad flitted across his mind as the wolf shoved him onto the mossy stones, the water shallow and running slower at the edge.

Elaine ran anxiously behind Rafferty. Cearnach cast her a look that told her to stay out of it. He'd be fine.

Baird suddenly yipped in pain, and Cearnach glanced briefly in his direction to see the wolf sitting on his ass, his injured leg lifted off the ground. Guthrie had torn the wolf's ligament. That had to hurt like a son of a bitch. It would heal, but he'd be limping three-legged on the long walk back home and for a prolonged time after that.

Vardon—his ears both torn, his throat a mess—
yelped when Duncan took a bite out of his flank.

After that, Rafferty's companions in crime lost their
urge to fight. Vardon sat on his butt near Baird, both
of them heaving, as Cearnach fielded another lunge
from Rafferty.

Cearnach and Rafferty's teeth connected again,
their forelegs shoving at each other, trying to get the
advantage. This time Cearnach lost his footing and fell
backward into the river. Cursing himself, he attempted
to stand, but he was already shoulder-deep in the water,
and it was carrying him away from Elaine. Panic drove
him toward the shore, even though he knew his brothers
would protect her from Rafferty.

Rafferty wasn't about to give up his lead in the fight.
He attacked Cearnach, getting the upper hand, though
he also was soon caught up in the swift-moving water.
That's when Cearnach gained the advantage. He pushed
the wolf farther into the river. Using his upper-body
strength to knock Rafferty off his feet, he lunged on top
of him. Cearnach quickly pinned him under the water,
his teeth at Rafferty's throat.

Drown, bastard, Cearnach silently prayed. Rafferty
deserved nothing less. Just as Rafferty had drowned
Elaine's parents.

The wolf fought him but couldn't get to his feet,
couldn't shake loose of Cearnach's fearsome grip,
couldn't save himself this time.

When the wolf stopped fighting him, Cearnach
dragged him to the shore. They couldn't let a dead
body be found in the river with wolf teeth marks in
the throat.

The damn wolf was fighting for air. He wasn't dead. Cearnach thought to pull him into the water again, but Elaine came running up, then slowly approached him, poking her nose at Rafferty's arm, as if seeing if he was really dying and could never be a threat to her again.

Elaine's heart was ready to burst out of her chest because she'd been so worried about Cearnach.

Rafferty looked like he didn't have long for this world. His face was gray, and he coughed water up as he shifted into his human form.

Him, the mighty pirate of the seas, whom she thought had drowned eons ago, was finally dying—this time at the hands, well, teeth of one of the good guys.

Cearnach growled at her, and she knew he didn't want her to get close to the man, as if he could suddenly hurt her. Or maybe he was afraid she'd feel something for Rafferty now that Cearnach had injured him fatally.

But Cearnach was her hero. He would always be her hero.

She poked again at the man, then growled at him, wanting him to tell her the truth before he was unable to. His eyes fluttered open, and he looked like he was trying to focus on her.

"You know," he said, his voice raspy, "I wanted you back."

She growled low, not liking what he might say in front of Cearnach or his brothers, gathered close to protect her if she needed them, listening to what the bastard had to say. Vardon and Baird had long ago limped off, knowing the fight would be in the MacNeills' favor. Whatever Rafferty had promised them, they wouldn't get the payment now.

Rafferty coughed, closed his eyes, and then slowly opened them and looked up at her with longing. He took a shallow, shuddering breath.

"You couldn't have suitors." He reached out to touch her. "You were always mine."

Never again.

His hand suddenly clutched his chest, his eyes wide, then he dropped his hand to the ground, his eyes staring at her, mouth parted on one last breath.

She listened for his heartbeat, for his breath, and hearing none, she knew he was finally truly dead. She wanted to collapse with relief but looked up at Cearnach, feeling horrible about all of this.

Cearnach came forward, nudged her face, and licked it, giving her comfort. She nosed his face, then rubbed her face along his cheek. They were mates. No one would undo what had been done.

Kelly Rafferty was dead. He would never hurt her again.

Her cousins were long gone.

Cearnach licked her cheek again, then shifted. He crouched down and wrapped his arms around her neck, and she couldn't tell him how much his embracing her made her feel loved, though she couldn't stop her tail from wagging. He smiled as her tail swishing so wildly caught his eye.

"Kelly Rafferty is dead, Elaine. You have nothing to fear."

She nuzzled his face and licked his cheek.

"You're coming home with us now."

She glanced back in the direction of Senton Castle.

"Seems that's our home also. If you're worried about

them taking your car again, your kin have a surprise waiting for them."

She looked up at him inquiringly.

"We'll go to my car. It's closer," he said, standing, then lifting Rafferty over his shoulder. He stalked toward the woods and Elaine ran beside him. "Then we'll drop Guthrie off at his vehicle to avoid Oglivie's farm."

Duncan and Guthrie raced ahead until they disappeared. She couldn't figure out why until quite a while later when she saw Duncan returning at a dead run in human form, fully dressed. He took Rafferty's body, and Cearnach shifted into wolf form. Then he and Elaine ran at their faster wolf pace to reach the car so no one would catch them running as wolves. She couldn't help worrying about Duncan if he was caught carrying a naked dead man.

When she and Cearnach reached the car, he shifted and opened the door where Guthrie was sitting, panting in the back seat. Then she joined him while Cearnach quickly dressed and popped the trunk. She was afraid Ian would be angry with her for bringing this fight to Argent Castle. That Cearnach and his brothers would be upset with her for running off. That the whole pack would be. What of Duncan's mate, Shelley? She had to be worried that he might not return in one piece. Then there were Cearnach's mother and aunt: she was certain they'd judge her harshly.

When Duncan joined them at the car, he put Rafferty's body into the trunk, slammed it closed, then got into the passenger's seat.

Cearnach drove to where Guthrie's vehicle was parked. Duncan got the door for Guthrie so he could change, dress, and then take over the wheel of his own vehicle.

Elaine thought that Duncan would stay with Guthrie and was about to jump over the seat to sit up front with Cearnach when Duncan returned to Cearnach's car. He climbed in and cast a smile over his shoulder at Elaine. She closed her panting mouth.

"I'm staying with the two of you. Ian's orders. He doesn't want anything further to happen to either of you, should some of the McKinley or Kilpatrick kin decide to attempt to waylay us." Duncan called Ian. "We're on our way home, Ian."

"Elaine's coming home… for good," Cearnach said.

Ian didn't say anything.

Cearnach glanced back at Elaine. She was watching him.

"Is Rafferty dead?" Ian asked Duncan.

"Aye, he is for good this time," Duncan said.

"Good," Ian said. "Because if he wasn't, he would be. Our mother's already planning the wedding without Elaine so if the lass wants to have any say at all in it, she needs to hurry home."

Elaine smiled and sat down on the seat. She really didn't care anything about the wedding… except that she had loved Calla's ceremony before Vardon ruined it. She was truly mated to Cearnach. That's all that really mattered. And she was relieved beyond measure that Calla was at Argent and had been safe all this time from that bastard Kelly.

"Aye. We're all headed back to Argent Castle. Tell Shelley we're all right."

"You can tell her yourself."

"Duncan?" Shelley said, her voice worried.

"Aye, lass, we're all fine."

Elaine smiled to see the look on his face. He was one happy mated wolf.

"Thank you for bringing her home," Shelley said, tears in her voice.

Elaine felt choked up. She'd thought everyone would be angry with her, but the only thing they were showing was that she was one of them now. A tear and then two rolled down her furry cheeks. She brushed them away with her paw. Cearnach looked up at the rearview mirror.

"Everything's going to be fine, Elaine. I love you," he said.

She poked her head over his seat and licked the back of his neck. He reached behind while he watched the road and stroked her head.

After Duncan had talked to his mate for a moment, he pocketed his cell.

"How did Ian know about Rafferty?" Cearnach asked, as Elaine settled back down on the seat. "Did you tell him?"

"Nay. He already knew."

Cearnach looked at his brother, questioning why. Duncan quickly shrugged.

Elaine knew Cearnach would have words with Ian.

Chapter 28

AS SOON AS THEY REACHED ARGENT CASTLE, EVERYONE came out to greet them, while Duncan directed a couple of their men to retrieve the dead man from the trunk of the car and bury him in the woods.

Cearnach only wanted to get Elaine settled in his room where she could shift, clean up, and dress, and then he wanted to confront Ian.

"I'll be right back," he said to Elaine before she'd even had a chance to shift. Then he shut the door to his bedchambers and stalked toward Ian's solar.

Ian was ready for him, sitting at his desk, looking weary after all the fighting that had gone on that day, and taking care of the aftermath of the battle and the mess left behind. When they'd arrived, the place didn't look like a wolf fight had taken place there hours earlier.

"How did you know about Rafferty, Ian?" Cearnach asked him.

"Our mother," Ian said, shaking his head, his arms folded over his chest. "I never would have guessed who was chasing after Elaine. Duncan left that part out when he called me. I assume you had all shifted to take care of the menace before you learned the truth." He raised a brow, questioning their actions.

"I was driving. Duncan was doing all the calling."

"Aye, and afraid that I'd be angered that Elaine was mated still to another wolf?"

Cearnach ignored the censure in his brother's tone of voice. He knew that anything that went on with the pack, particularly something that important, had to be shared with their pack leader. "How did *Mother* know?"

"Our lady mother learned the truth from the solicitor."

"Hell," Cearnach paced. "If she knew…" He shook his head. "Before or after I was mated to Elaine?"

"You'll have to question *her*. I didn't think to ask, assuming that she had only known after the fact. At this point, it doesn't really make a whole lot of difference. The good news is that I'm having Rafferty's properties transferred to Elaine's ownership. Seems appropriate since she was his mate and the closest family he had. It's little compensation for all that Elaine lost, but it's hers."

Cearnach closed his mouth, thinking the same, but then nodded, glad that the properties would go to good use. He turned to leave his brother's solar.

"If you're thinking of questioning our mother now, think again. She and Calla—who arrived a couple of hours ago—and the rest of the ladies are discussing wedding plans in our mother's sitting room. You know how she is when she's involved in something like that. No one will interrupt her," Ian cautioned.

Cearnach snorted and headed down the hall.

He heard women's laughter in the sitting room, even Elaine's, and he was glad to hear her enjoying herself after all that had happened. The women were having a lively discussion about the upcoming wedding, and Cearnach slowed his pace. He was still angry that his mother hadn't told him the truth. If she'd known before he mated Elaine, she shouldn't have encouraged the mating. He had to know.

He stalked into the room and saw Heather, Julia, Calla, Shelley, and Elaine seated cross-legged on the floor as they looked at catalogs of floral arrangements, his aunt and mother sitting on chairs, looking on. Elaine's hair was damp, and she wore fresh jeans, a red sweater, and a pair of suede slipper boots, as if someone had dragged her to the sitting room pronto to discuss wedding plans.

Calla beamed at him. His mother must have called her in to coordinate the affair. Calla looked so pleased to be here that he paused, glad she was no longer upset over the situation with Baird McKinley and the almost marriage.

Still, he scowled at his mother. "A word with you, my lady mother," he said, sounding like a snarling wolf.

His mother's brows shot up. "I don't think this is the time or place…"

"Now is the time, and as to the place, we'll discuss this elsewhere alone anywhere you choose to go, or the ladies can leave your sitting room while we speak of this matter here."

"Or everyone can just stay where they are," Elaine said, rising to her feet, folding her arms, and looking as though she was going to defend his mother. His mother, who didn't need anyone defending her at any time.

"Aye," his mother said, smiling up at Cearnach. "Did I tell you how much I like your wee lass? A true warrior she is. A real keeper. Did you know she left here because she thought Calla had been taken hostage?"

Cearnach looked at Elaine, his mouth agape, unable to contain his surprise.

"The last time I saw you look like this, like a dark thunderstorm approaching, you had run off the road and ruined two of your tires. Surely whatever it is can't be as important as all that," Elaine said lightly.

The last time he imagined he had looked like this was just a few hours ago when she had run off and her kin were trying to chase her down. "He lied to you about Calla?" Cearnach said to Elaine.

"He said he'd taken her hostage, and he said he'd kill you like he had my other suitors."

He didn't wish to discuss this matter with his mother in front of the other ladies. He didn't want to wait to hear her speak the truth, either. He didn't even want to say what he had to say in front of Elaine. Yet when his mate told him why she had run off, he felt his heart go out to her. She hadn't done it just to escape Rafferty, but to save Calla and protect Cearnach.

"What difference does it make, Cearnach?" his mother said, her smile warm. "She is yours, like she should have been the first time you went after her. In St. Andrews."

He scowled at his mother. "You knew, didn't you?"

His mother took a deep breath and exhaled. "I knew that she needed you and that you needed her. Now run along while we decide on the flowers."

He ground his teeth and looked from his mother to his mate, her brows raised as she waited for the storm to blow over.

"She wants purple flowers," he said to Calla, and then swept his gaze over the other ladies assembled there as if making sure they all understood. "That's all that needs to be said."

Then he stalked forward and scooped Elaine up in his arms, though she let out a small squeal of surprise at his action before wrapping her arms around his neck. "There are different variations of purple colors, you know," she said.

"Aye, and you've looked at the blasted flowers long enough." Even if she hadn't had time to look at them, purple was purple. "We need to discuss more important matters."

"Oh?"

"She'll see you ladies later." He turned and stalked out of the room.

She sighed. "Cearnach…"

"Aye, lass?"

"What in heaven's name was that all about?"

"I wished a word with my mother."

"Did you get what you wanted out of the conversation?"

He took a deep breath, nuzzled his face in her hair, and said, "Aye. My mother is a canny woman. She was right."

"About what?"

"That you were meant to be mine, no one else's, no matter the circumstances. You were wounded on the battlefield, weren't you?"

She took a deep breath. "Just a scratch. It'll heal."

"Vardon," he growled.

"Don't worry, Cearnach. Next time I see him, I'll kill him." She gave Cearnach a small smile.

God, how he loved his she-wolf.

He knew why his mother and even Flynn had been so insistent that he mate Elaine right away. She needed protection from the past and a family for the future. He was both for her.

Later that afternoon, the ladies gathered in the garden room to talk further about Elaine's wedding, this time without Cearnach's interference as his brothers were practicing sword-fighting with him, at their mother's request.

"I don't know what I should do," Elaine said to the women.

Julia and Shelley were sitting together on one sofa. Cearnach's mother and aunt had taken up another, while Cearnach's cousin Heather and Calla sat on a third one in front of the fire as it crackled and popped with welcome heat. Sheba's pups played in a bundle of teeth and fur and legs nearby, growling and woofing. Elaine's own puppy, Whiskers, named because of her funny little beard, was chewing on her shoelaces.

She was conflicted about wearing her own plaid at the wedding. "I've never worn the sett of my clan, but I can't just borrow someone else's for the wedding."

"You could wear a white wedding gown," Shelley said. "Some of the wolves do for their Scottish weddings. I thought of doing so, but my Uncle Ethan wouldn't hear of it."

Surprised that Shelley hadn't worn what she wished for such a special occasion, Elaine looked at Julia for her input.

"I wore my clan's plaid," Julia said. "It felt right to me."

Elaine chewed her lip as she watched Sheba's pups biting and growling and yipping in a variation on who's top dog of the heap. "All right," she said. "I'll wear my clan's plaid."

Julia and Shelley frowned at her, not looking too happy about her decision, although all along they had said the choice was hers.

"Think of it as *Romeo and Juliet*, only with a happy ending. I doubt the feuding families will be happy with the match, but it's kind of like mending fences… in a wolf way."

Shelley smiled but shook her head. "More likely it will be another reason for them to hate our clan."

Our clan. Elaine knew she was not only mating with a wolf from this clan, she was also joining them. Becoming family. Part of a pack. Who would have ever thought that a near collision with a wolf from an enemy clan would turn out so well? That he'd become her lover, her mate.

She was finally home. Not in a place she'd ever imagined. It felt right. Good.

"And," she said, "I want to hold the wedding at Senton Castle." She knew that would not go over well with Cearnach's people. Senton Castle was beautiful, even in ruins. It was her birthright. The kirk was still standing. No glass on the windows, no pews to sit in. A stone floor and a roof over their heads in case it rained. That's all that mattered.

"Not in our chapel?" his mother asked, her brows raised. She sounded more surprised than annoyed.

"I feel… I feel I must pay homage to my parents, to my uncles in some small way. What better way than to sanctify Cearnach's and my marriage in my family's chapel?" She thought it would feel like she was including her family in this joyous occasion. That the fighting between the clans had finally ceased. At least between her Hawthorn family and the MacNeills. The Kilpatricks and McKinleys were another story.

His mother nodded. "We will have to ask his lairdship

if he approves, but I will put in a good word for you."
She smiled and looked at Julia.

Julia sighed. "I will attempt to convince Ian that you
have your heart set on it."

Calla smiled brightly, and Elaine didn't think anything
was too daunting for the woman when it came to setting
up celebrations. "It's a brilliant idea. Not unlike weddings held where the bride and groom stand in the waves
at a beach or skydive into matrimony or scuba dive with
their friends. They share in the history of a place."

"But you've never shared anything with Cearnach at
Senton Castle," Cearnach's Aunt Agnes said. "You've
never been there with your family. I don't see why we
have to go to the ruins, truly."

"Cearnach and I did spend time there," Elaine said,
recalling fondly how they'd visited the ruins like two
lupus garous on a date. Their first. The way his hand had
held hers, keeping her from slipping on the wet, mossy
stones. The way he hadn't wanted to release her even
after she was safely inside the inner bailey. The way
he'd smiled at her when she'd raced all over the castle as
a wolf. "Have you ever entered a home and felt as if you
were welcome and that you weren't just a visitor? That
something about the place made you feel good, joyful,
at home?"

Shelley and Julia nodded. Cearnach's mother and
aunt had probably never considered going anywhere
other than their home at Argent Castle so no place else
would feel like home.

Elaine shook her head. "I don't know how to explain
it, but when I was there, I felt as though I'd been there
before. I didn't see it as a place of ruin, but a place

where once my people lived, broke bread, laughed, worshipped, worked, fought, and played. My parents were even wed in that kirk. They loved one another until the day they died. That's where I want to marry Cearnach."

Cearnach's mother quickly brushed away tears. "Something in my eye. *Blasted dust*," she said.

Julia tried to fight a smile. So did Shelley.

Calla didn't bother. Aunt Agnes's face reddened a little as if she was embarrassed for her sister by marriage.

On the day of the wedding, the sun was poking out of the light, fluffy clouds. Elaine knew it was going to be a grand day as Ian walked her down the aisle of the kirk, sunlight reflecting off the stained glass of the vases holding lavender flowers. The colorful flickering lights shimmered in the medieval gray stone building, like tiny winged fairies of some Celtic myth or legend.

The men all wore their kilts and Prince Charlie jackets, belted swords at their waists, dirks in their hose. The women wore long plaid gowns, mostly of the green and blue plaid and yellow of the MacNeills, while Elaine wore the McKinley plaid, predominantly green and blue and red, since the Hawthorn didn't have their own sett and had been allied with the rest of their McKinley kin over the years.

When the minister asked if anyone would object to the marriage, Elaine smiled at Cearnach who was looking down at her with such profound love that tears gathered in her eyes. She hadn't wanted to cry, told herself she wouldn't, but she loved him and couldn't help herself.

Growling between the hounds as they fought over something made everyone turn and look as Logan ran into the chapel dangling a piece of dirty blue silk from his fingers. He waved the torn fabric like a flag. "Anlan found it and Dillon was playing tug of war with him over it."

Elaine let out her breath and thought to continue with the ceremony, but then she remembered what Cearnach had told her. One of the goods her uncles had stolen from them was silk.

She rushed to join Logan. "Where did the dogs get it?"

Cearnach was close behind her.

His mother said, "What… what are they doing?"

Aunt Agnes said, "I told you we should have had the wedding in the chapel at Argent Castle. Nothing would have interrupted the ceremony there."

Logan led the way across the bailey to the cellar in the southeast tower and pointed to a place where the dogs had been digging. Two of the pups were deep in the hole, yipping and running around. "They smelled something in there. They were digging and… well, they opened up a wee passage."

"Let me see." Cearnach crouched down to get a better look. "It's too dark."

Ian leaned down with a flashlight, and Cearnach used it to peer into the hole. "Flynn, what are you doing in there?" He studied the silk, the shimmering gold, the pearls, the emeralds. His eyes widened at the sight of his sword poking out of the crate of green jewels—with the first carved handle he'd made, the one he had used in the fight against Elaine's Uncle Tobias and had lost to the older male. He shook his head. "Figures you put the dogs up to locating the hidden room, Flynn."

Cearnach smiled and looked up at Elaine, who was waiting to hear what they'd found.

"It appears your treasure…"

"Your stolen merchandise," Elaine corrected Cearnach.

"Was hidden in a secret room, buried for centuries. It's all there. Well, the pearls and gold and silk. The sugar I'm certain your kin used long ago. The loch surrounds the castle on three sides. During a downpour, water runs off the cliffs, making it appear like a waterfall. Here is where your uncle said the treasure was all along. And my sword," he said quietly, remembering when he'd fought so hard, determined not to give up while his *da* and clansmen and the pirate crew watched.

Her uncles had brought them together—the sword, their niece, and the Highlander who would one day steal her heart.

She touched his arm and stared up at him, her eyes wide with disbelief. "The one my uncle took away from you during a sword fight aboard your ship?"

"Aye."

"My uncles would be happy for me. Your sword will have a special place in our bedchamber," she said, taking a deep breath, her eyes misty with tears.

He loved her with all his heart, the she-wolf who would protect him. If she'd been with her uncles at that time, he knew she would have defended Cearnach even then and probably made her uncle return Cearnach's sword to him.

He handed the flashlight back to Ian, who returned it to Logan. Cearnach's gaze shifted again to the treasure before him. In her McKinley plaid wedding gown, she looked every bit the Highland lass, her hair pinned up in curls around her head, the bottom of her gown showing off lace-trimmed petticoats underneath. He wanted nothing more than to remove the McKinley plaid from her sweet body and the pins from her hair, and return her to their chambers at Argent.

"I thought to remove all weapons from our bedchamber and turn the room into a garden-like setting. The treasure is yours to do with what you will."

"No," she said, wrapping her arm around Cearnach's and tugging him out of the cellar and across the inner bailey to the chapel. Everyone hurried inside to take their places again. "I found my treasure, and it isn't merchandise but one hot-blooded Highland wolf in a kilt."

Smiling, he leaned down to kiss her, and his mother said, "There's time enough for that *after* the wedding, Cearnach."

He ignored her and kissed Elaine like there would be no tomorrow. She wrapped her arms around his neck and kissed him right back, deeply, passionately, with all her heart. She had evaded him all those years ago to finally find her way into his arms, into his life again, this time to stay.

Cearnach breathed in the scent of Elaine, the wind and wet breeze, the she-wolf's sweet fragrance. He tasted her wine-flavored mouth, felt her heated soft body pressed against his, and wanted nothing more than to take her home now and mate with her again.

He turned to address the minister. "Finish with all haste." He vowed they'd have the feasting done in the inner bailey in record time, and then he and his bonny lass would return to Argent Castle alone.

He loved her with every fiber of his being and realized as he saw Calla beaming at them near the front of the chapel that his plan to attend her wedding and change her mind about marrying Baird McKinley had brought him to this.

His own wedding—with the wolf of his dreams.

Acknowledgments

Thanks so much to my readers who made me a *USA Today* bestselling author! I can't thank everyone enough! To my editor, Deb Werksman, who continues to show me the way; to Danielle Jackson, who always keeps me straight on all the events I'm scheduled for; to the Sourcebooks cover art department that makes cover art, not just book covers; and to my Rebel Romance Writers, who keep me sane. And again to my fans. You are my inspiration!

USA Today Bestselling Author

Savage Hunger

by Terry Spear

———

He saved her once…

When Kathleen McKnight was caught in the crossfire during a mission deep in the Amazon rain forest, a mysterious man saved her life then disappeared. Kathleen returns a year later in hopes of finding her mysterious savior…

Now he wants to claim her…

Jaguar shape-shifter Connor Anderson is instantly intrigued by Kathleen's beauty and courage and thinks about her constantly. When she comes back to the Amazon to seek him out, he knows he has to act fast if he's to keep her for his own…

———

Praise for Terry Spear:

"Terry Spear knows exactly how to extract emotions from her readers… and keep them riveted."—*Love Romance Passion*

"Time after time Spear delivers, giving paranormal fans plenty of action, plenty of mystery, and, of course, love and romance aplenty." —*The Good, the Bad and the Unread*

For more Terry Spear, visit:

www.sourcebooks.com

USA Today Bestselling Author

Jaguar Fever

by Terry Spear

—◈—

She's a material girl...

Being the only jaguar shape-shifter in town was getting
tiresome for Maya Anderson. She's finally found a hangout
in a nearby city where she can go on the prowl with her own
kind—and she intends to make the most of it.

In a feline world...

Wade Patterson knew he could love her the moment he
looked into Maya's piercing eyes, but he thinks she's in
over her head with the big city cats. Wade's playing a deadly
game of cat and mouse with a different sort of predator, and
if Maya gets in the middle, they're all going to find out just
how wild a jungle cat can be.

—◈—

Praise for Savage Hunger:

"Spear paints a colorful, vivid portrait of the lush jungle
and deadly beauty... of jaguars."—*Publishers Weekly*

"A sizzling page turner."—*Night Owl
Romance* Reviewer Top Pick, 5 Stars

For more Terry Spear, visit:

www.sourcebooks.com

About the Author

A *USA Today* bestselling and award-winning author of urban fantasy romance and historical romance, Terry Spear pens fantasy and reality and historical works that are full of adventure, romance, mystery, and intrigue. She's a retired lieutenant colonel from the U.S. Army Reserves and has an MBA from Monmouth University. When she's not writing, she teaches online writing classes, gardens, plays around with photography, and creates award-winning teddy bears that have found homes as far away as Australia.